PATH
of
PROGRESS

One Man's Fight for Women's Rights

a novel

Flora Beach Burlingame

Path of Progress
First Edition

Book cover design by www.ebooklaunch.com

Book interior formatted by Debra Cranfield Kennedy

www.acornpublishingllc.com

Library of Congress Cataloging-in-Publication Data

Names: Burlingame, Flora Beach, author.
Title: Path of progress : one man's fight for women's rights : a novel /
  Flora Beach Burlingame.
Description: First edition. | Irvine, CA : Acorn Publishing LLC, [2019]
Identifiers: LCCN 2018061277 | ISBN 9781947392410 (pbk.) | ISBN 9781947392427
  (hardback)
Subjects: LCSH: Women--Suffrage--United States--Fiction. |
  Iowa--History--19th century--Fiction. | CYAC: Historical fiction.
Classification: LCC PS3602.U7583 P38 2019 | DDC 813/.6--dc23
LC record available at https://lccn.loc.gov/2018061277

*The coming of equal suffrage of equal rights and
duties irrespective of sex may be promoted or
retarded but it cannot be stopped. As well try to
thrust the dawning day back into the caverns of
night. It is part of that age long movement now
recognized and named evolution which is
carrying the race to higher things. If my
testimony or work can promote it in any degree,
however small, I shall be satisfied.*

John O. Stevenson

From his first editorial for *The Woman's Standard*, the
official organ of the Iowa Woman Suffrage Association,
September 1899 (later Iowa Equal Suffrage Association)

Chapter One

TRAPPED

Waterloo, Iowa

1889

The Reverend John Stevenson, pastor of the First Congregational Church of Waterloo, Iowa, stood, stretched, and stepped to his study window. He had been lost in time for two hours at his desk while working on a sermon. Pushing aside the curtains, he watched soft flakes of snow float down from the dark clouds.

Better put an extra log on the fire before the children get home from school, he thought, and was about to drop the curtain when an unexpected carriage pulled up in front of the parsonage. A woman, face hidden in a dark cape and hood, emerged from the vehicle and made her way cautiously up the walk. Something seemed not right. A sense of alarm stirred in John. Rolling down his sleeves and buttoning the cuffs of his white dress shirt, he reached for the well-worn black coat draped across a chair.

A rap sounded on the study door as he reached to open it. Mrs. Henderson, his middle-aged, part-time housekeeper stood there, eyes wide. "Sir, there's a Mrs. Cooper here to see you. She—she don't look so good, Reverend. She's hurt bad."

John's pulse quickened at this announcement.

Beatrice Cooper was a loyal parishioner of his church, a young woman involved in the Missionary Society. The wife of Leroy Cooper, a member of the board of trustees, she was not one to suddenly arrive ill or injured at his door mid-day. "See her right in."

Shock spiraled through John when the woman entered his study, swaying slightly as though she might faint. He rushed to steady her and led her to a chair. "Can I get you something? Hot tea?" He took a closer look. "A doctor?"

"No, Reverend. I need help, but I don't want a doctor." She lowered her hood, flecked with fresh snow, revealing her auburn curls and a mottled purple bruise on the left side of her face. A crimson stain splotched the lace handkerchief she pressed against her cut lip.

"My land, Mrs. Cooper. Who did this to you?" John turned to the housekeeper who still stood in the doorway wringing her hands in her apron at the unusual situation. "Please, bring a glass of water."

"My husband," the visitor sobbed into her bloodied handkerchief. "He did this to me, and it's not the first time. Only this is worse…I can't take it anymore." Tears of anger streamed down her cheeks. "Reverend Stevenson, he's taken everything that's mine, and he's destroyed my dignity. I feel like a trapped animal. I know I promised to love and obey the man, but I did not promise to be a slave nor to be humiliated and beaten. It's getting worse with each sip of the bottle. And as far as *until death do us part*, a piece of me dies every day, especially when he does this to me." She indicated her injured face. "And don't tell me those marriage vows were a covenant before God and cannot be broken. If God approves of Leroy's behavior, then he himself is cruel, and I will not believe in such a God." The woman's entire body trembled before John as she raged, and the pitch of her voice rose with each spoken word. The startling revelation spilled forth like icy liquid from a fractured jug in what, moments before, had been John's peaceful study.

A flustered Mrs. Henderson appeared with a glass of water, thrust it at him, then stood there looking on, nervously twisting a lock of her graying hair between her fingers.

"Thank you, Mrs. Henderson," John said. "Please shut the door on your way out." He waited for the woman to leave before offering the drink to his visitor. She pushed it away. He placed the glass on his desk and returned to his chair opposite her.

Shaking his head, he envisioned this proper lady, always fashionably attired, sitting in the second row beside her well-dressed husband on Sunday mornings, their two young boys on either side of them. If five-year-old Timothy dared squirm, a stern look from his father settled him. They seemed like a normal family.

As a pastor, John often found certain members of his congregation led hidden lives. Sooner or later, he was made privy to many of their troubles. Some were not surprises—such as the occasional man who carried excessive drinking to church on his breath. But learning of Leroy Cooper's out-of-control temper shocked him. Before this, John had no hint of the man's weakness for liquor. A church trustee and respected banker, Leroy was an upstanding member of the community. He was one who could be called upon to lead and be a good committee chairman. In fact, he was a person who always had things under control. Yes, *control.* That was the key word. He controlled whatever came his way, including his wife—even if it meant, as it seemed, beating her into submission.

Beatrice Copper stood and paced the room, dabbing at the tears and blood with her handkerchief. "I need help, Reverend. I can't go back there tonight, maybe not for a while. You have preached about equality. I thought maybe you had helped other women and knew where I could go—what I could do." She stopped pacing and looked at him, hope brimming in her eyes along with the tears.

The burden of her reliance pressed down on John like a heavy hand. Were Anna still alive, he would suggest Mrs. Cooper stay at the parsonage at least overnight, but with no other woman in the house, the scandal would only compound her situation. He pulled open a desk drawer, took out an address book, and sorted through a list of names. Noting one possibility, he reached for paper and pen, jotted down some numbers, and handed the notations to his visitor.

"Here is the name and address of an inexpensive boarding house that takes in women seeking refuge."

She studied what he had written. "This is out of town—Cedar Falls."

"It's not that far, and you'll be safer there. Do you have someone to take you?"

"My sister, Belva Parker. She's waiting for me now."

She looked back down at the piece of paper in her hand. "Will they take my boys, too? I plan to get my boys."

"That I don't know." Her remark alarmed John. It was common knowledge the law did not allow a wife custody of her children under any circumstances. He prayed a silent prayer. Perhaps after a brief separation Leroy would see the error of his ways and welcome her back with a changed attitude.

Beatrice adjusted her cloak and pulled the hood over her curls, preparing to leave. "Thank you, Reverend. I knew if anyone could help me it would be you." Her tears had dried, and her voice was resolute.

John took her elbow, guiding her out of the study and into the entry hall toward the front door. He reached into his pocket, brought out two silver dollars and handed them to her. "Here. You'll need this. I wish I could do more."

A chill wind blew scattered flakes of snow around them as he walked her to the waiting carriage. Her sister, also a member of John's congregation, opened the door, leaned forward, and offered her hand. She nodded to John but said nothing.

John helped Beatrice into the carriage. "Be careful, and God be with you," he said.

The driver gee-hawed to the horse pawing restlessly at the muddy street. Moments later, the sound of thudding hooves and the squeak of wheels echoed in the chill afternoon air as the two women sped on their way.

John returned to the house and slumped into his study chair. He ran his hands through his dark hair, now sprinkled with gray, and sighed. He caught his reflection in the window. The mutton chops gave him a mature look, but in spite of the laugh lines, his eyes looked tired. Times like these cut into the joy of bringing biblical messages to his parishioners. Mrs. Cooper's dilemma, and that of many women like her, angered him. Marriage for some *was* a trap, as she had so succinctly put it. He knew many determined women who had been fighting this for years, yet women could not vote to change the laws to allow them the same rights as men. John shook his head at the injustice of it. Here it was 1889, and the first women's rights convention in the nation had taken place in 1849. He was aware strides were being made, bit by bit, but not soon enough for women like Beatrice Cooper. She could divorce Leroy, the law allowed that, but that took money—of which she had none of her own—and was frowned upon by society. Most women chose to remain in torturous marriages rather than living with the scandal of divorce.

Now, as he sat at his desk, John attempted to refocus on the sermon interrupted by Beatrice Cooper's disturbing visit. The parsonage study, though small, contained all he needed to work: a bookcase along one wall for books and whatnots, two chairs, and a window for light, in addition to the kerosene lamp on the desk for when he wrote into the night. He also spent time at the church office on a daily basis, but at home there were fewer interruptions, and he preferred to work here if possible. He knew his parishioners expected challenging messages from him—words worth coming to church to hear, words to take home to mull over and stimulate their week—and his Scottish brogue seemed to add a bit of charm they liked. He put a lot of thought into these sermons and loved every minute of it, truly believing the Lord had put him on this earth to preach the truth from the Bible. The bookcase held bound volumes written by great thinkers—all good resources for gluing together the points John hoped to get across on Sundays. His gaze wandered now to those shelves. Not to any particular book, but to the photograph framed there of a woman who, as always, seemed to be gazing back at him.

Anna. Dear, dear Anna. John sighed. He looked down at the words he had just scrawled across the page on his desk. *What do you think of this sentence?* He had always tested his sermons on Anna and took to heart any changes she suggested. He started to read aloud, but his voice faltered and broke. It simply wasn't the same, quoting phrases to an angel in heaven. And he was having trouble concentrating, distressed over the troubles of a bloodied and bruised parishioner. If Anna were here, she would have gathered Beatrice in her arms and known what to do.

John felt a tug on his coat sleeve and looked down into the face of his youngest child.

"Papa, the lady was crying. Can't you take her hurt away?" Tears pooled in the blue eyes of four-year-old Irene, his precious girl. She stood before him, her pink dress and white pinafore wrinkled from her nap, a rag doll clasped in one hand.

He thought she had been sleeping while he dealt with his unexpected visitor, but apparently the commotion had awakened her, and she had come down the stairs from her room before Beatrice Cooper left, catching sight of the battered woman. John sighed and pulled Irene onto his lap. She snuggled against his chest, and he stroked her silky blonde hair. "I wish I could help the lady…how I wish I could." His help had been so little, and so temporary.

The housekeeper appeared at the study door. "Supper is started, Reverend, and I must be gone to my next job afore I'm too late." She hesitated a moment, curiosity written on her face. "Is the lady going to be all right?"

"Yes, Mrs. Henderson. I appreciate your help." He knew she wanted more, but it was none of her affair, something she had to understand if she was going to work in the parsonage. "Your pay is in the envelope on the foyer table. I'll see you next week."

Mrs. Henderson came every Monday, cleaned the house, and usually helped prepare the evening meal before she left. He needed her more than that, but once a week was all a pastor's salary afforded.

At supper John shoved the unhappy encounter with his visitor to the back of his mind. He had his own family to consider, and now, as their only parent, his focus must be on them while they were together. On this cold, winter evening, they gathered in the kitchen. The wood-burning cook stove cast off welcome heat, and the enticing aroma of the stew left simmering by Mrs. Henderson made the cozy space even more inviting. They sat around the table, draped with its yellow oil-cloth. Two kerosene lamps cast golden reflections on the faces of his four children—John's emotional sustenance. He held out his hands, and each in turn took hold of his or that of a brother or sister. Heads bowed, they repeated grace together. Immediately following the "amen," hot stew and buttered biscuits were served, and mealtime chatter commenced.

"So, tell me about your school day," John said, eyeing each of his three eldest.

"Me first," Irene said, before any of her siblings had a chance to respond. "A lady came to talk to Papa and she was crying. Big people aren't supposed to cry."

The remark unnerved John. Irene apparently couldn't let go of the scene she had witnessed. But it was more than that. She did know big people cried. It had been barely ten months since her mother had quietly slipped away to the Lord, and little Irene had seen plenty of adults cry that day and for days after.

"What lady?" twelve-year-old Margaret piped up with a toss of her brown braids.

Irene turned to her older sister, eyes wide with a tale to tell. "She was purple all over her face and bleeding blood."

"Did we miss something?" A spoonful of stew halfway to his mouth, Abram was suddenly alert to the remarks at hand. At age eleven, his mind often seemed to stray elsewhere, but the subject was catching fire.

John had to stop it from going further. "It's a personal matter, and you all know private concerns of parishioners are not to be discussed outside of this house."

"Well, we're not outside of this house. We're in it,

and we have a right to know what's going on." John Jr. snapped his suspenders against his blue cotton shirt as he spoke. The oldest at thirteen, he had become more and more outspoken lately.

John felt his jaw twitch. He would deal with the boy's comments later. Anna had always believed the moments together at the evening meal were the best time of the day. He was determined to keep it so. "You know the rules. Now, how was school today?" he asked again, steering the conversation as far away from his afternoon as possible.

He glanced around the table at each face, pausing for a wistful moment at the empty chair opposite him.

~ ~ ~

THE NIGHT WAS SOUNDLESS EXCEPT FOR THE OCCASIONAL clopping of hooves along the city's streets. From the parlor came the rustling of pages while John Jr. read the daily paper—a habit he had taken up recently. The other children lay tucked in their beds upstairs for the night. John sat in his study. Lamplight flowed onto the paper where Sunday's sermon lay scribbled across the page. He reread his words, occasionally scratching out a sentence and writing in new thoughts. But he found himself diverted from the task, pencil tapping against the desk. Beatrice Cooper's face and voice haunted him: *If God approves of such behavior, then he himself is cruel, and I will not believe in such a God.* There was a sermon there somewhere. Not against God, but against ungodly men and the curse of liquor, and for the rights of women.

A hundred thoughts spun through John's head as Sunday's sermon lay ignored. A sudden loud knocking at the front door jolted him from his reverie. Pulling his watch from his waistcoat, he checked the time—a quarter to ten, late for a caller. He heard Johnny open the door and the sound of voices. John stood as the boy appeared at the study door.

"It's Mr. Cooper." Johnny gestured toward the front hallway. In a low whisper added, "He says it's urgent, and he's angry."

John tensed. This was the last person he wanted to see. He muttered a quick prayer. Could he even be civil to the man? Taking a deep breath, he stepped into the hall to confront this unwelcome parishioner. "Good evening, Leroy. What can I do for you at this late hour?"

The visitor stood with defiance, his dark coat dripping melted snow onto the floor, a bowler clenched in his fist. "It's about Beatrice. I understand she came to see you today." The man's gaze bore into John—each spoken word filled with hostility, a whiff of alcohol scenting the hallway.

"Aye, Leroy, she did. But the content of our conversation is confidential."

"That's nonsense!" He flung out a hand almost knocking over the hall tree. "She's my wife, and she had no right coming here. Our problems are none of your business."

John turned to his eldest who stood by, mouth agape, taking in every word. "Go to bed, son." The boy clamped his jaw shut, turned and headed for the stairs. John knew there would be questions later.

Addressing his visitor, he motioned toward the parlor. "Let's discuss this in a civil manner, Leroy. Please, sit."

"No! I don't need your syrupy graciousness. Just tell me where my wife is. She has not come home."

They stood facing each other, John perplexed at what to say next, his visitor's face flushed with anger. "She's safe for now, Leroy, and you need time to calm down." John tried to keep his own voice level. "A little time apart will be good for both of you. Perhaps in a few days the three of us can sit down and discuss this rationally."

From the look in his eyes, John feared the man might strike out and hit him. But the moment passed, and Leroy's shoulders slumped slightly.

"Mind your own affairs, Reverend. We'll fix this ourselves, once she learns her proper place." And without further comment, Leroy Cooper slapped the now misshapen hat on his head, abruptly turned, and walked out the door, slamming it behind him.

Chapter Two

DILEMMAS

T houghts of Beatrice and her whereabouts scarcely left John's mind for the next two days. Had she gone to Cedar Falls? She had seemed hesitant due to the distance. Maybe Belva found a closer hideaway for her sister. Perhaps after a cooling-off spell, Beatrice would return home. John worried about their two young boys, Timothy and Peter. Surely their mother couldn't stay away from them for long. Maybe she could talk some sense into her husband, though that seemed unlikely. Leroy obviously was not the type to bend to the wishes of others.

Some of these questions appeared to be answered on Sunday morning. From the pulpit John met the steady gaze of Leroy Cooper. By his side sat the two boys. The space in the pew normally occupied by Beatrice remained empty.

John had struggled with the content of his sermon for this morning—at first setting aside the one he planned to give on "Imagination and the Christian Mind." Written and presented several years ago at Shenandoah when he pastored the church there, it remained a favorite of his. But with the plight of Beatrice weighing on his mind, the topic had seemed irrelevant. He sought biblical passages emphasizing respect of family and spouse, subtle yet powerful words that hadn't come. It was something he would have to work on and deliver at a more appropriate time. Today such a message would be too obvious and perhaps drive Leroy away. So, the original sermon was back in place.

When the service was over, John stood in the narthex greeting the congregants. Murmurs of "wonderful message, Reverend," and the like, were repeated as each member approached him before leaving the sanctuary. John waited for Leroy Cooper to appear, wondering what they would say to each other, but as the crowd dwindled, it was obvious the man and his two sons had slipped out a side door.

Then, next in line, stood Belva Parker, Beatrice's sister. Wearing her typical subdued brown schoolmarm dress, she smiled. "Good morning, Reverend. I appreciated your words this morning, as always." Her steady gaze seemed to relay a message, though exactly what John wasn't sure. She placed her gloved hand in his for barely a second and then moved on. A slip of paper lay in his palm. He hastily pocketed it before greeting the next church member.

A typical Sabbath day was full from dawn to dusk. Most of the congregants went directly from the church service to Sunday school. John taught lessons to an adult class, and the children gathered in groups by age. From there, the midday meal was often spent at the home of a parishioner, especially since Anna's death. This week the invitation came from Mr. and Mrs. Clyde

Alan, which was good, because the Alans had children close to the ages of John's four. It made for a crowded, boisterous, and cheerful gathering. They sat around a large oak table in the dining room of the old farm house. Sunshine filtered through the lace curtains covering the tall windows that flanked one side of the room. Glowing embers in a fireplace provided heat on this cool February day.

John was asked to say grace before bowls and platters of food began to make the rounds.

"I invited Leroy Cooper and the boys to join us," Mrs. Alan said following the "amen," "Beatrice being sick and all. But he declined."

John sensed his youngest was about to say something. He shook his head, squeezed her hand and, with relief, felt the moment pass.

As much as he appreciated the camaraderie, it seemed like a long afternoon. John was eager to read the note from Belva Parker tucked in his pocket. Finally, they said their thank yous and goodbyes and began the short walk home. John found the crisp, winter air invigorating. The older children chatted among themselves as they hurried along. Irene skipped, her mittened hand clasping John's. He liked the feel of Waterloo, a friendly river town. He and Anna had moved here three and a half years ago for two reasons. Something in the air in Shenandoah aggravated his lungs bringing on a hay fever that often made it difficult for him to breathe. Thinking a different location would be better, he approached other churches. Several had responded positively, but Waterloo had offered the best salary. They settled in and were warmly welcomed. John especially enjoyed the Cedar River that flowed through the community—the life-giving source that had originally created the town. Yet he soon learned this watery path also split Waterloo in two, often causing strong competition between the east and west—sometimes a good thing and other times not so good. Each side had its shopping districts, its prestigious neighborhoods, and those homes with a neglected look.

He and Anna missed Shenandoah and, ironically, it soon became apparent he had not escaped whatever it was that caused his breathing problems. "I'll simply have to live with it," he had told Anna, as they became equally fond of and immersed in their life at Waterloo.

Now she was gone, and he carried on the best he could. This Sunday afternoon in the warmth of the parsonage, they settled in the parlor reading Sunday school lessons. A year ago, Anna would have been holding Irene on her lap reading the primary lesson to her. Now it was Margaret's job. Sunday afternoons and bedtime were when the children seemed to miss their mother the most, and though John tried to appear stoic himself, the ache in his heart felt especially pronounced during what had once been his favorite family time together.

With the children settled, he was anxious to read the paper Belva Parker had placed in his hand after the morning services. He slipped into his study and withdrew the note from his pocket. He laid the crumpled square of paper on the desk, smoothed it with his fingers, and read the brief message:

Beatrice is safe for now. I will watch after the boys as much as I can until she is able to send for them. More later. B.P.

John paced, wondering how long a woman alone could stay in hiding before being recognized. Cedar Falls wasn't that far away, and what about money? Even if her sister had provided her with additional funds, John was certain it wouldn't be enough to go far. Belva Parker's earnings came from a teaching position at the public school, probably just enough to get by herself. She wouldn't have the means to give her sister much assistance. John was aware that both women had inherited a comfortable sum from their father. Belva invested hers in a small house, but Beatrice married Leroy and, according to law, that money was now his. Then there was the issue of the children. To John's understanding, though Beatrice had borne them, she had no legal rights to them. If she took them from her husband, it would be a criminal act. John dwelled on this for a moment, wondering at the accuracy of these thoughts. Some laws had changed in Iowa over the years, and the common law brought to America by the early settlers was gradually being outdated. He made a note to spend time at the courthouse researching the subject.

John shook his head at the injustices. Drink was what led to so many of these similar situations. Something had to be done. The struggle to prohibit the manufacture and sale of intoxicating liquors in Iowa had been an ongoing battle. In 1884, John had read anxiously in the weekly paper about the repeal of the wine and beer legislation which would return state-wide prohibition after an almost thirty-year license. Though he'd breathed many sighs of relief at the time, the next five years had proved how difficult enforcing such laws could be, not only in his hometown of Waterloo, but across the state as a whole. Even if the saloons were closed—and many failed to do so—men like Leroy still found drink. John bowed his head and prayed over the matter, as he had done many times before.

Monday morning brought the usual pandemonium—getting the three oldest children fed and out the door to school. John cleaned up the dishes, trying not to soil his dress shirt, while he mentally tallied the day's schedule.

Irene sat at the table, kicking her feet against the chair while licking jam off her fingers. "Where are we going today, Papa?"

John had anticipated this question. It always came after the other children left for the day, leaving the two of them on their own. Sometimes he took Irene to his church office where he allowed her to scribble on scrap paper while he tended to business. Other times she came with him when he made informal calls at the homes of parishioners. However, that wasn't always possible. When his schedule wouldn't allow Irene to be with him, he walked her to a neighbor's, Mrs. Pennyworth, a reliable older woman who was happy for the small amount of money John paid her. Today would be one of those days.

"I have to go out of town, Reenie. You will stay with Mrs. Pennyworth."

"No! I won't." She stood and stamped her feet. "Mrs.

Pennyworth is old and feeds me food I don't like. Please take me with you, Papa. Pleeease." Tears trickled down her chubby, pink cheeks.

"Not today, Irene. Papa has important business that would be too long and tiring for a little girl."

"I won't be tired. I promise." She hiccupped a sob.

John wiped his dishwater hands on a towel, sat down, and pulled her to him.

She hugged him tightly, clinging as though she couldn't let go. "Bring Mama back, Papa. Please. I don't want to go to Mrs. Pennyworth's."

Twenty minutes later, after leaving her and hurrying away from the neighbor's house, he could still hear his little daughter weeping. It broke his heart each time. It had been almost a year since Anna's death. Being a single parent and the pastor for a large congregation pulled him in too many directions. The emotional strain was taking its toll on him and the children. He often couldn't sleep, and hiring someone to watch over Irene, and to occasionally clean and cook, was a poor substitute for the warmth of the home they had enjoyed when Anna was alive.

Lately, thoughts he had never dreamed of during those first few months after losing Anna had been threading their way out of his subconscious into the forefront of his mind. The children needed a mother, and he needed a helpmate. But more than that, he was lonely and missed the presence of a woman with whom to share the give and take of daily living, someone to be there at the end of the day. Someone to love and return that love.

Chapter Three

A FRIEND FROM THE PAST

Dear Miss McDonald…

John sat at his parsonage desk, a sheet of stationery before him, pen in hand, deep in thought. For days, he had been mentally listing the names of unmarried women among his circle of acquaintances. Few came to mind, and of those, none he could imagine wedding. There was, however, one woman who had charmed him years ago: Ella Clara McDonald. They met at Oberlin College, Ohio, where he took classes after teaching the freed slaves in Texas. She majored in music while his studies centered on the required courses to get him into Yale's Divinity School.

John enjoyed Ella's companionship, intellect, and musical talent, but at that time, his heart belonged to sweet Anna Keen from his staff at Galveston, Texas, where they had both taught the freedmen. Anna had agreed to wait for him no matter how long it took to finish his education. On August 24, 1875, after completing his classes at Oberlin and prior to entering Yale, he and Anna were married at her parents' home in Fulton, Wisconsin.

Now, as John focused on a possible companion and helpmate for himself and the children, memories of Ella crowded into his thoughts—sensing affection had been there between them, just not allowed to surface. *Surely, she has married and now has a family of her own.* But then again, he didn't know for certain Was it too late to rekindle that spark? It seemed absurd. Still, what did he have to lose? So, after much thought, in a determined and crazy moment, he began... *I am writing to let you know of the death of Anna last May ...* as he labored, crumpled sheets of paper representing failed attempts at finding the right words littered the floor until a one-page message finally pleased him.

The envelope bore the only address he'd ever had for her, the home of her parents in Salem, Ohio. He immediately marched to the post office while his nerve held. Then a moment of panic overtook him when the clerk disappeared with John's message in hand—the silliness of it. Though they had lost touch, he and Ella had occasionally corresponded over the years, and as long-time friends, it was perfectly logical for him to write of Anna's death. Yet the underlying reason for the letter was obvious, and of course she wouldn't still be unwed after all this time. What had gotten into him?

The first week after the note had been sent, he scarcely paid attention to the envelopes that arrived—bills, occasional letters from colleagues, solicitations for money and advertisements for anything and everything a pastor of a church might need or want. The second week, however, he collected the mail with eagerness and trepidation, shuffling through the envelopes with shaky fingers, admonishing himself when disappointment dropped his heart a little lower each time the letter he hoped for did not appear.

One day when the mail brought only a slim envelope containing a bill, he scolded Irene for some trivial issue typical of a four-year-old.

She burst into tears. "Papa, don't be mad. I'm only a little girl."

He gathered his precious baby into his arms, close to tears himself. *What am I doing? I mustn't make my own anxiety spill over to the children. Dear God. Dear Anna. Please forgive me, I'm trying to do the right thing.*

Two days later, the letter arrived with the scent of lilac blossoms wafting from the paper. He waited a full five minutes before he opened the seal, unfolded the stationery, and began to read, aware of his suddenly rapid pulse rate.

Dear Reverend Stevenson,

Thank you for your very unexpected note. I am so sorry to hear of Anna's death and can only guess at the sadness this has caused you and the children. Please accept my heartfelt condolences.

As for me, much has happened since our years at Oberlin. In 1881, I married a man whom I met in Defiance while Cora and I taught there. We eventually had a little girl who lived but a few short months before dying of cholera infantum. Nothing compares to the heartache and emptiness that prevails once you have held your own baby in your arms and then she is gone forever.

Without going into details, my marriage was not happy, and six months ago, I was granted a divorce. I know the wedding vows say, "what God has brought together man shall not put asunder," and, as a member of the clergy, you undoubtedly believe what I have done is a sin. All I can say to that is there are worse sins. I hope you can find it in your heart to understand and forgive me for what I have done, but my sanity and happiness were at stake.

I am once again living with my folks in Salem. My father no longer works due to age-related health issues, and I help out financially by giving piano lessons and taking dictation for a local businessman.

Thank you again for your note. It means a lot to hear from you. Give the children my love.

Ella

John sat with the letter in his hand for a long time. He didn't know what he'd expected. That she was married with children? Certainly. That she was still single after all these years? Hopefully. But to have been married and then granted a divorce? This had never entered his mind. Marriage was a sacrament, a religious act. One didn't simply walk away from it. He sighed, said a prayer, and tucked the letter under the Bible on his desk. He would answer it later — or maybe not. With a heavy heart, he stood, put on his coat and left the house. A walk would help clear his mind, then he could get on with life as it was. To even think Ella was available had been a ridiculous notion.

But she was available. A fact he couldn't shake loose from his thoughts. He lay in bed that night unable to sleep. By now he had memorized the letter, attempting to read between the lines. The salutation, *Dear Reverend Stevenson,* was so formal. Hadn't he signed his note to her with his given name, John? Yet two phrases stood out in her letter: *I hope you can find it in your heart to understand and forgive me for what I have done…* and… *It means a lot to hear from you.*

First and foremost, could he forgive her for what she had done? Could he marry a woman who had already divorced one man? He didn't know the answers to these questions. He also realized he knew nothing of the circumstances. He was judging her before he knew the facts. His thoughts kept drifting back to the intelligent and attractive young woman he had known at Oberlin. Something just didn't fit. She was not a quitter. Ella must have been truly unhappy. When he finally dozed off at three o'clock in the morning, her closing statement lingered in his mind. If it meant a lot for her to hear from him, he knew he would write again.

"Papa, why doesn't Mrs. Cooper just divorce Mr. Cooper? I mean, if he is beating her and all." The question came from John's oldest daughter while they washed and dried dishes one evening.

John Jr., who sat at the kitchen table working on a school assignment, piped up, "Because she promised to obey him, that's why."

Maggie put her sudsy hands on her hips, ignoring the fact it meant getting her gingham school dress damp. "And he promised to love her. I've heard those marriage vows. Beating your wife is not love."

The boy shrugged his shoulders and returned his attention to his lessons.

John listened to his children's comments with interest. Beatrice Cooper still had not returned to

Waterloo, and her absence created an undercurrent of scandal among church parishioners. The subject seemed to be on everyone's mind, including his daughter's.

She turned to him. "Don't you agree, Papa? Surely you can see that Mr. Cooper is wrong."

John had been giving the subject of divorce a lot of thought lately himself, and not just because of the Coopers. He hesitated a moment before answering, wiped a dinner plate dry, and placed it on a stack in the cupboard. "Well, Margaret, I do believe marriage is a sacred union and should be treated as such, but I also believe God did not intend for marriage to be a hell on earth."

A snicker immediately erupted from Johnny—hell being a word not usually heard in their household. The boy dropped his pencil. It rolled across the table and fell to the floor. Maggie's flushed face bore a smug smile.

"Therefore," John continued, "I believe divorce is not always wrong. There are certain circumstances when it is a blessing. If divorce frees a man or woman from a terrible life, then it is right."

Johnny was back in the discussion. "What about 'what God hath joined together, man shall not put asunder,' or however it goes. I've heard you say that with great conviction while marrying a couple." He picked up his pencil and flipped it back and forth in his fingers, obviously waiting for his father's response.

"'What God hath joined together' does not mean what the justice of peace or the gospel minister has joined together, son. Both of these dignitaries frequently join together couples in whose union God never has taken a hand. And, what is more, he would contradict any such insinuation or implication."

The conversation with his children allowed John to say aloud what had been working through his mind for several days. It helped convince him not to rush judgment on Ella.

There are worse sins, she had written about her divorce.

A week after receiving her letter, John pulled out a piece of paper and began to write, *Dear Ella…*

Thus, the correspondence began, and with each letter, John's doubts and misgivings became more and more diluted. Each response from her felt less formal, more like the Ella he had known so long ago. She never explained the why of her divorce. He never questioned her about it. It mattered less and less to him. Finally, after several weeks, he suggested he come to call on her. She replied in the affirmative.

"Where are you going, Papa?" little Irene asked at supper the day before he was scheduled to leave.

"To see a friend from the past," John said. He had not mentioned his reason to the children, still not knowing how it would turn out. However, he didn't miss the looks exchanged among his three older children responding to what he hoped had been a casual remark. He knew they suspected something different from a church-related trip was afoot.

"Can I come, Papa?" Irene asked, making circles in her soup with a spoon that had yet to bring any of the warm liquid to her mouth. "I want to come."

"Not this time, Reenie. Ohio is a long way. I'll be

gone a whole week. Mrs. Pennyworth will stay here while I'm gone."

~ ~ ~

JOHN LEFT WATERLOO EARLY ON A MONDAY MORNING IN May, a year after Anna's death. A retired pastor who occasionally substituted in the pulpit when John's throat bothered him had agreed to preach the following Sunday.

The trip grew tiresome, involving several transfers from stage to train and train to stage. During the long ride, as the countryside drifted by, John had too much time to think. Fourteen years had passed since he and Ella last saw each other. He still felt fit and young—not yet developing a paunch like so many men his age. He tugged at his mustache and thought back to the man he had been during his studies at Oberlin. Certainly, he was mature then, especially following his challenges while teaching the freedmen in Texas. Yet now, at forty-eight, life's experiences had proven the naiveté of many of his convictions during those college years.

Ella had been raised in Salem, Ohio, and hadn't ventured much beyond that community except to Oberlin. She had two older sisters, Nell and Cora, and talked of Cora, three years her senior, with great pride—a teacher taking post-graduate classes at the University of Chicago and a strong advocate of women's rights. Ella, now in her mid-thirties, would not be the same person as that young woman he once knew. Her letters attested to that. John wondered again if perhaps this venture was simply folly. All during the trip his thoughts vacillated between an apprehension of approaching her and the longing for a companion to fill the deep void that had opened at Anna's last living breath. As his destination loomed, a rumbling lump in his stomach grew. He shook away the feeling. *Enough of this. I am on my way, whatever the outcome.*

Once in Salem, John sought a hotel where he washed off the grime of travel, ate a light meal and, surprisingly, slept well. At ten o'clock the following morning, he knocked on the door of a simple frame house in a pleasant, tree-lined neighborhood. *It's the same house where I grew up*, Ella had written in the letter giving him instructions on how to get there. *You will meet my folks, John and Fanny McDonald, but not my sisters, both still unmarried. They are off teaching in other communities.*

John held a small bouquet of yellow daisies, his sweaty palms crushing the stems. Having found no store that carried flowers, he had paid a lady fifty cents to allow him to pick a few from her garden. At his knock, footsteps approached from inside the house, and suddenly he felt himself a flustered sixteen again, wondering what he would say when Ella opened the door.

An older, heavy-set, pleasant-looking woman answered his knock. Her navy blue dress trimmed with lace seemed more appropriate for church than an afternoon visitor, but John sensed she had fancied up just for him. "Mrs. McDonald?" he managed to blurt in his disappointment—having expected her daughter to answer the door.

"Good morning, Reverend Stevenson. Please come

in. I'll call Ella. She's expecting you."

He stood in the entry hall, feeling awkward. Then, there she was, looking self-assured, her face a little older, of course, but dominated by the same warm smile, her wheat-colored hair draping to her shoulders in soft curls, pulled back from her face with mother-of-pearl combs. John's heart stirred at the sight of her. She wore a pale green shirtwaist featuring a row of vertical pleats from the high neck to where it was tucked into a skirt of darker green.

"Mr. Stevenson, how good to see you again. Please come in."

He handed her the flowers feeling the soft tug of a grin on his face, "Ella, you are as pretty as ever."

"Thank you—for the compliment and the flowers. They are lovely." She led him into the parlor. "Please make yourself comfortable. I'll put these in a vase and get some tea."

He didn't sit. During these few moments alone, he studied the room. A writing desk stood against one wall next to a grandfather clock. A settee and two chairs, upholstered in a matching, slightly faded flowered print flanked a low table. A piano dominated one corner. This made him smile. It was the very essence of the Ella he had remembered—a woman who loved and excelled in music.

She entered the room with the flowers in a vase, which she set upon the table. Her mother followed with a tray containing a tea pot, cups, and saucers, and a plate of what appeared to be ginger snaps. Behind her hobbled a gray-haired, bushy-bearded man, supported by a gnarled cane, his trousers held up with bright red suspenders. He held out his hand to John. "Reverend Stevenson, it's a pleasure."

John grasped the man's hand. "Likewise," he said.

They sat, Ella and John together on the settee, Mr. and Mrs. McDonald opposite them in the chairs.

"Well," Mrs. McDonald began, while pouring tea into the cups. "It is quite a trip from Iowa to Ohio. I hope the weather was nice. Cream and sugar, Reverend?"

"No, thank you. Plain is fine."

Mrs. McDonald handed him a cup and saucer. "Ella says you are from Scotland and had barely been here when you went to teach the freed slaves in Texas. That must have been something."

During the next half hour, John said very little, unable to squeeze in a word while the woman talked non-stop. Mr. McDonald said nothing, just sat there and wheezed as though breathing were a huge effort. John couldn't tell if he was even interested in the conversation, but surmised the man had given in to his wife's chatter years before.

John felt perspiration trickle along his temples. The small house was close and stuffy in the May heat, and the warm tea worsened his discomfort. He pulled a handkerchief from his pocket and wiped his brow.

Ella, who had added a comment or two when possible, finally interrupted her mother. "It's a little warm. I think Mr. Stevenson and I will take a walk. There should be a breeze about now." She stood and smiled at John. "Is that all right with you?"

"A fine idea." Relief at the suggestion brought a

different warmth. Ella was in tune with his feelings, just as he sensed she had been all those years ago at Oberlin. He felt himself relax as they left the house and strolled up the street.

They visited for hours during the next few days. And each moment John felt more confident his trip had not been made in vain. He and Ella thought so much alike on a variety of subjects. They took little trips away from town most days, and during the hours Ella taught music lessons or worked at dictation, John either walked on his own or wrote letters and sermons in his hotel room. Each evening he was invited to Ella's home for supper. As the days passed, he found Mrs. McDonald's prattle less frustrating. She was, after all, a pleasant woman and Ella's mother.

When he arrived at the house for his last evening in Salem, to his surprise, Mr. and Mrs. McDonald were absent. The table was set for two with candles flickering, a gardenia centered between them.

"My parents have gone to visit my Aunt Sadie. They haven't seen her in a while, and she isn't well," Ella explained. "I fixed our meal tonight. It's lamb. I hope you like it."

It was obviously planned so the two of them could be alone. Time was running short. John was scheduled to leave for home in twenty-four hours, and he had not yet had the courage to ask Ella to marry him. Even as they ate and chatted by candlelight, the subject was not broached. There were still questions in his mind and, he suspected, hers, too. When she rose to clear away the dishes, he stood, suggesting he help her clean up.

"I've had a lot of practice lately," he said. "We are usually invited to a meal at the home of a parishioner on Sunday, but on most other evenings, one of the children and I cook, and I have another child clean up afterward while I help. It gives us special time together."

"I would love to meet your children. They sound very responsible," Ella said with a smile.

"I want you to meet them, Ella." And suddenly it seemed the time to ask her. He had rehearsed it over and over in his mind. They would be in the parlor and he would get down on his knee—all very formal and proper. Yet here he was in his shirtsleeves, she in an apron with suds on her hand and a question in her eyes. She was expecting it now. It came easy, the asking. "They need a mother, Ella, and I need a wife and helpmate. You would do us a great honor if you would say yes to those roles."

She hesitated before replying—a moment that brought a queasiness to his stomach. Had he read her wrong? Did she not expect this? But then she spoke.

"I would be greatly honored to be Mrs. John Stevenson." Her smile was genuine, and tears accentuated the sparkle in her eyes. "Only..." She hesitated again. "But..."

He took her hand, suds and all, trying to read her mind. "I know it won't be easy. The children miss Anna terribly, but they'll adjust. It will be all right. You and I can make it work. I know we can."

"It's not that, John. It's, well, the fact I'm divorced. Would that be too scandalous for a preacher's wife?"

He smiled, and relief rolled through him like a burst

of sunlight. Ah, that was it. It was a fact that had totally left his mind during the past week. It had become a non-issue he had not even discussed with her. "It's none of their business. Besides, why do they have to know? That's all in the past. This will be your new life, a new beginning."

The tears in Ella's eyes spilled down her cheeks, and she laid her head against his chest. "Thank you. Oh, John, thank you."

He held her for a moment, then she stepped back and looked up at him. "I can't be Anna," she said, "but I will try to be the very best mother and wife I can be and understand the children's feelings."

Of that he had no doubt, but he had some other concerns he should voice. "You must also be aware it is difficult to be the wife of a minister." He paced the kitchen. "The parishioners will expect you to be perfect and always to be there when they have a need, no matter what trials and tribulations you might be experiencing in your own life. Also, I often must go on speaking trips and to meetings, taking me away from home." He stopped to control an unexpected welling of emotion, remembering how hard this had been on Anna. He cleared his throat and continued, "And you must be aware that not everyone agrees with my stand on certain issues."

Ella placed her hand on his arm. "Why, Reverend, I hope you are not trying to get me to change my mind."

"Not at all. I'm simply a wee bit nervous about bringing you into situations that might be difficult for you."

"I greatly admire your willingness to stand up for what you think is right. It's one of the things I admired about you at Oberlin."

Her encouraging remarks brought a tiny trickle of warmth circulating through him—the same sensation he had experienced when he first laid eyes on Anna Keen in Galveston so many years ago. *Thank you, Lord,* he whispered. He gently kissed Ella on the cheek. He felt his future blossom like the first rose of spring.

Chapter Four

A NEW MOTHER

The dishes done, they moved to the parlor. A rose-tinted glow flowed through a window from a setting sun that would soon dissolve into darkness. Ella lit a lamp and placed it on the tea table. John sat beside her on the settee and took her hand in his. There was a lot to discuss.

They agreed he would return to Ohio in July for the marriage vows. "I need time to prepare the children and tell certain members of the congregation who were once close to Anna about you. I can't simply show up at church one morning with a new wife," he said.

"Oh, my no," Ella said. "Please tell your parishioners. I will feel much more comfortable meeting them knowing they are aware of me." She hesitated a moment, fingering the lace on her sleeve. "I'm certain you'll be discreet about my past." It was almost a question.

John took her hand and nodded. This was obviously still a concern of hers. She would have to trust him.

Ella smiled and turned her focus to the wedding and her obligations in Salem. "I would like Cora and Nell to be here for the ceremony, if possible," she said. "They will need time to make travel plans. It might be difficult for Cora as a high school principal coming from Wyoming. Then there is my stenography position and the piano lessons to terminate, things to pack—oh my, much to be done, but it's all so exciting." She squeezed John's hand, sending a burst of sparks racing up his arm. He hadn't thought it possible to be this happy again. Still, there were serious concerns to address.

"I know you have been helping your folks financially. Will taking away your support hurt them?" he asked. "I wish I could contribute, but my salary is barely adequate for a family, and unfortunately won't stretch to another household."

"They'll be fine," Ella assured him. "Nell and Cora help a little, and mother takes in laundry and sewing. They've always been frugal and have a small savings account. My living with them has been an added expense, too." She beamed as she spoke the words, as though she could hardly believe how her life was about to change.

~ ~ ~

ON THE RETURN TRIP TO WATERLOO, JOHN'S HEART sang. He caught his reflection in the train window with a grin on his face. He rehearsed over and over what he would say to the children, praying: *Please, Lord, make them understand and be as happy as I am about this decision.*

It was the dinner hour when he approached the parsonage, and the clink of dishes and chatter of voices wafted through the windows, open to catch breezes on the warm evening air. John quietly entered the house, placed his valise on the foyer floor, and stepped into the kitchen. He stood in the doorway a moment, unobserved, enjoying the scene of his children gathered around the table—hope and excitement for their future catching in his throat.

Irene spied him first.

"Papa!" she squealed, and in an instant was in his arms.

The other three children pushed back their chairs, jumped up and crowded around, firing questions at him in a cacophony of voices, each hug a special reward.

"Welcome back, Reverend," Mrs. Pennyworth said. "There's plenty to eat, so pull yourself up a seat." She motioned to his empty chair at the end of the table. Back in their places with the clamor somewhat subdued, John gazed into each face. "You look well and happy. How's everything?"

For a moment, an awkward silence prevailed, then Irene, burst into tears. "It's been awful, Papa. Please don't go away again. Everything is too different." She looked down at her plate where a generous serving of succotash remained untouched. The other children said nothing, their gazes focused away from the woman who sat opposite John—formerly their mother's place at the table.

Mrs. Pennyworth laid down her napkin and stood. "I did my best, Reverend. I'm just not Anna." She picked up her plate and took it to the sink. "I do have some peach crisp for dessert. I know you all like that."

The tension of the moment eased as Mrs. Pennyworth handed out the warm, cinnamon-scented dessert. "Now, while you enjoy the crisp, I'll clean up and be on my way, Reverend. We can discuss payment later. I know you want to be alone with the children."

"Thank you, Mrs. Pennyworth. I greatly appreciate all you have done. The dessert is very good. Isn't that right, children?" He eyed them and received nods and a couple of "yes, sirs."

A few moments of silence followed while their mouths were full. They seemed at odds as to who would speak first. Maggie put down her spoon, flipped her braids and gave her father a cautious look. "And what about you, Papa? What did you do in Ohio? Did you find your old friend?" He sensed a wary note in her voice.

John swallowed a large bite of crisp and cleared his throat. The dessert seemed to plop into his stomach like a handful of pebbles. He was eager to share his news, yet his nerves felt taut to the point of snapping. "When we are through here, let's go into the parlor, and I'll tell you all about it. I have gifts, too."

Irene squealed again. "Oh, goody! Presents!" She clapped her hands and pushed away from the table. "Can we go now? I ate all my dessert." She held up a crumb-free plate.

Once in the parlor, a feeling of Christmas filled the air as they gathered around John. He handed each child a package especially selected with his or her interest in mind: a doll for Irene, perfume for Maggie, a tool for Abram, and a book for Johnny.

When the oohing, aahing and thank yous subsided, John cleared his throat again. "The best present is the good news I bring back from Ohio." Suddenly, the gaiety ceased, and inquisitive eyes turned to John. He took a deep breath and the words tumbled out. "I'm going to be married. We will once again have a woman in the house. Someone to love us and take care of us. A new mother."

No one said a thing. A thick silence dominated the room as though a heavy quilt had smothered them.

John forged ahead. "Her name is Ella, and I've known her for a long time. She is very eager to meet you, and you will like her."

Still no response. "Your mother knew her, too, and liked her very much. She, your mother, would be happy to know that someone like Ella is coming to complete our family." This wasn't entirely true. Ella and Anna had never met in person, but they knew of each other during the few years they had corresponded after John left Oberlin.

Irene broke the silence first. "A new mama? I won't have to go to Mrs. Pennyworth's anymore?" Her expression bore a mix of a question and the beginning of a smile.

"Aye, Reenie. No more Mrs. Pennyworth," John mentally crossed his fingers. "It will be like before. When Mama was here."

Irene's smile broadened. She jumped up, clutching the new doll in glee and twirled in a dance until she fell to the floor in dizzy laughter. John laughed, too, hopeful that his littlest child's enthusiasm would transfer to the others.

Maggie crossed her arms, her lower lip pooching out, tears swimming in her eyes. "No, Papa. It won't be like before, because she isn't Mama, and I won't call her Mama. I won't."

John reached for his older daughter and gave her a hug. "I know it's a new idea, Maggie, but give her a chance. This doesn't mean we will forget your mother or love her memory any less, but she would be happier knowing you are being cared for."

Abram said nothing, just opened and closed the new pair of pliers he held in his hand. It was as though he hadn't been listening. John could feel the boy's conflict over loyalty to his dead mother but sensed he would adjust. Of all the children, Abram was usually best at accepting new situations.

Yet it was his eldest son's reaction that caused John to choke up. Johnny came forward and held out his hand. "Congratulations, Papa. I hope she makes you as happy as Mama did. I will try my best to like her."

~ ~ ~

JOHN MADE THE LONG TRIP TO SALEM ONCE AGAIN SIX weeks later. He and Ella were married on July 18, 1889, in her parents' home. Nell was there, a taller, older version of her sister, whose modest dresses hung a little loose on her thin body. Unfortunately, Cora was unable to come, instead sending money for wedding clothes. Ella glowed in a mauve ensemble with black trim accents and a white blouse sporting a lace jabot—a lovely yet practical attire she would be able to wear again to church as the minister's wife. John thought his bride radiant and couldn't take his eyes off her as they exchanged vows. Mrs. McDonald cried, and Mr.

McDonald snuffled into a big, red handkerchief. John was touched at their obvious love for this daughter who, after some hard times, was now given a second chance at happiness.

~ ~ ~

LIFE AT THE PARSONAGE SETTLED INTO A NEW ROUTINE. There were awkward moments, of course, but Ella's piano music proved to be the adhesive necessary to bring the family together.

The large instrument took too much space in the parlor, causing other furniture to be crowded together, but it was a blessing. Irene often sat on the bench beside Ella, pressing the keys in counter tones to pieces her new mother played—creating noise that did not resemble music, yet was a happy sound regardless. Johnny sang in a choir at church, and Ella learned the accompaniment so he could practice with her at home. Maggie, who still refused to call her "mother," agreed to lessons. As her own talent grew, so did her resistance to this substitute for Anna. Abram seemed to tolerate these changes. As for John, when Ella sat down at the keyboard, the silvery melodies floating into every corner of the parsonage filled his heart, bringing a contentment he had not known in a long while.

Any worries he had about Ella's acceptance by the church ladies dissolved after their first Sunday at home. Apparently, many of the women had been concerned about his solitude and the responsibility of four children. Some had even felt it their duty to find him a suitable mate, and now that obligation was lifted from their shoulders. When Maggie relayed this to him one day after hearing it from a friend, John shook his head. "No one could force a wife on me," he said, "nor a mother for my children. It had to be my choice. The right choice."

Looking back, he felt his response had somehow softened Maggie's attitude toward Ella—that, and the fact that the church ladies were eager to welcome her into the congregation. Jane Logan offered to arrange a reception for them. An article in the *Courier* the following week told of the event:

On Tuesday evening of last week, a reception was tendered to Rev. and Mrs. J. O. Stevenson at the residence of J. W. Logan. A very pleasant evening was spent. A pleasing feature was the presentation of a flower of the night blooming cereus to the bride, by Mrs. J. N. Sweitzer. This flower was one of four which bloomed that evening on the plant owned by Mrs. Sweitzer. The plant is about ten years old and is blooming very prolifically this season.

Ella had gently carried the special flower home. "I'm going to press it and keep it forever as a wonderful remembrance of the friendly and accepting people of the Waterloo Congregational Church," she told John.

In the middle of their conversation, Irene skipped into the parlor. "Mama, could you please tie my bow?" She turned her back to Ella and pointed to the two long ribbons hanging from the waist of her blue calico dress.

"Why, of course, my lovely."

John watched with a lump in his throat while the new mother tied a perfect bow for her new little daughter.

Chapter Five

TEMPERANCE

John sat at his desk, shuffling through the pages of the next day's sermon. The clock chimed eleven. The children had long been tucked in for the night, and Ella tiptoed into the study.

"I'll leave you be, John. I'm especially weary this evening and will retire to bed."

He nodded, his mind elsewhere. Then, checking his rudeness, he stood and embraced his new wife. "I'll be along in a little while. I need to get this organized."

"I know," she replied, and he thanked the Lord once more for providing such an understanding woman.

Now, in the quiet of the night, two sounds stood out—the methodic ticking of the clock on the top shelf of the bookcase and the wheezing in his lungs. Of the two distractions, the one in his chest bothered him most. As had been the case in Shenandoah, something here in Waterloo, he knew not what, brought this on every year, often in the spring and always in late summer. At times breathing became such a chore, he simply had to leave the area for several weeks—usually to the cabin of a friend in Bayfield, Wisconsin, on the shore of Lake Superior. *Dear Lord, please don't let it come to that this year—so soon after Ella's arrival and with the household finally settling into a routine.*

He forced himself to return to the task at hand. It was time again to preach on the temperance issue. He had several sermons already written on the subject and selected one he had done while serving the church in Shenandoah. He still liked what it said, though it needed to be brought current. For most church members, this was a popular subject. Many of the ladies belonged to the Women's Christian Temperance Union. However, on the Sundays when John expounded on the issue, he noted a few men squirmed in their pews, some unable to meet his gaze.

His mind drifted to Beatrice Cooper. It had been six months since she had come to him bruised and bleeding at the hand of her drunken husband—a terribly long time. She had not reappeared, and rumors abounded at church as to her whereabouts, largely whispers of disapproval. The general feeling of both men and women was that, since Beatrice had vowed to love and obey for better or worse, her place was at home with her husband and children. John wondered how many knew of the beatings. But even then, the sentiment would undoubtedly be the same. A home was a man's castle. He was in charge. The "little" woman had no rights. John sighed.

He had done research on current laws, but information regarding a woman's rights in Iowa was mixed and confusing. The old common law of England regularly prevailed. Rulings in favor of women seemed determined by the thinking of each judge hearing a case. If a woman filed for divorce, she could be granted custody of her children, especially if certain reasons for her filing were evident—drunkenness of the husband being one of them. However, Leroy could also divorce Beatrice for desertion and therefore get custody of the children.

Leroy no longer attended services. John often asked Belva Parker of her sister's whereabouts. The usual answer, "She is doing all right," left John unsatisfied and worried.

"And the boys?" he would ask.

"I look after them as much as I can."

No real information was forthcoming. One Sunday, though, she startled him by offering a warning. "Reverend, you need to know that Leroy highly resents your meddling in his affairs and more than once has threatened to 'shut you up,' whatever that means. If I were you, I wouldn't take that lightly."

He shook his head at these thoughts while he pondered the sermon before him. Such a wrong. Such an unnecessary tragedy. Why couldn't Leroy see the damage he'd done to the poor woman? *Ah, the weaknesses of man. And society, and its saloons, are equally to blame.*

John picked up the introduction to his sermon and began reading:

Temperance

A few years ago today, a nonpartisan election was held on the moral issue of temperance, having for its object the promotion of temperance by constitutional prohibition. The men of the State of Iowa voted without regard to party lines or political measures and the result was an overwhelming majority for the insertion of a prohibitory law in our constitution.

Several years have passed away and still intemperance must be guarded against both in its manufacture, sale, and consumptions. Is this to be wondered at? Not at all. States are like persons. Absolute perfection is a dream, relative perfection a possibility and a reality; absolute holiness is impossible in our day, progressive holiness is possible and real. If the vote for constitutional prohibition had been an absolutely unanimous vote, and every vote the vote of an honest conscience, and every conscience the conscience of a saint, then the manufacture, sale, and consumption of liquor would have ceased absolutely in Iowa.

But the vote was neither unanimous, wholly honest, nor cast by saints and therefore we hear of difficulties local and sporadic that are met within the administration of prohibition and other temperance laws. Weak men voted with the majority and there was a strong minority against the measure, therefore we are called upon to continue to manufacture and to sustain with public opinion upon this important moral issue in behalf of the measures that have been thus far set afoot for its ultimate success.

John continued writing, adding what he felt was the meat of the sermon: that based on biblical verse. *Ecclesiastes, XII: 13-14: Let us hear the conclusion of the whole matter: Fear God, and keep his commandments: for this is the whole duty of man. For God shall bring every work into judgment, with every secret thing, whether it be good, or whether it be evil.*

John perused the pages before him, scratching out a few words here and there, inserting new ones. On page eight he read forward with approval:

Does not society owe to each individual the duty of surrounding that individual with an environment favorable to morality and temperance? A community that maintains saloons sins against every individual composing that community... If an act, or a business, or a place is wrong as seen by God, then "thou shalt not" is the only right thing for society to say. And this is God's commandment.

Once again John reflected on Leroy and Beatrice Cooper. Ideally, the man would stop his drunken rages, she would return to him and their children, and they would become a godly, happy family. Yet, the longer Beatrice stayed away, the more John doubted this would happen.

Reaching for the last page of the sermon, he read it aloud:

"It is proper to prohibit, and it is proper to obey.... He who fears God and keeps his commandments will have no trouble."

John closed his eyes, bowed his head and prayed that his message would reach out and touch not only those who needed it, but also those who could do something about curtailing the availability of liquor. He didn't object to a man's occasional drink for pleasure if that man could control his consumption. There was a difference between drinking and drunkenness. Unfortunately, saloons encouraged the latter, and drunkenness so often led to spousal abuse. Feeling satisfied with the words he had chosen, he closed the sermon booklet and set it beside his Bible in readiness for the morning.

The following day, John felt refreshed. The tightness in his chest had loosened and his breathing came easier. He stepped up to the pulpit full of resolve. He would get his message across. The current laws would be enforced as intended, instead of being ignored, and new, stronger prohibition laws voted in.

As he spoke his convictions, loud and firm, his gaze swept the congregation. Seventy-five percent of those present were women, and with them lay the strength of his belief in the matter of temperance. His thoughts spun. Women could not vote, yet there lay the answer. With woman suffrage it would be possible to control, manage, modify or abolish the liquor traffic. Without woman suffrage, such efforts simply beat the air. With these issues of suffrage in the home, the school, and the church, there could be a triumph at the ballot box. In that moment he realized without suffrage for women, any talk regarding what churches could do, about what schools ought to do, and about the sanctity and power of the home, was in vain.

~ ~ ~

HE AND ELLA STROLLED HOME FOLLOWING THE SERVICE. For the first time since Ella arrived, they had not been invited out for Sunday dinner. They had the afternoon to themselves. The normally hot sun had relented, conveying a hint of fall as a welcome breeze gently flipped the leaves of the trees lining the walkway. The children hurried on ahead.

Ella linked her hand through the crook of John's arm. "Your message was excellent," she said. "You hit the nail on the head, and I sensed most of the congregation thought so, too."

With Ella beside him, the refreshing air, and his hay fever abated, John should have felt serene. But the revelation that had come to him during the sermon dominated his mind. "I was preaching to the choir," he said. "Without suffrage for women, there is very little any audience can do about the problem, and yet women are the very ones whose vote could make the difference."

"Well," Ella said, giving his arm a squeeze. "Perhaps, then, you should pound the pulpit for a woman's right to have a voice in the government. Make it a goal. That just might solve a lot of problems."

He abruptly stopped, faced her and grabbed both her hands, his feelings of frustration turning to determination. "You are so right, my dear. You are so right." His head suddenly swarmed with ideas— sermons to preach, articles to write. He would join the suffragists who had worked so tirelessly for years, and perhaps in the near future, Iowa and even the nation would allow women to have a say and a vote in temperance and all moral issues.

Chapter Six

A SMART GIRL

John strode purposefully in the crisp fall air, enjoying the beauty of trees dressed in orange, red and golden hues. Hay fever season was finally over, and he had survived without being forced to leave the area. He hummed as he walked—something he was prone to do when his world seemed right. His morning meeting with the trustees had gone well, and his coat pocket held three letters delivered to the church, where he received mail related to his pastorate. He was ambivalent about the contents of these particular envelopes, yet was eager to share them with his wife.

As he approached the parsonage, he spied Irene peering out the window, a bright smile on her face. It was good that his youngest daughter was able to stay home—her day no longer dictated by his own schedule. Ella was sure to have a hot noon meal ready for the three of them. Yes, life was fine.

The little girl met him at the door. "Come, Papa. Come eat." She pulled him into the kitchen where Ella, drying her hands on her apron, came forward and gave him a kiss. "You are just in time, Reverend. Dinner is served."

They sat at the kitchen table, and John offered a

prayer of thanks for the warmth of the house, a hearty meal of chopped chicken with gravy on toast. He ended the prayer with, "and for my lovely, capable wife and charming daughter."

The four-year-old giggled. "Is charmin' good, Papa?"

"Aye, that is very good, and you are it."

"And how were the trustees this morning? Agreeable?" Ella asked between bites.

"Generally. Some voiced concerns about a few negative comments made behind my back regarding the subject matter of my sermons, but mostly things are fine, and John Leavitt as chairman runs an orderly meeting. How was your morning?"

"Well, after the other children left for school, Irene and I did some baking. And guess what? The postman brought a letter from Cora. She has applied for a position at the University of Wyoming to teach English. Isn't that something? She'll be a college professor!" Ella picked up an envelope from the table and pulled out several sheets of paper. "Cora also enclosed part of a speech she gives on the success of woman suffrage in the Wyoming Territory. What a forward-thinking place. They've allowed women the vote since 1869, you know. Cora says with women at the polls, some positive changes have been made."

Ella scanned a page until she came to a paragraph and began reading: "Previous to the enfranchisement of women, election day was marked by drunken riot and often by crime. Frequently a man took his life in his hand when he went to the polls. With woman suffrage came peace and order, clean polls, fair ballot, mutual respect and toleration."

John nodded at this comment. "Maybe we should get her to come to Iowa and give a talk. The Iowa Woman Suffrage Association could use a boost, and our general assembly needs to hear of the success in Wyoming."

"That would be grand if she could come." Ella's eyes sparkled. "I'll write and ask her. Ohio could use some of that success story, too."

John smiled at Ella's enthusiasm whenever this special sister became part of the conversation. "I have some letters to share, too," he said. Pushing back his chair, he stood and reached for his coat hanging on a hook by the door. He retrieved the three envelopes from a pocket and returned to his seat.

"What would you say about a move to Shenandoah? It's a little closer to Wyoming and your sister."

Ella looked taken-aback. "Are you serious?"

"Not really, but they do want me back." He held up a letter. "This is from Mr. Lake, one of the parishioners while I pastored there. I'm sure he knows what my answer will be. In addition to health issues, I had to leave because that small church could not afford to pay me enough to support my growing family, but it is nice to know I am still welcome." He picked up the other two envelopes. "Or we could move to Red Oak. According to these accounts, they would like me there, too." He removed a sheet of paper. "This is from a Mr. E. M. Carry who writes in part: I desire very much that your name may come up before the church by Sunday next and I am sure that a strong and quite likely unanimous invitation will be made to visit us …"

"A visit?" Ella asked, a puzzled look on her face. "Maybe they only want you to come and preach on a Sunday."

John shook his head. "A visit is required in these matters before a decision is made as to a new minister. But Red Oak can't afford me either, and that is why I am here in Waterloo. As much as I'd like to preach at one of these locations, our budget won't allow it, so don't fret over a move, at least not for now."

He set the envelopes aside. This type of letter was not uncommon—churches often sought new preachers. But the fact that Shenandoah wanted him back brought good memories and tugged at his heart. He and Anna had loved that little town and the church members. It was flattering to be asked back; his written responses, along with his polite refusals, would say as much.

He could tell from the expression on Ella's face she had more to say on the matter. "You have another question?"

"Not so much a question as a possible solution. If you truly want to return to Shenandoah or go to Red Oak, and money is the problem, I've been trained as a stenographer, you know. I worked in that capacity in Ohio to help out with expenses at home and could do that again to bring in additional income."

Her remark surprised John. In fact, he felt a bit offended. After all, he was the head of the household and the bread winner. But it was more than that. "I couldn't allow you to do that. For one thing, you are needed at home for Irene, and the older children after school. Then there is the issue of meals and other womanly responsibilities. No, I won't return to Shenandoah if it means you working outside the home. Waterloo is fine for now."

Ella stood abruptly and began clearing the dishes, her lips set in a firm line. "Well, Reverend Stevenson, congratulations on receiving those letters. Obviously, more people agree with your broadminded preaching than those who don't. But remember, when promoting woman's rights and suffrage, words mean nothing if you can't practice what you preach."

This was the first time she seemed irritated with him, and he wasn't quite certain how to respond. He did agree with women participating in the workforce when it was necessary. However, that was not the case for them. It was thoughtful of Ella to offer, but she should be grateful her homemaking talents were needed. John continually complimented her on her attention to the children, her meal preparation, and house cleaning. How could she be angry at him for appreciating the way she handled her place in his home? The minute that thought entered his mind, he felt an unpleasant jolt in his gut. Those were the very words Leroy Cooper had used the night he stormed into the parsonage looking for Beatrice, insisting their marriage would be fine when his wife "learned her proper place." But of course, this was totally different. *I would never, ever strike Ella to keep her in her place.*

Irene sat quietly spooning toast and gravy into her mouth while they talked. She swallowed several gulps of milk and plopped her cup on the table with a thud. "What is woman's suppage?"

"It's 'suffrage,' and is an important cause you need to know about," Ella responded with an atypical edge to her voice.

Irene wrinkled her nose. "What's a cause?"

John wiped his mouth with a napkin, placed it on the table and leaned back in his chair. "It's something people feel to be so important they work hard to make it happen. The word 'suffrage' means the right to have a vote—to change laws and make things better. Right now, except where Aunt Cora lives, women are not allowed to vote. Many folks think that is wrong and are trying to change it."

"We think it's time to show that we women are as smart as men," Ella said crisply. She didn't look at John.

Irene appeared to think about this for a moment. "I'm not as smart as Papa."

"Well," Ella said, "you do have a very smart papa." Her curtness seemed to have softened. "But you are a very smart little girl. By the time you grow up, we hope you will be able to vote and show the world just how smart you are."

Irene grinned, slid off her chair, grabbed a rag doll she had left on the floor, and ran to the parlor. John winked at Ella as they heard the little girl singing, "I'm a smart girl. I'm a smart girl. I'm a very smart girl."

"Surely she'll be able to vote when she is a woman," Ella said with a sigh as she picked up Cora's letter again. "How can a territory like Wyoming take the lead when the legislators in real states refuse to even consider enfranchising women? At least several states give women the right to vote on school issues, though in Kentucky, if I remember right, it's only for widows with school children. I guess Kansas allows women to vote on municipal matters. None of it is enough, but it's a start."

John's heart warmed at Ella's conviction. She certainly kept up on these issues. He had heard this before, even years ago when they were in school together at Oberlin. Her belief in equal rights was one of the things that most attracted him to her. He thought again about her suggestion to work outside of the home. This was really more about her beliefs and her eagerness to help, if necessary. He must understand it was a gesture of love, not an insult to his position in the household. Still he felt a little uneasy about her comment that he should practice what he preached.

Later that evening, as he sat in his study contemplating the new role he had thrust upon himself as a male suffragist, he mentally revisited his own conflicts on the matter. Was he really ready to accept full equality for men and women in every situation? Didn't men and women still have specific roles to play? In the years since his youth, he had encountered too many intelligent women to consider them inferior. And he certainly believed women in general held a higher moral standard than most men. Couldn't they retain their femininity, keep their "place," and express their opinions on a ballot?

He ran a hand through his hair and gazed out the window at the infinite scattering of stars. As random as they appeared, there was order and reason there—part of God's plan. And God's plan for men and women? John had to confess he hadn't always accepted the wisdom that women should have the same privileges as men, including the right to vote. His reasoning, he surmised, like most men, had been planted by heredity and training. It was generally accepted that, as one acquaintance so succinctly put it; "Men are the masters and women are intended to be our servants, to do our bidding, to obey us, to be ours. We are superior beings, and they are inferior beings."

Too many folks still clung to that outdated view, John mused. And it was this very element of society that kept woman suffrage from becoming a reality. In fact, right here in Iowa, there was a strong antisuffrage movement composed of both men and women.

Turning up the lamplight, John stared at the blank sheet of paper before him. What words could he come up with that would convince that element to change their minds? He was ready to take on the challenge.

Chapter Seven

THE MORAL RESERVE

1890

John carried the eight pages he had worked on all afternoon into the kitchen where Ella was preparing supper. He picked up a chair, set it on the table upside town and placed the pages between the wooden legs. His wife eyed him with an inquisitive look.

"It's a makeshift podium," he explained.

"Which means I'm about to hear a speech," she dried her hands on her apron and sat on an upright chair next to the table.

"Yes, I have been asked to give a commencement address to the young ladies at the East Side Public School. See what you think. I'll read what's in the middle, after the introduction, so you can get the meat of the subject." He shuffled the pages, cleared his throat, and began. "A woman is not a man... There is no woman who will say that a woman is a man; but there are many women and some men who will reply this way; a woman is equal to a man. This is true, and a sewing machine is equally valuable to a typewriter, but a sewing machine is not a typewriter.

"I continue to explain how men and women are different but equal, and tell the young ladies they have two choices in life: the single life or the married life." At this he glanced at Ella to see if he could read her expression. She wore her listening face which didn't tell him much. He read further: "Fortunately, all the callings of life are now open to woman. Let her choose along the line of her natural aptitudes. I tell them it is wise to train for a job appropriate for a woman, whether they plan to marry or not, but in either the domestic or working world, a woman's role is that of helpmeet."

He looked back at his speech and read on: "Man has been endowed for his life work by a superior material strength; woman for hers by a superior spiritual strength… It always has been the case, and it always will be the case that women prefer the married life to the single life, and therefore the married life is the one you all will live as a rule, and the one for which you all ought to be especially prepared… God made woman to be not the rivals of man, but the allies of man and the mother of man." He paused a moment, cleared his throat, smiled at Ella and said, "Then I tell them to choose for their life companion a noble man who has a firm physique, a good genuine character and a manly way of making a living. I advise them to never marry a sickly man."

At this his wife gave a little harumph. He laid down his speech. "You don't like that? It's excellent advice, Ella."

"Well, John, I am delighted that you support women in all their endeavors, married or unmarried, and I'm certain that is why you are called upon more and more to give commencement speeches to young girls. However, you don't know what is in a young woman's mind as far as if they want to marry or not, and some of your ideas are a little… too idealistic. There simply aren't that many perfect men out there for a woman's choosing. I just happen to be one of the lucky ones. Now, if you don't mind, I will return to my helpmeet duties."

John picked up the pages, replaced the chair podium and strode back to his office. In spite of Ella, he liked what he had written, and it was not only okay, but necessary for young women to set their sights high.

These subjects were still on his mind when the family sat down for supper that evening. After grace had been said and the food passed, John addressed his oldest daughter.

"So, what are your plans, Maggie?"

The girl looked perplexed at the query. "My plans?"

"Yes, your plans."

Maggie shrugged her shoulders and looked down at the peas on her plate in a moment of thought. "Well, tomorrow I plan to go to school, and in the afternoon I'll probably study with Gertrude. We have tests later this week."

"I mean beyond tomorrow—now that you are about to finish eighth grade. Do you plan to continue your education? Strive for a profession?"

Abram laughed at the question and answered for his sister. "She'll probably get married and have a passel of kids."

Maggie shot him a harsh look. "And what's wrong with that?"

Ella put down her fork and smiled at the bantering children. "Your papa is working on a commencement speech for young ladies. He has grand plans for the women of the future, which, of course, include his daughters."

"Well," Maggie said, her expression contemplative as though she were tugging hidden thoughts from her mind, "I have been thinking of going to normal school. I would like to be a teacher. That's a grand plan, isn't it? Then after that I can get married and have my own girl and maybe a boy, but he won't be like you." She stuck her tongue out at Abram.

Disregarding the spat between the two siblings, John continued, "Ah, teaching. A noble profession, one I would be happy for you to pursue. But we live in an enlightened age, and more and more women are standing shoulder to shoulder with men in a variety of fields—and married women at that." John's gaze swept the faces of his family members. "Do any of you know about Emily Roebling?"

Johnny swallowed a huge bite of buttered roll and entered the discussion. "Actually, I just read about her. She is the wife of Washington Roebling who built the Brooklyn Bridge. After he was injured, she studied mathematics and helped him supervise the construction. I think she got to be one of the first people to cross the bridge after its completion."

"Right," John said. "And that was only seven short years ago. Women have marched further forward in the work field since then. Another example of a married woman making her mark is J. Ellen Foster. She is not only an American, but an Iowan, and a lady of note. Do you know why?"

"Do I get to answer?" Ella asked. She hesitated a moment, obviously waiting for a response from one of the children. None came. "She is Iowa's first lady lawyer, a remarkable goal. I suspect she is high on your papa's list of notable women because she also feels strongly about a woman's right to vote… and she is married."

"She has actually partnered with her lawyer husband," John continued. "So, you see, Maggie and Irene, and hear this you two boys, marriage does not need to keep a woman from working outside the home when the necessity arises." A knowing glance from his wife caused him to flinch, prompting him to add, "Though a woman's primary, God-given role is that of being a wife and mother, it may be wise for her to study for a profession before marriage."

"That is very noble of Mrs. Foster," Johnny said, rising from the table and removing his supper dishes, "and if Maggie wants to follow in her footsteps, that's good, too. But does all this take away from the goals of us men? I am planning on becoming a lawyer myself, and as soon as I get out of high school I will go to college for a law degree." He set his plate and utensils on the counter and headed for the door, his involvement in the discussion clearly done.

"There," Maggie said, tossing her braids and crossing her arms. "I don't need to be a lawyer. One in the family is enough. I want to be a teacher."

John put up his hands in a gesture to calm things. "I'm proud of both of you and believe you will each accomplish your dreams." He enjoyed these lively conversations with the family, though he sensed Ella had some issues about this evening's subject.

Later, as he began work on a sermon prompted by the supper time discussion, his wife stepped into the study. "May I interrupt a moment?"

John put down his pencil and motioned toward an empty chair. "Certainly, have a seat and tell me what's on your mind." He noted she had removed her apron, her hair seemed freshly combed, and she shut the study door firmly behind her. Obviously, she came to express some serious thoughts. He braced himself. Now that they had been married for almost a year, Ella's opinions, especially if they opposed his, came more frequently.

"We heard some strong and important comments from two of your children this evening," she said.

He smiled. "Yes, and I like to think of them now as our 'shared' children, not just mine," he said. "They do form opinions of their own, of which I'm glad. I am pleased they are thinking ahead and toward admirable professions."

But Ella wasn't finished. "The closest normal school is in Cedar Falls, which means board and room. That costs money, to say nothing of law school." She looked John straight in the eye as she spoke. "I am again offering to find a job as a stenographer to help with the finances. I'm good, John. I can type long letters without errors. That is a rare talent, and employers like it." She paused, seemingly waiting for his objection. He said nothing, so she continued. "And to paraphrase your comments tonight, 'marriage does not need to keep a woman from working outside the home.' In the speech you read to me earlier, you said a woman had two choices: to marry or get a job to support herself. Have you changed your mind? It seems there are some conflicting ideas here, John."

John shook his head. *What to do about this strong-minded woman?* He could almost hear her thinking, *So there. I caught you in your own trap!* He cleared his throat and considered his response.

"I didn't read the entire speech to you, Ella. I told the young ladies there are exceptions. There are cases where a married woman, in her capacity as helpmeet, may have to work outside the home. That is why it is important for them to train for work appropriate for women." He felt he had not misrepresented his thoughts, maybe just hadn't explained them well enough. "Thank you for your offer, Ella, and I'm sure you are a good stenographer. But, for now, you need to be home, especially for Irene. I think we can swing normal school, especially if Maggie gets a job. And as far as law school goes, Johnny is already beginning to earn his way with his newspaper route. Plus, he has applied for a bellhop position at one of the local hotels. It's important they pay for their own education. It will mean much more to them in the long run."

Ella heaved a huge sigh, and John saw a glint of tears in her eyes. *It was this important to her to work outside the home? Did she not think she already contributed an enormous amount here?* He leaned forward, reached across the desk and took her hands in his. "I love you, Ella, and appreciate what you already do more than you will ever know. Can we leave it at that for now?"

She lifted her chin high and nodded, released his grip on her hands and stood. "Well, Reverend, I will leave you to your sermon. May I ask about the topic?"

"I've entitled it 'Path of Progress,' based on the fifth chapter of Judges. It's about Deborah and Jael, who were strong women, a subject on which I am becoming more and more familiar."

Ella strode toward the door. Her hand on the knob, she turned toward John with a parting remark. "And I'm learning more and more about stubborn men." She left the room, closing the door behind her.

He sat in thought for a few moments, tapping his pencil against the edge of the desk, then reached for the Bible.

~ ~ ~

SUNDAY BROKE THE WEEK'S PATTERN OF DREARY RAIN and dawned bright with the warmth and flowering scents of spring—the type of day that brought out the majority of church members.

This was the first opportunity for the ladies to wear their spring finery. Hats adorned with flowers, ribbons, and feathers bobbed throughout the congregation. True to his recent conviction to push for women's rights, John felt buoyed and ready with his well-thought-out sermon on the subject. Though, as he scanned the crowd, he wished more men were present. Several new faces smiled at him. One, a Mrs. Violet Cunningham, had introduced herself two Sundays ago. She and her husband were recent residents of Waterloo, though Mr. Cunningham had yet to attend a service. John guessed her to be in her forties. She seemed well-educated, wore the latest fashions, and came across like a tornado, whirling herself into conversations with strong opinions. *She'll be a good addition to the membership. A leader among the women,* John thought.

He opened by reading the fifth chapter of Judges, verses six and seven, then proceeded with his sermon:

The coming of the millennial runs where righteousness shall cover the earth as the waters cover the sea and depends upon our alliance with the powers above. Progress is never a uniform procession. It goes by fits and starts. This is true of all progress — material, moral, or spiritual... Some manufacturers are uncomfortable with progress, some rebel against it, but the end is sure. Automatic couplings and air brakes are ordered by law. The railways do not like it and rebel against it and hinder it because it is an expensive matter, but automatic couplings and air brakes on all freight trains are sure to come.

Today we have the woman question, the liquor question, and the labor question on hand. We may expect in all three questions times of conquest when the car of progress will go forward at a stride a great distance: we may expect times of apparent stagnation during which the conquered will revolt and gain a temporary advantage... But even this does not mean going backward. It means that we are adjusting ourselves for a new advance all along the line ... The question of woman's rights will move forward by agitation and legislation and election, and victory will crown them all at the last.

At this point he again referenced the strong women in the book of Judges: *For every Jabin and Sisera there awaits a Deborah and Barak. And every Heber has a Jael standing ever against him. The question of the hour and of the text is this, what is woman's public mission in connection with the coming of the millennium?*

A murmur rose throughout the sanctuary, and spring hats nodded. He noted one feather perched in the hat worn atop Mrs. Cunningham's brown curls, flickering in what he assumed was approval of his comments. John paused for a sip of water from the cup at the podium. The room quieted. The congregation was listening. *Woman is the moral reserve, the army reinforcement, not because she is better in herself than man, but because she is different in herself. In the extraordinary course of events some powerful woman will take the lead in her own person... But as things are now, how can Deborah be placed in the front of battle even when she has the capability that qualifies her for it, and when Jael has a treacherous husband whom she cannot persuade into the battle, how can she take the hammer and nails into her own hand and drive them home? There is one answer to these questions and but one. Give woman the ballot.*

Suddenly, the murmur in the congregation strengthened into audible remarks and even a few gasps. Men's voices mingled with the feminine. He'd hit the nail on the head. John concluded his sermon with one more strike: *There may be some doubt as to woman's action in general politics, some doubt as to whether woman in mass would even care to vote. There is no doubt in my mind as to woman's action in all affairs regarding the purity, temperance, and welfare of the home. Here she would cancel any husband's folly by driving the nail with her own hand through the head of any vice that was ruining the home. All else is open to woman now, all professions, all callings. Why should the ballot be withheld?*

Ella stood beside John in the narthex as the parishioners paraded by. Some greeted him with firm handshakes, "Good job, Reverend. You tell them." Others murmured politely about anything except the topic of his sermon. "Nice day today." Still others chose not to greet them at all.

Toward the end of the line, Violet Cunningham elbowed her way through the crowd and stood before him wagging her finger—her face flushed to nearly the color of her velvet trimmed lavender suit. "Well, Reverend Stevenson, that was quite a sermon. You will be hearing more from me on your misplaced opinions. You can count on that!" And she strode away like a soldier off to battle, her hat's purple feather fluttering as though to take flight.

John mentally re-examined his initial evaluation of the woman—strong, yes, but not necessarily in line with his thinking. She was going to be someone to reckon with.

Chapter Eight

THE COMMITTEE

Maggie answered the firm rap on the door. She, John, and Ella had watched from the parlor window as the group of women marched up the sidewalk to the parsonage—Mrs. Violet Cunningham leading the way. Maggie turned to John when the knock came, and he nodded. Reaching for his suit coat, he slipped his arms into the sleeves. "Let them in."

"I'll fix tea," Ella said, then hurried into the kitchen. The visitors had been expected, and John knew his wife and daughter had spent part of the morning baking cookies to sweeten the company who most likely came with bitterness.

A rush of cool air blew in with the guests, and Maggie quickly shut the door behind them. Five ladies crowded into the foyer. Mrs. Cunningham, with her signature hat's dominant purple feather, stood a mite taller than her companions. The blaze in her eyes betrayed her attempt at a friendly smile.

"Reverend Stevenson, we have come to talk to you about the sermons you have lately been preaching."

John smiled. He expected to enjoy this little confrontation, maybe even changing a few minds in the process. He motioned to the settee and several chairs.

"Certainly, ladies, please be seated. I'm always happy to explain myself and am eager to hear your remarks. Margaret, will you help Mother with the tea?" His daughter cast him a look he interpreted as *I want to stay and listen.*

Mrs. Cunningham immediately began her tirade. "Tea won't be necessary, Reverend. This is not a social call. It is a meeting of critical importance." The woman sat on the edge of her chair, and the other four nodded their concurrence.

"Suit yourself," John said. "How may I help you?" He noted that Maggie did not leave the room, easing herself instead onto the piano bench.

Scarcely taking a breath, Violet Cunningham continued, her hat feather bobbing in emphasis. "With all due respect, Reverend, you have no right to talk about suffrage for women, because you are a man. And because of that, you have no concept of what it is like to be a woman, and therefore what is best for us. It is our duty to take care of our families and households. It is the duty of our husbands to take care of us and make decisions about things political and financial. Men are much more suited for these things. Society is balanced the way God intended it, in spite of how you twist the words of the Bible to the contrary. I think it's what we object to the most, the blasphemy that spews from your mouth on Sunday mornings in the name of Christianity."

Maggie jumped to her feet. "How dare you talk to Papa that way!"

John sent her a sharp look. "Margaret. Mrs.

Cunningham has a right to her opinion. You may stay and listen—quietly."

His daughter plopped down on the bench, clutching the skirt of her dress in both fists, her gaze focused on the woman in the purple hat.

"The girl *should* stay," Mrs. Cunningham blared on. "It would be good for her to hear another side to the views forced on her in her own home."

John heard a quiet intake of breath behind him, and turning, he noted that Ella had brought in a chair from the kitchen and was now listening to the conversation. He directed his attention back to the issue at hand. "It's Margaret's decision whether to stay or not," he said, hearing tension creep into his own voice. He felt the need to shift the focus away from his daughter. "I'm sorry you think my sermons are irreverent, Madam. I preach the truth as written in the Bible."

"That is your own interpretation, not that of others," said Ida Jacobson, who before then had only nodded her head in approval of Mrs. Cunningham.

"Everyone has his or her own interpretation of the Bible," John said. "It is wise to listen to differing opinions."

"Wrong again, Reverend," Mrs. Cunningham said. "The Bible is very clear about what it says, and different opinions come from people who refuse to accept the word of God as written."

John scanned the faces of the women sitting in his parlor. Those present, as far as he knew, came from comfortable homes. Though not necessarily wealthy, their husbands had steady jobs and were reasonable men.

"Here's something to think about, ladies. What about the woman whose husband is a drunk? He beats her and the children, but laws dictate that if she leaves him she has no right to her children, and she cannot vote to change the law. And what about property? A married woman has no rights to property that was once hers before the marriage. Is that fair? Yet, again, a woman cannot vote to change that law."

For a moment, no one spoke. Once more John studied each of his visitors. They all met his gaze with serious intent.

Mrs. Cunningham interrupted the silence. "My husband handles property better than I. Why would I want to bother with it?"

"That is not the point," John said. "Not all women are as fortunate as you in that regard."

Mrs. Cunningham set her lips in a firm line, and the muscles in her jaw twitched. "Now you are getting personal, Reverend. That is uncalled for and out of line for a minister."

John shook his head. "Just something for you to think about, Madam."

Violet Cunningham abruptly stood. "Well, ladies, I think we have said what we came to say. The Reverend now knows our feelings, and that of many of his other parishioners, I might add. Being the intelligent man he is, I'm certain he will give this some serious thought and realize his mistaken views on the subject of suffrage. Thank you for giving us your audience." She turned her attention to Maggie. "And I hope you learned something today as well, young lady."

The girl said nothing in response, yet John was aware from the look on her face that his daughter was struggling to hold her temper. *Good for you, Maggie.*

Once the visitors were gone, John felt a collective sigh of relief within the household. Ella approached him, slipped her arm through his, and gave his hand a squeeze. "Mr. Stevenson, you are a man among men to remain so calm when confronted with the likes of Violet Cunningham's committee. I love you more each day."

He returned the squeeze and gave her a light kiss on the cheek. "It is easy to be strong when I have the support of my own women." He put his other arm around Maggie.

"I stayed in the room because of you, not because of that stuffy old woman," she said with a pout. "But, Papa, I don't understand, if giving women the vote is right, why do some women do nothing about it and others, like Mrs. Cunningham, act like they don't even want it?"

"Ah, that is a good question, and one I frequently ponder. Let me tell you a story." He led her to the settee and patted the seat beside him, indicating for her to sit.

"Wait for me," Ella said. "In the wake of that committee, I'd say we could use some nourishment." She disappeared into the kitchen and returned a few moments later with a tray containing a plate of cookies and three cups of tea. Offering some to John and Maggie, she set the remainder on the piano bench and sat opposite John in an over-stuffed chair. "Let's hear your story, Reverend husband."

John took a sip of tea, cleared his throat, and began. "Now there was a horse, so the story goes, that objected seriously to umbrellas, which made that horse useless both on shiny and rainy days. But a wise man bought him and cured him. Knowing that the horse loved fruits of various kinds, he impaled an apple or a potato on the sharp end of an umbrella and held it out to the horse. At first, and for quite a while, the horse shied at the umbrella. But he wanted the fruit and gradually accepted the alarming object to get it.

"Now there are some women like the horse. They object very much to the suffrage umbrella because it is a new idea to them, and maybe their husbands and other folks tell them it's not necessary. In the meantime, there are many wise and noble women who strive to set their sisters free, and their efforts will open doors these objectors haven't even thought of: the right to own the wages they earn, the right to own property in their name, the right to own themselves when single and their children when married, and other valuable fruits too numerous to mention. So, gradually, all women will find out that the umbrella and the fruit go together. But time is needed, and so there are still many women, like the horse, shying at the umbrella.

"And here is the end of the parable. After many days, that horse became so accustomed to the umbrella that he lost all fear of it and chased an umbrella whenever he saw one in the hope of getting an apple or potato. And so will it be with these good but fearful women. After many days, they will chase a suffragist, hunt a polling place, vote with eagerness, out-do their most strenuous efforts to obtain equal wages, equal rights, equal powers, and equal liberty with their brothers.

"In the meantime, we must be patient with women who think they do not want their freedom. We will just keep on sticking apples and potatoes and good fruits on the end of the suffrage umbrella."

When he finished, Maggie clapped. "Hooray, Papa! Do you really think that will happen?"

"Yes, it will. There are many women and men across the United States who have been striving toward this for years, and we will join them to see that it happens in Iowa, so you will reap the benefits. We can't give up. We must keep fighting."

Chapter Nine

AUNT CORA

1891

John had never seen Ella in such a dither. She raced around the house for a week, washing and re-hanging curtains, scrubbing floors, and airing rugs. The day before their company was due, she baked cookies, bread, and a cake. The house smelled delicious, but the air of anticipation was so brittle John feared it would shatter.

"Does your sister really expect perfection?" he asked. "Surely your home in Ohio was not always pristine."

"Men just don't understand," she said, scarcely stopping a moment from her labors to talk. "Special guests require special preparation, and Cora is a very special guest."

"That much I surmised," John said, and realized it was pointless to discuss the matter further. Thank the Lord he didn't feel compelled to scrub his study in preparation. That room was his domain exclusively and off limits to a feather duster operated by him or anyone else. Actually, he was looking forward to Cora's visit. He had heard so much about this extraordinary sister-in-law, and he was eager to engage her in conversation about her position at the University of Wyoming. He hoped he could get her to agree to give a talk at his church on Sunday evening. It was extremely important for folks of all ages and both sexes to be exposed to successful women.

John and Ella took the buggy to meet Cora's train. Once on the station platform, Ella clutched his arm in almost uncontrollable anticipation as passengers began to step from the rail cars.

"There she is. There she is!" The usually calm Ella shrieked. She released her grip on John and ran forth to embrace a woman in the midst of the crowd. Three years older and so adored by his wife, John had expected Cora to be Amazonian. She wasn't. In fact, she was shorter than Ella, and a few pounds heavier. However, the minute they were introduced, her self-assurance and firm handshake clearly conveyed she was a woman of authority.

During the ride home, John kept quiet and managed the horse. The two women sat behind him in the buggy's passenger seat talking nonstop. John knew he would have ample opportunity to become acquainted with Cora over the rest of the week.

They had left Maggie and Abram at home in charge of Irene while he and Ella fetched "Aunt" Cora. Upon their return from the station, John and the two ladies were greeted by the eager youngsters, curiosity and excitement written on each face.

"These are three of the children," Ella said. "John, the oldest, works as a bellhop at a hotel in town, so you won't get to meet him until tomorrow. We are very proud of them."

Cora extended her hand for each to shake. "It is

an honor to meet you. I feel I know you already from the many favorable comments Ella has written in her letters."

Maggie and Abram returned the formal greeting in a very adult manner. Irene, usually so bubbly, suddenly seemed shy and a little awed by the woman about whom they had heard so much. She timidly reached out her hand, then smiled broadly as Cora clasped her own around it.

"Abram, please help Aunt Cora with her valise," John said.

His younger son obliged, hefting the large bag on his shoulders, leading the way upstairs to the girls' bedroom.

Irene followed closely, once again her usual animated self, chattering the entire time about the arrangements. "You will sleep in our bed with Maggie, and I get to sleep with Mama and Papa."

After the traveler freshened up, the family gathered in the parlor. Cora handed out gifts of pencils to each of the children and they quizzed her about Wyoming and the long train ride from there to Iowa. John watched with amusement while his offspring clustered around this pleasant woman who had no children of her own yet seemed perfectly at ease with them.

At the supper table that evening, conversation kept drifting to Cora's teaching job at the university and to that distant part of the United States called Wyoming. "We are now officially a state. Did you know that?" Cora said with pride.

"Oh, yes. I pay close attention to what's going on

out west," Ella said. "But tell us how the women there convinced the men to allow them the vote. We need to do that same persuasion here."

"Well, it is rather long and complicated. But to put it simply, when the Legislature first convened in November 1869, they remained in session for sixty days, and provided the Territory with a general code of laws for its government. One act they approved gave women all the political rights, duties, franchises, and responsibilities of male citizens, as long as they were citizens of the United States and the Wyoming Territory. Then someone, almost in jest, suggested they go one step further and grant women suffrage."

Ella's eyebrows lifted in surprise. "It was that easy?"

"It sounds like there must have been a catch," John said, shaking his head. He found this difficult to believe having heard so many arguments against the idea of allowing women to vote.

"The catch, if you can call it that, is the author of the bill never dreamed it would pass. It was supposed that the council, at least, would defeat it, and if not, the governor would veto it, or congress would interfere somewhere along the way. But none of that happened, and it became law."

"I wish it were that simple in other states." Ella sighed. "We fight so hard for this right, and the men in the legislature here just don't seem to hear or care."

"The irony of all this," Cora continued, "is, as far as we know, no one was aggressively advocating women's suffrage in the territory—men or women."

John noted that Cora's enthusiasm for her subject

held even the children's constant attention.

"I know about woman's suff-er-age," Irene said, her eyes bright. "Mama and Papa have told me. It means I'm as smart as Papa."

Cora smiled at this and patted her head.

"We also know that the men in charge of the government in Iowa are not as smart as the men in charge of Wyoming," Margaret added.

Abram piped in, "Or if the men in Wyoming really didn't know what they were doing, the men here think they know too much and can't see their mistakes."

This provoked laughter around the table. "That comment calls for dessert. Come help me, Maggie," Ella said and rose to fetch an angel food cake.

The following day, John gathered together the trustees and asked for approval for Cora to speak Sunday evening. "She has some interesting facts to tell about living out west, especially as it pertains to women's rights, and she presents it in an intriguing manner."

Tom Jones balked at the request. "Don't you think this is going a little far, Reverend? It's not ladylike to stand up in front of a crowd and talk. Some folks might get the wrong idea about the kind of woman she is."

A couple of the other men nodded in agreement, uncertainty written on their faces.

"She's an instructor, and a good one," John argued. "This is what she does for a living. It is most honorable, and she has a message to give. The congregation will hang on every word. You'll see."

In the end, John prevailed. Not only could he be

persuasive, but he suspected curiosity about Cora McDonald helped his cause. Word had gotten out, and even the Sunday morning service was packed. The summer heat wasn't a deterrent as handheld fans swished constantly throughout the crowded pews. John introduced Cora, asking her to stand so the congregants could see who to expect for the evening program. As she did so, whispers rippled through the sanctuary. *They will come*, John sensed, *not only due to interest in the subject, but for the novelty of a woman speaking from the pulpit.*

During the social hour, a number of well-wishers immediately snagged Ella and Cora, so John stood without family members in the narthex while folks filed out of the church. The mood seemed positive. His sermon had been one of his better ones, and most congregants said they looked forward to the evening talk. Folks thrived on variety, and having Cora speak certainly fell into that category. Just when he was feeling comfortable about the situation, he noticed Violet Cunningham and several of her followers hanging back. They waited to approach until the line of greeters had diminished, then marched up to him, looking for all the world like a brood of chicks led by a sassy hen.

"You don't have us fooled, Reverend," Violet clucked. "The whole purpose of putting Miss McDonald at the podium is to promote this nonsense of enfranchising women. It is not only unnecessary and inappropriate, but demeaning. Proper women do not speak in public."

"The trustees have approved it, Madam. And that is

what Miss McDonald does for a living—a very honorable living, I might add—she stands up in front of an audience and teaches. I believe she has something of importance to say to folks in Waterloo. I hope you will see fit to be here. I think you will find it worth your while. Good day, ladies." With that he excused himself and walked off to join his family.

John felt the excitement ripple through the congregants that evening as members and visitors filled the pews. A hush fell when he escorted Cora to the lectern and introduced her once again before returning to the front row to sit with Ella and the children.

Cora looked over the crowd and smiled, both hands on the lectern, no evidence of a written speech before her. "Good evening, ladies and gentlemen. It is such a privilege to be in Waterloo and to share some of my experiences from America's frontier." Perfectly at ease, she began with an introduction about her career at the University of Wyoming. She described the area and the sturdy pioneers who had settled there. Then she segued into the history of woman suffrage in this remote and wild state, beginning with the same stories she told at the Stevenson dinner table.

"Not long after the enfranchisement of women in Wyoming," she continued, "a jury was selected which included the names of Laramie's most prominent ladies. This created a bit of excitement, and the ladies—who had not sought this privilege—were hesitant to serve. Chief Justice Howe, who was to preside over the court, made a long and eloquent appeal, begging the ladies who had been called to take their places and act in that capacity through the term of court, which was likely to prove a long one. His principal argument was that hitherto they had been unsuccessful in securing juries that could convict the well-known guilty criminals tried in their courts, because up to then our society had been led and controlled by lawless and desperate men and women. Consequently, public sentiment demanded criminals should not be punished for their deeds. The judges believed that women serving on the juries would remedy this flagrant evil and inaugurate a new era, and they so expressed themselves. They fully believed women would do conscientious work, and that a marked reform would follow.

"And what do you think happened?" Cora asked, pausing for a moment of anticipation. Murmurs could be heard in the audience. John half anticipated someone to jump up and loudly object to the whole idea, but no one spoke out.

Cora continued. "It must be remembered that Laramie was, in 1869, a frontier town. There was wickedness on every hand, but the breaking of Sunday [church traditions] and the sin of prostitution were especially prominent. No sooner had women received franchise, they turned their attention to these alarming evils. Through their efforts the laws against these crimes were published and indictments were secured against the offenders. In an incredibly short time, the open breaking of Sunday ceased, and keepers of disreputable houses were moved to more favorable locations. At the close of the court term the verdict was that in both civil and criminal cases, with women on the juries, even-handed justice had been done in every instance."

After a few more stories, Cora concluded to loud applause throughout the sanctuary. John considered the talk a great success and a grand step forward for woman suffrage, at least in Waterloo. In his mind, only one thing marred the evening. Mrs. Cunningham and her committee of antisuffragists were nowhere to be seen. They had boycotted Cora's speech.

Chapter Ten

Most evenings found John in the parsonage study working on either sermons for church or upcoming speaking engagements. One hot, sticky night, early in July, he sat at his desk scratching out thoughts on what to preach the coming Sunday. He alternated writing with one hand and mopping the perspiration from his brow with a handkerchief in the other. Earlier, he had lifted the sash of the only window in the room, hoping for a breeze that didn't seem to materialize. A chorus of crickets chirped their loud, summer song, which did nothing to alleviate the oppressive heat.

A tap on the open door to the hall caused him to look up. Ella entered holding a tall drink of mint tea. A chunk of ice clinked against the glass as she crossed the room. "I thought perhaps this would help the thinking process," she said, setting the tea on the desk. "And what, pray tell, are you working on so studiously this sweltering night?"

John picked up the glass, took several long swallows and held its coolness against his cheek. "Thank you, dear wife. This is most welcome. As for my project here, it's Sunday's sermon on one of my favorite subjects.

Three guesses as to what that might be."

"Well, now, let me see. Temperance? Woman's Suffrage? Keeping the Sabbath?"

"Right the first time. I'm entitling it 'The Saloon,' and I think it will be one of my better illustrations on why the issue is so important. It's based on the Second Epistle of Peter." John picked up the open Bible before him and quoted: "And beside this, giving all diligence, add to your faith virtue; and to virtue knowledge; and to knowledge temperance; and to temperance patience, and to patience godliness." He set the Bible aside and looked up at Ella. "There's more before and after, of course, but it fits the theme of the sermon and leads to a powerful Christian message."

Ella smiled and picked up his empty glass. "I'll be in the parlor if you need any advice. Maybe I'll do some reading in the Bible myself, perhaps the Epistles of Peter?"

John returned her smile, his gaze following her as she left the room, then he refocused on the papers before him. Reading through his written words one more time, he retrieved a sermon booklet from a desk drawer. On the cover he wrote the title, Bible reference, and date of delivery, and began to transfer his words onto the inner pages.

Part-way through he paused a moment to reflect on Beatrice Cooper, something he often did when the subject of temperance was at hand. She was still a motivating factor for these sermons, though he had lost all contact with her. Leroy no longer attended church and even her sister had not been seen at a service in weeks. Rumors, whispered here and there, suggested Belva, too, had moved away from Waterloo. John prayed silently for the entire family. What had become of the two boys? The question always pained him.

In spite of the heat, a good crowd showed up for church on Sunday. John noted, as always, the women outnumbered the men. Nevertheless, it was an audience, and hopefully his message would strike a new chord. This morning his sermon came off well, and following the service, he received many hearty congratulations. One woman, Sarah Ware Whitney, was especially enthusiastic at what he had preached.

"Splendid, Reverend Stevenson," she said. "I am going to suggest to the Woman's Christian Temperance Union that we recommend you as a speaker at the Northern Iowa Union camp meeting later this month. This is just what a gathering like that needs to hear."

"Thank you, Mrs. Whitney. I would be honored to present this particular sermon at the camp meeting." The idea pleased John immensely. Camp meetings provided a much wider audience, including more men. *Perhaps my ideas will catch fire, and some of the local saloons will actually be forced to close.*

John had become better acquainted with Sarah Whitney in recent months, learning she was not only active in the Woman's Christian Temperance Union but also involved with the Iowa Woman Suffrage Association. She was strongly on his side with these issues—a good advocate to have on board at the Waterloo Congregational Church.

Just a few days later, he received a note confirming

the WCTU had arranged for him to present his sermon "The Saloon" at the camp meeting. *The executive committee has scheduled you to speak on Friday afternoon, August 25,* the note read. The only caveat was they requested a synopsis of the talk in advance.

~ ~ ~

THE DAY OF THE CAMP MEETING DAWNED BRIGHT, breezeless, and humid. But the weather could not detract John from the good feeling he always enjoyed when he was about to share his thoughts on a favorite subject.

Ella fixed a hearty breakfast, "to fortify and give you a clear head during your presentation," she said.

His sermon was scheduled for the afternoon, but the entire family planned to leave for the meeting grounds early to attend other events. Johnny even had the afternoon off from bell-hopping. Irene, wearing a new white eyelet frock with yellow ribbons, seemed especially eager to leave. "Hurry, Papa must be in time for his talk."

A knock sounded on the door.

"Irene, will you get that please?" John called from the study where he was gathering the pages of his speech, curious as who had come calling. Everyone they knew planned to be at the camp meeting all day and would be headed there now.

Irene stuck her head in the study doorway, her eyes wide. "It's a tall, scary man," she whispered. "He says he has to see you."

John placed his papers back on the desk, buttoned

his waistcoat and strode past his daughter, who shrank against the door jam. In the entryway stood a stranger, tall indeed, dressed in a dark suit with a scowl on his face to match. He reminded John of a chimney sweep, minus the soot.

The man stepped forward, bowler in one hand his other extended to shake John's, then proceeded to speak. "Reverend Stevenson, I am Dr. Fullerton, secretary of the camp meeting association. I'm here to advise you that your talk scheduled for this afternoon has been cancelled at the request of the executive committee."

John felt blood rush to his head. "Cancelled? There must be some mistake. The WCTU told me it was all arranged. What is the problem?"

"The problem, sir, as I understand it, is your talk is of a political nature and would leave a disturbing effect upon the spirituality of the meeting. So, the decision was made to omit it."

"Political? It's based on scripture. Who's behind this?" John's astonishment quelled his anger for the moment.

"Judge Couch, also on the executive committee, said he felt the talk was not a gospel temperance sermon but a political harangue."

"A political harangue? Nonsense!" John's ears burned at the accusation as he made an effort to keep his voice controlled. "Has the judge heard the sermon? I have only given it once before on a Sunday morning, and I don't recall his presence in the congregation."

"That I cannot say. However, we, the committee, agree it would be impossible for anyone to give an address on the saloon in Iowa without making it political. We regret any inconvenience this may have caused you." With that the man plopped his hat upon his head and strode toward the door. He hesitated there a moment, his hand on the knob, and turned back to John. "We have posted a sign at the meeting tent announcing the cancellation of the talk. Good day, Reverend."

The front door closed with a determined thud, and Irene, cowering a few feet away, burst into tears.

Ella, hands on her hips, swept in from the kitchen. "Well, this is a strange turn of affairs."

Maggie, Abram, and John Jr. immediately crowded into the small entry way, full of questions and anger. No one in the family had missed a word of the short confrontation.

"Everyone into the parlor," John said.

Ella took the settee beside Irene, putting her arm around the weeping child. Maggie and Abram dropped onto chairs.

"Can they do that, Papa?" Johnny asked, still standing, a muscle in his jaw visibly twitching. "I mean, just tell you not to talk? There is such a thing as free speech, you know. It's part of the United States Constitution."

John put his hand on the boy's shoulder. "We'll work out something. The day isn't over yet. What dumbfounds me most is how anyone could come to the conclusion that the talk was political without hearing the sermon in the first place. There is more behind this than meets the eye."

"You did give them a synopsis," Ella said.

"It was an outline—nothing political about it."

No one spoke for a moment. Irene's sniffling dominated the room.

John sighed. "This won't be the end of it," he said. "And it won't keep us from the camp meeting. Everyone continue getting ready. We'll leave soon, as planned."

The group scattered, and John marched through the entry hall toward the study to get his coat. He stopped short upon hearing voices and footsteps on the porch. Ready to confront whoever it might be this time, he flung open the front door. There stood Sarah Ware Whitney and a man he did not recognize. Sarah's face glowed crimson in anger. The stranger, a short, round man of middle age with a neatly trimmed mustache matching his blond hair, held a notebook in one hand and a pencil in the other, a look of eager anticipation on his face.

"Please, come in." John motioned toward the parlor.

Sarah spoke first. "Reverend, we have been to the camp meeting and read that outrageous cancellation notice. I have learned of the reasons why from Dr. Fullerton and Judge Couch of the camp committee, neither of whom ever heard your sermon, and I have taken it upon myself on behalf of the Woman's Christian Temperance Union to make certain that the citizens of Waterloo know about this travesty of justice."

She turned to the man with the notebook. "This is Mr. Blake from the newspaper. He is prepared to take a statement from you on the subject."

"Please, be seated," John said, and pulled up a chair

himself. "I am unhappy about the situation, but we need to be rational about this."

"Now, Reverend, I've never known you to shy away from controversy, and this is certainly not the time to start," Sarah said.

"I'm not backing down, Mrs. Whitney. I believe in my talk and want others to hear it. We need to get the facts right in the paper and then set a new time and venue."

"Well, the facts are, Reverend, that the WCTU recommended your sermon to the camp meeting committee. It was accepted, then refused at the last minute by one member who happens to be the only Democrat on the committee. That's where the politics come in—not in your sermon." She turned to the reporter. "Take that down, Mr. Blake."

A half hour later, with further comments from John to the reporter on the biblical basis for his talk, their meeting concluded.

"This will appear in this evening's paper," Mr. Blake said on departing. The energy in his step confirmed an enthusiasm for the scoop he was about to dash off for his readership.

After the visitors left, John decided the family would not go to the camp meeting after all. "I'll only be bombarded with questions to which I do not know the answer, and so will each of you. In the words of the scary camp meeting executive, Dr. Fullerton, it will not be a spiritual experience for any of us." John entered his study and shut the door.

He emerged late that afternoon when Johnny was

about to head out to deliver *The Courier*. He handed the boy a nickel. "Here, son. Pick up a copy of Mr. Blake's paper. We'll see what he wrote."

Abram went with his brother, and just before supper the two boys bounded into the house holding up the front page of *The State Register*.

"Look at this!" Johnny exclaimed with a wide smile. John took the paper and began reading aloud: "Shielding the Saloon. A Waterloo Minister Barred from Preaching Temperance at a Camp Meeting. The manager is a Democrat and was afraid his saloon pets might get hurt."

Maggie cheered. "That will teach those scamps!"

"Those are just the headlines," John said. "Listen to this."

The family crowded around while he read the opening paragraph: *Camp Meeting Politics. A Temperance Sermon Barred Out. Waterloo, July 25. Special to the State Register. Something of a sensation was created here today by the refusal of the executive committee of the Northern Iowa Union camp meeting, under the management of George W. Willis, of Cleveland, O., to allow Rev. John Stevenson, pastor of the Congregational Church of this city, to speak at the camp meeting this afternoon on the subject of "The Saloon" although he had been requested to speak by the WCTU. The leading member of the executive committee is a Democrat, and he stated that he had been informed that Mr. Stevenson's address was of a partisan nature. He called the committee together, and they ordered Mr. Stevenson's address omitted.*

The remainder of the article explained how the sermon had been preached previously from the church pulpit. It quoted part of the synopsis submitted by John to the committee.

"Well, Mr. Blake interviewed both sides of the issue. That's good reporting," John said, beginning to enjoy this little conflict.

"And you definitely came out on top," Johnny said with pride.

~ ~ ~

BEFORE THE WEEK WAS OVER, MORE ARTICLES APPEARED IN other papers, and a large number of Waterloo residents, both Republicans and Democrats, signed a petition which stated:

We deem it propriety that the public should have the opportunity to hear the address of Rev. Stevenson on the saloon, and therefore the undersigned respectfully request him to name an early date at which he will give the address.

"Your reputation has been restored," Ella said upon reading the notice, and she gave John a hug.

The following Sunday afternoon, John delivered the sermon in the public square where a large crowd gathered in attendance. Laughter rippled through the audience when John introduced his subject by saying, "Oh, Lord, if thou dost not know anything about politics, and if we are not to pray for politics, make the politicians pray for themselves."

That evening John gave his regular sermon at church, his third talk within twelve hours. His throat throbbed, and his voice croaked, as it often did when overused, but the day had been satisfying, nonetheless. As he prepared for bed, Ella brought a cup of milky liquid up from the kitchen.

He cleared his throat and rasped, "And what, pray tell, is this?"

"Beaten egg white, lemon juice, and sugar. I understand it works miracles." She poured some into a tablespoon and handed it to him. "Here, take it or you won't be able to talk at all tomorrow."

He shuddered, let the repulsive stuff slide down his throat, and climbed into bed. A raw throat was worth the entire experience. Sarah Whitney, Dr. Fullerton, Judge Couch, and others had certainly added spice to his life the past few days. He held that good thought as he drifted off to sleep, trying to ignore not only a raw throat but the hint of a wheeze creeping into his lungs.

Chapter Eleven

HONORS AND WORRIES

Occasionally, when his allergies got the better of him, John would escape for a few weeks in the fall to Bayfield, Wisconsin, where the lakeside breezes cleared his lungs. Eighteen ninety-one was one of those years. It had been a worthwhile respite, and he returned to Waterloo with vigor, only to learn with dismay that during his absence, Ella's father had passed away.

"Why didn't you telegram me? I would have come home to be with the children so you could go to your mother." He felt terrible.

"It wasn't unexpected, John, in fact a blessing. He had been ill for so long. Nellie is staying with mother for a while. I wasn't really needed, and it was important that you get away."

He gave her a hug, sensing she was being stoic on his account, and thanking the Lord again for her presence in his life.

Though John sensed a melancholy since her father's death, nothing buoyed Ella's spirits like letters from her sisters. One afternoon before the children returned from school, they sat together in the parlor going over the day's mail which included a letter from Cora.

Ella's face brightened as she read. "I declare, Cora is almost as much in demand as you are." She handed John a newspaper clipping. "This was in her letter. It tells of the speakers at the Teachers' Institute for Unita County, Wyoming, and she received top billing. I'm so proud of her!"

John chuckled. "Your sister is quite a whirlwind. She never stops, yet still finds time to write."

While Ella reread the letter from her sister, John opened an envelope addressed to him from an old friend, N. H. Whittesey. He pulled out a short note and read silently to himself. The letter brought a warm rush of disbelief, and he read the message again before turning to Ella. "Well, here's something to write Cora about," he said with a wide smile. "Apparently Tabor College is considering conferring an honorary doctorate degree on me."

"Oh, John, really? That's wonderful!" Ella moved from the chair to sit on the settee next to him and eyed the stationery he held in his hand. "Doctor John Ogilvie Stevenson. It has a nice solid ring to it."

He handed her the letter. "This is a copy of a note written to Tabor by a former school acquaintance of mine. He must have been approached by the nominating committee for a recommendation."

As the Yale Seminary Classmate who had the pleasure of introducing Rev. John Stevenson to Shenandoah and to Iowa, I shall be very glad of any honor which may come to him. I have long regarded him as one of the freshest and strongest preachers in the state. He reads, studies, and thinks; and puts his thoughts into vigorous language.

Ella smiled as she read, then laid the note on the table. "He knows you well," she said. "What a good friend. I wonder how long the process takes and when it will be official?"

"I have no idea, and perhaps he overstepped his boundaries by letting me in on it before the fact. Either way, it's flattering to be considered and to know his opinion of me."

Ella gave John a kiss. They sat in silence for a moment savoring Whittesey's words.

A commotion out front caused Ella to rise and go to the window. "Are you expecting a package of some sort? A delivery van has stopped here." She paused a moment, then her voice rose. "What in the world? A man is helping someone down—Oh, my! It's Johnny, and he's hurt!"

John jumped up and followed Ella to the front door. It opened just as they reached the entry hall. John Jr., his face white and contorted with pain, stood on one foot, his right arm flung across the shoulders of Jack Burgess, who made deliveries throughout Waterloo.

"I was at the school picking up packages when your boy was brought into the office. Hurt his foot real bad at recess. I was there, so said I'd take him home," Mr. Burgess explained.

John's gaze swept to the injured foot. No blood, but obviously any pressure was painful. He reached for his son's arm and helped him to a chair in the parlor. "What happened, lad?"

"We were playing football, and I landed wrong. The pain is awful." Sweat beaded on his forehead.

John examined the swollen and bruised foot. "Hard to tell if it is broken. But we had better get Dr. Griffin."

Ella placed a cushion under the foot to elevate it, then glanced toward the foyer. "Oh, where are our manners," she said. "We need to thank the delivery man." She scurried from the room to where Mr. Burgess stood, twisting his hat in both hands, his eyes filled with concern.

John followed and held out his hand. "Thank you for interrupting your work to bring him home. What do we owe you?"

Mr. Burgess shrugged his shoulders. "Nothing at all, sir. I was scheduled to be in this neighborhood anyway and am glad to help." He hesitated a moment, then added. "You're the preacher at the Congregational Church, aren't you?"

John nodded.

"My wife sometimes goes there on Sundays. Says you have good things to say about giving women the right to vote. I guess I don't care about that one way or the other, but it seems important to her. Me and God, we get along okay without bothering with church, but I do respect the clergy," he added quickly.

The man's comments amused John. He had heard it all before, the guilt, the excuses. Many people, especially men, often felt compelled to explain to him why they didn't come to church. However, the man's lack of interest in the suffrage movement did concern him. It was this ambivalence among men, who could vote, that kept the enfranchisement of women from becoming a reality.

"Bringing our son home shows your heart is in the right place. Thank you again. Maybe one of these days I'll see you in the congregation with your wife."

"Doubt that, but glad to be of help. I could tell the boy was hurting bad."

John closed the door gently behind him and returned to the parlor where he found Ella kneeling before Johnny examining the injury. "It doesn't look good, John."

"Let's take him up to his room where he can lie down and prop the foot. Ice should help, too. Then I'll go fetch Dr. Griffin."

It took an hour for John to bring the doctor. In the meantime, Ella had made the boy as comfortable as possible.

"It's not broken, but the sprain is serious," Dr. Griffin told them after his examination. "He'll need to stay off the foot for at least three weeks."

"Mean job!" exclaimed Johnny, obviously disappointed but trying to remain stoic.

~ ~ ~

THOUGH ELLA WAS THERE MOST DAYS, JOHN CAME HOME as often as he could to check on things, especially during the first week when his eldest son was in so much pain. It was a time of renewal and re-acquaintance as the two of them talked alone—something that happened rarely with three other children in the house. One morning in particular, while Ella was out visiting a friend, Johnny hobbled down the stairs, and he and John sat in the parlor together.

"So, you want to be a lawyer?" John asked, thinking back on a dinner discussion not long before. "What made you decide on that profession?" This had come as a surprise to him, thinking the lad would follow in his footsteps and become a man of the cloth.

"It's important to know the laws, Papa, and if I study them, I might as well be a lawyer. Besides, they help folks who get themselves in a legal pickle."

John had to chuckle at the remark, but it did give him some insight into his son's mind. He guessed if Johnny felt he was helping people by being a lawyer, maybe the lad was following along the same line as a preacher after all.

"And I'd like to be a soldier if my country ever needs me," Johnny said. Again, this surprised John, but then perhaps it shouldn't have. Didn't every boy want to be a soldier? Yet, war was harsh, and with Johnny's sensitivity and desire to help others, it would be difficult for him. The thought was unsettling.

The boy wasn't finished with the subject. "Did you ever fight in a war, Papa?"

John shook his head no, and realized with a little shock that he had rarely if ever discussed his boyhood and youth with the lad. "There was no opportunity in Scotland, and I moved to America just as the great Civil War ended. So, I served my new country in other ways."

"Teaching the former slaves?"

"Aye, son. It was a difficult but rewarding time. Those people had been mistreated and would never get on an equal footing with white folk if they didn't get educated."

"I'm proud of you, Papa, and proud that you are now trying to help women get some rights, too. I think Mama and Maggie are smart enough to vote—and Irene, too, when she gets older."

They were both silent for a few moments, John pondering their conversation and, he suspected Johnny was, too. Then the boy spoke again. "I also agree with you on the temperance issue. Anything addicting like that must be wrong. I will never drink alcohol. I want my mind to stay clear so I behave properly. Did I tell you I saw Beatrice Cooper not long ago? She is back home with Mr. Cooper. I deliver papers there, and I think she recognized me because she turned her face away. I think she had a black eye and didn't want me to see it."

The front door opened bringing a whoosh of cold air as Ella walked in. "Well, here is the invalid downstairs with his Papa. You must both be ready for dinner. I'll get on it right away." She removed her hat and coat and headed for the kitchen.

The mood was broken, but John felt something valuable had been gained from the discussions with his eldest. For the remainder of the afternoon, and often for days later, his thoughts focused on Johnny's comments.

He also couldn't forget the boy's remark about the Coopers. Had Leroy struck Beatrice again? He cringed at the thought and stopped by their house at the first opportunity, determined to help their situation, if possible, and at the very least to check on Beatrice. No one answered the door. Frustrated, he turned toward home. Thoughts pulsed through his mind like the clip-clop of Blaze's hooves. *I'll come back — more than once if necessary. We need to know if Beatrice is all right.*

~ ~ ~

DECEMBER ARRIVED, AND WITH IT MANY EXTRA ACTIVITIES. Johnny had returned to school. He limped less each day until he no longer favored the injured foot.

"He's as stoic as his father," Ella commented.

John knew she was right. He was proud of his firstborn. The lad worked and studied hard. He would make a good lawyer someday, and a soldier, too, if it ever came to that.

Ella sang as she decorated the house for the season, and in the evenings she sat at the piano, filling the air with Christmas carols. Each day, gaily wrapped packages appeared under the tree in the parlor, mostly homemade gifts of appreciation from church members.

One evening, as a gentle snow fell outside, John and Ella sat together in the parlor enjoying the tree and the aura of the season. "We have much to be grateful for," Ella said. "The children are healthy, and you are doing well and receiving honors. We are very fortunate."

"Indeed, we are," John said. "Oh, and I have a surprise. Another good thing. This came in the church mail today." He pulled an envelope from his pocket and handed it to Ella.

She took out a formal notice and read aloud: "Dear Sir: I have the honor to inform you that you have been elected a member of the American Academy of Political and Social Science... It is our desire to have the Academy include in its membership all those who are interested in the progress of the Political and Social Sciences."

Ella looked at John with a mix of pride and mischief in her eyes. "I'm sure this is quite an honor, Reverend, but somehow you just can't avoid being mixed up in politics."

"This is a surprise," John said. "It's a young organization and its membership is very select, including some notables like Jane Addams and W. E. B. Dubois. I am flattered and humbled."

Ella handed the announcement back to him. "Congratulations. This is certainly a feather in your cap."

John couldn't help but laugh out loud at that, as an image of Violet Cunningham and her purple plume popped into his head. "I've wanted a feather in my cap for quite some time," he said between guffaws. "Thank you, American Academy of Political and Social Science!"

Two days before Christmas, Ella fixed up a box of festively wrapped canned jams, pickles, and peaches to take to the Coopers. Though she had never met Beatrice, after John had told her the story, Ella seemed particularly concerned about the woman. "We'll go together, John, and say we are making the rounds of folks to wish them a Merry Christmas. It will be less awkward that way."

"A fine idea," he said.

When they were ready to leave, John carefully carried the box of jars to the carriage, placing it on the floor. He and Ella rode up front. Abram had attached bells to Blaze's harness so that everywhere they went for the past few weeks, happy jingles accompanied them.

"I even feel like Santa Claus," Ella said as she snuggled next to John in the crisp afternoon air.

When they pulled up to the Cooper house, a moment of sadness washed over John. During Leroy's successful days as a banker, he and Beatrice had lived near West Fourth Street and Kingbard Boulevard in an impressive brick home. That prestigious position, now gone, necessitated a move to a modest, one-story building in a much poorer neighborhood. The exterior paint was faded and peeling in places. Weeds sprouted through cracks in the walkway. John climbed down from the driver's seat, tied the horse to a post, and helped Ella to the ground. "You lead the way," he said. "I'll follow with the box."

At the door, Ella rapped. There was no sign of activity inside, and no response. John set the box on the porch step and knocked more firmly. Still, no one came to the door.

"Maybe they're in the back of the house," he said. They waited several minutes more, to no avail.

"Well, this is a disappointment," Ella said. "Shall we come back later?"

"I have a meeting this evening, and other obligations tomorrow," John said. "I say leave the box here. They can't help but notice it when they return, and we did include a card."

Neither of them spoke on the way home. The jingle bells rang out, but somehow seemed less merry. Troubled thoughts circled through John's mind. There was nothing about the Coopers' home to suggest the season—no wreath on the door, no flickering candles, no Christmas cards displayed along the window sills. Something wasn't right.

He pushed the dark thoughts away as best he could during the next twenty-four hours—the day before Christmas. After running errands in the morning, he returned home to excitement. Irene could not be still, dancing and giggling and dashing from room to room. Secrets took place behind closed doors. Margaret had placed a sign on the girls' bedroom door that read *KEEP OUT ELVES AT WORK*. Ella spent hours in the kitchen, and festive baked goods appeared from the oven. The house smelled of vanilla, peppermint, and cinnamon. Their world seemed right, and John reveled in the joy.

That mood evaporated when Johnny arrived home from his paper route. In his hand he held a shard of glass and a limp red ribbon.

"What have you there?" John asked, though deep inside he knew, and his gut twisted.

"I found these in front of the Coopers' house," his son said. "The steps were covered with broken jars and fruit. It looked like the package Mama had fixed up, and I thought you would want to know. Who would do such a thing? It's Christmas!"

Chapter Twelve

THE CRIME

1892

As the glow of the holidays faded and a new year took over, John couldn't dismiss thoughts of the Cooper's destroyed gift from his mind. He stopped by the Cooper house several times, hopeful there was something he could say or do to persuade Leroy to come back to the church. Once or twice a light flickered in a back room, but when John rapped firmly on the door, no one appeared.

"I'm so worried about Beatrice and the boys," Ella remarked one evening as they prepared for bed. "I don't care about Leroy. He should be in jail. For all we know he has murdered his family."

The comment startled John so much that the shoe he was removing slipped from his hand and dropped to the floor with a thud. "Now, Ella, that's pretty extreme. I don't think Leroy is capable of murder."

"Humph!" Ella plopped onto the bed, lay down and pulled the covers up. "Of course he's capable. From what you described of her bruised face, he gave her some mighty hefty slaps. Greater force could prove fatal."

The following day John attempted another visit to the Cooper household. Finding the house dark, he thought about Ella's comment. He still didn't believe Leroy capable of murdering his wife, but the man could be in jail for drunkenness. It would be a simple matter to find out. The jail, located in the basement of the courthouse, was just across the river on Water Street. With little crime in the city, the two cells often remained empty. A quick check would settle the matter and put Ella's mind—and his own—at ease.

So, after his midday meal, he bundled up against the winter chill for the second time that day and left the parsonage for the courthouse. The sun shone through scattered clouds, and he decided to walk the few blocks. Crossing the Cedar River on the Fourth Street Bridge, he slowed his vigorous stride, stopping now and then to watch as chunks of ice bobbed along in the current. The river sometimes froze completely over, but it was not yet cold enough this winter.

Once across the bridge, he turned right onto Water Street, guided by the sight of the courthouse cupola. Entering the impressive columned building, John was reminded of the many events he had attended there. The interior served not only as a courthouse, but as a venue for social events, including concerts, lectures, balls, and church services. Meanwhile, in the jail cells beneath the gaiety often dwelled Waterloo's unlawful citizens. Today, the foyer was quiet and empty. John looked for someone on duty. "Hello," he called out. His voice and footsteps echoed back as he sought the door to the basement. Finding it, he descended into the stark and chilly interior. A slightly overweight, mustached man dozed behind a desk, chair tipped back. As John approached, the man jumped up, the chair legs clattering in place. A gold star affixed to his dark blue coat identified him as the marshal.

John removed his hat and held out his hand. "John Stevenson from the Congregational Church. Thought I would stop by to pay a visit to the incarcerated."

"Of course, Reverend. I recognize you. You're in luck. We have a full house today, though probably a waste of your time. Just keeping them both till they dry out." The marshal picked up a set of keys from his desk and motioned John to follow. "Looking for anyone in particular?"

"Not necessarily. I felt it was time to visit and perhaps give your guests a little hope." He doubted he'd find Leroy here and didn't want to muddy the man's name if he were not. John unbuttoned his coat so his clerical attire showed and made certain the Bible in his right hand was clearly visible.

The marshal unlocked a gate and pointed to the two cells. "Help yourself."

A jail always depressed John, its occupants so often wasted souls. He took a deep breath and walked the few paces to the first cell where a rumpled looking young man lounged on a cot and sneered at him. His voice slurred, "Hey, preacher, looking to save me from sin? Sorry, too late."

John stopped. "It's never too late, lad. I'll pray with you, if you would like."

The young man spit on the floor and laughed. His clothes reeked of strong drink. John shook his head and moved on. Until the lad was sober, no consoling words would reach him. He stopped at the second cell, waiting for his eyes to adjust to the dimness. Against the far wall, his face half hidden in the dark interior, slouched a familiar figure.

"Hello, Reverend," a low voice rasped from the shadows.

John's heartbeat quickened, and his throat went dry. "Hello, Leroy," he said softly. "I'm sorry to find you here."

"Maybe sorry, but I'll bet not surprised." The prisoner, once a respected banker and a member of the church's board of trustees, now wore soiled clothes and was in bad need of a shave. Leroy made no effort to rise or come closer.

"Sorry and disappointed," John said, the words hardly describing his emotions. "Can I do anything to help?"

"Help a drunk? Doubt you would do that." A short laugh accompanied this remark. "And don't try prayer. It's no good."

John swallowed his response. Instead, he asked the question foremost in his mind. "Where are Beatrice and the boys, Leroy? Are they safe?"

"You tell me, Reverend. You were the one who sent her off—you and your misguided ideas about a woman's place."

"I didn't send her away, Leroy. You did that, and I know she came back. Yet I've been to the house, and no one's there."

"Don't know. She took off with those boys. My boys. She's got no right to them. As soon as I get out of here,

I'll find her. You wait and see." He stood suddenly, took several steps toward the bars that separated them, and looked John straight in the eye. Fists clenched and trembling in anger, he spat: "And don't you go interfering. She has defied the law, and as much as you would like to, you can't change the law. Now leave me be." He slumped back down on the cot and turned his face to the wall.

John felt his own anger rise. "I think you're wrong, Leroy. If Beatrice sues for divorce, the courts are inclined to give children to their mother, especially if she or they have experienced abuse at the hands of the husband."

"Hah! That's what you hope. Just you wait and see. Besides, she can't sue me for divorce. She has no money. It's a crime to take my boys, and she'll pay for that crime."

There was no more for John to say. With a heavy heart, he headed toward the exit.

"Find what you were looking for?" the marshal asked as he turned the key in the lock.

John shrugged his shoulders. "Yes and no."

Outside, he stood a moment in the cold. The sun, so cheery on his walk over, had slithered behind a gray cloud. John raised his coat collar higher on his neck. His thoughts spun in dark circles. Leroy, arrested for drunkenness — was it really a lesser crime than that of a wife who took her children to protect them? John didn't know the answer, and possibly only a court of law would determine that. He shook his head and cringed at the thought of kindly, soft-

spoken Beatrice considered a criminal. Her crime—
being a loving mother.

Chapter Thirteen

THE DOCTORATE

John settled in a comfortable chair in the parlor and opened the most recent edition of *The Woman's Standard*. He subscribed to several suffrage publications, but this was a homegrown Iowan paper, and it kept him advised of the woman's movement in his own state.

Ella, wielding her feather duster about the room, stopped and looked over his shoulder. "That Carrie Chapman is certainly a strong up-and-coming voice for women. Iowa should be proud of her," she said. "I understand she's even involved in the National American Woman Suffrage Association now that they have reorganized. They need some new blood—so many of those who have fought for so long are getting on in years."

John agreed. Lucretia Mott, who had worked tirelessly for woman's suffrage, had been gone since 1880, and Susan B. Anthony, Elizabeth Cady Stanton, and Lucy Stone were now all in their seventies. A woman's right to vote would never happen if young crusaders didn't take up the fight. "Carrie has the right spark," he said, "and she is definitely spreading her wings. Now that she's married to Mr. Catt, she lives in

New York, you know."

"Humph! That's loyalty for you. Iowa needs her here." Ella gave her duster a vigorous swipe along the windowsill.

"The entire movement needs her, Ella, and according to this account," John indicated the article in *The Woman's Standard*, "she's keeping her promises to help organize conferences in Iowa this summer and fall. If at all possible, I think I'll try to attend one of the meetings."

He perused the rest of the newspaper, noting in frustration, how the wheels of justice not only turned slowly but sometimes seemed to go in reverse, in spite of all the men and women who worked tirelessly for the cause.

~ ~ ~

THOUGH JOHN CONTINUED HIS OWN CAMPAIGNS AGAINST saloons and for woman suffrage, often speaking outside his pulpit on these issues, he frequently had to decline opportunities as his overworked throat caused his words to come out in a squawk or whisper. And now the hay fever was striking early. Usually it was not a problem until late summer. But this year, springtime pollens attacked his lungs, bringing on the wretched wheezing. He often scarcely slept at night due to the laboring of his breath.

Though his health issues wouldn't go away, a celebratory aura brightened the household. As had been hinted the previous fall, John received a formal letter from Tabor College stating he was to be presented with an honorary doctorate degree at a ceremony the last Saturday of April. *It is our hope that you can be here to accept this honor in person,* the announcement read. A buzz ran through him as he read the notice enclosed in the gilded envelope. This was going to happen. By nightfall he made up his mind and announced to Ella, "I'll go!"

They were in the bedroom preparing for bed. She sat in the wicker chair next to the window, one long silk stocking in her hand, and shook her head. "I'm not sure you should, John. What if your breathing becomes a problem? I can help with tonics and other remedies for your throat while you are here." She pulled off the other stocking, twisted the two together, and plopped them next to her shoes with a firm thrust then sighed. "But I don't know what to do for the hay fever except keep the windows closed."

John ignored her comments. "Of course I'll go," he said. "If I don't, it will look like I don't care, and I do care, very much. I'll be fine. I can't simply fold up and disappear because I need to catch my breath now and then. You can come, too, and be my nurse. We'll leave Irene under the watch of the older children."

Ella threw up her hands in surrender—something she had started doing lately when there was no sense in arguing.

But as the date drew near, it became apparent she would not accompany him. The children each suffered from colds and bad coughs. Her nursing was needed at home. Shoving a twinge of guilt to the back of his mind, John felt relieved. Tabor was but a short distance from Shenandoah where he and Anna had first settled in

Iowa, a poignant piece of his life before Ella. Many memories centered there, among them the birth of three children, two buried in a Shenandoah cemetery along with little Louis, the youngest, born in Waterloo, but laid to rest with his tiny siblings.

John boarded the Chicago Great Western on a blustery Thursday morning. His breathing seemed almost normal—a relief to him and obviously to Ella as she kissed him goodbye. *The Almighty must have meant for me to go*, he mused.

"I'll return on Tuesday," he told her. The trip would take two days with an overnight stay in Des Moines each way. Arrangements had been made for a guest preacher to fill his Waterloo pulpit on Sunday, which would offer a welcome respite for John's throat. His acceptance speech for Tabor, tucked carefully away in his coat pocket, was short and to the point and would not cause any undue irritation to his vocal chords.

On Friday evening, John stepped from the car of the Tabor and Northern Railway after a short, hilly ride from a connection with The Burlington Cedar Rapids and Quincy in Malvern. Before him atop a plateau lay the small town of Tabor. The brick buildings of the campus stood out among the modest white clapboard houses. The founders, George Gaston and John Todd, had modeled the college after Oberlin in Ohio, thus enrollment was open to students of both sexes and to every class and race—a fact that made John especially proud to be receiving an honorary doctorate here.

A feeling of joy embraced him, and he took in a big

breath of welcome air. The terrain and atmosphere in this corner of Iowa felt like coming home. Picking up his valise, he strode toward Gaston Hall where he was to meet a member of the staff and be apprised of the following day's events.

~ ~ ~

COMMENCEMENT, FULL OF THE TYPICAL POMP AND circumstance, was held outside on the breezy college lawn. John, dressed in the appropriate academic gown provided for him, sat on a raised platform with other dignitaries and watched the small class of proud graduates file up to receive their diplomas. After a flowery introduction, John stood for his own recognition, and those in attendance rose to applaud him. A sudden lump in his throat, which had nothing to do with strained vocal chords, caught him off guard. How he wished his father was present. It had been a long journey from Bannockburn, Scotland, to this place and this moment. He swallowed the lump away and presented his acceptance speech with the best elocution he could muster.

The evening was filled with a formal banquet, music from the small college band, and many rounds of congratulations. At midnight John retired to a bed in Woods Hall, the campus dormitory. The excitement had been tiring. He slept soundly, awoke before dawn, and slipped away to the stables where a loaned buggy awaited his personal use.

The ribbon of road dipped and rose before him as the sun crept above the horizon. Crossing over the East

Nishnabotna River, John's gut tightened with anticipation. A few short miles later, he entered the familiar territory of Shenandoah. Memories rushed at him, and he wondered if coming here had been the right decision. But how could he not? Pulling the horse to a halt at Rose Hill Cemetery on the outskirts of town, he sat for a full ten minutes gazing at the green hillside dotted with markers before climbing from the buggy. His steps took him directly to the three child-sized graves. With an audible sigh, he removed his hat and bowed his head.

"Dear, Lord, I know you are taking care of these little angels and their mother."

He knelt and fingered the names engraved in granite: *Donald G. Stevenson, b. Feb. 5, 1882 d. Jul. 28, 1882; Ruth Stevenson b. Jun. 23 1883 d. Sep. 8, 1884, Louis Stevenson, b. Aug. 23, 1887 d. Oct. 27, 1887.* Tears spilled down his cheeks as he sensed Anna's presence beside him. The two of them had gone through so much together—the challenges and triumphs in Texas teaching the freedmen, starting a home, the joy and heartbreak of parenthood. John would have preferred to bury her here with her precious babies, but had given in to her parents' wish to lay her to rest near their home in Fulton, Wisconsin. Two family gravesites remained here—originally reserved for him and Anna. Now, he and Ella would be interred there.

He stayed for a while, pulling at a few weeds that had worked their way up through the damp earth in spite of the gardener's efforts. Muffled notes of a familiar hymn, "Nearer, My God, to Thee," wafted across the air as someone practiced on the organ that early Sunday morning. John smiled and wiped his cheeks with the back of his hand. He stood and returned to the buggy, driving the short distance to town to attend the Congregational Church and to greet old friends.

~ ~ ~

ONCE HOME, CONGRATULATIONS POURED IN FOR DR. John Stevenson. He tried, with difficulty at times, to squelch the pride accompanying his new honor. Ella, however, had no trouble displaying her pleasure in his accomplishment. When he showed her the doctoral certificate, she quickly announced, "We'll frame it under glass and you can hang it in the church study next to your divinity degree from Yale. The congregation will be so proud."

His new title confused the children, especially Irene. "If you are a doctor," she said, "we won't need Dr. Griffin anymore when we get sick or Johnny breaks his foot."

John chuckled at the remark, "Not that kind of a doctor, Reenie. It's just a title like mister or missus. I'm still the same preacher, still the same papa, and we will still need Dr. Griffin from time to time. Though we hope not too often."

The few weeks since he put "Dr." before his name became a wild ride—heady and humbling. The mail brought notes from old friends and colleagues. Whittesey, who had first hinted of the honor, began his letter with a quote.

My dear Stevenson,

"They that will live godly shall suffer persecution."

For a long time I have not hesitated to say that you are one of the freshest and strongest preachers in Iowa. You have earned your degree.

I sympathize with you in the trials through which you are passing. May the Lord make the storm calm and bring you to your desired haven.

John had heard rumors that a few folks felt his doctorate was not earned and therefore not legitimate. He wasn't certain if this last paragraph referred to the controversy regarding his doctorate or his battle with hay fever. He suspected the latter. Either way, the concern was gratifying.

~ ~ ~

HAY FEVER PLAGUED JOHN THROUGH THE SUMMER, BUT he chose not to escape to the Wisconsin shore. He missed the Iowa Woman Suffrage Association conference he had hoped to attend. Staying home meant no respite from sermons, and Ella treated his throat with every remedy she could find. He cut back on his speaking engagements outside of the church. By the time autumn colored the countryside, his breathing problems had abated, and because the soreness in his throat had grown tolerable, he accepted an invitation to talk at the laying of a cornerstone of the Congregational Church in Shell Rock.

Ella accompanied him, and it was a grand affair for such a small community. Posters touted the celebration of the new church as "The Event of the Season." After a splendid dinner at the Opera House, he was introduced as "Dr. John Stevenson, one of Iowa's most distinguished orators." The laying of the stone and other addresses followed his speech, and the day culminated in an evening concert featuring "the finest ability of the State assisted by home talent."

They retired to the home of the church's pastor. In bed that night, Ella snuggled up to John. "That was lovely, and I'm so proud of you," she said. "I'm amazed at the crowd that showed up. It's not as though Shell Rock is the center of the earth. I'm sure you were the big draw."

He was touched by her remarks. This had been quite an occasion for the little town, and he doubted he was the main attraction, but it was nice to know his wife thought so. He felt well—the best he had in a long time—and the fall air brought with it a sense of anticipation. Surely, good things were in store for the months ahead.

Chapter Fourteen

THE UNEXPECTED

1893

An air of excitement pulsed in Iowa and throughout the nation as Chicago prepared to open its long-planned-for World's Columbian Exposition on May first. Word spread it was to be a magnificent event with multiple buildings gleaming and covering acres of land. John had read as much about it as he could and had some definite thoughts on the fair's management, including the price of a railway ticket to get there.

"If they want the general public to attend en masse, like they hope," he remarked to his family one evening, "they should encourage the railroad to reduce the cost. To my knowledge, this is not in their plans. At least one thing is being done right, though. The management has accepted from the American people, through Congress, a large sum of money on the condition that the doors will be closed on the Lord's Day."

The family was gathered in the parlor around the warmth of the wood burning stove as March winds howled outside. John read excerpts from the daily paper, prompting his remarks regarding the fair.

"Wouldn't it be great to go?" Johnny exclaimed. "There will be things to see from all over the world!"

"I've heard the whole place will be lit up with electric lights," Abram said, his eyes bright with excitement. "That's the future, you know."

John had heard this from his younger son on more than one occasion. It wouldn't surprise him at all if the boy ended up in a profession involving Edison's new invention.

Maggie jumped into the discussion. "Mama was reading in *The Ladies' Home Journal* that there will even be an exhibit of an electric stove for cooking. Won't that be something? I would love to go. There will be so much to see. Can't we go, Papa?"

"Hooray! A fair!" Irene exclaimed. "Let's go, Papa."

John folded the newspaper and shook his head. "I don't know how we could. The cost to get there, plus any entrance fees and lodging and meals, sounds out of the question."

Johnny stood, thrust his hands in his pockets, and paced the room. "Then I'll go by myself, by golly. I'll go. I'm old enough to do something like that on my own, and I have some money."

"That's your college money, son. You can't throw your future away on a fair."

Now Maggie stood, hands on her hips in the defiant way she often expressed herself. "But it's not just any old fair. It *is* our future, the future for all of us! I want to see an electric cook stove…and other things I can't even imagine."

John tried not to smile at her dramatics, wondering, *did she think her brother would pay her way, too?* He noted that during this prattle, Ella said nothing. She sat on the settee working her embroidery, punching a needle strung with bright red thread in and out of the almost completed floral design for a dresser scarf. She knew the money situation. They lived on a tight budget. He was surprised she hadn't backed his comment about the expense of such a trip. After almost four years of marriage, she still often perplexed him.

A week later, John sensed Ella's mood change. He could feel it the minute he walked into the kitchen one evening as she added ingredients to a soup simmering on the stove. She stirred the pot with a determination he had come to recognize as a sign that a confrontation would erupt before the day was over. She had been especially quiet lately, and he sensed something brewed besides the stew.

During supper, while the children chit-chatted, Ella said very little, avoiding John's glance, her jaw set. After the meal, the boys and girls washed their own soup bowls and utensils, as was the custom, and left the room, until it was only Ella and John together for the remainder of the clean-up. He dried and put away dishes while she washed and remained quiet.

"Good supper, Mother," he commented, trying to be especially congenial, in an effort to reach what was going on under his wife's façade.

But it was much later when they were in bed together that she turned to him and whispered, "We are going to the fair. All of us."

John sat bolt upright. This was not what he was expecting. "Ella, you know we can't do that. What on earth brought this on?"

She sat up, too, reached for an envelope on the nightstand and pulled out a letter. John immediately recognized Cora's handwriting.

"She's going to be there. She's going to give a talk in the Woman's Building. We have to go."

John sighed and put his arm around his wife. "My dear, my dear. I understand your desire, but it's simply not possible. You know that."

Ella held the letter against her heart, and John heard her take in a big breath. "Yes, John. We can."

Had she lost her mind? "And just how do you propose to pay for this trip?"

"I will pay for it." She paused a moment, then blurted, "Today I got a job."

He sat stunned for a full moment. After numerous conversations on the subject, she had defied him. He pushed back the quilt, sat on the edge of the bed with his head in his hands, and said a silent prayer. Then, in as calm a voice as possible, said, "Tell me about it."

In a rush, Ella was kneeling on the floor at his feet, Cora's letter still in her hand. "It will work, John. It's perfect! I'll only be gone during the day while the children are at school. In fact, I will be home an hour before they are."

"And where are you to be employed?" He still couldn't believe what he was hearing.

"The law firm of Alford and Gates. I read an ad in the paper saying they were looking for a part-time stenographer. I went there this morning with my resume. I took dictation before we were married, you know. They had me do some sample typing and note-taking, and hired me on the spot. And the best part is, I'll be paid six dollars a week!" With this disclosure, she broke into a wide smile. Reflections of the oil lamp from the bedside table danced in her eyes.

The importance of this resolve and the totally unexpected move on Ella's part struck John as though he had been jolted awake from a deep sleep. He had not seen her radiate this much joy since they were first married. Her working outside the home would take some getting used to, and it might cause negative rumors at church, but he knew he had to accept her decision. He pulled her up onto the bed beside him and held her close. "Let's pray about this together," he said as his inner thoughts tumbled over one another. *Surely, God will help me through this newest revelation and the changes it will make in our lives.*

Chapter Fifteen

THE WORLD'S FAIR

They had decided to go to Chicago the end of May in time to hear Susan B. Anthony speak at the World's Congress of Representative Women. In the meantime, Ella had learned with disappointment that Cora was not actually going to be at the fair. Instead, a paper she had written, entitled *Literature for Young People*, would be displayed in the Woman's building along with other writings by women of note.

"That still makes it worthwhile, doesn't it?" Ella had pleaded with John when she learned the news. "And to hear Miss Anthony—what an opportunity!" The expression on her face, which he interpreted as a mix of concern that he might be cross over this revelation and her hope they would still go, made him agree. By now they had promised the trip to the children, and each was full of the anticipation that comes when something magical is within reach. Changing his mind was out of the question.

A jubilant mood hummed in the parsonage for weeks beforehand. There was very little bickering among the younger members of the family, and John noted how Ella seemed to breeze through her household chores, even after working several hours a day at the law office, when he expected her to be tired.

"It's a perfect chance for you to glean material for sermons and talks promoting a woman's right to vote," she said one afternoon. "Why, I've learned Congress even authorized the appointment of a Board of Lady Managers to represent the interests of women at the fair. And did you know a woman architect designed the Woman's Building? Her name is Sophia Hayden. She's from Boston, and she graduated from the Massachusetts Institute of Technology. This all simply proves women are capable of making important decisions."

At the conclusion of this little speech, Ella beamed as though she herself had had a hand in the creation of the building. Underneath, John sensed all the jolly talk was calculated to keep him from changing his mind. Though, by now, he found himself just as caught up in the excitement as the others.

~ ~ ~

AT LAST, THE DEPARTURE DATE ARRIVED, AND THE FAMILY boarded the Burlington, Cedar Rapids and Northern Railway early in the morning. Each was responsible for his or her own satchel containing a change of clothes and personal items. Additionally, John carried a basket Ella had prepared heaped with food to appease their hunger during the two-day trip.

At Elmira they connected with the Chicago and Northwestern Railway heading east, and at Clinton, Iowa, they changed trains again. Each transfer was an adventure in itself, especially for Maggie, Abram, and Irene, who had never before traveled by rail. During the long ride, Ella and the four children chattered non-stop. Their excitement seemed to generate an electric glow about them — something akin to Edison's light bulbs Abram was so bent on seeing. John tried not to worry about the cost of bringing a family this far. Even with Ella's job, which in the end only covered two fares, this once-in-a lifetime experience took a significant cut from his own pay. They had found a way to reduce expenses by staying the three nights with a fellow pastor and his wife in Chicago, which helped. *It would work out somehow. It had to.*

When they entered Jackson Park on the first day of their visit, John couldn't help but think of the words of the Queen of Sheba in First Kings upon seeing the wealth and kingdom of Solomon. *Howbeit I believed not the words, until I came, and mine eyes had seen it: and behold the half was not told me: thy wisdom and prosperity exceedeth the fame which I heard.*

This exposition, celebrating the 400th anniversary of Christopher Columbus's landing in America, far surpassed John's expectations. He knew it would be marvelous and a sight to behold, but the words of others had not begun to tell of the splendor and the exciting learning opportunities to be found upon these many acres. The massive buildings gleamed a white so brilliant it almost hurt the eyes. In the center glistened a pool large enough for boats to cross from one side to the other.

The children tugged John and Ella this way and that as they spied something new.

"Look," cried Abram. He pointed to a huge wheel-like structure that rose high into the sky. "It's Mr. Ferris' wheel. I've read that you can sit in little cars and be rotated up until there is a grand view of the fair grounds and beyond. There's never been anything like it. Mr. Ferris is a bridge builder, and this is his answer to the tower at the Paris Exposition built by Mr. Eiffel. I think it's even better because it moves."

"Don't get too excited, kid," Johnny said. "It's not finished yet and won't be for a couple of weeks. We should have come in June. But somewhere there's a moving sidewalk. Let's find that."

A gentleman passing by overheard the remark. "Forget it, son. It broke the first day and hasn't worked since."

In spite of those disappointments, there were plenty of other amazing sights. In the Electricity Building, Maggie and Ella spent time before a modern kitchen that displayed not only the stove they had talked about but an electric dishwasher as well. In that same building, John and the boys were particularly interested in displays of Thomas Edison's kinetoscope, search lights, a seismograph, and a Morse code telegraph.

And so it was with everything they saw—each exhibit thought to be better than the one before, opening the imagination until nothing seemed impossible. To add to the magic, a myriad of multi-colored banners flapped overhead in the breeze, live musicians strolled the grounds, and the aroma of peanuts and popcorn filled the air.

"It's like when the circus comes to town," Abram said, "only ten times more."

"Peanuts, pleeease!" begged Irene.

John relented, buying several bags to pass around. He popped a few in his mouth, the flavor adding to the festive feeling. Later, they received free samples of a new product called Cracker Jacks, a combination of peanuts, popcorn and molasses, that left them with sticky fingers, sticky lips, and wide smiles.

They stayed until dark to see electricity light up the white buildings — a wondrous iridescent sight. Finally, with their feet dragging and Irene asleep in John's arms, they retired to the home of their hosts, near collapse from exhaustion and delight.

The second day, May 27th, John and Ella planned to hear Susan B. Anthony. Her talk was part of a series of scholarly congresses held at the new Art Institute on Michigan Avenue, at a distance from the fairgrounds. The day's theme was the religious press.

"That sounds really boring," Abram said, rolling his eyes.

"I'll say," agreed Johnny. "Can't we go to the fair on our own? There's still so much to see. Maggie and I will watch Irene. We promise."

John relented, knowing there would be other talks at the institute in addition to Miss Anthony's, none of which would interest the children. The subject of the religious press intrigued him immensely. He was more than miffed that the fair's management had backed down on its promise to close the fair on Sundays and was eager to hear talks on the subject. Plus, he knew Miss Anthony was often at odds with the religious press — especially the more conservative newspapers —

and he was curious about her thoughts on the matter.

Thus, the children went their separate way with the understanding they would meet at the Woman's Pavilion at three o'clock. There was still that paper of Cora's to find.

John and Ella arrived at the great hall in the art building only minutes before the first speaker took the podium, and they felt fortunate to find two seats together in the large crowd. Once in place, Ella leaned toward John and whispered, "I didn't expect such a big crowd. Most must have come to hear Miss Anthony."

He nodded. In all his years advocating woman's suffrage, this was the first time he had seen any of the primary spokeswomen in person, and he couldn't deny a thrill at being there. Several speakers preceded Miss Anthony, and John was satisfied that some of them lambasted the fair authorities for not closing the gates on Sunday.

After a much-needed intermission, Miss Anthony was introduced to loud applause. The woman looked severe in a black dress and red shawl, her gray hair pulled back in a bun. She stood quietly on the stage until silence filled the hall. Then she began.

"I am asked to speak upon The Moral Leadership of the Religious Press. For one who has for fifty years been ridiculed by both press and pulpit, denounced as infidel by both, it is, to say the least, very funny. Nevertheless, I am glad to stand here today as an object lesson of the survival of the fittest, from ridicule and contempt."

She talked about her own religious upbringing as a Quaker, saying her early reform work was in the cause of temperance. "I had my first little experience with the religious press on that question. It was no light affair, I can assure you. As a delegate to the annual convention of the New York State Temperance Society, I was told that it was very well for women to belong to the temperance society, but wholly out of the way for them to be accepted as delegates or to speak or to take any part in the meetings, and I want to say to you that the majority of the men of that convention were ministers."

At this comment, muffled remarks rippled through the auditorium, and Ella poked John in the side. He smiled, eager to hear more.

Anthony continued: "The whole religious press of the country came down on my head for obtruding myself there, claiming that St. Paul had said: 'Let your women keep silence in the churches, and no one but an infidel would attempt to speak there.' I submit that was not leadership in the right direction."

She went on to chastise the religious press during the anti-slavery movement, saying, "The press used to make my hair stand straight for fear I might go to the bottomless pit because I was an abolitionist.

"Then the next great question has been this woman question. When we started out on that, the whole religious world was turned upside down with fright. We women were disobeying St. Paul; we women were getting out of sphere and would be no good anywhere, here or hereafter. And the way that I was scarified! The religious press, instead of being a leader in the great moral reform, is usually a little behind."

At this remark applause broke out, and John joined

in. His forward-thinking sermons often conflicted with the more conservative members of the religious community—something that frustrated him. But, like the admirable Miss Anthony, he was never afraid to speak his mind.

She had much more to say, and though many of her remarks were negative ones against the religious press, she did thank those religious newspapers who advocated for equal rights. "I do not believe," she said, "religious liberty can exist anywhere except where political liberty has been thoroughly and fully established."

Amen, John thought, but he stiffened when Miss Anthony concluded with remarks against closing the fair on Sundays. "I have stood with my friend Mrs. Stanton in favor of the opening of the gates on Sunday. Not because I do not venerate God and all his works, but because I do venerate God and all his works, and to say that for us to go there and study those wonderful productions of the hand and the brain of man is violating what we term the American Sabbath—is violating any injunction of God—well, I cannot understand it. To me, if I want to venerate God, and if I want to feel that man is rising and approaching divinity itself, I go there and look at those wonderful productions."

As he and Ella wove their way through the throng in search of the Woman's Building, John was already composing a sermon. As much as he had been invigorated by Miss Anthony's speech, she had one thing wrong. Sunday was the day set aside to worship in the house of the Lord. There were six other days of the week to "venerate God" by appreciating the "wonderful productions" of the hand and brain of man. And as wonderful as they were, these accomplishments did not make man divine. That status was reserved for God, and the public needed to honor that by filling church pews on Sunday. With all due respect for the Misses Anthony and Stanton, he thought, this had nothing to do with giving women the right to vote.

Chapter Sixteen

STRONG WOMEN

For weeks following their extravagant excursion to Chicago, the family talked about the sights they had seen. John was pleased that the children had been exposed to so much information that would stay with them and help them grow. However, the trip had severely drained their finances. Maggie and Irene would not have new frocks for school that fall. Ella stretched the grocery money as far as it would go, turning every meat bone into soup, and often making a meal out of nothing but dried beans, soaked, baked, and seasoned. But scrimping at the Stevenson residence wasn't due only to their trip. The entire nation suffered.

"They call it a Depression," John told the children one evening as they sat together in the parlor.

"It's not so bad. Other girls can't have new dresses, either," said Maggie as she mended a tear in last year's jumper. "But I don't understand how everyone can become poor at once."

"It's complicated, Maggie," John said, as he struggled to explain something he didn't quite understand himself. "It has to do with the decline of the gold reserves which causes major businesses like railroads and banks to shut down. That means fewer jobs. Everyone is hurt. It's like when you play dominos. The one at the top falls, it hits another, and another, and so on."

"It sounds pretty serious," Johnny said, shaking his head. He set aside the book he was reading to join in the conversation.

"It is, son, but we'll get by, and it won't last forever."

Ella said nothing, just listened as her needle wove in and out of her needlepoint. Abram, too, was quiet. He sat on the floor and studied a piece of paper in front of him. His youngest son had taken to drawing maps. However, he had no doubt the lad was listening to the conversation.

Unfortunately, the Depression also meant members of the Congregational Church put less in the offering plate on Sunday, cutting into the ongoing expenses of the church, the parsonage, and John's own salary. He had to admit that he appreciated Ella's job, even though, as he had predicted, there were those who criticized them for it.

Luckily, there were always those parishioners who, regardless of their own circumstances, understood that a pastor's salary was not cream on top of the milk jug even in normal times. One Friday, as he worked on a sermon in the church study, John's thoughts were interrupted by the sound of footsteps and a soft rap on the door. The late afternoon sun already cast dark shadows upon the walls, and he was about to finish up for the day. He lay his pen aside, leaned back in the chair and stretched, wondering who the visitor might be.

"Come in," he said.

Mrs. Alan stepped into the room with a calico-covered basket over her arm.

"Hello, Reverend. I'm so glad you are still here. I was afraid I might have missed you." Setting the basket on the desk, she pulled back the cloth to reveal a dozen eggs, a loaf of homemade bread, and a jar of preserves. "This was baking day, and I made plenty. I wanted you to have a loaf, and our chickens have been laying extra these days. Evidently they have no notion of a Depression in the coop. I hoped you and Mrs. Stevenson could use a few eggs. We've more than we need."

John doubted this last statement, considering the Alans' six children, but that made the gift even more thoughtful. "Thank you. I'm certain Ella will put them to good use, and the bread smells heavenly. In fact, I was just leaving for home, and it will be a temptation to nibble the loaf on my way."

He accepted the gifts graciously. Amidst all the conflicts and challenges faced by ministers and their families, food always seemed to appear, even when the coffers were slim. For this, John was eternally grateful.

He sang on the brisk walk home, surrounded by autumn. The smell of wood-smoke mingled with the scent of Mrs. Alan's freshly baked bread and lightened his step. He felt he could do a little polka on the fallen leaves that crunched beneath his feet.

Upon entering the house, he found Abram lighting the lamps in the hallway and parlor, his youngest son's self-appointed job. Glancing towards the kitchen, he noticed it was still dark. Ella usually lit the lamps there before starting the evening meal, but there was no sign of activity nor welcoming smell of a supper cooking.

"Where's Mama?" he asked.

Abram shrugged his shoulders. "Upstairs, I guess."

Just then Maggie appeared, worry lines etched on her young face. "She came home early from work and has been in the bedroom all afternoon with the door shut, Papa. I think I heard her crying."

"Crying?" This news took John aback. Ella never cried. Tough times before their marriage had made her strong and stoic. He couldn't imagine what could break her down to tears. Cora? Something must have happened to her beloved sister.

He took the stairs two at a time and entered their bedroom. Ella stood at the window, her back to him. John approached, put his hand on her shoulder and turned her toward him. Tears streaked her cheeks, and she clutched a wet, crumpled handkerchief. "What is it, Ella? Is it Cora?"

She laid her head against his chest. "No, no. Not that. Oh, John." She hesitated a moment, then blurted, "I lost my job."

"You were fired?" Her startling news felt like a slap. She was a good stenographer. He doubted the law firm could find a better one in all of Waterloo.

Ella dabbed at her red eyes with the handkerchief. "No. Not exactly, but folks aren't paying lawyers these days, so the money isn't coming in, and they can't afford me." She blew her nose and sighed. "They said they'd hire me back when things got better, but now is when we need the money, John, and it's partly my fault because I insisted we go to the fair."

He held her, knowing her tears were not only about

the money and the humiliation of losing the job. He had watched her blossom the past few months since she began working for Alford and Gates. During that short time, he had come to learn that she, and likely many women, needed fulfillment beyond the duties of a homemaker. This shouldn't have come as a surprise. He thought of Anna and her strength and devotion to teaching the former slaves. It had been her determination before their marriage to continue that for the rest of her life. And he thought of his own situation. What if his livelihood were taken from him? What if he could no longer preach or have a church full of parishioners to guide? He would be devastated. Maybe Ella's situation wasn't quite the same, but still, he recognized and understood her emotions.

A quiet settled over the house for the next few days. Conversation was scarce, and the children seemed to tiptoe around, as though noise would make the situation worse.

Each day, as John left the house, he did so with ambivalence, feeling guilty he could shut the door and enter his own work world, but also somewhat relieved he could escape the tension. Yet, as the week progressed, the atmosphere at home gradually warmed. By Friday things felt almost normal. When John climbed the stairs for bed that evening, he found Ella in her nightclothes, sitting up reading. She looked relaxed.

"Found a good book?" he asked, making conversation to keep things light.

She ignored the question and laid the book aside. "I hoped you would finish that sermon and come to bed before I was asleep," she said. "I have something to tell you."

Oh, no, here we go again. He removed his waistcoat and began unbuttoning his shirt. "And what might that be?"

"I have a new job." Her voice was firm, yet John noticed the hint of a smile at the corners of her mouth.

Tossing his shirt on the chest at the foot of the bed, he braced himself, not knowing whether to be pleased or upset at this newest announcement. He would wait to hear what she had to say. "You are quite the woman, Ella. What is it now?"

"I'm going to give piano lessons. I already have one pupil, the mayor's daughter. They can afford it, in spite of the economy." Now Ella's smile spread wide and her words flew. "It won't be as much money as I made at the law firm, but it's something, and there are probably other wealthy families in Waterloo who have children I could teach, too. I've done this before, you know, and I can do it again. Now what do you think of that?" She crossed her arms and beamed at him.

John could only shake his head and wonder at this unpredictable creature sitting in his bed, peering out from under her night cap. He advocated for strong women, and none were stronger than the one he married. He loved her music. Teaching piano would be far more socially acceptable than her previous work, and would serve to quiet those who clucked behind their backs about such things.

He finished readying himself for bed, turned down the gas light, crawled in beside his wife, and put his arm around her. "God bless you," he murmured in her ear. Then under his breath, he whispered a prayer, "Thank you, Lord," and fell asleep with a smile on his face.

Ella was right about one thing—by the end of October, two other little girls had signed up for piano lessons. John came home early one afternoon and decided he was thankful he wasn't there every day. From three o'clock to four-thirty, Monday through Thursday, piano keys plunked laboriously, often out of tune. This was not the same as the lyrical notes of Chopin, Beethoven, or the simple hymns Ella played in the evening.

Abram sometimes came by the church in the afternoons to do his school work. He grumbled to John, "It's noisy at home, especially when those girls hit the wrong notes." At this he would grimace and cover his ears as though the sound had carried the few blocks from the parsonage.

"Things could be worse, son," John said. "Your mother's happy, and it's only for an hour and a half a day. Plus, the extra money does help with the budget."

Maggie complained about it, too. "It's not pretty music. Why can't Mama go to their homes to teach?"

Maggie had always spoken her mind, which was a good thing, John thought. But at sixteen she had yet to use tact and diplomacy. Just the day before he learned she had exchanged sharp words with Mrs. Cunningham. Upon hearing this, he had called his daughter into his study. "Is it true you told Mrs. Cunningham she didn't know what she was talking about?" he asked.

Maggie put her hands on her hips. "Yes, Papa. She was telling people you were wrong about women being equal to men. She said the Bible says something different. And she made me mad."

"That may be so, Margaret Stevenson, but you have got to learn to control your tongue. You must not be rude to people. I don't want to hear of this kind of behavior again, do you understand? And you owe her an apology."

She glared at him, opened her mouth to object, then seemed to think better of it before stomping out of the room.

John sighed. He had no doubt Mrs. Cunningham may have said something negative about him. That woman was an enigma. He couldn't understand why she continued to be a member of his church when she seemed to disagree with so much of what he preached. As the subject of his sermons was usually printed in *The Courier* in advance of each Sunday, she rarely attended church the mornings he spoke on temperance, and never on those occasions he advocated for woman's suffrage. Yet she was very involved in the Ladies Industrial Society, an important church committee that raised money for a variety of needs. What's more, she seemed to like Ella—though John was discovering that most of the church women liked his wife.

"One of the reasons Violet is so effective in the Society is she has money, or her husband does," Ella told John as they strolled home from a Sunday service. "I don't know exactly what he does, but I think he's involved in the liquor industry."

"Well, that would certainly explain why she skips my sermons on temperance," John said. "But it deepens the mystery even more as to why she attends at all."

Ella shrugged her shoulders. "She has friends here. Everyone needs friends. And as far as you are concerned, you obviously offer something she agrees with, whether she makes it known or not."

But there was still the incident with Maggie. Even though his daughter had been defending him, it concerned John greatly that she had spoken to anyone, let alone a parishioner, in such a manner. It was imperative that she apologize.

He let the matter rest a while before approaching Maggie again on the subject. She was in the front yard picking chrysanthemums one day as he walked in the gate after a series of long meetings at the church. He put his arm around her shoulder.

"How is my Maggie today?"

She looked at him out of the corner of her eyes and mumbled, "Fine."

"And have you apologized to Mrs. Cunningham?"

He felt her tense. "Well, not exactly yet, but I'm working on it." She plucked at the petals of one of the blossoms until not much remained on the stem.

"Working on it? What does that mean?" John tried to control his irritation. "You either have or you haven't. This is very important, Margaret."

"I know, Papa. I know." She all but stamped her foot as she used to do when she was little. "I will, but I'm going to do it my way." She slipped out from under his arm and headed toward the house with the remnants of her bouquet.

John shook his head. Whatever her "way" happened to be, he had to believe she would obey his request. What *could* a man do with strong-willed women? He seemed to collect them — Anna, Ella, and now his oldest daughter.

Yet a week later, he rejoiced that there were women who were not afraid to speak up for their convictions. On November 7th, the women in the state of Colorado were granted the right to vote.

"Well, that's two states down, only forty-two more to go," Ella said upon hearing the news. "Now, what about Iowa?"

Chapter Seventeen

TO EVERYTHING THERE IS A SEASON

It took a while for the details of the victory in Colorado to trickle across the nation, but when the news hit the Iowa papers, John read it with relish. He sat back in the most comfortable chair in the parlor, his stocking feet propped up on the tea table, reading *The Woman's Standard*. *The Standard* gave a more detailed account than the local papers and was edited thoughtfully by Mary Jane Coggeshall, an Iowa suffragist he greatly admired.

"Listen to this," he said to Ella. "Fifty-five percent of the Colorado electorate turned out to vote, with 35,798 voting in favor and 29,551 against. That is a sizeable margin." He read on to himself, exclaiming here and there until Ella snatched the paper from him.

"If you are just going to chortle and ahem and aha without telling me what's going on, I will read it for myself." She plopped down on the piano bench and began studying the article, making the same unconscious noises as he had.

"Well?" he said, watching the expressions on her face.

Ella rattled the pages. "Here's an interesting tidbit. The women in Colorado asked for help from the National American Woman's Suffrage Association, but it was refused because the organization was short of money and Miss Anthony thought they had no chance of winning. Mrs. Catt disagreed and helped the Colorado suffragists organize their campaign. She even traveled all the way to the state and made speeches."

"We need five hundred more like her," John said.

Ella sighed. "I'm not sure even that would help. People are so set in their ways." She read on. "Look here, New Zealand and South Australia also recently gave women the vote. That's pretty forward for backward countries, if you ask me! Aren't these United States supposed to be forward? Something is wrong here."

The dialogue continued throughout the day and into supper. The children put in their two cents worth at the table, as they passed around bowls of barley soup and slices of buttered bread.

"Nobody's going to make me be a dormouse and grovel to some man," Maggie fumed between bites. "Even if I can't vote, I'm going to stand up for my rights, and when I'm a teacher I will tell the girls in my class that—and the boys, too."

John chuckled inwardly, giving her a silent hurrah, but hoping a little tact would become part of her stand. He wondered if she had apologized yet to Mrs. Cunningham for being rude. He'd give her a couple more days to come to him about it before asking her again.

"I'm not sure I'd want you for my teacher," Abram mumbled, his mouth full of bread. "You don't sound like much fun."

"I do," Irene said. "I want her to be my teacher.

She'll give me good grades because I'm her sister."

"You're getting off the subject," Johnny said. "This is about a woman's rights, not your sneaky way to get good marks. Pass the butter. Please!"

In the middle of the discussion, John put down his fork. Suddenly, the subject of enfranchisement seemed far off and unimportant. Something in the air since he arrived home had been irritating his lungs, bringing on the wheezing. That evening it seemed especially bad. For a moment, his breath wouldn't come, and he felt he might suffocate.

"John, are you all right?" Ella's voice, full of panic, interrupted the children's prattle.

John stood abruptly, knocking his chair backward with a crash to the floor.

Ella was immediately at his side, grabbing his arm. "What is it? You're turning white!"

He waved her away and stumbled from the kitchen into the hall and out the front door into the frosty night air. The bitter cold hit like a slap on the face and brought him to. He managed to gulp a big breath.

He heard Irene wailing in the background. "Papa! Papa!"

Ella brought his coat and put it over his shoulders as he paced the yard in the dark. "Should I send Johnny for the doctor?"

"No, I'm better. Don't know what it was. That was about as bad as it gets."

He stayed outside for a while longer until his breathing seemed easier and his fingers and toes began to tingle from the cold. Inside he found the family scurrying around at Ella's orders trying to find anything unusual that could possibly have brought on the attack. It was finally decided perhaps the last chrysanthemums of the season, a spindly bouquet Maggie had arranged and set in the middle of the supper table, had been the culprit.

"I threw them away, Papa, and tomorrow after school, I will pull them all out of the yard, I promise." Tears streaked his oldest daughter's cheeks.

His few moments of panic had frightened the entire family, for which he was sorry. And though he suspected the flowers had been the cause, there were other plants that also brought on his affliction. He had managed, for the first year in quite some time, to survive the spring and summer without having to leave the area, and for that, he was thankful.

Later that evening, after Ella played several soothing melodies on the piano, she sat beside him in the parlor. "I've been thinking," she said, and John couldn't help but smile. He never knew quite what to expect when Ella put her mind to a problem.

"You told me once you seriously considered working at an Indian mission, and even looked into teaching at the Santee Normal Training School in Nebraska. Maybe now is the time to reconsider a move—for the sake of your health, if nothing else."

She ignored his look of surprise.

"Cora is friends with the superintendent of Presbyterian Missions. I bet she could put in a good word for you. And here is the best part—they have missions in Colorado. Wouldn't it be great to live in that forward-thinking state where the air is pure?"

John took her hand. "It's a nice thought, Ella, but moving the family and all, I don't…"

"It's a good time, John, at least at the end of this school year. Next fall Maggie will be going to Normal School and Johnny away to college. Abram would love the adventure, you know that, and Irene is young enough that it won't matter. Please consider it. I'll write Cora and ask her to approach her friend. You gave us all a terrible fright tonight. We must do something."

He squeezed her hand, touched by her concern. "Yes, my love, I appreciate the concern, although I'm sure I'm no worse than in prior years. If it helps to ease your mind, I will give the idea serious consideration."

However, that night, John lay awake for hours. His attack had scared him as well, but once the bouquet was tossed he felt better. Perhaps paying closer attention to what caused these spells and then avoiding the offending plants was all that was needed. He was well established in Waterloo and liked the community. Yet, the more he thought about it, the more appealing Ella's proposal became. Ever since working with the former slaves in Texas, a part of him couldn't forget the satisfaction of pursuing benevolent causes. He and Anna had wanted to teach the Indians, but it would have been a difficult move in 1880 with three small children. That seemed a lifetime ago, but his yearning lingered. As for causes, he could promote woman's suffrage wherever they lived.

Morning brought cheerful sunshine, a day bright with promise. After a quick breakfast, the children scurried off for school. The concerns of the evening before seemed forgotten.

John pulled on his overcoat and picked up his Bible. "I plan on doing some visitations today," he said. "There are several elderly members who haven't been to church lately. I'm not sure Mrs. Jenkins will be with us much longer."

"And you, John?" Ella asked. "How about you? Are you going to continue being with us? I heard you wheezing during the night."

"I'm much better today." He took in a big breath to prove to her that he was still among the living. But before heading out the door, he turned to her. "I've been doing a great deal of thinking. Maybe you are right about Colorado. I'll write to Cora myself and ask her to contact her friend."

He mentally wrote the letter as he went about his day. That night he put his thoughts down on paper, explaining his background and his strong desire to work with the Indians. He also told about his family situation and added an amount he felt necessary for salary.

"That bit of information may make the request null and void at the outset," he told Ella as they readied for bed, "but I have to be honest in both my application and to the family."

After delivering the letter to the post office the next morning, a sudden sense of glee overtook him. Just the thought of living in Colorado was exciting. Sure, he would miss the folks in Waterloo. But the prospect of once more spreading the word of God to underprivileged people and bettering their lives with education gave the future a whole new glow.

December arrived with all its trappings, busyness, and celebrations. John loved the season, even though there never seemed to be enough time to fit everything in. Anxious as he was to hear from Cora or her friend, he couldn't dwell on a move until later.

But amidst the joyous singing of carols and colorful pageantry, a telegram arrived, settling a pall over the household. Directed to Ella, it tersely read: *Your mother near death. Please come if possible. I have notified Cora and Nellie. A. J. Strawn.*

"Mrs. Strawn is a longtime neighbor and friend," Ella explained to John, her hand shaking as she reread the ominous black print. "I'll send a return message saying I can't come." Her words seemed forced and tight.

John held her close, remembering how he had learned of his father's death in Scotland months after the fact, wishing with all his heart he could have been there to say goodbye. Nor had Ella had the opportunity to say goodbye to her own father when he died several years before. "Of course you'll go. You need to be there with your sisters."

"But the money..."

"We can manage it, thanks to your help with the finances."

"It means I may not be here for Christmas."

"We celebrate the Lord's birth all year," John said. "Death comes but once. You must go."

And so she left, and John went about his duties as a minister and a father without Ella. He tucked away thoughts of her missing on Christmas morning, reminding himself: *To everything there is a season, and a time to every purpose under the heaven.*

Chapter Eighteen

DECISIONS AND SURPRISES

1894

A new year blew in with snow and gray skies. Everyone bundled up to avoid frostbitten noses, toes, and fingers. Abram and Johnny complained about constantly shoveling snow, which was necessary to get from the house to the street. The one welcome respite was from John's allergies—naked trees, buried bulbs, and seeds hidden under frozen earth made it easy for him to breathe. His sermons took on a new strength. His throat bothered him less.

Fanny McDonald's final breath was taken on December thirteenth. Ella had reached her mother in time to say goodbye, and she stayed on in Ohio for several more days, visiting with her sisters. She returned to Waterloo on December twenty-fourth, a Christmas gift for John and the children, far more precious than any of the gaily wrapped packages under the tree.

John waited awhile to bring up the subject of Colorado. His wife had much on her mind, and he figured they'd get around to the subject sooner or later. However, he was anxious to plan for his future, and if there was to be a change, he needed to let the church know. One morning, when the children were back at school, he and Ella talked as they cleared away the remnants of the holidays. Open boxes cluttered the floor, waiting to be filled. John removed the last garland from the wilted tree and turned to Ella. "I don't suppose you had a chance to discuss my letter with Cora." He watched for her reaction as she gently placed a tissue-wrapped, glass ornament into a box marked *Christmas*.

She stood, moved to the window and sighed, looking out at the drab, January sky. "Cora, Nellie, and I talked about everything. It was so special to be together after all these years. There was hardly a moment when we weren't rattling on." Her gaze out the window seemed to go somewhere beyond Waterloo.

John waited for the melancholy moment to pass. He didn't want to push for an answer to his question at an inappropriate time, but his hope dwindled like fading embers with her silence. *She has no answer*, he thought.

Then she turned and spoke. "I'm sorry, John. I've been so thoughtless ignoring your question. Yes, Cora said she received your letter and sent it on to the Reverend Kirkwood before leaving for Ohio. She hopes there is a job for you in Colorado." Suddenly her mood shifted, and a smile blossomed on her lips. "Furthermore, she is thinking of moving there herself sometime in the future. Wouldn't that be grand? We would all be together."

John reached for his wife and gave her a warm hug.

With the flame rekindled, John once again grew restless in eager anticipation over the prospect of working in the mission field. A response to his query finally came in early February, arriving in an envelope from Cora accompanied by a short note:

Dear Rev. Stevenson,

Enclosed herewith is a reply from the Rev. Kirkwood, a disappointment for you, I am sure. But perhaps something will work out in time.

With sincere regards,

Cora

John unfolded the letter written on official stationery and began reading—already understanding there would not be a move to Colorado.

Rev. T.C. Kirkwood, D.D.
Superintendent of Presbyterian Missions,
Synod of Colorado
Colorado Springs, Colorado
January 16, 1894
To Miss Cora M. McDonald,
Laramie, Wyoming
Dear Miss McDonald—your letter at hand. I shall be most pleased if we can arrange to avail ourselves of your brother-in-law's assistance in our Colorado field. The only drawback that I can foresee is the matter of salary. We have no vacancies that give as much as he is now receiving. If at any time in the future I find an opportunity for him, I will write him. I am glad to hear from you again and to know that you are occupying a position of such great usefulness as well as honor.

Very truly yours, T. C. Kirkwood

John refolded the note, placing it back in the envelope. He wasn't surprised. Benevolent causes never had enough money to do what they set out to do—a fact he had learned while working for the American Missionary Association in Texas. Regarding Rev. Kirkwood advising him if something came up in the future, John knew it wouldn't happen. His pastorate at Waterloo was where he and his family belonged. He had to accept that—as long as his lungs and voice held out.

Ella tried not to show her disappointment, but John knew she had hoped, even more than he, that this move would happen. They discussed it at the supper table that night with mixed feelings. Not surprisingly, Abram seemed to regret the news the most.

"I really want to live out west," he said, mounding his mashed potatoes into a peak with his spoon, then squashing it flat. "I'll do it on my own someday if it comes to that."

"Not me," piped up Irene. "I like it here with my friends."

"I wouldn't have gone anyway," Maggie said. "I'm going to finish school here." She thumped her empty milk glass on the table as though to emphasize her point.

Suddenly, above the chatter, John thought he heard knocking. "Shhhh, listen," he said, holding up a hand to quell the voices. In the hush that followed, there indeed came a knock—more like a pounding. A loud voice, muffled through the walls, called out. "Stevenson, are you there?"

John immediately stood. "I'll get it," he said. "It sounds like Leroy Cooper. Ella, keep the children here."

John strode out of the room, shutting the kitchen door behind him. His anger rose at the thought of a drunken Leroy intruding on the privacy of his home. The pounding continued, and a fist, poised to knock again, almost caught John in the face when he swung open the front door.

"Leroy, I don't want you here. If you need to see me, send a messenger, and I will come to your house."

A closer look at the man standing before him caused John to reconsider. It was Leroy, all right, clean-shaven and wearing a freshly pressed navy blue suit complete with cravat at the high collar, looking every bit as respectful as when he had been a member of the board of trustees at the Waterloo Congregational Church.

The man held his hat in his hands, turning it nervously. "Forgive me, Reverend, I wasn't thinking. But I'm sober, and I need your help. May I come in?"

John hesitated a moment, then ushered his unwelcome guest into the study. He offered Leroy a chair and sat with the desk between them. The air in the small room felt heavy and hot, though a winter chill hovered outside.

Confounded by this new image of the man, John kept a steady gaze on the contrite and sober Leroy Cooper. "What can I do for you?"

Leroy cleared his throat, swallowed a couple of times, then blurted, "It's about Beatrice and the boys."

No surprise there, but had something happened to them? John's stomach muscles tightened.

Leroy continued, "I need to find them, Reverend, and you are the only one who can help me. I think you know where they are. I'm on the wagon now. For good. You can ask McLloyd at the saloon. I haven't been in for weeks."

John shook his head. "I don't know where they are, Leroy. I don't even know the whereabouts of her sister and haven't heard anything in over a year."

Leroy shifted in the chair and ran a finger around the inside of his collar. A flush crept up his neck and onto his cheeks as he appeared to stifle an outburst of temper. "You sent her somewhere, Reverend. You know where that is. If she's not there, then those people should at least know where she went."

"Not necessarily," John tapped a pencil against the desk waiting for Leroy to start shouting. Instead, to his surprise, tears sprang to the man's eyes.

"Please, Reverend, you must believe me. I've found the Lord again and plan to start attending church. I have my job back at the bank. I've been given a second chance, because I am good with numbers and they need me. They believe in my turnaround regarding drink. Surely, you, a man of God, can do the same."

John said nothing, carefully considering the facts, uncertain how to respond.

The few seconds of silence in the room caused Leroy to fidget. As though the thought had just occurred to him, he added, "I'll be very generous when the offering plate is passed on Sunday morning."

John felt a prick of irritation. Did the man think he could be bribed? Then again, a parishioner who comes to his minister for help should trust that a plea will be met with compassion. He struggled to squelch judgment.

"Of course the church doors are always welcome to you, Leroy, whether you fill the offering plate or not. That is beside the point. Living the life Christ taught is what's important."

Leroy squirmed a little. "Yes, sir. I know that. I promise I'm back on the right track." He cleared his throat and swallowed. "Now, about my reason for coming to you."

"The issue here," John said, "and my main concern, is the safety of Beatrice and the boys."

At this, Leroy jumped up. "Reverend, you have not heard a word I've said. I am a new man! Doesn't that matter to you? What kind of minister are you? You obviously don't care about me—about us as a family." His voice rose with each word, and he glared at John.

"Please, Leroy, sit down. You know that's not true. I care very much about your family, and I haven't said I wouldn't help you. What I have said is I don't know where they are. I'm very pleased that you have turned your life around, and I'll see what I can do about finding them. However, you have to understand that if I'm successful, the final decision to return home will be up to Beatrice."

The man slumped back into the chair and sighed deeply. "I apologize for the outburst, and I will appreciate any effort you make. I miss her so much, and the boys—my boys—they were my whole life. She has no legal right..." He bit his lip, seeming to know if he pursued that angle he might lose John's support.

John stood and held out his hand. "Thanks for

coming by, Leroy. I look forward to seeing you in church on Sunday. I'll get on this as soon as I can and will keep you informed of any progress."

Leroy stood and accepted the handshake. "Thank you, Reverend. I hope to hear from you soon." He plopped his hat on his head and strode toward the outer hall and the front door, shutting it firmly as he left.

John watched through a window as the man marched up the street and rounded a corner, disappearing from sight. A light touch on his arm caused him to turn. Ella stood beside him, concern wrinkling her brow.

"Well?" she asked. "What was that all about? I heard shouting. Was he sober?"

John sighed. "Indeed, he was. In fact, he looked surprisingly respectable and says he has turned over a new leaf. However, the issue is the same. He misses Beatrice and the boys, insists I know where they are, and that therefore it's up to me to bring them back."

Ella shook her head. "What are you going to do?"

"I told him I do not know where they are but promised I would see what I could do."

"And what if you find them, then what? They'll come back, and he will beat her or run away with the boys, or both." Ella's cheeks grew crimson as she spoke.

"Now, Ella, give me a little credit. I also told him, if I am able to locate her, the decision to return is up to Beatrice."

"You know what will happen. He'll have you followed," Johnny said. He stood in the doorway, obviously having overheard most of the conversation.

The boy had a point, but John had made a promise and planned to follow up not only with action but a lot of prayer. "Let's not upset our evening any further. Mother, how about some music?"

Ella nodded and headed for the piano, always a balm for stressful moments.

John spent most of that evening in his study as he often did. A half-written sermon lay on the desk, but he was not making much progress. Leroy's request continually interrupted any creative thought. Where to begin looking for the missing woman? She had returned once, so, contrary to her husband's comment, the boarding house where John had first sent her would not be the logical place to begin. Or would it? Johnny's remark that Leroy would have him followed was also worrisome.

The dilemma wouldn't leave him as he lay in bed that night, unable to sleep. A bright moon shone through the branches of a tree outside the window casting shadows of imaginary figures on the wall and ceiling. One looked like a small boy. Timmy Cooper? John sighed at the tricks of his mind. Timmy wouldn't even be that little anymore. He closed his eyes. Ella, who he had assumed was asleep, turned toward him, laying her arm on his chest.

"If you are intent on finding Beatrice, I may be able to help," she said.

John's eyes popped open. "How?"

"Not too long ago, Caroline Murphy said something that makes me think she is in touch with Beatrice's sister. She'll be at the Ladies' Missionary Society meeting here on Monday. I'll see what I can find out."

John had an idea of his own, too. But the next day being Sunday, with all the obligations for a pastor and his family, the search for Beatrice would have to wait for at least another twenty-four hours.

The following morning, while the organist played a hymn announcing the beginning of the service, John scanned the congregation from the pulpit. Loyal members filled the pews, from the youngest who squirmed and swung legs that didn't quite reach the floor, to the elderly who needed assistance down the aisle. John returned smiles and nods, watching as gentlemen removed their hats and ladies whispered to neighbors. His gaze continued to the end of the back row and stopped. There sat Leroy, all spit and polish, looking like Waterloo's most respectable citizen. John's pulse quickened. He desperately wanted this transformation to be real, yet found himself wondering if, in fact, it truly was.

Before the morning was over, one more questionable incident occurred. Violet Cunningham approached John in the receiving line with sugar and honey in her smile and voice. "Interesting sermon once again, Reverend." She handed him a small envelope. He pocketed it to read later, perplexed as to what its contents might hold and not certain he wanted to know.

Chapter Nineteen

SHEPHERDING HIS FLOCK

The entire family was invited to the Alans' for dinner. Once grace had been offered at their hosts' large table and the food passed, they began conversation.

"I was very pleased and surprised to see Leroy Cooper there today," Mrs. Alan said. "And he looked so …"

"Sober," her husband said.

Mrs. Alan ignored his comment and added, "so dapper, just like before. I wonder if it means Beatrice and the boys are coming home."

"Maybe he has a lady friend," Mr. Alan said, handing a basket of bread to John.

"Clyde, please," his wife cast him a warning look. "There are young ears here."

John glanced at his children. All except Irene looked intently at their plates. Was his youngest about to say something? He wasn't sure if she really understood Leroy's situation, but not much escaped her inquisitive mind, and it was difficult to have information others wanted and not say it. He noticed Ella give the girl a subtle shake of the head, and the moment passed.

Mrs. Alan, clearly having similar issues with her

husband, changed the subject. She nodded at her oldest son. "Please pass the preserves, Jacob."

Talk for the remainder of the meal concentrated on the weather, the approaching farming season, and other safe topics. It was pleasant enough, though a long afternoon.

John had coaxed the family to walk to church that morning and on to the Alans' instead of bundling up in the buggy, in spite of a winter bite in the air. Heading for home after hours of confinement, the children ran ahead. Mounds of sparkling snow lay about from the storm a few days past. Johnny scooped some up in his gloved hands, molded it into a ball, and threw it at Abram, who quickly returned the attack with a bigger, more compact weapon of the same. Maggie picked up a handful of loose snow, grabbed Abram by the collar, and pushed the icy crystals down the back of his coat. Irene followed with her own mischief, their shouts and laughter enlivening the hike toward home.

John chuckled. "Sometimes I wonder if growing up is a good thing," he said, squeezing his wife's hand. He and Ella strolled several yards behind the rambunctious children, ducking an occasional snowball tossed in their direction.

Ella smiled at his remark, but obviously had more adult things on her mind. "That was an interesting morning at church, to say nothing of the tensions at the Alans' dinner table," she remarked. "I must admit I was as surprised as they were to see Leroy during the service. I really didn't expect him to show up, regardless of what he promised you."

John was mulling over how to respond when Ella added, "And what a surprise for Violet to be so gracious to you after the service."

"Agreed," John said. He patted the pocket holding the as-yet-unread note from the lady he privately referred to as the "anti-woman."

"We may be in for more surprises. She handed me an envelope, the contents of which I plan to read the moment we get home."

Ella raised her eyebrows. "Really? You don't suppose she has changed her mind about woman suffrage. It would be so good to have her on our side."

"No. As much as I would like to think that's the case, I don't suppose it is."

Once in the house, wet over-clothes removed and hung to dry, the family gathered in the parlor to study church lessons and read the Bible as was their Sunday afternoon custom. John, however, slipped into his study to read the note that had weighed down his pocket with curiosity since morning. Breaking the seal stamped with a VC, he pulled out a folded paper—a small purple violet appropriately printed on the front. The lacy penmanship read:

Dear Reverend Stevenson,

I received a note from your daughter apologizing for her behavior toward me. She is a lovely young woman, and it is admirable that she defends her father regardless of the subject of his sermons; however, it would be a shame to destroy her femininity and God's true intent for women by pushing her into the world of politics intended for men. If you love your daughter, as I'm sure you do, I hope you will give this some serious thought.

Sincerely, Violet Cunningham.

John took a deep breath and resisted the urge to crumple the note and toss it in the waste basket. *Where in God's holy name does the Bible say a woman should not have a say in her own future?*

"Mrs. Cunningham," he said aloud, "it is because I love my daughter I preach about the things I do. And I am not pushing her; she is moving forward based on her own intelligence." Before joining the family in the other room, he closed his eyes and prayed, as he had done so many times, that all the antisuffragists would soon see the light.

He fell asleep that night with two parishioners on his mind: Violet Cunningham and Leroy Cooper. He had learned over the years that shepherding a church meant involving himself in the lives of his congregants — caring about them as Christ had taught — no matter who they were or what their circumstances. These two were no exception, but right now one required more attention than the other.

The following day, when John kissed Ella on his way out the door, he reminded her she had agreed to check with Mrs. Murphy as to the whereabouts of Belva Parker.

"I won't forget," Ella said. "And I will be discreet in my inquiry. The Missionary Society meets here at ten. I should have an answer when you come home for your midday meal."

All morning while attending to church business, John's agreement with Leroy interrupted his thoughts. At a quarter to one, he locked his study door and stepped outside. A blustery winter wind whipped at his coattails, and a promise of more snow chilled the air—a sudden change from the cool but pleasant walk earlier in the day. Not many folks were out, and he hoped the missionary ladies were able to convene at the parsonage in spite of the weather.

Movement to his far left caught his eye, and when he turned, he noticed a man wrapped in a heavy coat, scurrying up the walk on the opposite side of the street. The gait seemed familiar. Leroy? Probably not, or he would have acknowledged John—surely whoever it was had seen him leave the church. Johnny's remark of a few days previous rang in his thoughts. "He'll have you followed." Maybe it *was* Leroy, keeping a close eye on him, hoping to be led to Beatrice. John shook his head at his own paranoia and hurried on through the bitter gale for home.

In the warmth of the kitchen, John sipped a welcome bowl of steaming soup while Ella talked. "Caroline was at the meeting, and I was able to ask about Belva. I don't think she suspected why I was inquiring."

"And…?"

"She's living in Cedar Falls, teaching school there. Caroline said she had afternoon tea with her recently."

"I don't suppose she said anything about Beatrice and the boys."

"No, and I didn't ask. So, are you going to go visit

her? I didn't get an address, but I do have the name of the school where she teaches."

John swallowed a last spoonful of soup, wiped his mouth, and pushed back his chair. His thoughts focused on the man he had seen on the walkway opposite the church. Would he be followed if he drove to Cedar Falls? He would hate to be responsible for leading Leroy directly to his wife and sons.

"Well?" Ella sat across from him, elbows on the table, her gaze steady on his face. Patience was not one of her virtues.

John had been working on a plan. "What if I head out one afternoon as a decoy—say to visit a shut-in across town—perhaps old Mrs. Jenkins. Johnny could take Blaze to school that day, then afterward leave for Cedar Falls with a note to Belva Parker requesting the whereabouts of Beatrice."

Ella frowned. "It might work. Would you walk to Mrs. Jenkins' house? That is quite a way in this kind of weather. And what about Johnny's paper route? And what if Belva is gone from the school by the time Johnny gets there?"

"That's a chance we'll have to take, and the walk would do me good. It's not that far. Abram could deliver the papers. He has gone with his brother often enough that it wouldn't be a problem. All of this, of course, assumes Leroy is actually trying to follow me." He told her about the man he saw outside the church. "There's more to figure out, like how Beatrice or Belva will get a message back to me."

He gazed out the kitchen window. A few soft flakes

of snow drifted down from the gathering dark clouds. "I think I won't return to church this afternoon. I'll work from home." He turned to Ella. "Thanks for the meal, good as always."

She began collecting their dishes. "Oh, I almost forgot to mention, a package came for you. I put it on your desk."

In his study, John picked up the parcel wrapped in brown paper and tied with string.

Ella followed close behind, obviously curious about the delivery. "What is it?"

He ripped off the paper. "It's the book I sent for." He held up a copy of *Woman, Church and State* by Matilda Joslyn Gage. "It's rather controversial among my colleagues, and my curiosity got the better of me."

"May I take a look?" Ella reached for it and flipped through some pages.

"Certainly. I won't get around to it for a few days, especially with this Leroy Cooper situation on my mind."

Ella carried the book from the room and marched upstairs where John figured she would place it on the little table beside the bed. She read each evening before retiring. Once she started reading Mrs. Gage's book, John was sure he'd get an earful.

But his wife had other things on her mind, and the new book remained closed. When John crawled into bed that night, she started in.

"How about Wednesday?" she asked.

"Wednesday?"

"To send Johnny to Cedar Falls. By then the snow

from this little storm will have melted. And I've figured out how to get a response. It's simple. Just include a blank piece of paper in a self-addressed stamped envelope. You'll write two notes, one to Belva asking her to pass the other one and the stamped envelope on to her sister. The note you write to Beatrice can explain all about Leroy's turn-around and his request, but also that the decision is still up to her. She can return her answer in the envelope you provide."

John made a little involuntary harumph. Sometimes Ella's thinking didn't allow for him to have any brains himself. "The letters are written, my dear, and ready to go. Thursday works the best with my schedule and Johnny's." At that, he turned over and closed his eyes.

~ ~ ~

THE PLAN CAME OFF AS HOPED. BY THURSDAY THE SNOW had become only wet puddles, and the chill wind had abated. The boys were energized at the thought of being part of the conspiracy, and John prayed during his entire trek to Mrs. Jenkins' that all would go well. The frail woman was delighted with John's visit. As usual, she rambled on while he listened. It seemed fitting that he call on this particular parishioner while they plotted to get a letter to Belva Parker. Here was another example of a wife once abused by an alcoholic husband. Though this all occurred before John's tenure in Waterloo, according to whispers, the now-deceased Mr. Jenkins had not spared his wrath on his wife. "After one beating she didn't come to church for weeks due to a broken nose," Mrs. Alan had told John in confidence. "And she just took it like a good wife."

On his way to see Mrs. Jenkins and on his return, he frequently looked behind to see if he was being followed. Once he glimpsed a shadow behind a tree, and his heartbeat quickened; however, at second glance, nothing moved—some stationary object, a slender bush perhaps, stirred by the wind—definitely not Leroy Cooper.

John returned first. An hour later Abram burst through the front door shouting, "Is Papa home yet?"

"In here, Abram," John called from his study.

The boy's face glowed, and not just from the winter weather. "Well, I know for certain that Mr. Cooper did not follow you or Johnny," he said, hardly stopping to catch his breath. "He was home when I tossed the paper on his porch. I saw him. He came out and picked it up—was in his shirtsleeves and slippers, so couldn't even have been out in the cold before I came. I think we did it!"

John chuckled at the boy's enthusiasm for the ploy. "Thanks for helping, lad. I hope your brother's part in all this was equally successful."

The wait for John Jr. to return dragged on. The dark of the night was full upon them, and still he had not arrived. Ella frequently checked the front window, pulling back the curtains and peering out. "He should be here by now," she kept saying.

"Now, Mother. It takes a while to get from Cedar Falls to Waterloo, even on horseback. He's a grown boy and will be fine," John reassured her. Yet, he felt a surge of relief himself when he heard Blaze's whinny and the clop-clop of hooves as Johnny led the horse around back to the barn.

Abram pounced on his brother the minute he entered the house. "Well, was she there? Did you get the note delivered? I know you weren't followed." He repeated how he had seen Leroy Cooper at his house.

"Yes, all accomplished as planned. Now, is supper ready? I'm starved."

With the initial stage of their plot over and done, there was nothing to do but wait for a response—one that might not ever come. John knew this, but he would give it time, then let Leroy know that he had made his best effort.

At bedtime, John found Ella reading the book, *Woman, Church and State*. When he entered the room, she looked up at him, her eyes round with a look of shock. "Have you read any of this? Who is this woman, anyway!"

Chapter Twenty

THE RIGHT SPIRIT

John sat on the bed beside her. "Matilda Joslyn Gage? She's a strong advocate for woman's rights who has worked with Susan B. Anthony and Elizabeth Cady Stanton for a long time. The three of them wrote and published *The History of Woman Suffrage* a number of years ago. However, the book you hold in your hand she researched and wrote on her own. It's quite an accomplishment."

"But have you read any of it? The woman is criticizing your profession." Ella paused a second as though waiting for his response, then before he could take a breath, continued. "Actually, maybe you shouldn't read it. I wouldn't want it to change your mind about supporting a woman's right to vote."

John raised his eyebrows, surprised that Ella would think someone else's opinion could influence his thoughts so strongly.

"John, she is blaming the Bible for the reason women are considered inferior to men, and therefore why so many folks believe we should never have the right to vote. Here, read this." She thrust out the opened book, pointing her finger to a paragraph.

He held up his hands. "I won't read it out of context,

and you and I both know that every passage in the Bible has many interpretations. I am well aware there are those who quote liberally from the book of Genesis to the Epistles of Paul in an effort to convince themselves, and others, that women are inferior to men. It's what they want to believe, but it does not make it so."

"Well, according to Mrs. Gage, most people don't see it that way. Her book is almost irreverent, almost, almost..." She seemed to grope for a word. "Anti-Christian." Ella blushed, as though saying it aloud soiled her own thoughts.

"Unfortunately, she is right, Ella. Many folks do use the Bible as a tool to keep women from advancing in society. Remember Susan B. Anthony's remarks on the same subject during her talk at the World's Fair? I haven't read Mrs. Gage's book, but I intend to do so, and my understanding is she is trying to prove the antisuffragists wrong, not degrade the Almighty."

He reached for the book. "If it's upsetting you, perhaps you shouldn't continue reading it."

She pulled back, clasping the book to her bosom. "No, I'll finish it. And to tell you the truth, I can see her point. I was upset because I was afraid it would distress you."

John smiled and shook his head. Even after five years of marriage, they often did not understand each other. Perhaps that would always be the case. He doubted anything Matilda Joslyn Gage wrote in her book could shock him. He might disagree with some ideas, but he had heard all the arguments before. John often countered with his favorite Biblical passage, Galatians 3:28: *There is neither Jew nor Greek, there is neither bond nor free, there is neither male nor female: for ye are all one in Christ Jesus.*

Before even reading *Woman, Church and State*, John admired Mrs. Gage's tenacity for writing such a volume and the courage it took to speak her mind when so many people quoted the Bible as a means to suppress equal rights for half of the population.

John had strong views of his own he was not afraid to voice as a speaker and a writer. A letter he had submitted to a church publication earlier in the year regarding equality for former slaves, again using the quote from Galatians, provoked a number of responses—negative and positive. Publishing his thoughts provided an outlet that did not irritate his throat, nor was it difficult to sit quietly at his desk and write when the hay fever hit. He found this method to his liking and vowed to write more and speak less—at least beyond the pulpit.

The Scotch Irish Society of America in particular solicited papers from him on everything from poetry to politics. These, of course, were not necessarily controversial. In fact, they were most enjoyable to write, and the responses plus an invitation to speak about the poetry of Robert Burns spurred him on.

"You don't have to accept, you know," Ella said, when he read the invitation to her.

She had come into his study to inquire when he might be coming to bed. He motioned for her to sit, the flame in the lamp on his desk casting flickering shadows on her face. He still felt a little thrill when she came to him like this in the evening after the children were in bed—just the two of them. He knew her comment was suggested with his best interest in mind, but talking about the old country and his favorite poet—well, the temptation was too great. "An extra speech now and then won't hurt."

Each time he agreed to a talk outside of the church, in addition to his weekly sermon, Ella shook her head. "You must have been a difficult boy to raise—being blind to the wisest choices. I can just see your parents wringing their hands."

And so the weeks swept by with John writing commentaries, and gradually, once again, accepting speaking engagements. At the height of the pollen season, he often stopped mid-talk to catch his breath, sip some water and carry on. One Sunday, a coughing fit caused him to cut his sermon short. He apologized and sat down, his chest heaving, eyes watering, nose running.

The choir director immediately stood and directed the congregation in a number of popular hymns. Members responded with loud vigor, as though the clamor would help the problem go away.

Later, when he greeted the last parishioner following the service, John turned to Ella and remarked, "I think I got my point across before having to stop."

She shook her head and put her arm through his. "The point you got across, Reverend Husband, is you should not be giving sermons during this time of year."

Yet he continued preaching. This was his calling, after all, and his obligation. Though, as always, pastoring a church brought with it multiple challenges beyond that of spell-binding sermons—that of his flock and its many personal issues.

One sweltering Monday afternoon in July, John sat in his church office, his coat tossed aside, his shirtsleeves rolled up, and a soggy cloth nearby to wipe beads of perspiration from his forehead. Today his breathing came easily enough, but his other nemesis, the tight, painful throat, still throbbed from a particularly long sermon he gave the day before. He sipped frequently from a cool glass of water laced with a drop of iodine—one of Ella's medicinal concoctions. He wasn't sure it helped, but he was willing to try most anything. He was about to close up shop and head home for a nap when the outer door swung open with a resounding bang. In staggered a red-eyed Leroy Cooper. John immediately stood and rushed to grab the man, afraid he was about to fall.

Leroy jerked his arm loose and plopped onto a chair. "Don't be solishatatious to me," he slurred. "You're not my friend. In fact, you are a goddamned liar!"

John winced. "Now, now, Leroy."

"Now, now, Leroy," the man mimicked in a high whiny voice, the stench of whisky wafting into the air with each word. He leaned forward and pointed a wavering finger at John. "Where are my wife and boys? You promised me my wife and boys."

John lowered himself onto an adjoining chair and sighed. "I've told you, Leroy."

"You've told me what? Every time I talk to you about this you say you are working on it. It's been weeks, Reverend. Weeks! Where is she?" He attempted to stand but couldn't quite get out of the chair.

"I've done what I can, Leroy. Apparently, she doesn't want to be found. And look at you. Can you blame her?"

Leroy's ruddy face went from pink to red. "Judge ye not, Reverend! Don't you read that book you preach from?" He snorted. "Why, I bet you sneak a nip here and there yourself. That stuff you're drinking right now don't look like water to me." He reached for the glass sitting on the desk, missed, and knocked it to the floor, spilling its contents onto their shoes.

John watched the puddle spread, saying nothing as he groped for the proper words.

"Papa?" Johnny suddenly appeared in the doorway, his gaze darting from the drunken visitor to John and back. "Papa?"

John stood. "I was about to leave, son. Could you help me take Mr. Cooper home? He's not feeling well."

Leroy struggled to his feet. "That won't be neshesshary. I can get there myself." He staggered toward the door, shoving the boy aside on his way, then turned. "You know when she is found, and she will be, she'll go to jail for stealing those boys. You know that." He glared at John for another couple of seconds before swaying down the steps and onto the walkway.

"Well, lad," John said, once the man was gone. "You've seen a little bit of the coarser side of life."

Johnny shrugged. "I've seen it before, Papa."

John put his arm around his son and locked the door behind them. They walked silently home together, a sermon developing in John's mind with each step. Time for more words on temperance and the rights of women.

~ ~ ~

JOHN CROAKED HIS WAY THROUGH THE REMAINING summer from the pulpit, ignoring Ella's demands that he take a break from speaking engagements and Sunday sermons.

"I still have so much to say," he told her in frustration.

"Give the throat a rest," she said, "or you won't be saying a word of it ever again."

After a Sunday late in August when once again his voice gave out, he finally agreed. He made arrangements for guest speakers and prepared to escape to the lakeside retreat in Wisconsin. As he readied to go, his eldest son filled a satchel with his own belongings. School would soon start, and John Jr. was on his way to Tabor College.

"Eventually to study law," he told anyone who would listen—excitement ringing in his voice. Like so many young people, he was off to make the world a better place.

John thought about his own youth—sailing to America for an education—and a six-year interruption to teach the freed slaves. He believed he *had* made a difference. He understood Johnny's eagerness and, in a way, envied him the challenges of the unknown future he was about to explore.

The entire family took the young man to the station

to see him off, then they waved and waved until the train was nothing more than a speck on the horizon. John's mind wandered back to the chubby baby he had played with eighteen years before. He and Anna had been so proud, marveling at the miracle of creation produced by their love for each other. She was then a robust, happy mother recovering quickly from the birth of their firstborn. So many babies had been born since then, the birth of each one silently stealing a bit of Anna's health, until she had no strength left to care for those living. He choked back tears as he boarded the buggy for home with Ella and the other three children.

Ella squeezed his hand. "It's hard, isn't it?"

He sensed she knew his thoughts were on Anna. He was aware with his own strength ebbing low that this parting was harder on him than it might have been. He also felt his congregation was growing weary of a preacher who couldn't talk and would welcome a change—a younger man without health issues. Johnny had departed in eager anticipation. John verged on despondency.

"I'll write some letters while in Wisconsin, seeking a pastorate elsewhere," he told Ella.

Her eyes brightened. "There is still Colorado," she said. "Your work doesn't have to be in the mission field. Surely Congregational Churches throughout the state would welcome your fresh sermons—though there is the issue of your throat."

He promised he would look into Colorado churches, but he also planned to write to those not so far afield where his reputation as a forward-thinking preacher who gave thought-provoking sermons was well known; someplace away from whatever irritated his lungs. A fresh start would be good, and surely after a respite his voice would regain its strength.

He left for his retreat with new hope. He would write sermons and articles, armed with reading material, including Mrs. Gage's history of woman's oppression. He still had much more to say and was inspired by *Woman, Church and State*.

And the time was right. Things were looking up for women in Iowa. Recently the state legislature had granted women the right to vote on bond issues. They still couldn't vote for candidates running for public office, but having a voice on money to build schools or libraries was a step in the right direction. This milestone, though small, gave John a new surge of determination. He would join hands with Matilda Joslyn Gage and others to show the public what the Bible did say about women. A sermon on the account of Adam and Eve would be timely. He would branch out and find new venues for his message—whether in Waterloo or elsewhere—as soon as his throat and hay fever got better.

Chapter Twenty-One

SLOW AND STEADY

1895

His lungs clear, John returned from his respite full of enthusiasm and eager to share his ideas. He had written copious notes, essays, and full sermons, and immediately embarked on a series of winter lectures for Sunday evenings. Whenever Maggie or Abram were available to stay with Irene, Ella attended the sessions, too.

"There is always such a good crowd. You obviously have something to say that people want to hear," she said one evening as she bundled up to walk to the church with him.

It delighted John when his wife seemed proud of his work. Since his return from Wisconsin, they had spoken little about his hunt for a new church. He had written letters, as promised, and though responses acknowledged his reputation as an exemplary speaker, there were either no vacancies or the churches he approached could not afford his salary request. Besides, the Waterloo congregation seemed genuinely pleased he had returned, fully rested and ready to pick up where he had left off. Attendance both at the morning and evening services on Sunday attested to that.

True to his promise to himself, he focused more and

more on the rights of women, both in articles wherever they could be published and in sermons and speeches. And, the Lord be praised, the flowering springtime brought less hay fever this year. Unfortunately, he couldn't say the same about his throat, but Ella's tonics helped a little. Occasionally, when she left the room, John pulled open a desk drawer and took out a small packet of cocaine—a remedy prescribed by a doctor several years before. Pinching a bit between his fingers he held it up to his nose and inhaled. The drug came with a warning to use it sparingly as it could become addictive. This concerned John, yet the powder was the one thing that seemed to ease the pain and open his throat. It provided the added bonus of making him feel increasingly alert for a while. But later, it had the opposite effect, fogging his mind when he tried to write.

When he confessed this to Ella, she responded in horror. "Then for heaven's sake, quit taking it. You have enough trouble with your lungs and your throat without muddling up your head, too."

He agreed she was right, and he eased up on it, but sometimes relief from the pain and the inability to speak was worth a few highs, lows, and a little confusion. He never took the drug before church, and when he resorted to using it at home, he usually napped once the good effects began to wear off and was able to carry on afterwards.

~ ~ ~

THE CAMPAIGN TO WIN WOMEN THE VOTE CONTINUED TO be a steep uphill battle. Even after years of determination from those dedicated to the cause, the antisuffragists seemed stronger than ever and more organized. Many came from influential families—old money, well-educated leaders of the community. Though many women were the leaders against enfranchisement, their husbands often held positions of influence: journalists, lawyers, and politicians.

"It's like swimming against a strong tide," Ella remarked after reading an anti-suffragist piece in the paper. "Those ladies live very comfortable lives and don't feel the need to have a say in government—not like the women employed in the factories springing up in Waterloo, or those who have abusive husbands who take away what is rightfully theirs. You would think the anti's would at least want a say in their own property rights."

She set her lips in a firm line in apparent disbelief at the thought. Bustling about the kitchen preparing a meal, her anger against those who opposed the suffrage movement became evident as she slammed a cupboard door and banged a pan on the stovetop.

One evening, as John half dozed in the big armchair in the parlor, his shoeless feet propped on the tea table, Ella stormed into the room and thrust a copy of *The Ladies Home Journal* at him. "Here, read this by the Reverend Charles Parkhurst. He's been doing a series of columns endorsing antisuffrage sentiment." She plopped onto the piano bench, crossed her arms, and tapped her toe against the floor, obviously waiting for a response.

As John perused the article, the cobwebs of sleep in

his brain spun away. Here was a devout Christian man who, as president of the Society for Prevention of Crime, had recently cleaned up urban corruption in New York. Powerful men like this who worked against giving women the vote only made the drive more difficult. John laid the magazine aside and shook his head. "We'll still do it, Ella. Misguided folks like Parkhurst will eventually see the light. As Aesop demonstrated in the story of the tortoise and the hare, slow and steady wins the race."

Ella smiled, reached over and squeezed his hand. "Dear Dr. Stevenson, as I have said before, you are a man among men. You are right. We'll beat folks like the Reverend Parkhurst yet."

John pulled her onto his lap. "It's not a matter of beating them, Ella. It's a matter of changing their minds. That means our argument needs to be better, more thoughtful, and convincing. I'm working on it."

She put an arm about his neck and kissed him gently on the forehead. "Of that, I am certain."

Her pride in his work spurred John on, though even then there were limits to her patience. Later that same evening, while deep in thought, a light rap on his study door caused him to look up. There stood Ella in her nightclothes, sleepy-eyed. "Do you realize it's almost one o'clock in the morning?" she said, a hint of irritation in her voice.

John glanced at the clock ticking away on the bookcase. He had not even heard it chime twelve. "No, I guess I wasn't aware of the time," he said, leaning back in his chair, stretching to relieve a kink in his back.

"I'm working on a sermon to clarify the biblical meaning of the creation of man, woman, and their equality. That should please you."

"It does, John, but this is Thursday. You have two more days and evenings to work on it."

"I'm inspired now, Ella, and I want it right. Sit down. I will read parts to you and see what you think."

He ignored her sigh as she sat wearily in a chair.

John cleared his throat and picked up the papers before him.

"Let me give you the gist of it." John paused and made a note to himself on the paper, then continued. "Our concern is with the physical creation. This is treated in Chapter One, Verses 26 to 3, and Chapter Five, Verses 1 to 2. *God created man in his own image.* The word *man* means humanity in this connection. *God created humanity in his own image, male and female created he them.* This means that humanity was created in the image of God, the woman as well as the man. *He called their name Adam.* The man's name was Adam; the woman also was named Adam, thus they were equal in faculties, capacities and qualities. Again, the Bible's account of physical creation gives us a doctrine of quality between the sexes.

"*God blessed them.* He did not bless the man and curse the woman; he blessed *them both. God bestowed upon both an equal dowry.* He gave them the earth and its fruits. These gifts were not to the man apart from the woman, and to the woman through the man; they were equally given to both. *God bestowed upon both an equal mission.* Both were commissioned to be fruitful, and multiply, and replenish and subdue the earth. *God endowed both with equal powers*. He gave them dominion. He did not give dominion to him and subjection to her, but dominion to *them*. In our physical creation, as revealed in the Bible, men and women received the same image, name, blessing, dowry, mission and powers. No description of equality between man and woman could be made stronger than this."

When John finished reading, he looked up from his written work. "There's more, of course, but this is the point of the subject. There it is in everyone's Bible in black and white. Man and woman were created equal."

A smile brightened Ella's face that only moments ago had been clouded with sleep. "I can hardly wait for Sunday," she said. "How can anyone argue with that?"

After the service, John could tell who did and did not agree with his remarks. Mr. and Mrs. Alan, always on his side, both shook his hand heartily. "You tell them, Reverend. We can still be good Christians and believe in a woman's rights."

Those members who approached him were most often in accordance with his thoughts. A few avoided him. He looked about for Violet Cunningham, eager to engage her in a discussion; however, she apparently had skipped church that morning. A shame, he thought, though none of his sermons on the subject seemed to have swayed her yet.

Others had been convinced all along, and several women in the congregation were active in the Iowa Woman Suffrage Association. Sarah Ware Whitney in particular had become a close friend. She held out her hand on her way out of the church that morning and smiled. "You should write for *The Woman's Standard* after that well-worded sermon," she said. "You need to meet Mary Jane Coggeshall. I'm sure you know of her. She is a pioneer for woman's suffrage in Iowa. Are you planning on attending the annual conference in Des Moines this September? She'll be there."

The idea appealed to John. The event was still a couple of months away, but he tucked the thought in the back of his mind.

The humid days of summer crawled by, and the atmosphere at home felt different. Both boys were gone. Johnny stayed on in Tabor working and taking classes. Abram found a job in the country for which he was paid fifteen dollars a month, plus room and board.

"I'll be rich!" he had exclaimed. He talked of nothing else since receiving the job offer, his enthusiasm evident as he dashed about the house deciding what to take with him, whistling happy tunes as he tossed things into a valise.

The evening after they saw him off, a melancholy took hold of John. He sat in his sweltering study attempting to work, his collar open and sleeves rolled up, occasionally fanning himself with the blank paper on which he could not put words. Finally, he gave up, tidied his desk, and headed upstairs to join Ella. In their room she had opened all the windows. A slight breeze fluttered the curtains, pushing out a little of the day's heat. Once in his night clothes, John settled next to his wife who lay on top of the coverlet.

"You've come up early," she said, eyes closed,

though very much awake. "The sermon finished already?"

"No. Too hot, and too much else going on in my mind."

"Abram?"

He didn't answer, but she knew him well, and obviously her thoughts were centered there, too.

"He'll find farming to be hard work, but good for him," she said.

"It will toughen him up," John agreed. He thought back to his days in Minnesota, pitching hay on the Cranston farm when he first arrived in America. "He'll return tan, muscular, and more of a man."

~ ~ ~

"I THINK I'LL GO TO DES MOINES FOR THE IOWA WOMAN Suffrage Association meeting," he announced one September evening, "and on the way I'll attend the Woman's Christian Temperance Union convention in Boone."

Ella kept on knitting, and he wondered if she had heard his comment. But of course she had. She never missed a thing. "That's a rather roundabout way to get to Des Moines, if you ask me." Then she sighed and for a moment her needles stopped clicking. "I suppose, considering your stand on temperance, it's not a bad idea."

"It means I'll be gone longer, but I feel it's important." Men like Leroy Cooper weighed heavily on his mind, plus he knew WCTU members were pro-suffrage, which could be part of their platform worth hearing.

The morning of his travels, Ella helped him pack, rushing around like the mother hen she had become, suggesting things to include in his satchel, surprising him with new collars for his good shirts. "The others are getting a little frayed," she said. "You need better ones, for Sunday, too."

He pulled her close and kissed her. Though she hadn't said so, he suspected she would have liked to come. With Ella's piano lessons, they could probably have managed it financially. Yet this would be too many nights gone from Irene. Though ten years old and more responsible, she was still not ready to be on her own, and John and Ella could no longer rely on the older children to be home with her. Abram, back from his summer job, delivered papers after school. Maggie often watched young children for pay or did housecleaning in the afternoon and on weekends.

Early on September 9th, John boarded a train for points north, leaving Ella behind at home. The next day, he strolled the streets of Boone, a bustling coal mining town. At the church where the meeting was to take place, members of the convention crowded through the door with chattering enthusiasm. Once seated, John noted the large audience was comprised mainly of women, as were the participants listed in the program. This should not have surprised him. After all, it was the Woman's Christian Temperance Union—and he applauded them for their leadership—but somehow he had expected more men.

The first day's agenda took care of organizational

business—minutes from former meetings, a treasurer's report of the purpose of the WCTU. John felt a lot of it redundant but necessary. The second day he found more beneficial, especially a talk on the organization's stand on woman suffrage and committee reports on a temperance hospital and mercy missions they supported. One woman spoke at length about the Benedict Home in Des Moines, a reformatory for "fallen" women. Inmates were pregnant women, many of them former prostitutes. They had to be free of venereal disease and promise to receive Christian training while residing there, and of course, give up their babies for adoption. WCTU chapters funded the home and the State of Iowa also provided some money.

At the conclusion, John was glad he had attended, though tired of sitting. After the convention adjourned, he stood, stretched, and began to file out of the hall with the other attendees. As he stepped into the aisle, he bumped elbows with a lady who seemed intent on getting ahead of the crowd. "Pardon me, ma'am," he said.

She turned and stared a moment before each was struck with recognition. "Why, Reverend Stevenson," Violet Cunningham stammered. "I had no idea you were here."

"Nor I, you," John said, hardly believing he had not observed her for an entire two days. It was then he saw her plumed hat had been replaced by a smaller and more sedate style—a lighter shade of lavender sporting a bow instead of a feather. He might have noticed her had she been wearing her signature chapeau.

She seemed at a loss for words and hurried on her

way, pushed forward by a crowd eager to depart. Later, as John mulled over the surprise encounter, he wondered about her reaction to the strong stand the speaker had taken on woman suffrage. Violet's presence seemed a contradiction to all he knew about her, especially with her husband's involvement in the liquor industry. Perhaps he was an abusive drunk like Leroy. John had never met the man. Like so many of his parishioners, the wife attended church, not the husband. Yet, Violet's cream-like complexion was never marred with bruises.

With other thoughts roiling through his mind, he didn't dwell on the Cunninghams for long. His next destination, the Iowa Woman Suffrage Association convention, lit a fire in him. The city itself generated excitement. With a population of over twenty-five thousand, the streets bustled with horses and carriages of every size and make. In addition to the clamor, the aroma of restaurant foods, horse excrement, and an assortment of other odors John could not identify filled the air. Modern structures several stories high lined the streets, and along Grand Avenue stood the State Capitol building, its gold dome glistening in the sunlight. Built on a hill, John likened it to a queen overlooking her subjects.

Inside the hotel where the IWSA convened, John felt invigorated to be surrounded by people so intent on forging ahead for the rights of women. He scanned the noisy foyer for familiar faces. Violet Cunningham would definitely not be here, that he knew, but there were others.

A hand waved and beckoned above the crowd. "Reverend Stevenson, over here," a voice called.

John recognized Sarah Ware Whitney and pushed his way through the throng to greet her. "Hello, Mrs. Whitney. I had hoped to find you. This is quite amazing and encouraging, isn't it?" He gestured toward the men and women flowing into the building.

"Oh, yes, and I am so glad you could come. There is someone I want you to meet." She turned to a woman standing quietly beside her. Slender and dressed modestly in beige, the plain blouse adorned only with a small brooch at the neckline, she appeared to be about John's age, perhaps in her mid-fifties. Her graying hair, slightly fluffed over her ears, was pulled back in a bun. Wire-framed spectacles perched on her nose. John thought her rather severe looking until her smile sparked an immediate change.

"This is Mrs. Coggeshall of whom I have spoken so highly," Sarah said. "She was the first editor of *The Woman's Standard,* former president of Iowa Woman Suffrage Association, and just recently elected to the board of the National American Woman Suffrage Association." Sarah's face glowed with pride as she introduced her companion.

John held out his hand in greeting, awed and humbled in the presence of this diminutive, but obviously powerful woman. "I am deeply honored and have looked forward to meeting you."

Mrs. Coggeshall took his hand in hers. "And I you. Sarah has told me how strongly and eloquently you promote women's rights from the pulpit and in your writings. We need more men like you, especially in the clergy."

The three of them sat together throughout the convention, and at the conclusion, John agreed to write occasionally for *The Woman's Standard*.

As they left the hall that evening, a group of banner-carrying antisuffragists attempted to block their way. John searched for the familiar face of Violet Cunningham. If she had traveled all the way to Boone, might she not have come here also? But she was not to be found.

Chapter Twenty-Two

THE VISITOR

Highlights of the two conventions John attended stayed with him. Since meeting with Sarah Whitney and Mary Jane Coggeshall in Des Moines, he had already sent an article for *The Woman's Standard*, as promised. As for the WCTU event, he couldn't forget his chance encounter with Violet Cunningham. He often found himself thinking about her. She had not been to church since then, and a myriad of questions racked his mind.

The answers came one day in late October when he returned home from an afternoon making the rounds of shut-ins. As he opened the door to the parsonage, his senses were assailed by the scent of expensive perfume. Ella greeted him in the entry hall with a kiss on the cheek. He sniffed the air. "You've had a visitor?"

She put a finger to her lips and whispered. "She's still here, arrived a few minutes ago. It's Violet Cunningham."

"Well, this is a surprise," John said, his own voice low. "Is she upset?"

"No. A bit nervous, perhaps, but I wouldn't say upset. She's here to see you."

"Well, I'm glad she's here. Fix us some tea, will you

please?" He hung his hat and unbuttoned his overcoat. Ella reached for it, placed it on the hook, and headed for the kitchen.

Violet, dressed in a gray suit trimmed in lavender, stood looking out the parlor window, her back to the door, the purple plume once again in place, quivering slightly.

"Mrs. Cunningham," John said upon entering the room, "how nice to see you. Please have a seat. Ella will bring us some tea."

She turned, attempted a smile, and lowered herself onto the settee.

John sat in a chair opposite her. "I've missed you in church. I hope things are all right at your household." He meant this sincerely—wondering since the Boone convention about her relationship with her husband.

"Fine, Reverend. Just fine." She did not look at him directly, but opened her mouth, then shut it again as though something might escape that shouldn't.

John had never known this woman to be at a loss for words. He waited, not sure himself how to proceed.

Finally, her voice came in very measured tones. "I feel I owe you an explanation for my presence at the WCTU convention."

John held up a hand. "You don't owe me anything, Mrs. Cunningham, especially if it makes you uncomfortable. We all have our reasons for what we do, and they are not always the business of others—though I do hope it means you have changed your mind about certain issues."

Ella entered with a tray containing a teapot, a sugar

bowl and creamer, and two cups and saucers, which she set on a table.

Violet studied the tray. "Only two cups? Will you not be joining us?"

Ella gave John a cautionary look. "I didn't want to intrude on a private conversation."

"Nonsense," Violet bristled. "Please, get a cup for yourself. I would like you to be here. I trust anything said to a pastor can be said to his wife with the same assurance of confidentiality."

"Absolutely," John said as Ella hurried to the kitchen. He sensed his visitor needed the presence of another woman for what she was about to say, which added to his curiosity.

When Ella returned with a third cup, she poured tea for the three of them, then sat next to John.

Violet took a sip of tea, set the cup down on its saucer with a determined clink, and started in. "About the temperance convention," she began. "I'm sure you have been wondering at my presence there. I have a niece, Reverend, of whom I am very fond, who currently resides at The Benedict Home in Des Moines." She revealed this fact with her head held high, yet a flush crept up her cheeks.

Now the words tumbled from her mouth. "She's a good girl, a young woman who was on an outing with a male acquaintance. He took advantage of her. She tried to fight him off, but he was strong, determined, and somewhat drunk. Now she is in a family way. Her reputation and future are ruined."

John shook his head. Here it was—laid out without

mincing words. He had to admire the courage it undoubtedly took to reveal this family secret. With a husband in the liquor industry, Violet lived a good life—a lovely home, expensive clothes, the wherewithal to give generously to charitable causes. Now someone she cared about had suffered greatly because a man could not control his drinking and behavior. In addition to the shame of it, Violet must be wrestling with the fact that her husband's generous income, from which her life benefitted, contributed to situations such as had befallen her beloved niece.

"Have you discussed this with your husband?" he asked.

"Oh, heavens no! He wouldn't understand. That's one reason why I came here, to tell you please not to spread word that I was at the convention. I was there trying to get more information about the Benedict Home—knowing it was a project of the Temperance Union. I feel I can support them without my husband's knowledge and, and ..."

She suddenly stopped as though shocked to hear her own words of deception. The color drained from her face. She picked up her tea cup and sipped, her fingers trembling. "I guess I sound like a terrible wife. I do love my husband. I just find myself wishing he were in another type of business." She put down the cup, her lips pressed together in a determined line that looked as though it had been drawn there. "I shouldn't have come and burdened you with this. I just felt you should know."

Ella stood, stepped over to the settee and put her hand

on Violet's arm. "We're glad you did, Violet. We all need someone to talk to, and your secret is safe with us."

The severe, no-nonsense Mrs. Cunningham seemed to have wilted. She managed a weak smile and placed her hand on Ella's. John sensed Ella's compassion rose from her own difficult past, and because of it, she could pass on an understanding to others.

"One more thing," Violet said, "I plan to drop my membership at the Congregational Church. Under the circumstances it would be best."

John's response was immediate. "My dear lady, that may be a grave mistake. Considering the concerns of your niece, this is a time when you most need the support of the Lord in your life."

Violet stood, her jaw again set in the familiar *I have made up my mind* attitude. "I didn't say I was forsaking the Christian religion, Reverend, just your church. I plan on joining the Baptists. It's my understanding that they follow the Bible a little more in the manner God intended."

Taking Ella's hands in hers, she seemed to soften again for just a moment. "You are a lovely lady, and I will miss your friendship. My deepest prayer is that you will one day sway your husband from his misguided convictions."

She turned to John. "Thank you for listening. I sense you are a good man and will find your way, but until then I must follow my own conscience."

They said their goodbyes, and the unexpected visitor left, marching up the walk in her familiar resolute manner. No one watching would ever suspect the woman had just bared her soul to her pastor — ex-pastor.

Several moments passed before Ella said, "Well, she may be wrong, but she is human after all."

"Everyone is," John said. "Some simply hide it better than others." He put his arm around his wife and they returned to the parlor where they sat together.

"You know," Ella said. "As strong a woman as she appears to be, she is still under her husband's thumb. All the good things she does are due to the allowance he gives her. She really isn't her own person. He controls her, but she can't seem to see that."

John found this remark revealing. It shed more light on Ella's need for independence and why earning money of her own was so important to her. It further explained her strong stand for women's rights.

Chapter Twenty-Three

REVIVAL PHILOSOPHY

1896

In January, the many folks pushing for women's rights rejoiced when Utah entered the Union with full woman suffrage written into its State Constitution. John read it first in *The Waterloo Daily Courier* and hurried home from a day of work at the church to share the news with Ella.

His wife opened the door with a wide grin on her face. "Guess what I just learned?" she said. And as was her custom, did not wait for him to answer. "Utah, of all places, has given women full suffrage!"

Sometimes John wondered if his wife was psychic, she had such an amazing pipeline to current news. He suspected it was because she had a cadre of friends who shared things with one another immediately.

"That *is* good news," he said. "I was just reading about it myself. The pro-suffragists there had some strong leaders. Women in the Utah territory were originally given the right to vote in 1870, but that was later rescinded. It's rather complicated." He handed her the paper tucked under his arm. "Here, you can read the details for yourself."

They talked of nothing else for the remainder of the day. Surely, with Utah joining the ranks of those enfranchising women, other states would follow in rapid order. The future for a woman's rights in the United States looked rosy.

In spite of what he considered misinterpretations by some folks, John still believed the Bible was the path to proper living and equality for women. The more converts to the faith who understood God's real message through Christ, the sooner women would be on an equal footing with men.

With this conviction a constant in his mind, he presented the idea of an all-city revival to the Ministerial Association in Waterloo. Someone suggested inviting the Reverend M. D. Williams of Atlanta, Georgia, to be the main attraction. "He comes highly recommended," one of the other pastors said, "and is assisted by Billy Sunday, an up-and-coming young evangelist. As a fellow Iowan, he'll be a big draw."

With this, the planning began. Revivals were commonplace, but this was to be the biggest event of its kind held in Waterloo in quite some time. Because of his enthusiasm and leadership, the committee chose John to be the event coordinator.

Mr. Sunday sparked Abram's attention. "Isn't he a baseball player?" the boy asked John one evening when supper conversation came around to the revival.

"I believe so, son, but I understand he gave that up a few years ago to spread the word of the gospel."

"I'll bet Williams is bringing him along just to fill up the meeting hall. Maybe he'll throw a few balls. That would be dandy." Abram picked up an apple from a basket in the center of the table and tossed it at John who managed to catch it before it hit the wall.

Ella shook her head. "Boys, please! This is not a ball court."

John chuckled at his son's enthusiasms, but still wished the lad showed the same passion for religion as he did for sports, adventure, and new inventions. John, himself, was not particularly impressed with Mr. Sunday's sports career. He was more interested in what the two evangelists had to say, especially Williams as the key speaker.

~ ~ ~

THREE WEEKS IN ADVANCE, WILLIAMS' ASSISTANTS arrived in town with a crew of workers to build the tabernacle — a huge, temporary facility constructed of wood and canvas. Its rise on an empty lot created a buzz of excitement, and on the evening of March 22nd, the revival began.

On opening night, John's gaze swept the large room. He was proud of his part in organizing the event. Electric lights — still a novelty in Waterloo — crisscrossed the ceiling on long cords, casting a glow on the faces of the enthusiastic audience. A loud anticipatory hum filled the space. Sawdust scattered about the floor scented the air like a pine forest, and stoves kept the interior as warm as possible. John noted with great satisfaction that only a few of the 3,000 chairs remained empty. The local ministers sat in a row on the stage and were to share the pulpit with Billy Sunday for the first sessions until the arrival of the Reverend Williams a few days later.

On March 27th, M.D. Williams himself took the stage—with flair and to loud applause. John thought the man's attire a little flamboyant for a revival: a gray suit with flashy gold cuff links and matching pin on the maroon tie. *Judge ye not,* he mused. That evening the curious and reverent of Waterloo filled all the seats. This was what the congregants had been waiting for. The evangelist's introductory sermon was directed to both male and female alike. After this, the sessions would be split into special topics for women and men respectively.

John and the other preachers continued to sit on the platform behind Williams, demonstrating the ecumenical and community endeavor that brought such an opportunity to Waterloo. One evening, after two hours of listening to the guest speaker addressing a room of men, a sense of foreboding crept over John. It wasn't Williams' topics that disturbed him—social purity, temperance, gambling, and the like. It was his presentation.

Later at home, John paced through the rooms on the lower floor, knowing if he went up to bed he would simply lie there awake.

"What is it?" Ella demanded, her voice cross and groggy from sleep. She had come down the stairs in her nightgown, her hair up in rags, hands on her hips.

John let loose. "He lectures rather than preaches, and rambles in his subject matter. He tells stories of conversion and brags to the last degree of his meetings. Tells all his family affairs." John stopped for a moment, wondering if he should go on. "He says his daughter is a natural born liar, or rather was, but is now converted. That is a personal matter, not something one announces from the pulpit. He advertises and sells books, especially his own. One member of his staff is a bookseller. He's going to make a pile of money off this revival, and we've already paid him a pretty penny."

"Come to bed, John. You're tired from all the effort it has taken to set this up. Things will look better in the morning. Williams must have something worthwhile to offer, or he wouldn't have been so highly recommended." Ella turned and led the way up the stairs.

Yet each evening John grew more troubled with the evangelist's words. John believed a revival was an awakening of interest in and a concern for the welfare of the soul. After a successful revival, folks should come away with an abiding and spiritual renewal. In John's mind, Williams was not leading a revival at all, but a crusade.

At the parsonage one morning after the previous night's session, John paraded from one end of the parlor to the other flailing his arms, his voice louder than usual. "It's reform by religious attack," he told Ella. "I call it cleaning out the town. It's not a revival at all and should not be called that. A revival emphasizes spiritual conditions and sins, a crusade emphasizes carnal conditions and sins—artificial sins, such as dancing and the theater. He is blaspheming culture. He says Waterloo is honeycombed through and through with sin and is as rotten as hell."

Ella sat working on her needlepoint. At one strong

emphasis in John's rhetoric, she jumped, pricking her finger. A drop of blood stained her work. Licking her finger, she set her project aside. "I hope you are writing all these words down for a sermon, dear."

"I'm doing that. And keeping notes in a book with my thoughts each evening. I may write an article for the paper if this keeps up."

Ella frowned. "Does everyone feel the same as you do?"

"It's hard to tell. The chairs are filled every night."

John made one more round of the room and stopped by the window. Dark clouds bunched overhead, matching his mood. Rain splattered the panes. Maybe the weather would keep folks away for the next revival session. Yet, that was not what he wanted. He wished, with fervent prayer, that Williams would present a different tone. When Billy Sunday preached, the mood seemed to change. However, the young evangelist had not been in the pulpit enough. He seemed to be only an apprentice or assistant to the more experienced Williams.

Still, at each session the audience appeared to be enthralled. John wrote comments regarding the sermons in his notebook as the evangelist pounded the podium and railed against sinners. *Two hours on dancing. Says dancing is responsible for nine-tenths of all prostitutes, all social vices. Someone spoke up saying that Black Hawk County had a larger number of inmates in the Benedict Home than any other county in Iowa.*

Finally, John couldn't stand it one minute longer. He called out, "That is your opinion."

"I am talking facts," the man volunteered.

"Names," John said, and regretted it immediately. They didn't need names, numbers maybe, to disprove all this maligning of Waterloo.

Williams jumped in and said he could certainly give names, and what's more could "preach a corker that would cause thunderbolts to fall in places where least suspected."

John cringed. He knew not all women at the Benedict House were prostitutes — were not all there as the result of a harmless dance. What if Williams did have names? Lightning truly could strike and destroy some folks in its flash.

The evangelist closed the meeting with the comment, "The brothel is a necessity to the man who frequents the dance."

This tone continued throughout the presentations, and John found it more difficult each evening to remain calm. The revival was not at all going in the direction he had hoped for. Then during a session the second week of April, Ron Henderson, a reporter for *The Courier,* challenged a remark made by Williams. The evangelist took offense, and in a heated response called Henderson a "black-hearted liar," asking those in the audience who endorsed his sermon to rise. A large number of those in attendance stood, and a smug Williams shouted, "See! Two thousand call you a liar."

At that the Methodist pastor, Reverend Scott, seated on the stage beside John, turned to him and said, "Let me get out of here." He and John stood and walked off the stage.

"I wish I had been there," Ella remarked later, after hearing John's account of the unpleasant episode. She stood in the kitchen at the ironing board, flat iron in hand as she pressed wrinkles out of one of John's freshly laundered shirts.

"No," John said, still shaken. "You would not have wanted to witness that terrible scene. Don't burn the shirt." He noted she had been so intent on listening to him she had neglected to move the iron.

She quickly replaced the iron on the stove, stepped to the chair where he sat, and laid her hand on his arm. "To support you, John. That is what I meant. I'm sorry this is turning out so opposite of what you envisioned."

He shook his head. "I'm glad you weren't there, but thank you, Ella. I feel your support regardless." He felt badly that he had scolded her about the shirt. He mustn't let frustrations and anger at others spill into his family life.

An account of the impulsive exit from the tabernacle stage of two of Waterloo's better-known clergy appeared in the *Courier* the following day. Ella handed the paper to John as he pulled on his overcoat to leave for a meeting regarding the issue. He quickly read the article. The reporter had gotten it amazingly correct, and a surge of righteousness coursed through him. He was not sorry for what he had done. He tucked the paper into his coat pocket.

"The meeting is at Scott's church," he told Ella. "His board of trustees and mine will be there, plus members of the Ministerial Association. We'll see what kind of support we get."

When John entered the basement room at the unfamiliar church, a dozen or so people milled about. A long table flanked by uncomfortable-looking chairs centered the room. Two gas wall sconces barely enhanced the light seeping from a gray sky through a small high window. The space felt claustrophobic and too warm. John ran a finger around his collar, looking for one of his own church members in the group.

Once everyone was seated, John's anxiety eased. Mrs. J. H. Leavitt, a strong promoter of the meeting and a loyal member of his congregation, sat among them. Though there were mixed feelings as to whether John should have challenged Williams and whether the subsequent abrupt exit by the two pastors was proper, these were friends who wanted the best for the whole community.

Ella must have been watching for him out a parsonage window, because the front door swung open before he had a chance to turn the knob. "Well?" she asked. "How did things go? Are you and the Reverend Scott to be run out of town?"

"No, at least not yet." John could tell by her tone that she wasn't worried, just curious as always. He removed his scarf and hat and handed them to her while he unbuttoned his coat. "The consensus was that Mr. Henderson should apologize to Williams for his scathing reporting, and Williams needs to apologize to Mr. Henderson for calling him a black-hearted liar. Until then, neither Scott nor I will return to the revival platform."

"Of course," she said. "They have to realize you

were only right to show your support for Mr. Henderson. Surely Williams will see the error of his remarks and apologize."

John hoped she was right, though wasn't certain. He started to follow her into the kitchen when a rap sounded at the door. Upon opening it, a courier handed him an envelope. Recognizing the handwriting of Sarah Ware Whitney, he felt a surge of relief. Here would be more support for his actions. He sat near the comfort and warmth of the cook stove and opened the seal on the envelope while Ella bustled about preparing supper. The message was not what he expected.

Dr. Stevenson:
Dear Friend,
If you wish for information on Waterloo's moral rottenness, I think I can give you enough to show that Mr. Williams' language was true if not arguable. I will be glad to inform you at any time and place that you may name.
Very Sincerely,
S. W. Whitney

John lay the note on the table and put his hands together, releasing a heavy rush of air that had been building in his lungs since morning. Absentmindedly, he steepled his index fingers—bringing a wry smile to his lips. *This is the church and this is the steeple, open the doors and see all the people.* He twisted his hands and wiggled the interlocked fingers. The tabernacle did not have a steeple. Maybe that was the problem. The goings-on inside weren't reaching for or even trying to find God, and John refused to believe Waterloo was as rotten as some folks suggested.

He sent Sarah a hasty reply, saying he appreciated her thoughts but felt all the negative assessment of their community was untrue. What's more, he wrote, the emphasis of a revival should be on an awakening of interest in the welfare of the soul. That is not what they were getting.

Two evenings passed with no apology from Williams. John began receiving notes and visits from church members asking him to return to his seat on the stage. On the third afternoon following the revival debacle, he opened the parsonage door to a committee of three women, Mrs. Leavitt leading the way. He ushered them into the parlor, a little wary as to what this group had in mind. The first sunshine in days streamed through the windows, though he sensed the brightness of the room was at odds with the mood of his guests. The minute the ladies sat, their leader spoke.

"Doctor Stevenson, we have word that a reconciliation between Williams and Henderson is to take place this evening, and we feel it would be a nice thing if you could go forward at the same time and take your place on the platform. We need your leadership there. It matters to those of us in your congregation and to new converts as well."

John felt his muscles tense. "Ladies, I appreciate your kind remarks, but if this is a promise by Williams, I prefer to wait until after it has actually happened rather than assume it will before the fact."

For a moment, a strained silence chilled the room.

The women glanced at each other with a *what now?* expression. Mrs. Leavitt sat a little taller, then looked directly at John. "Could you at least come to the meeting and hear for yourself?"

He said he would think about it.

Ella had been out shopping with Irene, and they arrived in time to see the committee hurry silently away from the parsonage.

"More people on your side?" she asked John as they entered the house. "I noticed Mrs. Leavitt was among them."

John nodded. "They believe there is to be a reconciliation tonight and said I should be there."

"And will you?" She removed her hat and gloves and helped Irene off with her coat.

"Are you still fighting?" Irene asked. They had tried to tone down the situation in front of their youngest child, but the matter dominated their conversations, every word stoking a furnace of frustration throughout the parsonage.

John put his arm around the girl. "It's not a fight, Reenie, it's…" He groped for an appropriate explanation. "…a disagreement that needs to be fixed."

"Here," Ella said, handing him a piece of mail. "You can add this to your arsenal. A messenger handed it to me as we approached the house."

Once again he held Sarah Whitney's bold handwriting in his hands. John took the thick envelope into his study where he sat and opened the seal. After her other note, he wasn't certain he would want to read this piece of correspondence. It was a rambling four pages, surprisingly written on stationery bearing the Iowa Woman Suffrage Association letterhead. Were her points made on behalf of that organization? After reading it through twice, he thought not, though she may have used the official paper to help push her point.

In the first half, she re-emphasized the moral downfall of Waterloo as she had hinted at in her previous note, naming names—as she had indicated she could—of men, not women, who had gone astray. Their wickedness, she said, was not dance, card playing, nor the theater, as Williams insisted, but drink. She said the men needed to hear what the evangelist was saying, yet were using John's exit as an excuse not to attend the revival. *I am praying for you and our church and myself and family and most of all for the men of Waterloo… Now is the accepted time for us all to be in Christ's image at work,* she wrote.

He supposed her concerns were legitimate, but even after his response to her first letter, she was missing the difference between a revival and a crusade. Still, her final sentence touched him deeply, and he sat in prayer until Ella called him to supper.

During the meal Ella asked. "So, are you going tonight—to hear the apology?"

"Yes. I will sit in the back of the room and hear for myself what Williams has to say to Henderson. That much I will do."

"Then I'm going with you," Ella said.

It was an apology, of sorts. Williams said, "Let past be past—forgive and forget." Not what John had hoped for. At a Ministerial Association meeting the following day, however, he agreed to return and support Williams to the end of the campaign.

"It is the lesser of two evils," he told Ella. "I am pocketing my feelings for the sake of the church. The converts who prefer the Congregational Church need a pastor, and all the churches and the city need peace and harmony."

At the end of the revival, the tabernacle came down and the evangelists moved on to a new community. The entire affair left John unsettled, especially when he later learned that Williams made $3,000 during his "crusade" in Waterloo. Yet the Congregational Church did have new members, for which John was thankful. He just hoped they didn't expect a continuation of the same kind of preaching they had witnessed in the tabernacle the spring of 1896.

Chapter Twenty-Four

CHANGES

As much as the Williams affair disturbed John, everyday life in Waterloo continued unabated. For more than a year the church trustees had discussed improvements to the parsonage, and decided May 1896 was the right time to tackle that job. Under Ella's direction, a crew arrived with paint and wallpaper. First on the agenda was the master bedroom, which seemed most in need of freshening up.

John avoided the project as best he could, but Ella stayed right in the middle of it, enjoying every second of the renovation. He marveled at how new surroundings lifted her spirits.

To him the whole operation was a nuisance, but he supposed it had to be done to keep the parsonage presentable—not that anyone ever entered their bedroom. For days, members of the trustees traipsed through the house hauling ladders, buckets of paint, and rolls of wallpaper. John worked in his study with the door closed or took long walks to get away from the noise of banging hammers as windowpanes were repaired and damaged flooring replaced. The smell of paint crept into every corner of the house. During the transformation, he and Ella slept in the boys' room—

Johnny still at Tabor and Abram once again off in the country making money pitching hay.

"It's just the beginning," Ella said as she danced through the house like a giddy child. "The trustees plan on doing the other bedrooms next. The downstairs will have to wait. It was done more recently — well, you can tell."

The very second the work was completed, she pulled John from his study and pushed him up the stairs to show him their room. "Isn't it beautiful?"

He had to admit it looked a mite better. In addition to the new paint, brightly flowered paper freshened the walls. Ella had even talked the committee into hanging crisp, white curtains at the windows. What had been a dingy though acceptable space to him, now radiated light and cheerfulness. And it felt good to sleep in his own bed again despite the smell of new paint.

John wondered if perhaps the church was sprucing up the parsonage with the thought of asking a new pastor to come on board. There were his ongoing health issues, and now he had added the turbulent episode of the Williams revival—not that he would have responded any differently to the evangelist's behavior even if he felt his congregation might toss him out because of it.

When he voiced these concerns to Ella, she put her hands on her hips and stared at him, disbelief smoldering in her eyes. "Don't be ridiculous!" she sputtered. "They wouldn't think of letting you go. They know a good man when they have one. They love you. I hear it all the time."

John threw up his hands. "You are the pastor's wife. No one is going to say negative things to you about me."

"I would feel it in the air, John. I would know." She turned from him to continue her dusting, the conversation obviously done in her mind.

He had to smile at her response and wondered if she really did feel congregational attitudes floating around in the atmosphere like wispy spirits. He decided she probably could.

~ ~ ~

CHANGES OTHER THAN FRESH COATS OF PAINT WERE occurring at the Stevenson home. Maggie graduated from Normal School the end of May with high marks and immediately began looking for a teaching job. Any number of elementary schools in Black Hawk County could be looking for teachers. John knew his oldest daughter had applied at several, and assumed she would begin teaching at one of them in the fall while living at home.

On a Monday evening in late August, when Abram had returned from his summer job and they sat around the supper table, John sensed Maggie had something important to say. She fidgeted, eyeing each of them, John in particular, but waited until they had blessed the food and passed the dishes before speaking up.

"I have a teaching job," she blurted, her gaze still intent on John.

"Why, that's wonderful," Ella exclaimed. "Where will it be?"

Maggie looked like she might burst apart any

moment. "Shenandoah."

"Shenandoah?" John thought he surely must have heard wrong.

Ella looked at John, wide-eyed. It seemed she couldn't quite believe it either. She turned to Maggie. "But that's clear across Iowa. Where will you stay? We thought—we just assumed—you would find a teaching position near here."

"A woman provides a room in her house for the teacher. It's all part of the contract. We have friends there, and I'll be near Johnny at Tabor."

"You lucky dog," Abram said, staring at his sister, his voice tinged with jealousy.

John knew they both missed their older brother, but the news still took him so aback he wasn't sure how to respond.

Tears sprang to Maggie's eyes from their unexpected reaction. "Are you mad, Papa? I thought you'd be glad. I've saved enough money from childcare and housecleaning. I can even pay my whole train fare to get there. Aren't you glad?"

Suddenly, the meaning of the conversation hit Irene. "Are you going away, Maggie?" She burst into tears.

John finally found his voice. "No, Margaret, I'm not mad. In fact, I'm very proud of you for venturing out on your own. You will be a fine teacher, and Shenandoah is lucky to have you." He *was* proud; he just needed to adjust to this totally new idea.

~ ~ ~

TWO WEEKS LATER THEY STOOD AGAIN AT THE TRAIN

station and waved goodbye to another family member.

"We're dwindling," Ella said, as they returned to the buggy.

"That's the way it is supposed to be," John replied in his most stoic manner. "We raise them to be responsible adults so they can make their own way." He tried not to think of Margaret, still in her teens, who had never ventured anywhere beyond her hometown without a family member — alone and changing trains twice before reaching her destination. *She can do it*, he thought. *She has to.*

Irene cried quiet tears during the ride back.

Abram poked his little sister and teased. "I don't know why you're so unhappy. Just think, you get the bed all to yourself now." Then he fell silent, looking out at the countryside as Blaze trotted toward home.

Abram often seemed to be in another world. John wondered where the lad's mind wandered off to this time.

As though reading his thoughts, the boy turned to him and said, "I'm not sure what I want to do now, but I may not keep on with school. Do I have to have a diploma to be an electrician?"

"I don't know, son, but I expect so."

John exchanged glances with Ella. He knew she was also concerned with what Abram had in mind. He had taken over the paper route when Johnny went off to college, which kept him around and helped him build his growing bank account. That seemed to be most important to him for the moment.

"He will take off one of these days," John told Ella

later. "I only hope he finishes school first."

~ ~ ~

The trustees completed the work on the remainder of the bedrooms by September, just in time for the church's forty-year celebration—open house at the parsonage being one of the many events planned for the special anniversary.

A week's worth of festivities focusing on the history of the Waterloo Congregational Church culminated in a ceremony the evening of September twenty-fourth. Folks dressed in their finest church-going attire crowded into every pew. The organist put on her best performance while the choir sang old-time favorites. Long-standing members read biographical sketches of former pastors and related the background of the church from its humble beginnings in a log school house to when it shared services with the Presbyterians to the present day. John gave a talk on "The Ten-Year Pastorate"—a composite of his years behind that pulpit. The evening ended with "The Anniversary Ode" written by Mrs. Julia Richards, a poem put to music and sung with enthusiasm, after which the congregation responded with loud and vigorous applause.

At breakfast the following day, Ella laid the local paper on John's place at the table as he sat down to eat. "Two pages on the history of the church," she said. "Someone really dug into the archives to get all that information." She had folded the paper and circled in pen a special section for his attention.

He picked it up and read to himself:

… The society is out of debt and is prospering in a financial as well as spiritual way. Dr. Stevenson, the pastor, has the respect and esteem of the citizens of Waterloo generally, as well as of his own congregation, and is, it is hoped, destined to live and labor here for many years to come.

He smiled, acknowledging to himself Ella's sixth sense about people. He tried not to think of his bouts with hay fever and troublesome throat.

One day in early October, John half-dozed in deep thought at his church office. Sunlight poured in from a window pooling around him and onto the desk like a warm mantle. A rap sounded on the door, forcing him out of his stupor. He sat upright, but before he could answer, Moses Cross, chairman of the ministerial committee, let himself in. This parishioner, a little on the heavy side, always dressed like a banker regardless of the weather or time of day. A chain, attached to an expensive gold watch, looped from his vest pocket. Moses frequently pulled out the timepiece and checked the hour, as though he were always on his way to some important appointment. Though a friendly and supportive chap, John found him to be a little intimidating, never quite certain what the man might be thinking.

"Morning, Dr. Stevenson. I hoped I would find you here." Moses handed John an envelope. "Here is the annual review of the pastorate. Read it over and get back to us with your response." He smiled, tipped his hat, and left as quickly as he had entered.

John tucked the envelope in his coat pocket to take

home to read. In the past he felt confident about the predictable message inside, but now a tiny stream of unease rippled through him. Despite the glowing report in the newspaper, this year had been somewhat rocky.

At home in his study, he sat at his desk for a few moments pulling on his mustache in contemplation before breaking open the seal. He took a deep breath and began to read the flowing handwriting:

Dear Doctor Stevenson,

I have been requested to write you a brief statement of the proceedings of the meetings called on Sunday last...

The report announced that the debt of the society was all paid or provided for, then stated that a motion to renew John's pastorate resulted in thirty-four ayes and zero noes.

The letter bore the signatures of all those present, representing the "aye" votes, with a promise of more signatures to come. John's spirits lifted with each paragraph as he continued to read:

...the church then voted to pay you a salary of $1,100 and the use of the parsonage, per annum, quarterly in advance; with a vacation of four weeks annually.

We earnestly hope for a favorable response from you at as early a day as may consist with your judgment.

In behalf of the church, Moses K. Cross.

Nothing was mentioned of his health issues nor his philosophy on what constituted a revival. In fact, the salary and vacation time allotted were more than in previous years.

With a feeling of relief, John left his study, letter in hand, to find Ella. Sitting down next to her on the piano bench where she prepared for a student, he handed her the report. "You should read this."

She took it, a cautious look in her eyes. When she finished reading, she folded the pages and handed them back with a smile. "I don't know what else you expected, John. Of course they want you to continue. I never doubted it."

He gave her a hug and retired to his study to write an acceptance of the generous offer.

~ ~ ~

JOHN'S FRIENDSHIP WITH SARAH WARE WHITLEY SEEMED not to have suffered, despite their disagreement regarding the morals of Waterloo. She still complimented him on the articles he wrote for *The Woman's Standard,* and the two of them had stimulating conversations regarding woman's suffrage. This spurred him on, keeping the movement foremost in his mind.

In the evenings, after Abram brought home their copy of *The Courier,* John often read articles aloud, especially those that pertained to the rights of women. In November, the cause received another big boost when Idaho adopted a Woman's Suffrage amendment to its constitution.

"Those western states keep surging ahead of the rest," John said, while in the kitchen reading a lengthy article on the subject. He set the paper aside and picked up a potato Ella had handed him to peel.

"That makes four states," she said. "I've been reading about some of the key women in Idaho who made this happen. Kate E. Nevile Feitham, originally from Iowa, by the way, was a teacher in Ackley before moving to Idaho. She reminds me of Cora. She teaches English at the College of Idaho, and has been very active in the National American Woman Suffrage Association."

Ella chattered non-stop extolling the virtues, strength, and determination of the women in Idaho who worked tirelessly for their rights. She turned to John, waving a mixing spoon about as though she were chasing giants. "And with you working for the enfranchisement of women locally, surely Iowa will be next."

In spite of Ella's insight about things, John didn't share her optimism regarding Iowa. He was too aware of the contrary feelings among the men in the state legislature. One would think when a state accepted woman's suffrage, it should weaken the stand of opponents in the others. However, statistics showed that lately the antisuffrage movement seemed even stronger. He shook his head as an image of Violet Cunningham popped into his thoughts.

Chapter Twenty-Five

THE CAT AND MOUSE GAME

1897

"I think I'll make another trip to Des Moines," John announced one evening as they sat in the parlor. He always felt charged when a new year began — full of hope, plans, and aspirations for the months ahead.

Ella looked up from the book she'd been engrossed in since supper. "And what is the occasion this time?"

"The National American Woman Suffrage Association is meeting there the end of this month. It will be the first time they have met west of the Mississippi and only the second time outside of Washington D.C. Carrie Chapman Catt will be there as well as other big names, including Susan B. Anthony and Alice Stone Blackwell, Lucy Stone's daughter." He handed Ella the copy of *The Woman's Standard* highlighting the information.

She scanned the article, her face brightening. "Oh, John, this is wonderful! I'm going to come with you. This is too good to pass up."

He didn't reply immediately. He hadn't expected this response from her — hadn't even thought to include her. They didn't take out-of-town trips together without family, and in January both Irene and Abram were in school and not able to leave.

Ella flared at his hesitation, and standing, she let the book fall from her lap onto the floor. "I know what you're thinking. *I need to be here with the children.* Well, I have a better idea. You stay home, and I'll go. It's all about women, you know. Yes, it's more important I go."

Her fire caught him off guard. She had always been so supportive of his stand on woman's rights. He just assumed she would be delighted at his decision to go to the convention. But of course, this was part of it, a woman's right not always to be trapped at home, her right to be out voicing her opinion on things that mattered. He heard it often, and truly felt he agreed and understood this aspect of the argument. In fact, the idea of women out and about ignoring their wifely and motherly duties was a huge bone of contention to the antisuffragists. According to them, a woman's involvement in politics would destroy the family. John did not agree with this mindset and yet here he was guilty of it himself. Ella's comment on another occasion rushed at him: *"Practice what you preach, John."* As his wife stood there and glared at him, he knew he needed to rethink his plan for the Des Moines trip.

So they both went. Arrangements were made for Irene to go directly to Mrs. Pennyworth's after school and stay until Abram was through with his paper route. In the evenings and mornings before school, they would be on their own. At age eighteen, Abram should certainly be responsible enough to look after his eleven-year-old sister for a few nights. John felt comfortable with this arrangement. He sensed Ella was a little reluctant to leave Irene, though not enough to miss out on the convention.

In Des Moines, the delegates gathered at the Central Christian Church. Green palm branches lined the room, and a suffrage flag was prominently displayed boasting four stars to represent Wyoming, Colorado, Utah, and Idaho. Susan B. Anthony, president of the National American Woman Suffrage Association, led the sessions—as strong in her presentation as always, despite being seventy-six years of age. She vigorously chastised the Iowa legislature for their inaction regarding a woman's rights, saying they had played with the idea "like a cat plays with a mouse."

But still, she was optimistic that by the year 1900 Iowa would join the ranks of those states enfranchising women, believing others would have joined by then, too. "We'll be in the company of the forward western states of California, Nevada, Oregon, Washington, and Montana," she said, pounding the lectern. At this, a cheer erupted from the large crowd.

John and Ella walked back to their hotel, ignoring the horse-drawn cabs to save their money. The January breeze stung their cheeks, and though encased in fur-lined gloves, their fingertips tingled with cold. The chill seemed to heighten Ella's enthusiasm for the conference and everything it stood for. She rambled on about the events of the day, fairly skipping along the walkway. John had to increase his pace to keep up with her.

"Wasn't Miss Anthony something?" Ella said. "And to think I actually shook her hand, and Mrs. Catt's, and they seemed genuinely pleased to meet me. What remarkable women they are!"

John never showed emotions as fervently as his wife, though something akin to the feeling of a locomotive speeding down the track toward equality filled his senses. The cause was definitely on its way.

Mrs. Catt had announced she was to begin an intense campaign throughout Iowa to bring women's rights to the forefront, and invited those in attendance to assist in any way possible. Ella had not missed this opportunity.

"I told those women I would help with petitions and whatever it takes to promote the cause," she said, as they hurried along to the warmth of their hotel room. "It's the least I can do. Mrs. Catt wants every county in Iowa to have a suffrage club by the end of the year."

John smiled as his wife's words tumbled out one after another. He was glad she came with him. They would be better partners for the crusade because of it. The possibility had been there all along, but John admitted he was sometimes blind to Ella's talents outside those of homemaker, mother, and music teacher. She seemed an unlikely daisy blossoming in winter as the passion for women's rights grabbed hold. Their zeal remained while they headed for home.

John and Ella were greeted on their return by an exuberant Irene. "Can we vote now?" she asked flinging herself into Ella's arms.

"It's not that simple, dear, but Iowa has the best people working to make it happen. We must convince the men in our state government how important it is."

"Can I help?" Irene asked.

The question from his young daughter touched John. He was proud of his women, and if Susan B. Anthony's predictions were correct—the year 1900 being so close—he was convinced Iowa would soon give equal rights to women. Surely the legislators would finally see the wisdom in that.

Chapter Twenty-Six

CONSULTATIONS

When John arrived as pastor in 1886, the existing sanctuary was, in his own words, dirty, dingy, and dilapidated. However, he had been warned when he accepted the ministry there if he expected to stay any length of time he would do well not to say anything about building a new church.

He told Anna at the time, "Something must be done about this if we want the membership to grow." He saw the old building through the eyes of a newcomer — a wreck that had passed through flood and fire. Regardless of the warning, he knew something had to change. How best to approach the congregation about a new building, he wondered? Then, quite unexpectedly, Mother Nature stepped in with an answer to the problem.

Later, John loved to tell how one Sabbath evening "a wind storm shook the building so violently the congregants fled outside, afraid ancient beams and walls might fall upon them and send them to heaven prematurely."

Shortly after that nerve-racking episode, a committee formed and started a campaign for a new church building. In November 1887, only a year after

John's arrival, the old sanctuary was demolished and a new one began to take shape at the same location on Fifth and Jefferson. Dedicated the following September, it was a striking edifice, with a tall, stately bell tower—a handsome addition to Waterloo architecture.

But Waterloo didn't remain a little mid-western town. Factories found their way there. Smokestacks rose on the city's skyline bringing workers of varied nationalities into the community with a tide of prosperity. By the spring of 1897, the church had outgrown its new building.

"We'll make it bigger," John remarked to Ella following a Sunday service when members spilled into the narthex with no more room in the pews

The congregation raised $4,000 and construction began in June. John was elated with the thought of a larger sanctuary. Even so, an ominous cloud hung about him. In addition to his croaking voice, the hay fever came early that year, bringing on the dreaded wheezing. By early summer he left for Wisconsin to ease his labored breathing.

The family and the entire congregation prayed the time away would help John's lungs. A break from sermons for several weeks would surely cure his troubled throat. And at first, upon his return at the end of July, this seemed to be the case. The hay fever had abated. But it took only two Sundays of preaching for John to realize his throat required more than a break. Sips of water during sermons no longer helped. There were times when his throat seemed to close altogether, and no words came out—not even a croak.

He knew he must seek serious medical help or risk permanent damage.

When he approached Moses Cross with the news, the man was aghast.

"We don't want to lose you, Reverend. Let me speak with the committee and see what we can come up with."

By evening, John had their decision. "They are giving me a leave of absence for a year," he told Ella. "During that time, I will find the best doctor and treatment available. By next summer I'll be back in the pulpit."

~ ~ ~

JOHN IMMEDIATELY SOUGHT THE ADVICE OF DR. CASE IN Waterloo, a physician he'd seen in the past. The receptionist ushered him into the examining room and instructed him to sit on the table. "The doctor will see you shortly," she said.

The dark paneled space felt cold and impersonal, and the air smelled acrid. Cabinets with glass doors held an array of instruments for probing and poking, some of which appeared downright threatening. After a long fifteen-minute wait, Dr. Case entered, greeted John, and peered down his throat, muttering undecipherable hums and ahs.

At last the man stood back and shook his head. "What remedies you are using don't appear to be helping, Reverend, and throats are not my specialty. Would you be willing to travel to Chicago? The best doctor I know of in this field practices there."

The idea took John aback for a moment. Chicago was quite a distance to travel to see a doctor, but a specialist was obviously what he needed.

"His name is Fletcher Ingals, and he has done extensive study on diseases of the chest, throat, and nasal cavities. In fact, that is the title of his book on the subject." Dr. Case pulled a bound volume from a shelf and handed it to John. "Look through this and see what you think. I would be happy to send a letter to him regarding your particular affliction, including a history of your treatments, and I can set up an appointment for you."

John took the book home and spent the afternoon reading its contents. Ella was away having tea with a friend. When she returned, she stuck her head in the study door while removing her hat and gloves, anxiety written on her face. "Well?" she asked, "What did Dr. Case have to say?"

"He recommends I see the author of this book, who happens to practice in Chicago. Look through this and see what you think."

She took the book and immediately headed to a chair in the parlor. It didn't take her long to return. She placed it on John's desk and stood there a moment, as though formulating her words before speaking them.

He fiddled with a pencil, not sure how to interpret the expression on her face. "Should I go see the man?" His mind was already made up. He would go, but he wanted her blessing. A trip to Chicago called for unbudgeted expenses, and he knew this would concern her.

Ella lowered herself into the chair opposite his desk, then burst forth with her reply. "By all means! Our goal is to have you cured so you can get on with your life's work. We have a little savings. We can afford it."

Dear God, Thank you. He breathed a sigh of relief, wondering why he thought, even for a moment, her response might be any other way.

Yet money *was* part of the problem. The church promised John a token salary during his leave of absence, and in addition, the membership would be paying guest preachers. This limited the amount they'd be able to give John. The small savings he and Ella had put away wouldn't tide them over for extras very long. Yet, right now healing John's throat was a priority. Without that, his income as a preacher—his livelihood—would cease.

They waited for Dr. Case to connect with Dr. Ingals and hoped for the best. John spent much time in his study at home, always having something to write about. He missed his daily trek to the church, though he occasionally set out for a walk and stopped by to chat a bit with whoever was there. He also continued visiting shut-ins—an arrangement made with the ministerial committee. Not only did the congregation appreciate this, but it also justified the small income he received. Praying with individuals for their personal concerns put far less strain on his voice than preaching.

One blustery day in early November, he had hoped to visit an elderly parishioner, but awoke barely able to swallow, the pain more intense than usual.

Ella put her foot down. "You stay in. I will treat your throat," she insisted.

He settled in his study and worked while she

brought him warm, wet towels to wrap around his neck, frequently reheated by tucking them into the oven. She served him hot tea, enhanced with a spoonful of honey and a squeeze of lemon, a luxury fruit hard to find and beyond their budget, but one she deemed necessary. For good measure, when she left the room, he added a pinch of the cocaine to the morning's treatments. Hot soup for lunch in the warm kitchen completed Ella's special care.

"Thank you, my dear," John said as he finished the last spoonful. "You have been very attentive, and I do believe my throat is better." He meant it, though it could have been due to any number of reasons—the hot concoctions his wife pressed on him, something as simple as not talking for several hours, or of course, the cocaine. He felt drowsy and took to his bed upstairs.

Two hours later, he awoke to a strangled rendition of "Row, Row, Row Your Boat," as Ella's newest student plunked laboriously on the piano keys downstairs. John sat on the edge of his bed trying to shake the haze from his head, each wrong note a painful, vibrating gong between his ears. Then the fractured melody stopped. He heard voices, and minutes later footsteps on the stairs.

The bedroom door opened, and Ella stepped in. "John? Oh, good, you are awake. A messenger just brought this." She handed him a piece of paper.

John took it from her, unfolded it, and read the few words, nearly illegible, scrawled across the page: *Dear Pastor, I am in an awful way. Please come. Leroy Cooper.*

John's sluggishness vanished, and he was suddenly

wide awake. "It's Leroy. I need to go to him."

He washed up, thumped down the stairs, put on his coat and hat, and stepped out the back door. An early storm buffeted Waterloo, and a few flakes of snow suggested more to come. At the barn, John connected Blaze to the buggy and headed for Leroy's. The wind whipped at his coattails, and he had to hang onto his hat to keep it from whirling away. He knew Ella was distressed at his going out, especially after all her attention to his throat earlier in the day. He also knew she would not keep him from his ministerial duties. Visiting Leroy fell right in line with his continued commitment to the church.

Fifteen minutes later, John pulled up in front of the Cooper house. After securing the horse and buggy, he hurried along the walkway and rapped loudly on the door. When he got no response, he tried the door knob and, finding it unlocked, stepped into the dark interior where he was immediately assailed with the unpleasant odors associated with the sick.

It had been months since he had seen Leroy, and word around town was the man was not doing well. The whereabouts of his wife and children remained a mystery. John was not interested in another conversation about them. It only led to anger and frustration. If Leroy was on his deathbed, they could talk about the forgiveness of sins, thus opening the gates of heaven to the poor soul. That was where John's expertise lay—not in the detective work of finding runaway spouses.

He called out, "Leroy? It's Reverend Stevenson."

A faint reply drifted from the rear of the house. "Here."

John followed the sound to a small bedroom. Shock swept through him as he entered. Leroy lay in bed, hollow-eyed and diminished. He stared up at the ceiling as though seeing nothing. John approached and gently touched his emaciated arm.

"Leroy?"

The man turned his head slowly in John's direction, blinked, swallowed, and spoke in a rasp. "Hello, pastor. Thanks for coming."

John pulled up a chair and sat close to the bed. "Is it time to confess your sins, Leroy? You appear not long for this world."

The man sighed and looked away. "You may be right about that, pastor. I don't know. No more drink, that's for sure." Each word seemed to take great effort. There was a long gap of silence, as though he forgot John was there.

"Shall we pray, Leroy?"

More silence. Then another sigh. "If you want, though I don't think God really cares about me."

"You're wrong. He hears your prayers, but they must be sincere. He knows when you're pretending."

Leroy turned and gazed at John with rheumy eyes. "Does he know where my wife and boys are? If so, he's been hiding them from me. That's not a caring God. That's a deceiving God."

John rubbed his forehead. *Here we go again.* "Do you want redemption, Leroy? If so, you have to admit your wife and boys are gone due to your wrongdoing. That's the only way."

"I want to see them one last time, pastor. Bring them to me." For a dying man, he suddenly seemed to have a burst of angry energy.

"We've been through this before, Leroy."

The man glared at him, turned his back, and began a coughing fit that wouldn't stop, gasping for breath between each hack. John shook his head. The man needed to be in a hospital, but the nearest one was miles away in Dubuque.

John stood. "You need help, Leroy. Let me get a doctor."

"No! No doctor, and if you can't do what I'm asking, get out. Get out!" His sudden explosive rant brought on another uncontrollable coughing fit.

John whispered a quiet prayer. *He's in your hands, Lord. I've done all I can.* He retraced his steps out into the cold, shutting the door firmly behind him.

At home, he related the visit to Ella.

She shook her head. "John, you are too good. Forget the likes of Leroy. They never change. They just make life miserable for everyone else." Anger snapped in her voice. "You have your own problems. You don't need Leroy's, too." And with that she pushed through the door to the kitchen and left him standing in the hall.

He trudged to the parlor and slumped in a chair, head in his hands. The strain of his own health issues was beginning to show in Ella's manner. They were both on edge waiting to hear from Dr. Case. And though he felt compelled to counsel his flock, Ella was right. He did not need the added stress of Leroy

Cooper's uncontrollable drinking problem.

Even so, he couldn't leave it at that. He arranged for a nurse to stop by and check on Leroy daily—her fee to be paid from his own meager pocket, though the church would probably take up a collection to reimburse him for such a cause. He expected a call to Leroy's deathbed any hour, and of course, he would go. Several days later, to his dismay, John learned Leroy had dismissed the nurse and had been seen out in the community.

"That man's a ghost," he told Ella. "I'm surprised he has the energy to get out of bed. He undoubtedly needed supplies. We should at least take a hot meal over."

At first she refused. John didn't argue, knowing her feelings about Leroy were personal. Still, she would come around. Regardless of the circumstances, it was the right thing to do. He often preached from the Gospel of Mark where Jesus said: *Verily I say unto you, in as much as ye have done it unto one of the least of these my brethren, ye have done it unto me.*

Later, he and Ella together delivered a jar of hot soup and a loaf of freshly baked bread to Leroy's house. When the door did not open to a dozen firm knocks, they left the meal on the porch.

~ ~ ~

It was several weeks before John heard from Dr. Case regarding an appointment with the throat specialist, during which time John continued with the various remedies prescribed in the past, including the cocaine and whatever Ella concocted. Word finally came that an appointment had been set for December 9th at Dr. Ingals' office in Chicago.

John left Waterloo on an icy day early in the month, his throat wrapped in a woolen scarf knitted by Irene. His youngest daughter, now a grown-up twelve-year old, accompanied Ella to the train station.

"I can hardly wait for you to come home all well!" Irene exclaimed, hugging him tightly.

"Don't expect that, Reenie. It won't happen overnight, but maybe this new doctor will know what to do to make things better."

Ella kissed him goodbye, and he boarded the car where he found a seat by a window to return their waves. The train lurched and the engine chugged, spitting out steam and coughing smoke. It picked up speed, and John, full of hope, was on his way. If anyone could help his throat it would be Dr. Ingals.

~ ~ ~

HE RETURNED A WEEK LATER WITH A WHOPPING BILL FROM the doctor, partially paid, with promises from John of more money to come later. He also carried with him a letter of diagnosis and treatment to be delivered to Dr. Case of Waterloo. John's satchel contained a muriate of ammonia inhaler with eucalyptol as prescribed by Dr. Ingals, a remedy John felt already afforded some relief. He spent a good deal of the train ride home rereading the letter, attempting to understand the medical terminology. Dr. Ingals wrote:

I regard his trouble as due to want of co-ordination in the action of the laryngeal muscles, resulting from irregular supply of the nervous force. There is no evidence of paresis, but on the contrary spasmodic action of the muscles, when he attempts to utter the lower notes. This probably results from the nervous strain which he has been under for some years, possible partly due to cocaine.

Dr. Ingals had been greatly alarmed and astonished that another doctor would have suggested the use of cocaine, saying it was enough to account for a host of misfortunes. He told John, "I cannot understand how anyone could have been so thoughtless as to order it."

The letter closed with a sentence that held John in a paralyzing-grip:

I apprehend that if the patient continues to preach, his voice will continue to grow worse, in spite of treatment.

Chapter Twenty-Seven

HOPE

1898

Though improvements to his throat were slower than John hoped, frequent use of the inhaler, as per the doctor's orders, brought some relief. He refused to dwell on the ominous closing sentence in the letter from Dr. Ingals to Dr. Case. In fact, he had not mentioned it to Ella. As always, with the turn of the new year, John experienced a burst of enthusiasm. He clipped along on his daily walks, humming hymns, even enjoying the bite of winter weather.

Ella continued to be optimistic about his future. "That trip to Chicago was the best decision we ever made," she said. "You'll be back in the pulpit by the first of summer."

He hugged her for that. Life would be normal soon—it had to be. In preparation for those days, he spent hours in his study writing sermons, papers, and articles.

They scraped up the balance owed Dr. Ingals, and with the check, John enclosed a message stating he felt his voice had improved, albeit more slowly than he had hoped. The doctor responded within days, writing:

Improvement of the voice in cases such as yours is always extremely slow.

He suggested John return to Chicago the end of

January so he could personally monitor the progress and make any necessary adjustments to the treatments. Another trip to Chicago was an additional expense they hadn't counted on, but both John and Ella felt it worthwhile.

"He's the only doctor who has ever helped you," Ella said at supper one night. "It would be foolish to stop seeing him now. We'll just have to do it somehow."

"Yes, you need help, Papa," Irene said. "You must go."

John appreciated the passionate and eager support of his youngest, yet knew she had no idea of their finances. He smiled at his daughter as she rose to help Ella clear away the dishes. The two women seemed excited about a dessert they were about to serve. Abram, on the other hand, had remained quiet during most of the meal. While the ladies busied themselves at the kitchen counter, the lad flipped a spoon back and forth between his fingers, his mind obviously preoccupied, as was often the case.

"Hot gingerbread with vanilla sauce," Ella announced with a flourish. She and Irene set a bowl of the special treat at each place. "In celebration of us."

Dessert in the household was rare, except for an occasional Sunday, but John knew Ella had been trying extra hard lately to maintain a cheerful spirit. He took a bite of the spicy cake.

"Hmmm, delicious. Thank you. This is the perfect ending to the day."

"I made the sauce," Irene boasted.

"Extra perfect," John added.

Abram emptied his bowl in four bites, wiped his mouth with a napkin, and cleared his throat. "Papa, I want to help pay for your return trip to Dr. Ingals. I'm actually quite rich, you know."

A rush of pride swept through John at this unexpected and generous offer. The lad had two jobs, and since completing school had been paying a small monthly sum to them for board and room. He would be gone one of these days and was saving his "riches" for when he was off living on his own, an idea John contemplated with mixed emotions. He loved this boy and his unpredictable nature. He would dearly miss him.

"That's very generous of you, but we can handle the cost for now."

Abram ignored this, pushed his chair back from the table, stood and pulled a small leather purse from his pocket. He snapped open the clasp and counted out twenty dollars, laying the money on the table. "Here, Papa. Please take it."

Ella gave John a look that said he should.

John reached for the money, folded it, and put it in his own pocket. "Thank you, son." The huskiness in his voice at that moment had nothing to do with an ailing throat.

~ ~ ~

IN THE WEEKS LEADING UP TO HIS TRIP, OTHER OBLIGATIONS occupied their time. John continued with his visitations to church members and his writing. Ella kept her promise to be involved in the suffrage movement in Iowa. For weeks, from late autumn through the beginning of the new year, she spent hours attending meetings and going from door to door gathering signatures on a petition favoring a constitutional amendment for the enfranchisement of women in the state.

One Saturday morning she dressed in her best—including a hat she had embellished with a multi-colored feather plucked, with permission, from a neighbor's colorful bantam chicken.

"What do you think?" she asked John, as she strutted around the room like some exotic bird.

"It looks to me like you have been cavorting with Mrs. Cunningham," John said, looking up from his paper. "I fear that whatever ails that woman must be catching."

"That's exactly what I'm doing," Ella said. "Today Irene and I are cavorting, as you put it, with Violet and her friends. In fact, we have been invited to tea at her lovely home, and I plan to return here with a page of new signatures on my petition. We've kept in touch, you know, and are still friends."

John frowned, remembering his last encounter with Violet before she changed churches. "Aren't you being a trifle optimistic?"

"She's changing, John, you know that. Both Irene and I feel it. I think a little persuasion is all it will take. And whatever she does, her followers will... well, follow."

John folded his paper and set it aside. "I don't know, Ella, you may be in for trouble. Being a member of the

Woman's Christian Temperance Union doesn't make Violet a suffragist. I think it's more likely she's trying to change you and Irene to antis. And speaking of Irene, does she need to go with you? It might end up being unpleasant."

"Irene has been helping me with this project and is becoming a die-hard suffragist herself. This will be a good experience for her. She is very good at driving home a point with the charm only a sincere young lady possesses."

John shook his head in resignation. No sense in arguing with two women, and perhaps Ella was right. Irene just might be able to win that stubborn woman over.

That evening when John wandered into the kitchen where the ladies of the house were preparing supper, he asked how the tea had gone.

Ella shrugged her shoulders. "Violet has a beautiful home."

"And the signatures on the petition?"

"We got one," Irene said with an air of victory.

"And was it Mrs. Cunningham?" John asked, trying to keep an "I told you so" smile off his face.

Ella feigned deafness. Irene, however, was eager to talk.

"No, but she let us give our little speech on a woman's right to vote before changing the subject. As we were outside leaving later, her niece Polly came up and asked if she could sign the petition. Isn't that good?"

John hugged his daughter. "Aye, it certainly is. One is better than none, especially from that camp." For a moment, his thoughts centered on this "Polly." Was she the niece who had resided for a while at the Benedict Home? If so, she might be just the influence needed to sway Violet to their side. The thought brought a smile to his lips.

The next day, John took Ella in the buggy to a part of town she had not yet canvassed, accompanying her to each house. As always, there were those who shut the door immediately upon hearing their opening statements, others who listened politely but didn't sign, and the reward of a few who wrote their names with great enthusiasm. It was a long afternoon. Nonetheless, by sundown the petition was filled.

"This is very exciting," Ella remarked on the way home. "My petition is only one of many from all over the state. Members of the legislature will receive hundreds of signatures. When Mrs. Coggeshall and other key ladies of the Iowa Woman's Suffrage Association attend the hearing of the House and Senate committee on constitutional amendments, the men will sit up and take notice. Surely this will be the year Iowa will pass an amendment in favor of women's rights."

The following morning Ella promptly mailed her petition off to Des Moines.

John left for his second trip to Chicago the last week of January and was gone when the Iowa suffragists met with the committee on February 3rd. Wishing he were in on the excitement, he watched for word of the outcome in the Chicago papers, but found nothing.

Perhaps Iowa news, no matter how great to Iowans, might not get to Illinois immediately.

On his return home, after welcome kisses and hugs, he headed up the stairs to the bedroom to unpack. Ella followed close at his heels. He placed his travel bag on the bed and began removing clothing, expecting an immediate barrage of questions from his wife related to his visit with Dr. Ingals. However, John felt there was time for that later. His curiosity regarding the outcome of the constitutional amendment had gnawed away at him for days. He got his question in first. "Well, how'd it go in Des Moines?"

Ella exploded. "Can you believe it? Both houses refused to approve a woman-suffrage amendment. We must get those thick-headed lawmakers out of there and vote in a new slate." She plopped onto the bed, arms crossed, a scowl creasing her forehead. "But how to do that if women can't vote? It's downright maddening."

"In case you've forgotten, there are men who believe enfranchisement for women is important." John tossed soiled clothing into a pile on the floor. "We simply have to work harder on recruiting them to vote favorably and get the right candidates into office."

Ella cast him a cynical look. "So, are you planning on running for the senate?"

John put up his hands in protest and said nothing. There were a hundred reasons why he couldn't run. Aside from preaching—his first profession—a throat that prevented him from swallowing or speaking stood at the top of the list.

His wife knew this and didn't wait for a reply. "Then find some men who will." She stood. "I'm going for some fresh air." Storming from the room, she thumped down the stairs. Moments later, the front door slammed shut with a bang.

She wasn't mad at him, John knew. She simply needed to vent her frustrations. Never down for long, Ella seemed to have a penchant for finding rainbows. She returned later with a head full of ideas on how to pursue their goal.

John's health rallied too. Dr. Ingals had sent him home with additional medications and a note to a new doctor in Waterloo to whom John would now report, eliminating the necessity of trips to Illinois. The evening of his return, as they prepared for bed, John held up three bottles to show Ella. "In addition to the inhaler, I am to take an internal prescription I can get as needed from this new doctor. Then there are these for you to swab on my larynx daily. This is a solution of sulphate of zinc with boric acid, and this is carbolic and tannic acid with a little morphine."

She frowned as John named off the ingredients. "Well, I hope he knows what he's doing. Morphine?"

He knew she was thinking of the cocaine he had taken before. "This is different. It's a very small amount and is regulated. Dr. Ingals seems confident it will help."

She reached for the bottle and the swabs. "Show me what to do."

~ ~ ~

ONE AFTERNOON IN LATE FEBRUARY, ELLA TAPPED ON John's study door, opened it and peeked in. "Are you busy?

He put down his pen and yawned. For two hours, he had been feverously writing a paper entitled "The Free Woman."

"I could use a break," he said and flexed his fingers.

Ella scooted into the room and handed him a cup of hot tea. Obviously not in a hurry to leave, she stood quietly beside the desk. John felt excitement radiating from her body.

He took the cup, thanked her, and began sipping the hot beverage. "What is it, Ella? What do you have up your sleeve now?"

"I think we should take a trip to Scotland."

John about choked on the tea, clanked the cup down on his desk, and looked at her in amazement. "My, dear! You are addled in the head. Have you not forgotten how we had to scrimp to get me twice to Chicago and back? That was small change compared to a voyage to the old country." He shook his head in disbelief. She never ceased to surprise him.

"Don't be so hasty," she said. "I've written Dr. Ingals, and he thinks it would do you a world of good. You know he believes much of your health problems are the result of nervous exhaustion."

"You wrote to Ingals?" That she would do such a thing without consulting him seemed an intrusion into his private matters. It astounded him, even angered him a little, but he immediately checked his reaction. She was doing this because she loved him. The whole idea was overwhelming. Yet he knew a trip to Scotland was impossible. He reached out and pulled her onto his lap and nuzzled her neck.

"Thank you, my dear. It is a most thoughtful gesture. But surely you know we can't."

It was a moment before he realized her cheeks were wet with tears. "Somehow we will afford it," she said, her voice soft. "It would be the best thing for you."

John wished for her sake they could go. He had always dreamed of taking her to Scotland — showing her where he grew up, introducing her to his half-brothers and old friends. Yet he knew it wasn't possible, and there was no sense in dwelling on it. All he could do for now was love her for the thought and pray the new remedies would cure his throat so they could simply carry on as before.

Chapter Twenty-Eight

CROSSROADS

One Sunday in late March, Abram surprised the family by accompanying them to the evening services at church. John should have figured something was afoot. Though his youngest son often attended the morning service, he usually skipped evening vespers—always with some reason for not going. Yet on this night he sat in the pew between Irene and Ella, singing the hymns with unusual gusto.

He had seemed particularly restless on their return home from church. While the family sat reading in the parlor, he repeatedly clamored up and down the stairs to his room, sometimes talking to himself, even whistling. On his third or fourth trip, he hurried into the kitchen reappearing with what looked like a loaf of bread and a hunk of cheese, half hidden in his arms. He headed in the direction of the stairs yet again.

Ella put down her church lesson plan. "Are you hungry, Abram?"

The young man stopped, his foot on the lowest step, and mumbled, "No. Not right now."

"Are you expecting to be hungry later?" Ella motioned with her head, indicating the items in his hand.

Abram removed his foot from the stairs and turned to face the room, his gaze first settling on Ella, then John.

"I'm going to Alaska," he said.

No one spoke.

Abram hesitated a moment, as though waiting for a response. When none came, he added, "Tomorrow."

Ella gasped, and John closed his Bible. "A little forewarning would have been appreciated, son."

For a moment Abram seemed chagrined. "I suppose, but I didn't want you to try and argue me out of it. I was going to tell you when I finished packing. There's gold there, you know. Lots of it. And I've saved enough money to go. I've figured it all out."

Irene was the first to slice through the thick silence that followed. "Isn't it cold there?"

"It's cold *here*, Reenie. Anyway, it's a long way, and by the time I get there it will be summer."

"They have summer in Alaska?"

The girl was full of questions, none of them the ones piling up in John's mind. The first on the list spilled out before he gave time to think.

"How do you plan on getting there?"

"By train to Seattle. Then I'll take a ship. I have it planned out. Look." He walked to the center of the room, took a folded paper from his pocket, opened it up and laid it on the tea table. It was a map of the United States and beyond, including Canada and Alaska. "Here's Waterloo." He placed a finger at one point and followed a red, squiggly line he had drawn across the country and up to his destination. "And here's the Klondike. I already have my train ticket." His voice quivered with excitement.

Ella's face turned as white as her linen collar and cuffs. "What about electrician's school? Have you given that up?"

Abram didn't seem to notice her concern, or perhaps didn't care. John wasn't sure.

Abram just shrugged his shoulders, his grin as wide as ever. "I'll still do that—when I get back. And I'll have plenty of money from the gold fields to pay for my schooling." He refolded the map and stood. "Guess I'll head for bed. Morning will be here soon."

They all watched as Abram thumped up the stairs one last time, Irene following close behind, still asking questions.

Ella rubbed her forehead and sighed. "Guess I'll go to bed, too. I'm suddenly very tired."

"I'll join you shortly," John said.

But once in bed, he couldn't sleep. He sensed Ella lying beside him, also wide awake.

"He has no idea what a hard life that will be," she said, tension tightening her voice. "And the men he'll encounter—thieves, drunkards, murderers…"

John reached over and patted her arm. He was thinking the same thoughts regarding his son—so young, naive, and sensitive—but he knew better than to object. "The lad has to get this out of his system. He'll be okay and will come home with wonderful stories to tell."

He heard Ella sigh. "You men are all alike. You have no sense." She turned her back to him and said nothing more.

John lay for a long time staring at the dark ceiling.

I suppose she's right — men and women do not think the same. Is this really any different from the young lad who left his family in Scotland for a new life in America more than thirty years ago? In his mix of thoughts and emotions, he felt a twinge of jealously, wishing for a quick moment he were the one heading off again for a great adventure.

This time Abram's dreams had turned to reality, and he did indeed leave early the next morning, reducing the family to three. Though Abram's departure happened abruptly, John sensed it had been in the works for a long time. The adjustment for the rest of them would be a slow process.

There were national worries, too. John had been following the news with interest for weeks as tensions grew between Spain and the United States over Spanish rule in Cuba and the Philippines. On February 15th, the USS Maine, sent to Cuba to protect Americans there, sank due to an unexplained explosion that killed 260 of the crew. Though not determined for certain, everyone assumed Spain was responsible, and the prospect of a conflict had escalated since then.

John had taken to walking to the newsstand each morning to check the headlines, even though *The Evening Courier* was delivered to their doorstep later in the day. Spain had declared war on the United States, and everyone waited for what would come next. On April 25th, John returned from his morning sojourn, a paper tucked under his arm. Ella sat at the piano reviewing a lesson plan for one of her more advanced students. John propped the paper in front of her on the music rack.

"Well, it's happened," he said. "Congress has voted to go to war."

When Irene burst in the door after school, she brought the same news and seemed particularly upset. Gasping for breath, she appeared to have run home, face flushed, her curls asunder. "America is at war! Isn't that awful?"

John couldn't quite fathom this bit of inevitable news upsetting his daughter so much. Even if battles ensued, they would be far from Iowa.

"The boys are all leaving to join the army and go fight. What if they find Abram and make him go, too?" Irene asked.

John led his daughter to the settee, where he sat beside her. "They can't make a man go to war, Irene, and Abram probably doesn't even know about it. Anyway, he has his heart set on Alaska right now." John wondered how true his statements might be. Abram would learn about the war soon enough, and knowing the lad's adventurous nature, he just might abandon the notion of Alaska for something he considered more exciting.

John squeezed Irene's hand. "You're just like your mother, supposing something will happen and worrying about it before the fact."

Irene pulled a ribbon from her hair, fiddled with it in her fingers, and sighed. "Maybe, but war is serious. People die in wars." She seemed to think for a moment before adding, "Besides, Mama doesn't do that—worry. She finds a way to fix it. But she can't fix war."

A tiny pain stabbed John deep in his chest when he realized they were talking about two different women. Irene meant Ella, but John had been referring to Anna, the mother whom the girl didn't even remember. Stifling his hurt, he continued to reassure his daughter that Abram was not in danger, and, though people generally did not want war, sometimes it was the only way to right a wrong.

Papers for the following days were filled with news about preparations for the war. No state was exempt from its duty to provide soldiers, and that included Iowa. The state fairground in Des Moines was hastily converted to a military base named Camp McKinley, and Iowa guardsmen from the four corners of the state began arriving to be mustered in. Of special concern and pride were the local boys, Company B of the 49th Volunteer Infantry. Headlines for *The Evening Courier* on April 26th shouted: *FOR HUMANITY'S SAKE! REMEMBER THE MAINE! This was the battle cry on the Lips of Our Brave Boys! Waterloo's Gallant Soldier Lads Are Off to the War at Their Country's Call.* This referred to all those leaving by train for the camp in Des Moines, not the actual battlefield — yet.

Irene read the blaring words over John's shoulder. "Well," she said, "Abram's not in Iowa, so I guess he's safe."

Abram had been gone a month, and they had heard nothing from him yet. John tried to allay his daughter's fears. "He's halfway across the United States by now, probably exploring as he goes. It takes time for a letter to get from there to here." *Wherever that might be,* John thought, trying not to worry about his younger son.

And then a letter arrived on May 25th, but not the one they were expecting.

"Oh my, land. It's from Johnny, and the postmark is Des Moines," Ella exclaimed. She ripped open the seal and began reading:

Dear Folks,

This may surprise you. I have joined the guard in Shenandoah, as have a number of my classmates. It seems the right thing to do. We arrived at Camp McKinley by train yesterday and are to be mustered in on the 30th. We are the 51st Volunteer Infantry. I am in company L. I don't know yet where we will be shipped to. Some from here expect to go to a camp in Florida and from there to Cuba. The feeling is the war will not last long. So, who knows, I may not get any farther than Des Moines. If that is the case, I will come home for a few days before returning to Tabor.

More later, Johnny.

In all their concern for Abram running off to the gold fields at such a critical time, no one had thought about John Jr., safely ensconced, they assumed, at Tabor, studying for his future.

John admonished himself for this unbelievable oversight and was reminded of a long-ago conversation with the lad as he recovered from an injured foot. "I want to be a lawyer, and a soldier, should my country ever need me," he had said. That need had arrived.

John read everything he could on the situation. On May 1st, the first battle of the war was fought in the

Philippines. An American squadron, under the command of Commodore George Dewey, defeated Spanish naval forces at great cost to the Spaniards. Ten of their warships were either lost or captured, and 400 of their sailors killed. Six Americans were wounded.

"That is a promising start for us," John said. They were seated around the supper table, and, as usual, conversation turned to the war.

"But if the Spanish lost, doesn't that mean America won the war?" Irene mumbled, her mouth full.

"No, Irene," John said. "Unfortunately, wars are more complicated than just one battle. And this is the Philippines. Cuba is where they expect the real war to take place."

"Well, wherever Abram is, he's a long way from either place. I think he'll be all right, but now we have to worry about Johnny."

"At least Johnny has written," Ella said, "and he has promised more letters. It's about time we heard from Abram."

Ella's extrasensory perception seemed to be in tune again. The very next day, they received the long-awaited word from Abram, a postcard a little bent at the edges, from some place in Wyoming, the date and name of the city smudged. The front of the card showed a photo of jagged mountain peaks. On the back the lad had scrawled a brief message:

The Rocky Mountains are as high as the sky and stretch for miles! A sight to see! On my way to Seattle. More later, Abram.

"He's been on his way to Seattle for a month, and it

looks like he tucked the card in his pocket and forgot about it," Ella sighed. "At least it's something, though he should have stopped to see Cora on his way through Wyoming."

Two weeks later they heard from John Jr. again. A letter, dated June 5th, bore a few hurried words;

We are heading out today — destination San Francisco. Looking forward to seeing the west coast. Johnny.

At least his unit had missed the first encounter with Spain's forces, and Iowa's 51st Volunteer Infantry was obviously not headed for Cuba. Perhaps, John thought, his son's prediction that it would be over before they could get to the battlefront was an accurate guess.

Within days, word came that U.S. troops had landed at Guantanamo Bay in Cuba, and on June 22nd, more arrived near the city of Santiago. Fierce fighting ensued, with many losses on both sides. But America prevailed in the battle at San Juan Hill, and on July 3rd, Spain's Caribbean fleet was destroyed.

"Well, I hope that's it," Ella said, "though I won't be relieved until Johnny and the other Iowa boys are back where they belong."

Tension held the parsonage in its grip for reasons other than a son marching off to war and another seeking adventure. John's one-year leave of absence from the pulpit of the Waterloo Congregational Church crept closer — July 31st. Neither he nor Ella had spoken of this for several months. The last serious conversation had occurred the end of March, when John felt Dr. Ingals' remedies seemed to be helping. He had even obliged the pastoral committee on a couple of Sundays and preached when a substitute could not be found or failed to appear. These rare occasions boosted John's morale, especially when parishioners greeted him following the service with positive reactions.

However, as the weeks passed, John became more uncertain of his future in the pulpit. The lining of his throat often swelled to the point where he could hardly swallow. He spoke in raspy tones, sometimes making it difficult for others to understand his words. Eating was a problem, too. Soup went down, but not much else.

One hot, sticky Sunday morning in early July, John delivered a sermon when the substitute did not show up. At the last minute, to save the day, he pulled a reserve talk from his files, stepped up to the pulpit, and began with the usual belief and conviction that what he had written needed to be said. He stopped often for sips of water, wiped the perspiration trickling down his brow, and carried on. As his voice cracked and broke, he resorted to Dr. Ingals' inhaler tucked in the pulpit shelf. It was not one of his better presentations. Following the service, he stood in the narthex greeting parishioners, most of whom smiled in support and, he suspected, sympathy.

As the well-wishers thinned out, Moses Cross approached him. "Well, Dr. Stevenson, how is the throat? We need to have your answer soon. As much as we hope it is not to be the case, in the event you are unable to return, we need to start looking for a permanent replacement."

The words stung. Even though other preachers had stood in John's designated place at the front of the sanctuary for most of that year, it wasn't the same as being replaced permanently. This was his church, and the thought of turning it over to someone else brought a dull ache that kept spreading until there were times when it seemed to suffocate him. It would be a painful and difficult decision. Yet he knew he couldn't put it off any longer.

"I'll have an answer for you next week," he told Moses.

At that he turned and greeted Mrs. Alan who took his hand in hers, searching his eyes with a pleading look in hers. "We are praying for the healing of your throat, Reverend. Mr. Alan and I do so miss your wise words and wonderful wit."

That night, after Irene had gone to bed, John and Ella sat in the parlor, reading the Scriptures.

"You've been extra quiet tonight, John," Ella said.

He set the Bible aside and pinched his nose between his thumb and forefinger, attempting to swallow in a throat that wouldn't always allow it. "The committee needs to know if I plan on returning to the pulpit. I promised I would give them an answer in a week."

"And…?"

John sat in an attitude of prayer, his eyes closed, his breathing shallow. Minutes passed. Ella did not press him further.

Finally, with a huge sigh—more of a shudder—he replied, his voice soft and broken. "I think I must say no. I simply don't see how I can do it. There seems to be no cure for my throat."

Chapter Twenty-Nine

TRANSITIONS

John tendered his resignation on July 30th in an official letter to the membership of the Waterloo First Congregational Church. Much to-do was made over his decision, though it was no surprise. John found the many tributes spoken from the pulpit that last Sunday morning embarrassing but gratifying. The pastoral committee presented him with a testimonial, compelling him to stand before the congregation and make one last brief speech. He sipped water and cleared his throat, hoping his voice would not be too raspy, and ended with the comment, "I may be leaving as your pastor, but my wife and I intend to stay in Waterloo and be vital members of this church." He motioned for Ella to join him up front.

A standing ovation followed with loud cheers, even whistles. John waved and smiled at his "flock," and Ella dabbed at her cheeks with a small handkerchief.

A potluck followed the service, and by the time John and Ella left for the parsonage, his arm and fingers felt limp and sore from the many handshakes. His voice was completely gone.

They kicked off their shoes in the parlor and sat in silence. When the clock struck five, Ella rose. "I'll fix us a light supper before we go back for vespers."

"Play something first," John said, motioning toward the piano.

"Any special requests?" Ella asked, as she slid onto the piano bench.

John thought a moment. "Something from the hymnal." He lay his head back against the top of the over-stuffed chair. "How about "I Need Thee Every Hour"—and anything else you can think of. Let's skip vespers. I can't stand the thought of hearing 'we'll miss you' one more time." A giddiness took hold of him, a feeling of release. No longer the official minister, he could now occasionally skip a service like any other parishioner. Surely, under the circumstances, the Lord would understand.

Ella played for an hour, turning pages in the hymnal, blending one song into the next. John listened with eyes closed. Of all the tonics and remedies prescribed to him for his physical maladies, none soothed the soul as the God-created gift of music. Here he was at the end of a huge chapter in his life—the essence of his existence, the reason he left his familiar homeland, the reason he furthered his education for a divinity degree—to spread the words in the Bible as he believed God intended them to be told. He felt exhausted, but also relieved. He needed rest.

At breakfast the following morning, Irene chattered away as usual, talking of her plans for the day. "I would like to go to Gertrude's. She has a new dress she wants to show me, and I want to watch her brother ride his bicycle. Henry's very good, you know. He even competes in races."

John smiled at his daughter, thinking about how life goes on for the young. She was enjoying her summer break from school and seemed totally unaware of the worries and decisions confronting him and Ella. That was a good thing.

Ella poured more coffee for herself and topped off John's cup. "That sounds nice, dear. Have a good time. Just be back for dinner at noon."

A quiet settled over the kitchen after Irene left. John had slept well but spoke very little all morning. His mind seemed to alternate between being totally empty or filled with thoughts so jumbled he couldn't sort them out.

Ella stirred her coffee, put in more cream, then stirred again, the clinking of her spoon against the side of the china cup the only sound in the room. She stared into the beige liquid before lifting her gaze to John. He recognized that look, and a little alarm buzzed in his head.

"A letter came from Cora on Saturday," Ella said. "It was full of news, but you had so much on your mind that day, I didn't want to bother you."

"Bad news?" he asked with a twinge of anxiety. He couldn't imagine Ella keeping a letter from Cora a secret. Usually any word from this beloved sister ignited his wife to the point where she couldn't stop talking about it for days.

"No, not at all, but a lot to digest. She has been to Hawaii, of all places, to lecture. Can you believe it? But the real news is she has moved to Colorado where she will be teaching at another university."

"Well, that is something." John continued to be amazed at his progressive sister-in-law, though he still wasn't quite certain why Ella waited to bring this up until now, unless it was to keep his mind off their own indeterminate future. She answered that question in her next breath.

"I have an idea, John."

Oh, oh. Here it comes.

"We should take a trip. You need to get away from Waterloo—to sort things out. It would be a good break for both of us." Her face held that *don't argue with me* expression.

John chuckled and shook his head. "I knew you were up to something. You might be right, but don't count on it being Scotland."

"No, I realize that is not financially possible. How about Colorado Springs?"

The idea settled on John like soft silk. A trip to Colorado. "Maybe," he said, liking the idea better each moment. "We'll have to see about the cost. We'd bring Irene, of course. That would be three train fares." He did some quick mental calculations. Worrisome figures swam in his head. One of the financial dilemmas facing them was housing. The parsonage would have to be vacated before the new minister arrived. John had never paid rent or a mortgage since receiving his divinity degree. Living quarters were provided by the congregation of each of the churches he had pastored— a compensation for a meager salary, a benefit that would soon be gone.

While all these thoughts skated through his mind, Ella scooted her chair closer, entwining her fingers in his. "And I have another surprise."

He squeezed her hand and looked into her eyes. They held the dangerous sparkle that appeared when she glowed with anticipation, but also something else. A hint of nervousness?

She clung to his hand as though it were a lifeline, closed her eyes for a moment, then blurted, "I have approached the Gates and Liffring law offices about work. I am being hired as office assistant full time starting next month."

John let out a long breath. So, that was it, and this time she knew he would not, *could not,* argue. For years he had been preaching that men and women were equal—even stressing it was biblical truth. Ella had dutifully served at home with the children when she was needed there—a woman's first calling, he still believed. But now he recognized her talents were required beyond the home. Her abilities as a stenographer were the solution to their financial worries.

John swallowed his pride and hugged her. "God bless you, dear wife. God bless you." The future suddenly seemed less bleak, and a much-needed vacation a real possibility. A look of relief in Ella's eyes replaced the anxiety John had seen there moments before. She returned his hug and smiled. Nothing more needed to be said right then. But once the idea of a trip had settled in their minds, they talked of nothing else for hours. Ella's job began in early September, so they decided to leave Waterloo in a week. There was a lot to prepare.

Meanwhile, John continuously kept track of information related to the war. After victory in Cuba, peace terms were being negotiated with Spain. John felt a weight lift when he read the account in the paper. Perhaps his oldest son would not have to go to war after all. He looked for Ella to share the news and found her in the garden, kneeling beside a row of carrots, her hair tied back with a large kerchief, a trowel in her hand. She sat back and wiped her brow and listened while John relayed this latest information.

"Well, that is very good news," Ella remarked. "It looks like Johnny's military career will be short-lived. Praise the Lord."

John squatted beside her and began pulling weeds, pondering the war situation. He wanted to believe the troops were coming home, but were they? He wouldn't feel complete relief until his son showed up on their doorstep. There were still thousands of soldiers stationed in San Francisco—a long way from Cuba, but closer to the Philippines and unresolved issues relating to Spanish rule.

A message from John Jr. dated July 15th did not explain the military's intent for these troops. However, the letter brought with it the welcome knowledge the lad was still safe.

Dear Papa,

We arrived at Camp Merritt on June 11th — a sad excuse for a camp. Part of it was a race track before it was set up for organizing the military. Many of the soldiers have gotten sick with a form of small pox. I heard that 80 men from our unit were in the hospital and I know of at least one death. I am well.

Rumor has it that we are to be transferred to nearby Camp Merriam in a week or so, and none too soon. I hear it is a much better camp.

I don't know yet when we are to be shipped out, if at all, but will keep you advised.

Your loving son, John Jr.

Three days later, as John and Ella prepared for the trip to Colorado, the postman brought another letter. "Looks like you hit the jackpot this week," he said. "This one's from your other boy."

The envelope, a trifle smudged, bore Abram's unmistakable penmanship, postmarked Seattle a week prior. They had received several postcards from the lad since he left home. He had meandered—stopping here and there at places that particularly interested him, and maybe, John guessed, with the intent of reaching Alaska when the weather might be a little warmer. This was the first real letter from him, four pages long, in which Abram exclaimed over the countryside he had passed through. His enthusiasm for mining gold had not waned.

I am in Seattle waiting for a ship to take me to Alaska. Today it is raining. Yesterday it rained, also, and the day before that. I plan to buy a slicker. It may be raining in Alaska, too, even though it is summer. The next time I write I should be digging up gold. Hope you are all fine. Everyone is talking about the war.

Your son, Abram K. Stevenson

Knowing both boys were safe was the perfect send-off for their trip to Colorado.

"We will see Abram's Rocky Mountains for ourselves," John told Ella, as they boarded the first of many trains that would take them to Colorado Springs. His sense of adventure stirred, reconfirming this escape was a good idea.

Irene had not come, opting instead to stay with her friend Gertrude's family. John sensed her decision was influenced by a crush on Gertrude's brother Henry. John smiled at the thought of his youngest daughter growing up. Her staying behind saved a train fare, but everyone's satisfaction with the arrangement was what mattered most.

Once they arrived in Colorado Springs, John relaxed and enjoyed the different terrain. It was more barren than he had imagined, but the magnificent mountains dominated the horizon, an awe-inspiring contrast to the gentle hills of Iowa. John busied himself by visiting the local newspaper office, searching for anything he could find on why the woman's suffrage movement had been successful in this forward-thinking state. Cora and Ella swirled in their own little world, oblivious to his absence and explorations. The two women talked on and on.

The only negative incident during the visit occurred one evening as they prepared for bed in the privacy of the guest room. Ella had approached John with hope etched on her face. "Once you dreamed of moving here because of your hay fever. It didn't happen because none of the churches contacted had a vacancy for a man with a family, but that has changed, John. You are retired. And we would be close to Cora."

He shook his head. "Things are different now, Ella. My breathing seems better, and no place will help my throat. Waterloo is our home, and you have a much-needed job waiting for you there. It would be hard to uproot Irene, and then there would be the expense of moving…" Ella turned away with a sigh. He sensed she knew it wasn't going to happen even before she asked, yet her disappointment stirred the air like a chill wind.

Ella slept most of the long way back to Waterloo, lulled by the rhythm of the train, while John refocused on other concerns. During their trip, Spain signed an armistice and the United States troops captured Manila in a mock skirmish. The war seemed to be coming to a close. Surely, on their arrival home, there would be a letter from Johnny saying he was being mustered out and returning to college. John tried not to worry about Abram, who likely was already in the wild Alaskan gold fields.

The first full day home, he strode in the muggy August heat to the church. As he entered the rear door, the sound of hammering banged from the direction of the pastor's study.

"Hellooo," he hollered over the pounding.

The noise stopped, and Moses Cross appeared in the doorway, coatless, his shirtsleeves rolled up. "Reverend, it's good to see you. How was your trip?"

"Fine. I came to check on the racket going on here. We could hear it way over at the parsonage."

Moses laughed. "Well, I didn't think it was that

loud. We're putting up a few more shelves for the new pastor."

John flinched at this. He had asked for more shelves several times, then given up, knowing it was one more expense for the church. Instead of adding pressure, he kept several boxes of books shoved in the corner where he could get to them if needed.

"That's why I'm here," he said, slipping into the familiar chair at the desk, his chair, where he had spent so many hours writing sermons and counseling parishioners—*no, not his chair anymore.* He must adjust to the idea. "About the new pastor," he continued, "have you found someone? Ella and I are wondering when we will need to vacate the parsonage."

Moses laid down the hammer and pulled up another chair and sat. "We're not certain, but we're hoping the Reverend Allen Tanner from Pueblo, Colorado, will take the job. If you recall, he filled the pulpit once as a guest preacher and was well received. We're waiting for a definite answer from him."

"When have you proposed that he come?" John felt his heartbeat accelerate. Suddenly things were moving too fast, and the irony of the new pastor coming from Colorado almost seemed a mockery.

"Well," Moses said, "there's bad news for the church but probably good news for you and Ella. Tanner has indicated if he comes it won't be until after the first of the year, so the parsonage will still be rent free for you until then. And another thing, we planned to approach you about this in a few days after you had rested up from your trip. We're thinking it's time for a new parsonage. Would you be willing to buy the old one if we give you a good deal?"

John nearly flew home. Not only would they be able to stay in the parsonage, but the church wanted him to continue in his role of visiting the shut-ins for pay until the new minister arrived. He burst through the front door. "Ella!" He called out in as loud a voice as his ailing throat allowed. "Ella!"

She rushed into the entry hall from the kitchen, drying her hands on her apron, concern etched on her face. "John, what is it? Are you all right?"

He picked her up and swung her around, kissing her hard on the mouth.

She looked up at him in astonishment. "My word! Have you gone crazy?"

They sat at the kitchen table while he explained to her about the parsonage.

"That's wonderful news, but do you think we can afford to buy it? What terms have they offered?"

"Moses said he would get back to me on that. However, they know our situation and will do everything they can to be fair."

"We can do it, John," Ella said, her jaw set in determination. "We have to."

He knew she was right. Things were falling into place. Now if he could only find a focus for his own uncertain future. Ill health had snatched his true calling like a malicious thief. Yet he had been a loyal servant of the Lord. Surely, God must have a plan.

Chapter Thirty

A DARK WINTER

Ella started work the following week. At first things seemed topsy-turvy. John saw Irene off to school in the morning and greeted her when she arrived home in the afternoon. He was not a cook, but Ella left instructions each day on what to prepare ahead of time, so she and Irene could complete meals in the early evening. John was good at washing dishes and sweeping the floor. If any visitors came to the house, he made certain he was not wearing an apron when he answered the door.

He clung to his one official connection to the church—visitations. For those shut-ins reasonably close by, he walked, humming hymns along the way to keep his spirits up, his gait matching the cadence of the musical notes. The cool autumn air helped his mood. He enjoyed this part of ministering—always had. And if he was careful not to overuse his throat prior to the visits, he felt—in spite of a squawk now and then—his voice was understood well enough. Of course, some homebound parishioners were easier to see than others. Mrs. Thompkins offered cookies and tea and asked a multitude of questions, mostly he suspected, to keep him there a little longer. Old Mr. Davis, hard of hearing, smiled and nodded in agreement, no matter what John said, and occasionally dozed off. Mrs. Nelson, in the last stages of dementia, never knew he was there, but it meant a lot to her daughter, Rachel, who knelt with John beside the bed and prayed.

John made notes regarding the visitations, and at the end of each week presented them to Moses—not required, but a self-satisfying confirmation he was doing his job.

One bright fall afternoon, when he had completed his regular rounds, he decided to check on Leroy. It had been some time since he had done so. Hearsay about the man's health came and went. John usually wasn't welcome. Leroy rarely came to the door. Yet John couldn't give up on the man. He rapped at the door, waited a moment, then knocked again to no response. He was about to leave a note under the mat when he heard footsteps and the door swung open. To his astonishment, there stood Beatrice.

"Hello, Reverend." She looked older, of course, and wan—wearing a faded blue cotton dress and soiled apron. She appeared to have lost weight, but she smiled, tucking a wayward wisp of hair behind her ear. "It's good to see you, though I can't ask you in. Leroy is not doing well today."

"What a nice surprise to find you here," John said. "Is… is Leroy failing?" he couldn't bring himself to say dying. Yet he couldn't erase the image in his mind of the man so near death during his last visit.

"No, not really, though I heard he might be and felt it my duty to come care for him." She hesitated a moment, twisting her apron in her hands. "Rumors also said he had stopped drinking, and I thought maybe there was hope we could return home."

"And the boys?" John wasn't sure how much he should ask, but curiosity clawed at him.

"They're not here. They're older now, you know, not as dependent as when we left."

Yet, she had said "we." So surely, John thought, they were here sometimes.

"Well, if there is anything Ella and I can do, please let us know. I've always had hope for Leroy. I'll continue to keep both of you in my prayers."

"Thank you."

Without further comment, she closed the door, leaving John standing on the porch, full of questions, and feeling unsettled about the situation. Beatrice seemed worn down. He wondered how long she had been there. Had Leroy stopped drinking? He had promised to so many times.

Later that evening, John relayed the encounter to Ella. "She said she came back because she heard he had stopped drinking and wasn't well, and thought she should be home to take care of him." John shook his head. "She's tried it before only to leave battered and bruised."

"She should have divorced him long ago," Ella said impatiently, obviously tired herself from working at the law firm all day. "She could have remarried and had a good life for her and the boys."

John let her remark pass. They had held this conversation before, and he wasn't in an arguing mood.

He decided to leave well enough alone and not return to the Cooper home—at least for a while. He still felt unwelcome, even with Beatrice there. As promised, he prayed daily for things to improve in their household, hoping finally, after all these years, the couple could find some peace and happiness together.

But John couldn't dwell on Leroy and Beatrice's problems. Bigger concerns occupied his mind. A recent letter from John Jr. hinted his unit might be shipped out soon, and days later the news confirmed that on November 3rd, the 51st Iowa Volunteer Infantry had boarded the transport *Pennsylvania,* scheduled to arrive in Manila Bay in early December.

Irene turned ashen upon hearing the news when she returned from school. Dropping her homework, she plopped onto the parlor floor, fingering a page of one of the books that had flung open. "Does that mean Johnny's going to fight?"

"Probably, Irene. That's why he volunteered, to help where he could. For young men, that usually means fighting."

She obviously didn't like the answer, and at supper that evening, after John blessed the food, Irene added, "and please keep Johnny safe. Don't let him get killed."

Later that evening, in their bedroom with Irene out of earshot, Ella voiced a concern that had dangled in the shadow of John's mind for weeks.

"From reports and Johnny's letters, I'm more concerned about him dying from smallpox or typhoid fever than being killed in battle. Have you read the statistics?"

"Yes," John said, his tone solemn. The local papers frequently listed the names of soldiers from Iowa—dead from the dread diseases while they waited in makeshift camps to be sent off to battle. "Those men are exposed to so much, and they haven't even been to war yet. It's such a tragedy."

On December 10th, the Treaty of Paris was signed wherein Spain relinquished its claim to Cuba; Puerto Rico, Guam and the Philippines were placed under American control. John handed the newspaper account to Ella when she walked into the house from work.

"I've already heard. It's the talk in the office." She removed her gloves, took the paper to the parlor, lowered herself onto the settee and read, while John sat on the piano bench watching her expression. She looked up at him and sighed. "Maybe this will be the end of it. They'll pull those ships out of there and send our boys home."

John shook his head, wishing he were that convinced. "Let's hope so. But the Philippines, and especially its self-appointed governor Emilio Aguinaldo, want to be an independent country. I suspect things aren't over yet."

~ ~ ~

THE UNCERTAINTY ABOUT JOHNNY CAUSED AN UNEASINESS to hang over the old parsonage during the month of December. Christmas lost some of its cheer with both boys gone, and bad weather kept Margaret from making the trip home for the holidays. War news dominated the household. Daily reports said the

Pennsylvania seemed to languish, first in Manila, then in Iloilo Bay. A letter from Johnny expressed dismay and boredom.

Nothing's happening here. And we're not quite sure what's going on. Rumors are that General Aguinaldo is gearing up to fight for independence.

John wrote letters of encouragement and news of home to the lad often. He also occupied his time by writing magazine and newspaper articles, especially to *The Woman's Standard*, the editors of which seemed particularly eager to receive his work. Some papers paid him for his work; *The Standard* did not, but he found his submissions to that publication the most satisfying.

~ ~ ~

EARLY IN 1899, TO THE RELIEF OF ALL THE PARISHIONERS, the Reverend Allen Tanner arrived to lead the Waterloo Congregational Church. John knew the members were more than weary of guest preachers and empty pulpits when substitutes were not available. The Reverend Tanner's coming also meant any church allowance for a parsonage went to the new pastor. John and Ella began paying a mortgage for the first time. It was quite a pinch, but with Ella's salary, John's income from writing, and a few donations from generous and faithful friends, they managed. It felt satisfying to know the only house they had lived in since coming to Waterloo was permanently theirs.

On Reverend Tanner's first Sunday in the pulpit, John, Ella, and Irene arose extra early and donned their best clothes. "We don't want to be late for the Reverend's opening remarks," John said as he buffed his shoes to a high shine. Something akin to a small whirlwind spun in his stomach, unsettling his breakfast. He tried to still it by filling his head with calm thoughts: *Why should I be nervous? It's Reverend Tanner's big day, not mine.* But they didn't assuage his feelings in the least. In fact, John suspected part of his anxiety was fear that the congregation would embrace the new pastor with great enthusiasm, leaving the memory of their fondness for him to crumble in the dust. Guilt grabbed him when this realization crossed his mind, and as he redid his tie for the third time, he murmured a silent prayer, *Dear Lord, please forgive me for these selfish thoughts.*

"You look fine, John," Ella said upon observing his struggle with the tie. She reached over and perfected it for him. "What's your concern? Reverend Tanner is the one who should be nervous. You should be relaxed and relieved it's not you up there searching for the perfect words to please the congregation."

She was right, but she also didn't understand. He had relished writing those words and sharing them with his flock.

The morning went well, despite John's misgivings, though it was evident from the morning's sermon that members of the Waterloo Congregational Church would be receiving very different messages from those of the Reverend John Stevenson. It appeared some different views would be replacing those John and preached, but he supposed that was to be expected. The morning ended in a welcome potluck where everyone hovered around the new pastor. John and Ella slipped away before the meal ended.

"It's his day," Ella said. "We should leave so we are not a distraction."

They had taken the buggy, as metal gray skies promised snow. Homeward bound, Blaze plodded along the icy roadway, an occasional crystalline flake landing on the horse's dark rump. Irene, who sat bundled up between the warmth of John and Ella, spoke only once. "The Reverend Tanner seems very nice, but I like your sermons better, Papa."

John transferred the reins to his left hand and gave his daughter a hug. "Thank you, Irene, but it's Reverend Tanner's turn to preach, and the people need to hear new thoughts."

Winter teased Waterloo for two days offering a few flurries here and there. On Wednesday afternoon, the weather got serious—snow falling steadily, quietly covering shrubbery, walkways, and streets with soft, clean layers of white. John stood at the window marveling at God's seasons and the reasons for each. He had settled in his study early that day to write. Perhaps putting pen to paper would somehow propel him toward his future, though he was still uncertain what that might be. As he gazed out at the wooly weather, he was startled to see an official-looking horse-drawn wagon pull up in front of the house. A burly man climbed down from the vehicle and skittered up the icy walk, slipping once, almost taking a tumble. John hurried to the front door to let him in.

In the entryway, the man removed his hat, gloves,

and overcoat, shaking fresh snow onto the rug. John motioned to the hall tree where the visitor hung the wet items before offering his hand for John to shake.

"Reverend Stevenson?"

John nodded, then gave a start, recognizing the man and the familiar star on his chest: the marshal from his visits to the jail.

"How may I help you? This must be an important errand to bring you out on such a wintery afternoon."

"Is there a place we can talk in private?" The man glanced toward the stairs leading to the second floor. Irene, obviously hearing the voices, was making her way down toward them, curiosity highlighting her face.

John ushered the officer into his study, gave his daughter a look that said she was not invited, and closed the door. He sat at his desk and motioned to an empty chair. The man sat heavily and began talking. "I believe you are acquainted with Leroy Cooper and often visit that household?"

The immediate thought racing through John's mind was, *Poor Beatrice. Leroy is back to the bottle and in jail again.* Yet something seemed a little off-kilter. Never before had John been approached by the authorities when Leroy was picked up for being drunk.

"I'm well acquainted with the Cooper family and Leroy's problems. However, I haven't visited there recently. Frankly, I'm not welcome."

The marshal pulled a pad of paper from a vest pocket and began to scribble notes. "Are you aware that his wife and sons are back living with him?"

"I knew Beatrice was there, at least she was the last

time I tried to see Leroy, but that was several months ago. I don't think the boys were there the day I visited."

"And when exactly was that—the day you were last there."

An alarm went off in John's head. He didn't like the way the questioning was going. This wasn't a routine follow-up from a drunk arrest. He tried to think back to the date of his encounter with Beatrice at their home and shook his head. "I can't tell you specifically right now, but if it's important, I'm sure I could get that information. The church has written reports of my in-home visits. May I ask what this is about?" A vision of Beatrice's bruised face, so long ago, flashed through his mind.

The marshal scratched more notes, cleared his throat then looked John steadily in the eye. "Leroy Cooper is dead—found this morning in his home. Looks like he's been there for quite some time."

John rubbed his hand across his forehead—*Dear God, no*. He couldn't speak for a few moments, absorbing the enormity of what he had just heard. He released a deep breath. "Poor soul. I knew the drink would catch up with him sometime."

"Doesn't appear he was done in by drink. He was bludgeoned to death—lots of dried blood, his skull bashed in. No sign of the wife or boys. We were hoping you knew of their whereabouts."

Chapter Thirty-One

LETTERS

1899

"Was that the marshal?" Irene asked, wide-eyed, as John closed the door behind the deputy.

"Yes. He had some information and questions for me."

"You couldn't have done anything wrong," she said, with a nervous but inquisitive quiver to her voice. "You're a minister."

"No, Irene, it didn't have to do with me. It's about Mr. Cooper." *Should he tell her? Of course, she is thirteen years old, and the news will be all over the city in hours.* "He was found dead this morning. In his home." John decided he wouldn't mention the gory details.

The girl plopped onto a chair, her face white with shock. "Oh, my goodness gracious. Dead? Really dead? What happened?"

"They don't know yet." John sat, too, picking up the Bible that always lay on the tea table in the parlor. It was then he realized his hands were trembling, and the thoughts pouring through his mind did nothing to calm his emotions. *Why was the marshal so sure Leroy had been murdered? He could have fallen in a drunken stupor and hit his head — a perfectly logical explanation. Where were Beatrice and the boys? Did they know Leroy was dead? Had Beatrice hit back when attacked by a drunken husband, or did one of the boys try to protect her?* These last thoughts made John cringe. How many beatings would a person take before something snapped, resulting in a defensive blow strong enough to be fatal, whether intended or not?

John hadn't offered any of these questions or suggestions to his visitor, but sensed the authorities thought family members were responsible. All he could say to the marshal was he honestly knew nothing of the whereabouts of Beatrice and the boys. And for the first time, after all his searching for the woman in the past, he was glad he had never found her hiding place.

John prayed daily for the family. Surely, they were still being sought, but nothing indicated they had been found. In the meantime, Leroy's remains were laid to rest in a pauper's grave. John, Ella, and several parishioners who had known the man in his better days drove their carriages to the forlorn site in a fierce windstorm. The gale cut through their winter clothing like icy daggers as the small group hovered around the grave. John recited Psalm 23 and asked the Lord to forgive Leroy for his sins—words that blew away in gusts, as did the notes of "Abide with Me" sung by the clutch of mourners.

On their return home, Ella, her features somber and her voice heavy, said, "I think the devil was there today. I'm sure I heard him laughing."

"Now, Ella, don't be harsh. That was only the wind. There was good in Leroy's soul. There is in all of us. Let the poor man rest in peace. Some folks simply can't handle drink, and I believe it is something beyond their control. That's where the devil comes in."

John had not sensed the presence of Satan there. However, on the periphery of the cemetery stood the same marshal who had brought the news of Leroy's death—watching, John suspected, for Beatrice and the boys to appear. They had not.

The troublesome events surrounding Leroy's death spurred John to write. Thoughts on temperance, divorce, and a woman's rights, poured from his pen. Some of his essays appeared in the local newspaper and some in *The Woman's Standard*.

Ironically, the murder of Leroy Cooper, supposedly by his wife's hand, wasn't the only murder by a woman in the news. A year before, Mrs. Martha Place of New York had been tried and convicted of murdering her step-daughter. Now in Sing Sing Prison, she awaited the electric chair. Mrs. Place was destined to be the first woman in the United States to be executed. The papers were full of her pending death, and John couldn't help but think of Beatrice Cooper. If she were found and convicted, would she face the death chamber? He couldn't imagine this once lovely lady being subjected to such a fate—all because of unfortunate circumstances. She did try to be a good wife.

Over the years, Elizabeth Cady Stanton had stumped for women on trial for murder and, in tandem with other suffragists, had succeeded in reversing the sentencing of a couple of women who had been victims of a society dominated by male standards. Now, with Mrs. Place's probable execution looming, Mrs. Stanton once again voiced her thoughts publicly on the subject, saying that a woman shouldn't be executed for murder when she had no hand in making the law that condemned her.

In response, the editor of the *Waterloo Courier* wrote, *"This is an argument that has no top or bottom. It can easily go on forever. Why punish or restrain women at all if they have no voice in making the laws? Why punish children? Unless women can do as they please in the making of the laws, they must be allowed to do as they please in breaking them. The whole pivot of Mrs. Stanton's argument is woman – not justice."*

John read these comments to Ella while she worked in the kitchen kneading dough for loaves of bread. "He failed to catch Mrs. Stanton's point," he said, tapping at the paper he held. "The pivot of her argument against the execution of women *is* justice. It is unjust to cause one to suffer under laws in the making of which they have neither voice nor vote. That's exactly what I'm going to say in my rebuttal."

John knew Ella was listening by the way she set her jaw. He waited while she divided the dough into several pans before stopping to wash her hands. Then she turned to him, her voice sharp. "I take offense at how he lumps women and children together. Women are not children. It is unjust to punish them as if they were."

"A very good point, Ella." John hammered one fist into the other as the gears in his head turned. "I'll use that in my argument. The writer apparently thinks of all women as inferior to men in some way." He left his wife with her project, marched into his study and sat at his desk. Picking up his pen, he immediately put his thoughts to paper.

Satisfied with his response, he sent a copy to the *Courier, The Waterloo Democrat,* and to *The Woman's Standard.*

The following day, the editor for the *Democrat* had more to say on the subject and countered John's response, writing: *That Rev. Stevenson thinks women oughtn't to be punished for breaking a law which they had no voice in making. An untenable position for a preacher. If it is unjust to exact obedience to a law from individuals who had no voice in making the law, then God is unjust when he demands of us obedience to His laws.*

John quickly wrote a rebuttal: *The position taken by Mrs. E. C. Stanton is quite tenable either by man or woman, preacher or layman. If man were God or Creator and woman were his creature it would be just for man to punish woman for breaking his laws, but man is not God nor Creator and woman is not his creature and therefore it is unjust for man to treat woman either under law or in any other way as if she was his creature.*

He had a lot more to say, and said it, sending his response again to the *Waterloo Democrat and The Woman's Standard.*

"I'm going to send copies of all this to Mrs. Stanton, too," John told Ella. "I also wrote a review of her book, *The Woman's Bible,* for *The Woman's Standard* and I'm going to include it in my mailing."

"I think that is a marvelous idea," Ella said. "Mrs. Stanton needs to know the suffragists have such a staunch male supporter as yourself. She needs to know who you are. And she's not getting any younger. She needs to know now." She reached into her knitting bag and pulled out a copy of *The Woman's Bible*. "Here's the copy you borrowed from Sarah Whitney. It's an amazing piece of work. The dedication of that woman is astounding." Ella paused a moment, a pensive look on her face, and sighed before she continued. "And to think she has fought for our equality for years and has not yet seen her efforts come to full fruition."

John posted his packet to Mrs. Stanton the following day. His steps to the post office held an energy he hadn't felt for months. Purposeful goals gave him the drive he had sought since his retirement from the pulpit.

~ ~ ~

IN THE MEANTIME, THE REVEREND TANNER HAD SETTLED into his duties at church. John didn't always agree with the man's sermons, but the congregation seemed to thrive on a new approach. They raised funds to add classrooms, a new pastor's study, a dining room and a kitchen to the rear of the existing building.

John wrote to his three children of these improvements, trying to sound open-minded about the whole situation. Maggie's responses from Shenandoah always came immediately. The boys were another matter. John was never quite certain where to send letters to Abram or whether he received them. It seemed forever before they heard from him and always a relief when they did.

"He doesn't say too much about getting rich," Ella

commented, after reading one of Abram's notes, "and the thought of him having to hide any gold he finds so it won't get stolen is very disturbing."

"It's a good experience," John said. "He needed to learn for himself that even finding gold has its price." Yet John felt Abram had been gone too long, and he wished the boy would come home.

Notes from John Jr. brought a different mood. He was good about writing, and they had a general idea of his whereabouts, which added to the stress. Though the clashes in Cuba had ended in an armistice in August, and the war was officially over in December with the signing of the Treaty of Paris, things were not quite settled. In February of the new year, the Philippine-American War broke out, involving the Iowa 51st Infantry in its battles. Letters from Johnny told of the brutality he witnessed. In one letter, he wrote that the campaign in the deep mud of the great Candaba swamp had been very trying to the health of the regiment and had put more than half of the men in the hospital.

It's all very hard on account of the heat. I have seen boys laid out, crazy, trembling and shaking, oblivious to all their surrounds. I have experienced thirst before, but not such a blind, raging desire as I have under the Philippine sun. The water is foul; the food is the same. We have to carry our food. In the morning we wrap up some bacon in a paper and fill our pockets with hard tack, but after wading through swamps and creeks, you can imagine what the condition of the bacon and hard tack is.

He mentioned that the casualties among the

Americans had been light so far, but many insurgents had been killed, adding:

It is horrible to see a man die no matter which side he is on. I suspect I will have nightmares about this for the rest of my life. It is not what God intended for man to do — slaughter our fellow humans.

John's heart constricted in pain for what the boy was witnessing. He bowed his head and whispered a prayer not only for his son's strength and safety, but for all the young men involved, and for peace in the Philippines.

The battles continued and, according to reports, the Iowa 51st Infantry fought at various Philippine locations throughout April. Each night John, Ella, and Irene held hands and prayed for the war to end. By mid-May some reports said the war was over, but a letter from Johnny dated early June told of units being fired upon. He also complained about the food, lack of proper clothing, and inferior rifles.

Though mail delivery at the Stevenson household often became a source of anxiety, there was also good correspondence to be had. One day, a special surprise arrived in a simple envelope—a personal letter from Elizabeth Cady Stanton responding to John's packet of several weeks before, her bold, nearly illegible handwriting scrawled across three pages:

250, West 94th
N.Y. June 7, 1899
John Stevenson,

Dear Sir,

*Many thanks for the copies of the Woman's Standard &
for your most complimentary review. It is the very best I have
had from either English or American Press. It is evident in
the case of most reviewers that they have not read the book.
But you have read, marked, and invariably digested the
contents.*

*I will send you a copy to give your mother, wife, or
fiancé... I believe I sent both of my books to the Woman's
Standard, if not let me know & I will do so.*

With kind regards,
Yours Sincerely,
Elizabeth Cady Stanton

Ella seemed even more thrilled than John at this
piece of personal correspondence from the great lady
herself. "Oh, John! I think you should frame it. I can
hardly wait for the book to come."

The package arrived a week later accompanied by a
tidy and readable letter dictated by Mrs. Stanton to her
secretary:

Dear Mr. Stevenson,

*In dedicating my book to your wife, you perceive I leave a
place for her maiden name which she must insert in the best
possible chirography. It is one of my principles that every
married woman should claim her own name, adding her
husband's merely as an appendix. I shall be thankful for your
efforts to extend the circulation of my books.*

Sincerely,
Elizabeth Cady Stanton,

Per sec.

Ella immediately penned in her maiden name, then hugged the book. "Thank you, John, and thank you Mrs. Stanton! This shall be one of my most prized possessions. I think we should give it a place of honor by the King James Bible on the tea table."

John chuckled at the irony of the gesture. "That should raise the eyebrows of any guests who come visiting."

"Well," Ella said, "it will be a great opener for conversation."

A rap on the front door interrupted the moment. John glanced at Ella. "Were you expecting someone?"

Ella shook her head and glided to the door, obviously still in a mood of enchantment over her personalized copy of *The Woman's Bible*.

John followed close behind, taking a step backward as Ella swung the door open. There stood two formidable women, Sarah Ware Whitney and Mary Jane Coggeshall.

Sarah smiled and spoke first. "Hello, Doctor and Mrs. Stevenson. Pardon us for arriving unannounced, but Mrs. Coggeshall happened to be in town, and we've been engaged in an important conversation. Could we please come in?"

John's heart flip-flopped. He had a feeling his future was about to change.

Chapter Thirty-Two

SHADOW OF DOUBT

"Why, of course. Please come in. What an honor to have you ladies stop by." Ella ushered the unexpected guests into the parlor. "I'll fix some tea for you to enjoy while you and the Reverend talk." She gave John a triumphant glance as she whisked out of the room.

She senses it, too, John thought. He settled in a chair opposite the two ladies on the settee. Sarah Whitney removed her gloves, gave a little cough, then turned to the older woman sitting primly beside her. "Do you want to do the honors, or shall I?"

Mrs. Coggeshall, smiled and nodded her consent. "You may."

"Reverend—Doctor Stevenson," Mrs. Whitney began, "the members of the Iowa Woman Suffrage Association and the readers of *The Woman's Standard* have been impressed with the quality and forthrightness of the articles you have submitted. You may or may not know, in February I offered to buy *The Standard* in order to continue publication. The executive committee of the Association agreed unanimously. We are now looking for a new editor and hope you will take on that responsibility."

"Though it is currently published in Sutherland," Mrs. Coggeshall jumped into the conversation, "for your convenience we can move it to Waterloo."

"There will be some pay," Sarah Whitney continued, "though I'm afraid not much. It will depend on the subscription base."

"And we feel with your talents, you can build that," Mrs. Coggeshall added. She looked directly at John as she spoke, her expression full of anticipation.

Ella arrived carrying a tray with cups and saucers, a pot of tea, and thin slices of cake, happily left over from a church meeting the evening before. After she poured tea for each of their visitors, John stood and offered her his chair. He cleared his troubled throat, wanting to speak as clearly as possible.

"These ladies are asking me to take on the job of editor for *The Woman's Standard*," John said. "What do you think?"

Ella's face almost glowed. "It's your decision, but surely you know I approve. It's a very wise choice on their part."

"Well, ladies, there's your answer," John said. "You know I would not do this without the approval of the woman in my life. I am honored you asked, and I will be happy to accommodate your request."

Sarah Whitney turned to her friend with a victory smile. "See, I told you he would. There is no one as capable and sincere in his desire for woman's rights as Doctor Stevenson. His writings attest to that."

They chatted for a half hour more. John would begin his responsibilities in September, a month away, and prior to that would meet with the executive committee of the Iowa Equal Suffrage Association in Des Moines to discuss details and sign any necessary agreements.

After the ladies said their goodbyes and John had closed the front door behind them, he took Ella in his arms. "Well, my dear, you are still the major breadwinner in this family, but at least now your husband can add a little more to the household kitty. And, best of all, he finally has direction and will be working toward something worthwhile."

She gave him a tight hug. "I am so happy for you, John, and equally happy for the cause. We can only go forward from here."

~ ~ ~

THE FALL OF 1899 BROUGHT MORE PROMISING NEWS. ON September 22, the Iowa 51st Infantry left the Philippines for San Francisco. John Jr. wrote:

We are scheduled to arrive about October 22. I'm not certain yet when we will be mustered out, soon I hope. But at least the horrors of war are behind us.

"His tone certainly changed over time," Ella said. "I doubt he will ever volunteer to fight again."

"Once he is back in college working toward his real future, he can leave those bad memories behind," John said. The boy's letters had concerned him, and he hoped those experiences, perhaps not forgettable, would at least become dormant.

"Thank God, he didn't get killed or die from sickness like so many others," Irene said, visibly relieved after reading this latest letter. John knew the girl had lived in constant fear of losing her brother during the past year and a half.

And so, buoyed by good family news, plus the editorship of *The Woman's Standard,* John felt solidly upright for the first time in months. He spent hours in his study, writing, thinking, re-writing, and loving every minute of it. After meeting with the committee in Des Moines, he soared even higher. The suffragists of Iowa were eager to have him on board.

At suppertime on the eve of his first deadline, he gulped down the last spoonful of stew, wiped his mouth with his napkin, and stood. "Delicious as always, Ella, but I must excuse myself to finish up an article so it is ready to send to the printers tomorrow."

Ella put her hands on her hips and tisk-tisked. "I do declare, Reverend, you have holed up in that room of yours longer in the past weeks than you ever did while preparing sermons. These editorials had better be good."

"Would you like to hear what I have to say? I could read a few excerpts to you."

Irene quickly ate the last two bites of her meal, rose, and began to clear the table. "Why don't you and Mama go into the parlor while I do the dishes. I'll read your words when the paper is published."

"As you like," John motioned to Ella to follow him, sensing his daughter's lifetime of hearing him preach had made her slightly weary of it all.

He strode to his study, collected several pages of his work, then joined Ella in the parlor. "I'll just give you bits and pieces," he said. "I've written a lot for this first edition."

He cleared his scratchy throat, scanned a page, and spoke. "I feel the readership needs to have an honest assessment of its new editor, so I begin by saying I didn't always believe in suffrage for women due to my heritage and training on a man's point of view. You've heard the story, how my real conviction came after giving a series of talks on temperance and realizing most of my audiences were made up of women—that segment of society who could not vote on the issues at hand. I go ahead and say, I am wide awake now to the fact that equal suffrage is a moral, political, social, and religious necessity."

He paused and looked up from his writing. Ella stood and kissed his forehead. "You are off to a good start, and I like your positive approach. You've got me convinced."

John returned the kiss and laughed. "You were already convinced. It's those men and women standing in the shadow of doubt I need to sway."

~ ~ ~

ONE AFTERNOON, SOON AFTER THE FIRST WATERLOO edition of *The Woman's Standard* was released, John and Ella took the trolley to the eastside where they shopped at Black's emporium above the music hall. Afterward, they strolled arm in arm along the walkway window shopping. He carried a package containing new hosiery for them both.

"How nice it will be to have unholy stockings," Ella said, then giggled. "Is it sacrilege for a minister to have unholy feet?"

"We will have warm feet," John countered, "not unholy ones."

"Oh look!" Ella pulled John to a stop and peered at a window display.

John's gaze caught not what Ella saw in the window, but the reflection of who was approaching them from behind. "Brace yourself," he said. "We're about to have company."

They both turned around to see Violet Cunningham marching toward them with what appeared to be a new purple feather atop her head jerking in time with a determined step. "This should be fun," he said under his breath. He took off his own hat in greeting. "Good afternoon, Mrs. Cunningham, what a rare pleasure."

"Good afternoon to you, Reverend" — she never addressed him as Doctor — "and Mrs. Stevenson, how nice to see you." She smiled at Ella before directing her attention to John in her usual assertive manner. "I see you have a new responsibility."

The remark at first puzzled him, then he noticed the folded paper in her hand. "Indeed, I do, Mrs. Cunningham. Am I to understand that you read *The Woman's Standard?*"

"As a matter of fact, yes. It is wise to keep abreast of news, and I have found good things in the *Standard*. At times, your words are almost convincing, but I'm not swayed yet. I agree there are some rights women should be entitled to. However, I still stand firm in my conviction that politics belong to the man, and a woman's place is in the home." Without further ado, she strode on her way.

John could feel Ella stiffen beside him. "That was a deliberate jab at the fact I now work outside the home," she murmured.

He gave her arm a squeeze. "Don't let her get to you, my dear. You have to admit, there is a softening in her attitude."

"Well, I certainly don't see it, and I once considered her a friend."

"Friends can have differing opinions," John said, "and she, and those like her, are the very reason why *The Woman's Standard* is so important."

"And makes the goal of suffrage for women so difficult." The enticements in the store window forgotten, Ella tugged at John's arm. "Let's go home and try on our new stockings. I am feeling unholy."

~ ~ ~

TIME MOVED MORE SWIFTLY NOW THAT JOHN WAS preoccupied with *The Woman's Standard,* and before he knew it, the holidays were upon them. What a different feeling rang in the air this December compared to last year. Johnny had been mustered out of 51st Infantry on November second, and came home within weeks, intending to stay until January. Margaret arrived the week before Christmas, and it almost seemed like old times. The only one missing was Abram. Apparently, he still hankered for gold, and his letters now talked of leaving the Klondike for Nome, which was, according to him, "the newest diggin's."

Upon hearing this latest news about his brother's

adventures, Johnny shook his head. "I don't know about that kid. He surely gets restless. At least he stayed out of the war."

Christmas Eve they gathered in the parlor to sing carols while Ella played the piano. Earlier that day, Johnny had gone with Irene to get a tree. It now stood by the window, furniture moved aside, filling the room with its fresh scent. Colorful paper chains made by the girls the day before twined throughout the boughs, and glass ornaments, each bearing a special memory from years past, glittered from the branches.

"Tell us about the war," Irene asked her brother." We just got bits and pieces in your letters."

Johnny shook his head. "You don't want to hear about it, Sis."

"Oh, but I do. It was such a courageous adventure."

"No, Irene, it was not, and it wasn't pretty." His face darkened, and muscles in his jaw set firm and twitched. Tension grew in the air, stealing from the gaiety of the season. Ella rolled a chord and began to play a soft rendition of "Silent Night." The somber mood passed, and the cheer and warmth of the celebration of the birth of Christ prevailed throughout the evening and into Christmas Day.

Margaret left December 26th, and Johnny departed for Tabor on New Year's Eve. Irene said goodbye to her brother earlier that day before joining her friend Gretchen for a party. John and Ella took their eldest to the station, and waved and waved as the train chugged away from Waterloo. They were silent during most of the carriage ride home, the tired, old horse plodding through the streets with a slow gait. John noticed the trappings of Christmas suddenly seemed to lack their original luster. He hated goodbyes.

Beside him, Ella heaved a huge sigh. "Wonder when we'll see Johnny next. He seems different. I'm worried about him."

"He'll be all right, Ella. He has a good future ahead of him."

Inwardly, however, John sensed something he couldn't quite put a finger on. He prayed a long, silent prayer for his eldest before turning his thoughts to a more positive vein. Tomorrow began not only a new year, but a new century full of promise.

Chapter Thirty-Three

A DOUBLE STAR

1900

John chewed the end of his pencil, the eraser about used up. Before him lay the results of an article for the January edition of *The Woman's Standard* entitled "To the Honorable Senators and Representatives of Iowa," bringing to their attention a piece of legislation that would "please more than half the citizens of our great state." Once again, a petition had been handed to the legislators requesting the question of equal suffrage be submitted to the voters.

John had struggled to get the words just right, being firm but not wanting to antagonize this group of lawmakers who held the future of Iowan women in its hands.

He heard the front door open and close against the winter wind, checked the clock on the wall opposite his desk, and realized the afternoon was late. Ella had returned from work. His wife appeared in the open study doorway, her slender frame silhouetted by the fading light.

John stood, lighting the lamp on his desk. "Welcome home, my dear. How was your day?"

She entered the room and settled into a chair. "Fine. It was a good day, busy but good." She removed her gloves as she spoke, having already deposited her coat and hat on the rack in the entry hall. "It's nippy out there." She blew on her fingers. "How was your day?"

"Good. Busy but good."

"John, don't tease." Ella pretended she didn't like his banter, but her eyes sparkled, and he knew it pleased her.

He held up the paper he had been laboring over. "Want to hear a little?" He felt better when he had shared his thoughts with her, and she often gave helpful comments from a woman's point of view.

She nodded, and he read aloud the end of his article:

Our forefathers believed that the earth was the center of the universe, and for a long time it was very irritating to a man to be told that it was not so. Our present fathers believe that man is the center of animated nature, woman included, and it is irritating to some men to be told that it is not so. But a legislator should be, and as a rule is, a man of a judicial frame of mind, one who can consider women's modern claims and requests with a calm and balanced judgment, one who is open to conviction on every new issue. Man is not a planet and woman his satellite; man and woman together form a double star whose revolutions are around each other…

There was more, there always was, but at this point, John looked up from his reading for his wife's reaction.

Ella smiled. "John you should have been a poet, or maybe a senator." She stood, stretched, and headed for the kitchen to prepare supper. As she did, he heard her repeating, "Man and woman together form a double star. Hmmmm, I like that."

That same evening in the kitchen, supper finished

and the clean-up done, they continued to discuss the content of *The Woman's Standard*. Part of John's responsibility as editor was to fill the pages with appropriate writing by others than himself. It was heartening to learn how much material surfaced, and a satisfying challenge to decide what to use and where to fit it in. John mentioned this to Ella while he relaxed, his stocking feet propped up in front of the wood-burning stove, the welcome heat warming the room against the frosty air outside.

"Look for good information for me," he said. "Little bits and pieces like poems, quotes from famous people, any news related to women you may come across, no matter how small."

Ella pulled up a chair beside him, shuffled through a few papers on the table, and handed him an envelope. "How about asking your son to submit an article?"

Johnny, now working toward his law degree at the University of Iowa in Iowa City, wrote home weekly. In his most recent letter he alluded to the women he encountered during his war experience—nurses, Red Cross workers, and simply good-hearted ladies who reached out to the soldiers along the way with *baskets of provisions, packages of sewing material and many useful things which only a woman would think to provide.*

"I see something there for your paper," Ella said. "And with the war still fresh in people's minds, I think the timing is right. It would certainly promote the importance of a woman's role, no matter what the situation."

The next morning John put a note in the mail to his

son, requesting such an article. Johnny responded post-haste with enough material to fill two columns of the next edition of *The Woman's Standard*. He entitled it *Woman's Work in War* and proudly signed it J. O. Stevenson Jr., Co. L, 51st Iowa.

Ella's eyes held tears as she read it. "This is very positive, John. I think he is finally recovering from the horrors of his war experiences."

On the fifth of February, John left for Washington, D.C. to attend the National American Woman Suffrage Association's thirty-second annual convention. "This is a great opportunity," he said to Ella as he packed an extra shirt into his satchel. "One I hadn't expected, but it will give me exceptional material for the paper."

"Sarah Whitney has great confidence in you, and rightly so, or she wouldn't have helped finance this trip," Ella said. "Here, I bought you a little something extra to take along." She removed two monogrammed handkerchiefs from a package and tucked them next to the shirt.

He smiled at her thoughtfulness. "I wish you were coming. I reckon it will be quite the occasion, with the celebration of Miss Anthony's eightieth birthday and all."

Nothing had been said about Ella's going, though John suspected she ached to accompany him. Now the tables were turned. As the main breadwinner of the family, she was locked into a schedule, and he was more free to travel, no longer restrained by his pastoral responsibilities. He tried to let her know how indebted he was to her for assuming this role, though he could find no way to express his true feelings.

She kissed him. "You can tell me all about it when you get back, and I'm sure I will read your wonderful accounts in *The Woman's Standard*. It will almost be like I'm there. You are so good with words."

During the three-day journey, John tried to quell the anticipatory flutter in his stomach, but the feeling prevailed, even accelerated, as he stepped from the train and strode to the nearby St. James Hotel where he planned to stay. Though the time was late, he spent part of the evening walking, savoring the awe of the nation's capital—his first time ever to be there. Though his Scottish heritage ran deep, he felt very American and proudly so.

He arose early in the morning and hurried to the Church of Our Father, the meeting place of the convention, having been told tickets were limited and required for entry, even for delegates.

"Hello, Dr. Stevenson. I heard you would be here. Let's find seats together."

John turned to face Mrs. Belden, President of the Iowa Equal Suffrage Association, who appeared as starry-eyed as he felt over the excitement of it all. Her presence pleased him, as she knew of his speaking limitations, and thus he was not as uncomfortable talking to her as he did with those who were unaware of his handicap.

"Isn't this crowd something?" she said. "How can anyone deny women the right to vote with this kind of enthusiasm!"

"I only wish the Iowa legislators could be here to see

this," John said. "Especially since our own Carrie Chapman Catt will be receiving the presidential gavel for the organization from Miss Anthony." He took Mrs. Belden's elbow and guided her toward two seats as near the front as they could get. He liked the fact the event was held in a church. It seemed appropriate—fighting for what was right in a house of God. John believed the spirit of the creator was everywhere in a church. His presence felt tangible, as though one could almost reach out and touch Him. Yes, this was a good thing.

By the end of the week, however, it became apparent a much larger venue would have served better.

The convention lasted six days. Each evening John sat in his hotel room and re-wrote the pages of notes he had taken during the sessions while still fresh in his mind—there was so much to tell. He emphasized the crowds that grew each day, many delegates having to be turned away.

It was the special events on February fifteenth that astounded him. That afternoon at Lafayette Square Opera House, a committee of suffragists hosted Miss Anthony's eightieth birthday celebration. The enormity of it was hard to express. John wrote: *The place was packed from galley to pit to hear speeches made in her honor.*

There was no way he could get everything down in writing, though with pad and pencil in hand at the event itself, he made a point to scribble Miss Anthony's own closing remarks: *I have passed as leader without a tear, but I am not through leading, for I shall work to the end of my time, and when I am called home, if there exists such a thing as a spirit, that spirit will still be with you and watching you.*

That same evening, the Corcoran Art Gallery opened its house of treasures for a private viewing in honor of the suffrage convention, featuring a full-size oil painting of Miss Anthony and marble busts of Miss Anthony, Lucretia Mott, and Elizabeth Cady Stanton. For two hours Miss Anthony and other Association officers received the crowd. John noted many more were turned away. The following morning, *The Washington Post* estimated 2,000 people shook the hand of Miss Anthony. To his own pile of notes, John added *The Post* account and other articles highlighting the week's event.

The evening of the sixteenth, he packed his bag in preparation to leave early the next morning. As his thoughts lingered over the last six days, he took several pieces of the hotel stationery and penned a letter to his benefactor.

Mrs. S. W. Whitney,
Dear Friend,
The convention has been held. It was a great success, crowded at the beginning, overcrowded long before the close, and suffocatingly insufficient at the end. The birthday celebration for Miss Anthony yesterday threw a glory over it that cannot be expected again at any other convention...

As for her successor, Mrs. Catt, time will tell. She has mental ability and is so far as I can see the best that could be done, but she is no second Anthony and the cause has passed into another stage in its evolution...

His remarks to Mrs. Whitney covered five pages,

and as he folded them into an envelope, he mused, *I won't have any trouble filling the March edition of the Standard. My problem will be where to stop.*

The weather during the convention, though cold and wintery, had been reasonably good. But as John prepared to leave, snowflakes drifted from a dark sky. Yes, it would be good to be home. He was bursting to tell Ella all about everything. Then he would shout in his loudest written words to the lawmakers in Iowa what he had just witnessed. The time was now to enfranchise women.

Chapter Thirty-Four

BAD NEWS – GOOD NEWS

John had been home from Washington, D.C. only a few weeks before he left again, this time for Des Moines to witness the Iowan House of Representatives vote on the equal suffrage amendment. He carried the optimism still burning in him from the National Convention.

"This could very well be it for the women of Iowa," he said as he kissed Ella goodbye. "The petition's pages and pages of signatures will surely be a big enough influence to make those men stop and think."

"It was a lot of work filling those pages of signatures," she said.

"I know, and I will add an extra cheer for your efforts when the amendment is finally put on the ballot and passes."

In Des Moines, John's hopes ran high as crowds of observers filled the gallery. Ninety-nine of 100 members of the house filed in and took their seats in the chamber below. John was awed by the surroundings. Ornate woodwork embellished the high ceiling, and elegant chandeliers provided additional light to what streamed in from the huge windows gracing one wall of the impressive room. It was a place befitting life-changing decisions.

The man sitting next to John leaned over and whispered. "This is highly extraordinary. Never have I seen so many representatives here for a vote on any issue."

John could feel the tension in the air—a sense that something unusual was about to happen. Dr. Hinkle, Chairman of the House Committee on Amendments, a large man from Wayne, Iowa, stood to present the measure. He told the house that at least 100,000 citizens and voters had petitioned for the right of speaking their minds at the polls, and that submission of the measure was only "just, and fair, and right."

At his comments, loud cheers and clapping erupted from the visitors as a feeling of "success at last" rumbled through the gallery. But, as John later wrote in *The Woman's Standard*, the battle had just begun.

Several representatives stood to express opposition to the amendment, each declaring to be friends of moral suffrage, the home, and women. John fidgeted in his seat, wanting to jump up and shout, "You are the enemies of all three and the antagonists of the liberties of the people!"

Others made speeches in support of equal suffrage, but it wasn't enough after years of prejudice and falsehoods. When the dust settled, the vote stood at forty-four ayes and fifty-five noes. Once more the general public was denied the vote on an amendment allowing suffrage for women in the State of Iowa.

"It was everywhere in the local papers," Ella said. She poured John a cup of hot tea as he fumed over the outcome upon his return. "I hoped you would have calmed down during the long ride home, but I should have known better."

"When things make you mad, Papa, you write better," Irene said. "I don't blame you for being upset. I am, too. I want the right to vote."

"I'm not really mad, Reenie, just frustrated. This has happened so many times. It would have been a miracle if it had passed. Yet it felt for a while that it might—we were so close."

Frustration spilled from his pen for the April edition of *The Standard.* He called the representatives who opposed the measure "political hoodlums" and wrote that when the proposed amendment was voted down, *liberty was defeated, woman's emancipation in Iowa was delayed, and progressive Iowa was placed in an untrue light before her sister states.* He proceeded to print the names of the friends and foes of freedom with the counties they represented or misrepresented, as the case might be, *in order that their suffrage constituency may intelligently apply their praise or blame to the proper persons.*

His initial anger subdued, John enjoyed his rebuttal. "I'm listing each and every legislator in this edition," he told Ella, "those who voted for and those who voted against. Mrs. Belden gave me her comments on the proceedings to be included in this issue. She is more philosophical than I about it, and gives us a good balance."

John's energy and determination climbed each day as both he and members of the Iowa Equal Suffrage Association received numerous letters and calls of encouragement. These positive responses worked their way into the next *Standard. Mrs. Catt — our Mrs. Catt,* John wrote, *urges us to be of good cheer, and George W. Catt telegraphed from New York, to "keep up your courage and count on double my contribution of last year."* One woman in Louisa County wrote: *Never give up the battle. I have never been an out-and-out suffrage worker, but now I am one.* There seemed no end to the support from friends and strangers alike.

The accolades filled two columns. When the paper finally went to press, John felt, despite the defeat by the House — or maybe because of it — Iowa suffragists were on an upward swing.

He encouraged stories on women who had made outstanding contributions to society, and the May edition would include a piece on the life of the late Dorothea Dix who had created mental asylums for the indigent insane. And, of course, any encouraging news regarding the enfranchisement of woman always found its way into *The Standard.* Under the title, *A Suffrage Victory,* John added good news from Australia. He wrote: *A few months ago, it was announced that both houses of parliament in West Australia had passed a resolution in favor of full suffrage for women. This was an earnest promise that they would pass a bill to that effect as soon as the necessary red tape could be untied. Now news comes that the bill has finally passed both houses. So, one by one, the Australian provinces join the procession.*

He added more promising news from the state of Oregon, where in June the "public" would vote upon a constitutional amendment to give women the right of suffrage. He told how the amendment had been *twice voted upon favorably by the legislature and will now go to the people for the final test.* He also noted that the Ohio House of Representatives came close to approving a suffrage amendment with fifty-four votes in favor and forty-eight against, but lacked the constitutional majority of three-fifths.

Now a bona fide suffragist, Irene would spout and fume whenever a step backward occurred in the women's rights movement. She and Ella were in the kitchen preparing the evening meal when John announced the defeat of the Oregon amendment.

Upon hearing the news, Irene almost dropped the plates she was carrying. "What is wrong with people? We're not moving forward at all—just standing still!" She thumped the plates down at each place on the table, the last one with such force John was surprised it didn't crack.

"Word is the antisuffrage folks did a better job campaigning against the ballot issue than the suffragist did for it," he said. "A lesson learned."

~ ~ ~

LIFE SETTLED INTO A NORMAL ROUTINE, AND THOUGH John had occasional bouts with the asthma and hay fever, it was tolerable. He was back to taking his daily walks. Fall had always been his favorite time of year, and these outings energized him. The red and gold of the turning leaves and a nip in the air suggested frost was just around the corner, and spoke of adventures to come. He sometimes stopped by the church to say hello to whoever was there, chatting a bit before he continued on. Though he still missed being a pastor, the angst had diminished, and he now felt comfortable with his new roles of editor, writer, and yes, housekeeper. Additionally, he served as registrar for the general Congregational Conference, a job that especially pleased him, because it continued his official connection with the church.

It was not unusual for John and Ella to be home alone at night, Irene often out doing childcare to earn money. So, he savored the mood one rare September evening when the three of them relaxed together in the parlor. The scent of new rain floated through an open window on a cool breeze, mingling with Ella's soft piano melodies. Irene sat on the settee punching a needle in and out on a needlework design.

Without warning, the front door opened and closed with a loud thud, disrupting their gentle mood. In the entryway, a stranger stood peering at them—a handlebar mustache topping a shaggy beard. His buckskin jacket hung loose over dirty denims tucked into boots laced high up his legs. His hands fingered a stained, felt hat.

Ella stopped playing, John lowered his book, and Irene looked up from her handwork, wide-eyed—the air suddenly loaded with surprise and puzzlement. No one even breathed for what seemed a full minute. Then the apparition spoke.

"Isn't anyone going to say hello?"

Irene recognized him first and let out a scream. "Abram!" Spilling her needlepoint onto the floor, she raced to her brother who grabbed her and swung her about like a rag doll, then held her out in front of him, giving a low whistle.

"Well, look at you little sister. You are all grown up. I haven't been gone that long."

"Yes, you have. It's been forever." She wiped the tears streaming down her cheeks. "And look at you! You're as brown as an Indian. I wouldn't have known you if I met you on the street—hiding behind that beard and all. Well, maybe after a second glance." She hugged him again.

John set his book aside, rose, and approached the boy, his arm outstretched in greeting—relief, joy, and thanksgiving tumbling through him like a creek during snow melt. "Welcome home, son."

Chapter Thirty-Five

NEW HORIZONS

1901

Abram stayed through fall and into winter, adding new life to the household. He found odd jobs in town to keep busy, even joining an amateur theater group. John didn't ask what his son would do next. He could tell from the familiar restlessness that Abram had something on his mind, and they would learn of his plans soon enough. In the meantime, they simply enjoyed his being home.

Then, on a blustery New Year's Day, while the family sat around the table in the warm kitchen, chatting and predicting what 1901 might bring, Abram leaned back in his chair, wiped a smudge of gravy off his now clean-shaven chin, and said, "That was mighty delicious Mama and Irene. I'm going to miss this wonderful home cooking."

Ella put down her fork, a frown wrinkling her forehead. "And where are you off to now, young man? We haven't seen much of you as it is in the few weeks since you arrived."

"Don't go back to Alaska," Irene said, with a pout. "That's too far away."

"Nope, won't do that. This time it's the navy, probably New York. I've been doing some investigating.

They will train me to become an electrician. What do you think of that? I'll be serving my country like Johnny did, getting educated, and being paid, too."

John swallowed his last bite of pie, digesting this newest bit of information along with his meal. "Well, son, that sounds like a mighty fine plan. I think you'll be glad you did it."

The boy wasn't through with his little surprises. With a big grin on his face, he said, "I would like to take Irene with me as far as Chicago—show her the sights of a big city."

Irene let out a screech, jumped up, ran to her brother and hugged him, knocking over his chair, the two of them landing in a laughing heap on the floor. Abram stood and helped her up. She hugged him again. "Oh, Papa, can I go, please? The school holiday lasts another two weeks, so it would work out fine."

John glanced at Ella, whose expression he couldn't read, while he mulled over this unexpected idea. "You need to tell us exactly what you have in mind, and Mother and I will discuss it."

Abram had all the particulars worked out, and the plan seemed safe enough, so the answer was yes, with certain caveats. So, a few days later, the two of them set off for their adventure.

As the train chugged into the distance, John took Ella's hand. "Things will feel different at home with only you and me."

She sighed. "I guess it's something we need to get used to. I doubt Abram will be coming back, and Irene is only a year or two from being gone herself."

John knew she was right, but for now, Irene would be back shortly. Although that familiar empty feeling each time a child left home plagued him, this time he felt Abram had made a wise choice. The boy's future looked good.

Irene returned from the trip all bubbly, talking constantly of her experiences in Chicago, until John grew weary of it and wished there was some way he could turn her off. Abram had bought her a new dress—yellow with ribbons—which she wore to church, glowing and flouncing at each compliment, while her friends hovered around to hear of her adventures.

In bed that Sunday evening, John lay back and sighed. "She was only gone a week, but does she seem older to you?" he asked Ella.

"Well, yes. That was an important week, John. She got a glimpse of the world beyond Waterloo, and she made the trip home all on her own. You should be proud."

Yes, and my little girl is slipping away. He turned on his side and closed his eyes, doubting he would sleep.

The remaining days in January and those into February sped by, and that old quandary of where Abram might be and what he might be doing continually lurked in John's mind while he waited for some word.

"Don't fret. He'll write when he has something to write home about," Ella said, a remark that made John chuckle. She was the fretter, not he. At least not openly, though as each morning dawned, he hoped it would be the day the postman brought a letter.

Finally, the anticipated note from Abram arrived. They each read it twice.

"So, he's in the Brooklyn Navy Yard on a ship," Ella said. "I guess he found what he was looking for, and they took him in." She smiled and set the letter down. "That lucky rascal, he always has a plan that seems to work out for him."

John laughed. "You're not giving him enough credit, my dear. I don't think luck has much to do with it. He knows what he wants and goes for it." A touch of pride tinged his words, and for a minute his thoughts turned to Anna. She would be proud, too.

The following morning, even before he started work on suffrage articles, John wrote to Abram.

Dear Son,

Your letter of February 26 is at hand. We are glad to know that you have reached your present destination safely… I would think it advisable to make the Navy a life work, climbing as high as you can for as I understand it, after a certain number of years (twenty-five or thirty) you can retire on two thirds pay for the rest of your days.

He added more advice, and upon re-reading it wondered for a moment if he had been too preachy. Ultimately he decided that was what parents were for, and left it as written. He pondered his words a minute more, adding:

Irene seems to have enjoyed herself very much with you in Chicago and will always remember it with pleasure.

> *With love from all,*
> *Your affectionate father.*

Irene had taken to reading *The Daily Courier,* pointing out what she felt newsworthy. She had announced the news to him before he had a chance to read it, that Queen Victoria had died. "Does that make you sad?" she asked.

It did. Irene was very much aware that this formidable lady had been a part of John's early years living in Scotland. He was touched by her concern.

Much to John's delight, his daughter also read *The Woman's Standard* — not just John's editorials, but the entire published paper. She always had a comment or two, usually favorable, often impatient because an Iowan woman's right to vote still floundered unresolved. It became evident that the articles increasingly influenced her thinking and her actions.

One weekday afternoon, Irene's friend Gretchen accompanied her home from school. The girls popped into John's study for a moment to say hello. "Gretchen is going to stay for supper. I asked Mama this morning, and she said it would be fine, as long as we helped." They settled in the parlor to chat while Irene did some hand sewing. John could hear their conversation through the open door.

"Did you get a rip in your beautiful new dress, Irene?" Gretchen asked, a tone of surprise in her voice.

"No. I'm making it shorter. Two inches, to be precise."

"Whatever for? It will look, well — wrong, unfashionable."

John chortled. He had a feeling he knew where this was leading.

"Judge McAuley of Kansas City thinks there should

be a law compelling women to wear shorter skirts so they don't drag around spittle and spread germs. I think it is a very wise idea."

"Kansas City? Irene, this is Waterloo."

"Men spit in Waterloo. I've seen them."

Gretchen laughed. "It sounds to me like the law should be against men spitting in public places, not against women and their skirts. Where do you get some of your absurd ideas?"

"*The Woman's Standard.* And the judge did say there should be a law against spitting in public. The skirt idea is to protect women and any place they drag their germy dresses."

"I thought that paper was all about giving women the vote. What's spitting got to do with it?"

"*The Standard* is full of articles of interest to women and about their rights. It is excellent reading."

John heard a rustle of papers. "Here," Irene said.

The room went silent, and after a few minutes, Gretchen said, "Can I borrow this? I'd like to show my mother."

John smiled at one more step toward spreading the word. *Now if Gretchen and her mother can convince the man of the house to vote in their favor...*

~ ~ ~

THE SUMMER OF 1901 BROUGHT NEW JOYS. MARGARET came home and stayed a spell. The house seemed to hum as three women busied about. And it was a boon for Ella to have extra help.

"I would like to further my education," Margaret

told the family one evening. "I won't be going back to Shenandoah to teach. I plan to attend Nebraska State University at Lincoln."

John's response was instantaneous. "That's a splendid idea, Margaret." Then a splinter of fear crept into his thoughts. *Would she expect money from them? That would be an impossibility.*

She answered this question immediately, as though she read his mind. "I have been putting aside a little money each month from my teacher's salary and have enough to get started. I will find work in Lincoln."

"I'm going to be a teacher, too, Maggie," Irene said. "I have one more year of high school, then I will do exactly what you did and find a teaching job somewhere."

John knew this was inevitable—a good thing—but secretly he hoped his youngest would find a school nearby to fulfill her dreams.

The summer heat was more oppressive than usual, causing crops to wither—devastating for the farmers— but in turn kept John's hay fever at bay. However, poor crops only postponed his health issues. By September a cough racked his chest until it hurt.

"You didn't have me fooled," Ella said, as she prepared her steamed herbs. "But I knew you didn't want to make an issue of it while Maggie was here."

~ ~ ~

NORMAL LIFE FOR THE ENTIRE NATION CAME TO A GRIM halt on September sixth, as the president of the United States was struck by an assassin's bullet. The paper stated, *President McKinley is Fatally Shot,* though rumors spread that he wasn't dead. At day's end, people stood out in front of their homes and on sidewalks and streets talking.

"It happened at the Temple of Music at the Pan American exposition in Buffalo, New York."

"That man was too relaxed while in a crowd. He should have listened to his security people."

"He was a good president who liked being out in public. He felt it important because it made him closer to the people."

"You make it sound like he is dead. I heard he is alive."

That was the unanswered question hovering like unwanted storm clouds. Was McKinley dead?

Though John's asthma made sleep difficult that night, it was the ominous feeling of the possible death of the nation's leader that kept him awake. When he looked out across the neighborhood, lights shone in the windows of most houses, where sleep obviously eluded others. The newspaper the following day brought a surge of hope. The front page displayed a huge photo of McKinley topped by headlines that read: *Our Beloved President Still Lives, May Recover.*

John left on September 10th for Bayfield. He couldn't wait any longer to find relief from the torment to his lungs. The mood of the nation was cautiously optimistic, hopeful the president would survive, and that everything would be as before.

John had hardly unpacked his things at the cottage on Lake Superior when the news spread throughout the small community. McKinley had died of gangrene to his gunshot wound. As a nation mourned, a new president stepped to the helm: Theodore Roosevelt. John whispered a prayer for the nation and wondered, what now?

Chapter Thirty-Six

ONE IDEA

1902

As the nation adjusted to a new administration, John was faced with another unexpected change. A letter from Abram said he asked for a discharge from the navy and planned to seek additional electrical training elsewhere. In the meantime, he found a job and place to live in Brooklyn.

John shook his head and sighed. What does one do about independent-thinking children? Just be thankful you have them, he supposed. He mentally wrote half a dozen responses to his son—some expressing his disappointment, some giving fatherly advice—but in the end, he simply wrote a short note wishing Abram well in his new ventures.

John's stay in Wisconsin was shorter than usual as winter arrived early. With frost glistening on the grasses at dawn, he packed his bag and headed for home. He was pleased he had not missed the deadline for the October issue of *The Woman's Standard,* and that much of the articles for November were well underway.

The early frost proved to be the precursor of an extra cold winter, but a letter dated January 19, 1902, brought warmth and excitement to the household.

Mr. and Mrs. Stevenson,
Dear Friends,
I take this opportunity at this time to ask you for your daughter Margaret to be my wife. I will say this, that our home will be a Christian home, and I assure you that Margaret will not be hindered in trying to live a Christian life, but I hope to be a help to her and I know she will be a help to me. Margaret tells me she always wanted to live on the farm, so I think we will be happy together.
Will close for this time. Hope to hear from you soon.
Very truly yours,
F. M. Wood

"I knew it!" Irene exclaimed. She read the announcement while curled up in a chair in the parlor, wrapped in a wool shawl on that wintry evening. Jumping up, she waved the letter for emphasis, the shawl slipping from her shoulders. "Maggie kept mentioning Mr. Wood in her letters, and when I asked about him during her summer visit here, she just smiled and got all sparkly-eyed and told me he was nice. Imagine her being married. When they have children, I'll be an auntie. Won't that be something?"

Ella looked up from the needlework in her lap. "It's time for Margaret to settle down, though the letter doesn't mention a wedding date, which is best. A girl needs to be sure. Marriage is a big commitment. You can't be too careful, and sometimes it's wise to wait."

Irene paused in the middle of an exuberant waltz across the room. "You and Papa didn't wait long. I really don't remember because I was so little, but that's what Abram told me. It was a big surprise when you got married."

"I had known your papa a long time before that and knew he was a good catch." Ella cast a bright smile at John.

He put down his paper and returned the smile. "And vice versa," he said. "I was lucky she was interested in me."

~ ~ ~

IT WAS TIME AGAIN FOR A PLEA TO THE MEN OF THE IOWA General Assembly. John put his pen to paper for an article.

… Our women must rise with us or we must go down with them. The movement is in line not only with the demands of civilization, but also with the principles of American government. "Taxation without representation is tyranny," and women are taxed. "Governments derive their just powers from the consent of the governed," and women are governed. "The right of petition is a sacred right," and women have petitioned the Iowa legislature for many years for a referendum on the question of woman's suffrage.

He never ran out of things to say on the subject, and with the 24th Annual Convention of the National American Woman Suffrage Association convening in February, there would be volumes of fodder for subsequent issues of the paper, especially since this year it was to be an international convention, the first ever for the NAWSA. John looked forward to everything this event would offer the cause.

He planned his days in an orderly manner,

designating the morning hours for working on editorials and organizing articles for *The Woman's Standard*. After lunch he took a short nap, then spent a couple of hours stuffing envelopes for the L & T Trust Company, a new project which brought in a little extra money. The work was tedious and repetitive, and he often stopped to stretch. One afternoon as he stood at the study window rotating his arm to get a kink from his shoulder, he observed a wagon pulling up in front of the house. A familiar figure jumped down, lifted a grip from the back, handed the driver something, and waved as the rig pulled away. John's heart rate accelerated, and he headed for the front door to greet his eldest son.

"Well, John. This is a pleasant surprise. Come in. Come in! What's the occasion?"

Johnny put down his satchel and clasped John's hand. "Hello, Papa. I've got news, and since it may be a while before I get home again, I thought I'd drop by for a few days."

"Come into the kitchen where it's warm. You must be hungry. Have you had lunch? I'm pretty good at fixing a meal now that Ella is gone during the day. In fact, I was just about to get something for myself." He led the way, curiosity gnawing away at him as he talked.

Johnny paced while John sliced and buttered bread and heated up some leftover pork and beans. As he worked, he eyed his son who seemed fidgety. Nervous maybe? Excited about something?

Once the food was ready, they sat and John said

grace. Then the questions poured out. "Now, what's this about, not seeing us for a while? What's going on with the lawyering?" He thought he might fall apart any moment from not knowing.

Johnny grinned. "Lawyering is fine. That's what this is all about. I just received my law degree—in record time, I might add. It took many long hours and hard work, but now I am free to practice. I'm moving to Washington State."

John's eyebrows shot up. "Washington State?"

"Yes. A fellow I met while I studied at Tabor, Ozro Gaston, has invited me to partner with him in a law firm in Everett—a town up a ways from Seattle. It's a swell opportunity. Ozro knows a lot about the law, and I am honored that he wants me. I am on my way!" Johnny scooped some beans onto a slice of bread and stuffed it into his mouth, grinning while he chewed, and mumbling, "What do you think of that?"

The name meant something to John. "The founder of Tabor was a George Gaston. Surely there is a connection there," he said, still astonished at the news.

"Yes, Ozro is George Gaston's grandson. He's very proud of his lineage."

"And well he should be. I think you must be a pretty good lawyer yourself if Mr. Gaston wants you for a partner. I'm proud of you, son."

Irene arrived home later in the day, and once she recovered from the happy shock of seeing Johnny, she riddled him with her own questions. "Tell us about Mr. Gaston. Do you know anything about Everett, Washington? How long can you stay?"

"Whoa, little sister, One thing at a time. I'll tell you more when Mama is home. As far as my visit here—how about a week?"

At supper, they learned Mr. Gaston was a few years older than Johnny. He had a wife and three sons, and for a number of years practiced as a court stenographer in various locations before serving in the same capacity in Council Bluffs. "He and his family lived in Tabor and attended the Congregational Church there," Johnny said. "I met him while studying for one of my pre-law classes. He knows a lot about the law and is highly regarded in his field. When I moved on to the University of Iowa, we kept in touch."

"Wow, a real lawyer," Irene said, gazing at her brother with adoration. "Only, I wish Washington wasn't so far away."

"It's the new frontier, Reenie. It's the place to be and is growing by leaps and bounds."

Ella stood and began clearing away the dishes. "Speaking of places that are growing, why don't you take Johnny for a ride around Waterloo tomorrow, John? There are so many changes in town. He'll be surprised."

"I saw a new bridge being built over the river on Fourth Street on my way in. That's an improvement. And every time I visit there's another smokestack in the industrial section. What else?"

"Progress is humming here, son. A new courthouse was just completed. That's something to see. The old brewery on the West Side up toward the Black Hawk is being pulled down, and extensive shops are to be erected on the site. And Carnegie has given $30,000 to build a library." John stopped a moment, shook his head, and chuckled. "Now comes the fight of locating it on both sides of the river, or in the middle of it. Also, the U.S. voted $150,000 for a Federal building on the West Side."

Johnny gave a low whistle. "Pretty soon I won't know the place."

The next morning, they hitched old Blaze to the carriage and took a grand tour of the new Waterloo. When the promised week was only half over, Johnny began to grow restless. Apparently, he had done all the visiting he felt necessary, and was eager to get on with his new life far to the west.

"Well, he's gone," Ella said with a distinct tone of finality after they said their goodbyes. "I wonder if we will see him again. He'll be so far away." She choked a little on the last comment.

"He's ready to be a lawyer, now, Ella, off to make his own way in the world. That's what we wanted, wasn't it?" He felt impatient with her melancholy. Yet, as eager as the lad was to begin his career as a lawyer, John sensed something was amiss.

Ella voiced it first. "Did his restlessness seem abnormal to you?"

"A little."

He thought about the fact that Johnny had pushed himself to finish school in record time, also keeping a job after classes to pay for expenses. "I think he's overly tired, Ella. He plunged right from the exhausting, negative experiences of war back to school, where it sounds like he hardly slept."

But Ella's remark about Johnny's odd restlessness lingered in John's mind. That night he said fervent prayers for the well-being and future of his eldest, a young man with so much promise.

~ ~ ~

JOHN KEPT BUSY WITH WORK FOR THE TRUST COMPANY AND his ongoing editorials. Plus, by mid-May he had put in a good garden: corn, beets, peas, beans, lettuce, onions, potatoes, tomatoes and radishes. This had been Ella's project before she worked outside the home. Surprising himself, he found satisfaction digging in the dirt, keeping the weeds out, and watching the seeds sprout and grow. A soft peace tiptoed through him while he labored in God's world.

John took time to write often to his children. He addressed Maggie's letters to Lincoln, Nebraska, and John Jr.'s to Everett, Washington, but he still never quite knew where to send correspondence to Abram. Since his Brooklyn address, the boy had had two different ones in Chicago, and his latest letter home indicated he might be moving to Alpena, Michigan. John could only shake his head at that news, hoping Abram would find his calling soon and settle down.

There was also regular correspondence with Sarah Ware Whitney. Though still publisher of *The Woman's Standard,* she and her husband had moved away from Iowa and now resided on a ranch in New Mexico. "She's invited us to join her there sometime during the summer," John told Ella after reading Sarah's most recent letter. The invitation was tempting. "It would be good timing for my allergies." So far this year his hay fever stayed under control, but he knew the affliction would catch up with him sooner or later. "Do you think you could get some time off from the law firm?"

Ella stood at the kitchen counter, cutting up a chicken. "Oh, John, that would be such a wonderful break for me. New Mexico—it sounds like some exotic land. I would love to go." She stopped her task for a moment and stared out the window as though picturing a southwest landscape. "I suppose I could ask, but I would hate to jeopardize my job."

"You have worked for Gates and Liffring for almost three years now and hardly taken a break. You deserve it, and they appreciate your abilities. Surely they will be reasonable about this." John felt himself getting a little riled up at the thought that perhaps they might not. He wanted so much to go to New Mexico—and with Ella.

He needn't have worried. Mr. Gates granted Ella a month's leave of absence with the assurance her place in the office was secure and would be waiting on her return. As the date of their departure approached, Ella couldn't sit still. Normally worn down in the evenings after a day at the law firm, she pranced about the house, humming, and finishing her chores in record time with nary a complaint. One warm evening as they sat on the porch, she announced. "I have a wonderful idea."

John, who was enjoying the relaxing to and fro of a rocking chair, braked the motion with a sudden clomp of his feet. Turning to her with a wary eye, he asked. "What now? Isn't a trip enough satisfaction?"

"That's part of my idea, John, to make the trip even better. As long as we are in the neighborhood, I think we should go to Colorado and visit Cora. We have the entire month. It will be perfect!"

He shook his head and chuckled at her plans, as though Colorado Springs and somewhere in the middle of New Mexico were a hop, skip, and jump from each other.

"I've been studying the map," Ella continued. "We'll take one route to get there and another to come home. It couldn't be easier."

He had been studying the map, too, and she was right. Making a loop of their trip would work and probably not add any more miles. It was decided they would do just that.

~ ~ ~

THE WHITNEYS' RANCH WAS AN HOUR'S WAGON RIDE from the train station in Albuquerque. A mile higher than any place in Iowa, the altitude taxed John's already compromised lungs. But the view, stretching from the Sangre de Christo Range to the north and glimmering plains and mesas, silver rivers, and more mountain ranges in all other directions, couldn't be matched. As John later observed, "it was worth the thin air to stand in the presence of the super-human, the divine forces of nature, and the wonderful painting of God's color brushes."

He and Sarah spent many hours discussing *The Woman's Standard.* "The Iowa Equal Suffrage Association is very pleased with your work," she kept reassuring him. "We couldn't have made a better choice for editor."

They stayed a week at each of their destinations, the Colorado Springs visit bringing its own satisfaction. John found pleasure in watching the two sisters eagerly embrace and then talk non-stop from dawn until a late bedtime each day. He also enjoyed making his own observations of a place that allowed women the right to vote—writing later in *The Standard* that, contrary to the fears of the antisuffragists, it didn't appear family values had been damaged in a state where all people were "free and equal."

~ ~ ~

ON THEIR RETURN TO WATERLOO, THEY LEARNED THEY had missed a Dry Run flood—a low watershed originating in the marshes that sometimes brought a torrent of water through the town during a major rainstorm. "It was so scary!" Irene said with great dramatics. "The water came whooshing down the streets tearing up sidewalks and a lot of other stuff. It was awful. By Sunday, there was still so much water we waded to church barefoot, lifting our skirts way up to keep them from getting wet."

It may have been scary, John thought, but she was making it sound like a great adventure. Yet he knew it must have been serious. Evidence of the flood remained with muddy high-water marks on the buildings. These floods hit every now and then, but apparently this one was considerably worse than usual. It had covered twenty-four square miles, and because of it, a much needed sewer project in Waterloo was underway.

After the travel break, and with a cool autumn approaching, John felt refreshed and eager to settle back to a normal routine. Sarah Whitney's positive comments on the work he was doing for *The Standard* caused him to tackle it with renewed fervor. Sadly, the November edition focused on the October 26th death of Elizabeth Cady Stanton. In addition to his own glowing account of her extraordinary life, John included a number of other tributes, among them an article from *The N.Y. American:* "A Splendid Life for a Great Purpose." *Elizabeth Cady Stanton, at the ripe old age of four score years and seven after a life of extraordinary activity and of unfaltering devotion to the main purpose, passes out into the darkness that is called death. Mrs. Stanton was a woman of ONE IDEA, and that idea was the elevation of woman.*

Meanwhile, letters from Abram bore good news. He remained in Chicago and was now employed as an electrician by the Stromberg-Carlson Manufacturing Company.

"What do you think of that?" John asked Ella and Irene at the supper table the day they first heard the news. "He knew what he wanted, went for it, and got it!"

"What I think," Irene said, "is we should get him to come home and put electric lights in this house. Wouldn't that be grand?"

"Yes," Ella agreed. "And we could get an electric cook stove and a washing machine. Now that *would* be grand!"

"All of which costs money," John said.

The two women glowered at him.

Then, in mid-November, a letter arrived from Abram that caused John's emotions to plummet before he had even opened the envelope. The return address? Ottumwa, Iowa, of all places. Whatever happened to the job in Chicago? John left the envelope unopened on his desk for a full thirty minutes while he finished an editorial, not wanting to darken his afternoon with disappointment. Finally, setting his writing aside, he picked up the letter and tore open the seal. When he unfolded the one-page note, a photograph dropped out and fell to the desk. Looking up at him was the image of a young woman with dark, swept-up hair, a lovely oval face, and a shy, beguiling smile. Surprised and curious, John quickly commenced reading the accompanying message.

Dear Papa,

I am in Ottumwa, sent here by Stromberg-Carlson to superintend the installation of equipment at the new office of the Ottumwa Telephone Company. During my few weeks here I have become acquainted with Ada Lee Walker, a stenographer for the telephone company. We have fallen in love and plan to be married sometime early next year. I am enclosing her picture. I hope you approve. She is the most wonderful woman I have ever met.

Fingering the photograph, John closed his teary eyes and said a prayer before marching into the kitchen where Irene and Ella were preparing supper. "Have I got news for you!"

Chapter Thirty-Seven

HAPPINESS AND TORMENT

1903

Abram and Ada set their wedding date for February 15, 1903. John could feel his son's joyful anticipation dancing on the pages of his letters. He and Ella shared the news with close church friends on Sunday and spoke of nothing else on the ride home.

"Everyone seems as happy for him as we are," Ella said, pulling the wool robe around her in the winter chill.

"This must be the right girl," John said. "His letters sing."

"He certainly seems sure, so I'm very happy for him."

"Me, too!" added Irene from the rear seat, obviously not missing a word. "Although it's hard to imagine Abram married." She giggled. "Somehow he doesn't seem the type—you know, running off to Alaska and all."

Ella turned to respond, her words white puffs of breath in the icy air. "Your brother has grown up since then, Irene. He's been in the navy and has a responsible job. He's ready."

"And marriage will settle him down," John said. He clicked Blaze forward, scarcely feeling the cold in his contentment.

One afternoon in early December, another letter

came from Abram. The words still radiated off the paper, but they left John concerned. The dusk turning to night felt more like a dreary fog rolling in through the once bright windows.

He heard Ella return from work and waited for her to check on him as she always did. Moments later, she tiptoed in. "John, are you napping?"

"No, simply thinking."

"You are always thinking. But why are you sitting here in the dark? Is something troubling you?"

She placed a hand on his shoulder, and he reached up and covered her fingers with his, giving a little squeeze. "Abram wants me to conduct the marriage ceremony. It would be an honor, but I don't see how I can without embarrassing him. I would hardly be able to croak out the words." He heaved an involuntary sigh. "I don't know what to tell him."

Ella remained at his side for a few minutes, though she said nothing, and he reckoned she didn't know how to respond. Finally, in the silent darkness of the room, she pulled her hand from his, patted him on the shoulder, and stepped away. At the door, she paused. "Do what you think is best, dear. Either way, you know Abram will understand."

John sat and thought on the dilemma for a while before lighting the lamp and putting his pen to paper.

My Dear Son,

I will be glad to come down and officiate at the wedding on some conditions. Miss Walker should know that it is with great difficulty that I can say anything at all. She might be shocked to hear me try to talk if she were not aware of it beforehand. If this is satisfactory to her then I will do the best I can to say what is necessary to constitute a marriage ceremony.

At supper that evening, Ella didn't ask about his decision. However, she did have something to say.

"I've, been thinking, John."

He smiled at these now familiar words from his wife. He lay down his fork and waited for what would come next.

"Remember when we were at Cora's, she mentioned a doctor in Colorado Springs who she was certain could help you?"

John started to object, but Ella put up her hand. "Hear me out, please. I think you should go see this doctor, the sooner the better. Who knows, maybe he can at least make talking a little easier and more understandable. Then you'll be able to officiate at the wedding."

John shook his head. "Ella, several specialists have done what they can for my condition. I seriously doubt another one has some magic up his sleeve that will do the trick." He could tell from the look in her eye that she wasn't convinced. "And then there is the cost of the trip."

"Now, John, you know we spent very little money on our travels in August, what with the generosity of Mrs. Whitney and Cora. Most of our savings for the trip are still in the tin under the bed. Cora practically begged me to have you see this doctor. She has great faith in him. It would be so worth it. Please go—if not for yourself, then for Abram and Ada, and," she continued in a soft, tear-choked voice, "for me." The pleading in her eyes cut into John like a razor just sharpened on a strop.

He left a few days later with the understanding he would not return until January—to give Doctor Wonderful time to perform his magic. And though John had serious doubts about the outcome, he prayed, for the sake of his family, the trip would be worth it.

He enjoyed Colorado, especially the company of his sister-in-law and her many friends, among them college professors and other highly educated men and women. In their presence he could relax and listen quietly with pleasure. He dutifully visited Cora's doctor, whose main instructions, in addition to hot, wet towels around the neck, all of which John had tried before, was "don't talk." Of course this helped, but as before, proved temporary, and frustrated John no end. What about the times he wanted to participate in conversations with what little voice he did have?

He returned to Waterloo in January with those directives, plus a horrible tasting concoction he was to gargle with twice a day. His throat felt better when he adhered to these remedies, but his speech remained abnormal. Close family members and friends had grown accustomed to his squawks and indecipherable guttural sounds, but the surprised and often sympathetic looks from strangers more than bothered him.

It was decided Ella and John would not attend the wedding. In addition to the raw throat, money was more of an issue now that he had emptied the tin to go to Colorado. Abram wrote that he understood. The marriage would be solemnized by the Reverend F. G. Davis, pastor of the First Baptist church where Ada regularly attended.

"That's probably best, anyway," John told Ella swallowing his disappointment. "I'm sure Miss Walker will be much more comfortable with her own pastor officiating."

The family was to be represented by the girls, each able to pay their own way. Margaret arrived in Waterloo a few days early, and she and Irene filled the house with happy chatter. As they packed to leave for Ottumwa, John overheard Irene ask her sister a question that had flickered in and out of his own mind. "When are you and Mr. Woods going to tie the knot, Maggie? You're letting Abram and Miss Walker get ahead of you."

Margaret seemed to toss off the question with nonchalance. "We haven't set a date. He is waiting to have enough money to support me."

John felt that was a good enough answer. In the meantime, he couldn't dwell on his regrets about not officiating at the marriage of his son and new daughter-in-law.

His saving grace, as always, was his focus on the continuing campaign to bring the right to vote to one-half of the nation's population. A constant challenge for him and other suffragists was the antisuffragist movement, which seemed to become stronger as the years progressed.

Occasionally, he and Ella would encounter Violet Cunningham on the streets of Waterloo. John actually enjoyed greeting the woman, and couldn't help but sense she was just one argument away from being convinced women deserved the right to vote. Yet, she always quoted something from the Bible, shaking her finger at him. "I don't understand how you as a holy man are so blind to God's true intent," she said at their last meeting, then turned in a huff and marched on her way.

Afterwards, John told Ella, "It's time for me again to clarify some points about the Bible and women in my writing,"

"You can't say it enough, John, though unfortunately the right people don't seem to be hearing it."

"I'll keep repeating it until they understand," he said, undaunted. So, he set about composing an editorial he entitled *The Bible and Women*, beginning with background information about the Bible. He first stated it was a compilation of history, poetry, philosophy, and theology written over several thousands of years, *not dictated from Heaven to a stenographer and written out on a typewriter. As Victor Hugo says, "God imparts his will to men by visible events, an obscure text written in a mysterious language."* And in John's words: *Of this obscure text... men have made manuscripts, transcripts, translations, revisions, versions, and editions; from these translations and versions have sprung parties, sects, factions, and misunderstandings. Men taking their stand upon Bible selections have argued in favor of slavery, polygamy, the subjection of women and other outrageous absurdities.*

But when the whole of the Bible is taken instead of a

selection; when the spirit of the Bible is taken instead of the letter; when the laws of interpretation are observed instead of the caprice of the moment or the fad of the hour, a far better argument can be made for liberty than ever was made for slavery, for monogamy than for polygamy, for woman's equality than for woman's subjection.

When his thoughts were focused on his editorials for *The Woman's Standard,* all other concerns evaporated. Expressing himself brought great satisfaction, and the fact that he did it with pen and paper instead of voice didn't seem to matter.

Letters from Abram, now less frequent with his marriage and a responsible job, told how he had completed his work with the Ottumwa Telephone Company. The couple made their home in Chicago, and John wrote to them often, immediately answering any correspondence—most of it from Ada who seemed to have taken up that responsibility.

Margaret still wrote regularly, but since Johnny's move to the west coast, letters from him were rare.

"I suppose it means the law practice is doing well," John told Ella. "And that's a good thing." He didn't voice his continued concerns regarding his eldest since he had left Iowa—now far from home and out of touch.

"That's no excuse!" Ella huffed. "He is still your son, and you deserve an occasional word from him. Success should not make him shun his family."

Finally, in July, after a long bout of silence, a letter arrived bearing the return address of Gaston & Stevenson, Attorneys and Counselors at Law, Everett, Washington. A spurt of joy flared in John's heart as he hurried to his study to open the envelope. Its thickness promised volumes of news.

He pulled out five pages of neatly typed pages and sat down to digest their contents only to discover the letter was not written by his son, but by his law partner, O. C. Gaston, which began: *Rev. Stevenson, Dear Sir and Friend, I feel under the necessity of writing you a letter which I regret to say may bring you disappointment and anxiety.* Alarm coursed through John creating a chill that left him immobilized for a long minute. A photo of his eldest, dressed in military garb, stared at him from a shelf opposite his desk. Closing his eyes, John prayed, "Please God, give me strength for what these pages reveal." With a deep breath, he refocused on the words before him.

… I think you should be fully apprised of the facts for the best interest of your son, and my friend, John.

As John read the entire letter, his hands began to shake, and his heart grew heavy. Mr. Gaston explained in great detail how John Jr. suffered from bouts of hallucinations, and in the young man's own words was often "batty."

To my mind, the attorney wrote, *it grows out of nothing except morbidness and a lack of strenuous exertion and the tense activity which, as you know, has heretofore marked his life. It may have been aided somewhat by the exposure of army life and the opium given him then as a remedy, as that, you are aware, tends to weaken the will and morbidly excite the imagination.*

Mr. Gaston said John was well-liked and had a group of close friends who were very concerned about him. Mrs. Gaston had arranged for treatments through the Christian Science faith that seemed to be helping. But then the letter told how John Jr. said doctors were after him and were going to "do him in." He himself felt this resulted from his job at the University of Iowa College of Law where he interned. During that time, to bring in much needed funds, he took care of the building for the College of Veterinary Medicine where he helped chloroform the dogs used in vivisection and then disposed of them afterwards—work he hated and now felt he was being punished for.

Mr. Gaston continued to say, *John's condition has been serious; so much so that I have been told that I ought emphatically to put him in an asylum or sanitarium, but that I am loath to do… We have no fear that John will do any harm; he thinks everything of us apparently and is perfectly at home with us, having the utmost confidence in us and taking our advice as good. We trust you will not worry over the matter, for we think he is going to get through this all right.*

John set the letter aside and for the first time in longer than he could remember, he wept like a child.

Chapter Thirty-Eight

MARKING TIME

1903-04

John sent an immediate response to Gaston, thanking him and asking to be kept advised of the situation. He also wrote to his son, careful not to reveal what he had learned from his law partner. This letter he labored over, leaving crumpled piles of paper in the wastebasket and on the floor. He wasn't totally satisfied with the final results, but basically said he and Ella were concerned because they hadn't heard from him in some time. He told him they loved him, and to please write.

John felt numb for days after reading Gaston's remarks. Silence hung heavy in the old parsonage. Ella's words of comfort and encouragement didn't help, and the two of them spoke little of the affliction suffered by John Jr., partly because it was painful, and because they had decided not to mention it to Irene. In addition, John couldn't get his mind off Anna. As much as he loved Ella and appreciated her support, he longed for Anna to be there to hold her and share this burden. What had become of their firstborn? Three little babies lay in graves in Shenandoah. Those losses were painful enough, but to lose an adult son because he was no longer cognizant seemed even more cruel. The lad held such promise. This affliction had to be temporary.

John's drive to write for *The Standard* and other publications somersaulted daily. There were times when it simply withered and deserted him like fragile leaves caught in an autumn wind. At other times, words crowded into his mind begging to be released onto paper. One such afternoon, as he reflected on Johnny's war experiences—surely the cause of his son's mental anguish—John's thoughts settled on the image of soldiers in training, marking time. We're all marking time in one way or other, he mused, not only men preparing for war, but women especially as they march to gain the right to vote. Yet little progress is made. John picked up his pen and began to write.

Military drill has an exercise called marking time. The feet are lifted and set down as in walking, but no step forward is taken. The experience teaches the soldier to keep step with others and thereby keep in time. It is also used when columns of troops are swung to the left or to right to maintain the line and present a solid front to a new direction.

John leaned back in his chair, waiting for more to come, then stood and walked to the parlor and back, three times.

"You're pacing," Ella said. "Does that mean the wheels in your brain are turning? Or have they stalled?"

He leaned against the piano where Ella sat studying a new piece of music. "I'm organizing my thoughts," he said. "I'm working with the theme *marking time.* Suffragists have maintained the line for years. They have turned to new directions to help their cause, yet they still seem to simply be marking time."

"How about including Mrs. Hansen's remark at the church meeting last week? I'm sure you could add some spice to that."

"Hmmmm. Good idea. Maybe you should be writing these editorials." He kissed her on the cheek, marched back to his study, and picked up a pen.

We were present in a religious gathering recently when a petition was being circulated for signatures in the hope to bring the moral forces into play against the unmoral forces that were violating the moral law. The minister exhorted the women also to sign the remonstrance. Many women did so, thereby marking time. Some women did not, saying, "What is the use of a woman signing this? Women do not vote. Women's petitions have no force in Iowa."

Such a woman has grown tired of marking time. We cannot blame women for tiring of marking time, since they have been at it a good many years in Iowa—as has most of the nation.

The preacher began to preach, and we began to think. What if women should go on strike and refuse to mark time any longer? What if they should all quit signing such petitions, running missionary circles and patronizing the moral and intellectual leagues of the day? What if the WCTU should disband and all benevolences be turned over to the men? Could they be blamed after their treatment at the hands of legislators and administrators and executives? Hardly. Men do not like to mark time forever. Why should women enjoy it? But let us continue to mark time. We will be able to march better when the order comes to go forward.

Whenever John wrote about moral issues and the WCTU, his thoughts paused for a moment on Beatrice

Cooper. No one had heard from her since Leroy's violent death. Where was she? Was she still alive? Such tragedies spurred him on.

He reread what he had written. Marking time was a good theme, but still there was hope. Over the years, many states had gradually allowed women to vote on select issues such as tax increases for public buildings—like Iowa's 1894 decision to grant women the right to vote on bond measures regarding schools and libraries. These positive steps needed to be acknowledged in the editorial.

Let us continue to mark time, for we are not wholly without progress. The world is awake. Men are discussing the cause of woman's rights, women are voting more and more, the press is more and more favorable to the cause, new doors are opening, bands are loosening, chains are falling, men, even in Iowa, are beginning to realize more and more that they need the help of the moral elements of society to secure a moral cause, a moral election, a moral municipal and state government.

~ ~ ~

FAMILY ISSUES ADDED TO THE JUMBLE OF THAT JULY. IRENE, after one year at the State Normal School, now headed for the Preparatory School of Denver University. John had long ago resigned himself to the fact that his children would not stay close by as he had once hoped. Opportunities abounded elsewhere in this growing country. Spreading their wings was a good thing. He must remember that, and toss away his selfishness.

Ella had been philosophical about Irene's decision,

her much-loved sister having a hand in the situation. "You and I don't seem to be able to move to Colorado," Ella told John. "So, Irene can represent the family there. Bless Cora's heart for arranging this opportunity."

Once the decision was made, Irene danced about in a gleeful dither. "I'll need some new clothes," she said, frowning at the meager offering of her wardrobe. "Especially winter ones. But with my housekeeping and childcare, I don't know how I'll ever find time to get anything sewn."

"I'll help," Ella said. "We'll do it on the weekends."

John observed with pride the camaraderie of his two special women. Ella had come into Irene's life when the girl was so young that they were as close as a mother and daughter could be. He knew this separation would be hard on both of them, but especially for Ella. Fortunately, two letters kept the mood in the old parsonage upbeat. Maggie was coming home for her summer break, and the day after that, Ada was due to arrive for a visit.

"Isn't that wonderful?" Ella said, her eyes aglow. "She is in Ottumwa visiting her family while Abram is off on a job for his company and will stop here on her return to Chicago."

John welcomed the news. The household would blossom with the two extra women, and they had yet to meet their new daughter-in-law. Ella's excitement seemed to ignite his own senses as he watched with humor while his wife sped around the house washing bedding, rearranging furniture, and baking—reminiscent of her preparations for Cora's visit years ago.

Ada proved to be as congenial as her photo suggested. There was a soft elegance in her young face and her intelligent blue-gray eyes seemed to hold questions asking to be answered. The brown hair, piled in soft curls on her head, added extra height to her stature. John could immediately see the allure she held for his son.

During Ada's stay, John gargled judiciously several times a day to keep his voice understandable, but the lovely young lady made no indication there was a problem. She and Maggie were most companionable. In fact, they returned to Chicago together, a good arrangement for both.

"Well," Ella said, as she and John stood at the doorway, arm in arm, seeing the girls off, "Abram certainly made a wise choice. Ada seems to handle his being gone much of the time. I know how difficult that can be for a wife."

John pretended to ignore that little dig. "Yes, I like her very much."

~ ~ ~

ONE MORE YEAR HUMMED BY, THIS TIME WITH JOHN AND Ella adjusting to a household without children. Frequent letters arrived from Maggie, Irene, Abram, and Ada. Occasionally one appeared from John Jr., though with never a mention of his mental state. John hoped that meant things were better but suspected the lad simply didn't want to worry his parents. The most honest communication regarding him came from his law partner—some letters more encouraging than others. Then, in late February of 1904, the note they dreaded was delivered.

O. C. Gaston wrote: *Dear Dr. Stevenson, I deeply regret to inform you that John has been institutionalized. We put it off as long as possible, but it became obvious over time that this was the only recourse. If you wish to contact him, he is now residing at Tacoma State Hospital, Lakewood, Washington.*

John had always prided himself that no matter what the circumstances, he could pull himself up and carry on, but there were moments when the weight of this news was almost too much to bear. In the past, Ella's positive spirit had helped. Now it seemed neither could bring themselves around. At the supper table, usually a time of reflection on the day and anticipation of tomorrow, he and Ella engaged in very little conversation. Finally, one evening John pushed his empty plate away, wiped his mouth with the linen napkin, laid it aside, and took Ella's hand.

"I need to let the others know," he said. "It's only right."

She nodded her agreement.

He rose from the table and headed toward his study. At his desk, he pulled out paper and pen and began the difficult task. By bedtime, three letters lay ready for the next day's post. John sat for a while longer, pondering the situation. He couldn't help wonder what he might have done differently as a parent. Had he been too hard on Johnny? The lad never seemed resentful of the work required of him during his growing years. It always came back to the war experiences and the opium. That was the only explanation.

As the weeks passed, John forced himself to focus on more cheerful subjects, even suggesting to Ella that they entertain. "Let's have the Alans over for dinner on Sunday. They are alway good company."

She sighed and shook her head. "Maybe some other time. I just don't seem to have the energy right now."

One day in late April, John forced himself out of the house and into the warm sunshine. Spring was late, and suddenly everything that had delayed blooming seemed to burst forth with color. Bees busily worked the blossoms of the cherry tree in the front yard — frothy in pink. A line of daffodils brightened the walkway like little welcoming sentinels, and the lilac bush stirred in a light breeze, a hummingbird dipping its beak into a lavender plume. At the risk of triggering his allergies, John inhaled deeply, intoxicated by the beauty. He could feel his spirits lifting. *I need to get out here more often.* He sat in the wicker chair on the porch, relaxing in the wonder of God's world, and dozed.

A voice startled him awake. A young man stood on the porch steps. "I'm looking for a Reverend Stevenson at this address. Is that you, sir?"

John abruptly stood. "Yes," he rasped. "How may I help you?"

"A telegram for you, sir." The boy held out a familiar-looking yellow envelope, then thrust a clipboard and pen at him. "Sign here for it, sir."

John felt his heart constrict. This had to be from Gaston, and it wouldn't be welcome news. With trembling fingers, he scrawled his name, then reached into his pocket and gave the courier a coin.

The boy grinned. "Thank you, sir."

He turned and strode down the walk, flipping his reward in the air while whistling a cheery tune.

But for John, the magic of the morning had evaporated. He returned to the chair, his legs suddenly leaden, the thin paper message clutched unopened in his palm. With his free hand he pulled a handkerchief from a pocket and wiped his brow. The spring sun had turned hot. With a silent prayer, he opened the telegram. Black print jumped out at him:

A baby girl, Josephine Ogilvie Stevenson, born this a.m. to Ada. Stop. Mother and baby doing fine. Stop. I am recovering. Abram.

Chapter Thirty-Nine

WHAT NEXT?

1904-1905

The feeling of new life surged in the old parsonage in Waterloo. Ella took to calling John "Grandpa."

"Yes, Grandma," he responded with a chuckle. How good it felt to be lifted up again.

After a day at the law office, Ella's fingers worked busily at knitting a pink shawl in place of stroking the piano keys. "Don't worry. You'll get your evening music back," she assured John, "but first things first."

A granddaughter, John mused. More reason to continue pushing for women's rights. Surely by the time Josephine was a young lady, she would be voting alongside the men of her generation. The importance of enfranchising women had come to the forefront in John's mind even more when, just weeks before, typhoid fever swept through Waterloo. Hundreds had been sickened and lives lost, this epidemic finally alerting public officials to the need of a clean water supply. He remembered that two years previously the Waterloo Civic Club spent an evening discussing the dangers of impure water and that of public buildings with no fire escapes. "And to what avail?" John had spouted to Ella. "Only an article in the daily paper by someone pooh-poohing the fears of the Civic Club, advising it to go and learn something about what it was discussing. If women had more voice in public matters..."

"I assume you are putting all this in a *Standard* article, dear," Ella said. This was often her response to his outbursts.

"Aye, indeed. I am."

He had much to say on the topic in the April edition. He wrote: *The point we make is this: In every community, there is an element alive to the dangers of disease and immortality... it is made up mainly of women... were they enfranchised the voting power would then include the domestic interest as well as the commercial interest and disasters such as theater fires and epidemics would be less likely to occur. The legislation along the lines of health and morals would become, by woman's vote, much more effectual than it now is. At any rate, the awakening of public interest on such measures would neither need a fire nor a fever.*

The year 1904 was also important for women's rights in Iowa, in that suffragists had once again presented to the House of Representatives a resolution for the submission of an amendment to the voters asking for equal suffrage. Forty-two representatives voted for it, a healthy number; however, thirty-nine nays meant it lacked the required constitutional majority to pass, so it lost by nine votes.

"As before, I will print the names of those antediluvians who stalled this important decision," John said as he stood beside Ella at the kitchen sink drying the evening supper dishes.

She smiled and scrubbed another plate. "I guess that response is working," she said. "Each time around a few more of those high and mighty men back down and join the smart ones. It's just that it's taking so long." She sighed and wiped her brow with a sudsy hand as though to clean away the creases forming there.

For the May edition, John included a blistering commentary written by Mary Coggeshall regarding the legislative defeat. He placed her words right up front on page one: *Dear Comrades*, she began, *again we have been called upon to pass through our biennial Gethsemane, of agony, and see our hope for an early enfranchisement go down before a legislative majority. Anyone who is even half intelligent knows that the legislature is not asked to grant woman's suffrage. It is only asked to permit the men of the state to decide by their votes whether they will grant it or not... It is evident that legislators are being driven into the last ditch. For years they simply feared to allow the question to go before the voters. They now fear for the question to have a chance even upon the floor of either house. For the last three sessions, the great effort was made to kill the bill in committee. The party word was: Strangle it at its birth.*

In the June *Standard*, John continued to expound on the narrow-mindedness of the legislature. *Our request for a referendum has been met in the usual way. Two years lie before us ere we can try again, and the question is "What Next?"* He gave his column that title, then continued with a multitude of ideas on how to move forward, ending on a positive note: *If we can maintain the integrity of our ranks and sustain our enthusiasm, we will shorten the time between the discouragements of the present and the sure encouragement of the future.*

On the fourth of July, John and Ella packed a lunch and, along with a crowd of others, spent the afternoon at nearby Washington Park. Ella spread a blanket on the cool grass. A brass band played patriotic music throughout the day, and during one interlude in the music, a gentleman stood and recited the Declaration of Independence, his deep basso voice booming across the revelators. "We hold these Truths to be self-evident, that all Men are created equal, that they are endowed by their Creator with certain unalienable Rights, that among these are Life, Liberty, and the Pursuit of Happiness. That to secure these Rights, Governments are instituted among Men, deriving their just Powers from the Consent of the Governed…"

Ella leaned over to John and whispered in his ear. "Do you suppose he is taking it literally? That only the male species are created equal? We should have brought the article you wrote on the subject for *The Standard* and read it aloud here. That would have caused some brilliant fireworks!"

In the July edition she referenced, John had written a strong editorial entitled *The Spirit of Seventy-Six,* inspired by what he considered misquotations and misinterpretations of the Declaration of Independence by men undermining its principles. Following an introductory paragraph stating that fact, he had continued with: *These are the truths which we hold to be self-evident. "All men are created equal." The word men as here used is the same as the word humanity, which includes women as well as men. The equality here predicated, means equality before the law. "Governments derive their just powers from the consent of the governed." And it makes no difference whether the governed be male or female, white, black or yellow, American or Asiatic, a just government will ask the consent of the governed. "Taxation without representation is tyranny," and the tyranny of a male majority, or a white majority, or a partisan legislature, is just as galling, just as tyrannical as that of a Czar or a king.*

Whenever a stack of an issue of *The Woman's Standard* was returned to John from the printers ready for him to mail to subscribers, he often delivered copies to the *Waterloo Courier* and other publications. If the papers chose to print his words, which happened more and more frequently, it reached a wider readership. *The Courier* seemed particularly pleased to receive them. If Ella got to the paper first, she always made a point to look for one of John's editorials.

"Here are your words for all to read again," she said with pride in her voice. "This ought to prompt a few letters to the editor."

"Good," John said. "I hope so." He enjoyed any comments generated by his writing. It meant people were paying attention. Folks he met at church and on the street let him know they had read his work. These were friends, many of whom agreed with him. Some of the responses printed in the paper often didn't, but this was to be expected.

One muggy summer morning, John left early for the church office to work on the books for the General Association. This connection to his former pastorate and the Congregational Church membership throughout Iowa brought an added energy to his step, and despite the weather, allowed his spirits to remain high. He stayed through the lunch hour, snacked on bread and cheese brought from home, and visited with the church staff.

On his return home in the mid-afternoon, jacket flung over his arm and perspiration tricking down his neck, he hummed a hymn as he strolled up the walkway to the old parsonage. Upon unlocking the door, he glanced down and stopped short with surprise.

"What is this?" An envelope had been jammed into the crack under the door. Leaning down, John pulled it loose, exposing large red letters scrawled across the front. *Read your Bible!* The first thought to sweep through his mind was someone canvassing the neighborhood promoting their own religious convictions; however, the bold words implied more of a threat than proselytizing. John entered the house and made his way into the parlor. Laying his coat on the arm of a chair, he sat and ripped open the sealed envelope. A newspaper clipping fell onto his lap—his latest reprint in *The Courier* of an article from *The Woman's Standard*. The accompanying single sheet of paper bore bright red sentences. *How can a man of your education and background so misconstrue the words of God?*

John studied the message in his hand. Words were spelled correctly, the letters large for obvious emphasis, and the penmanship good. Whoever was responsible was probably as educated as he—though of an entirely opposite mindset. He was accustomed to viewpoints that differed from his own. This just happened to be a new method of delivering disagreement. The one thing that rankled him was its anonymity. He preferred discussing his point of view person to person, and had lower respect for anyone who chose not to face him with their argument. He sat for a while pondering the unexpected note, then set it aside. This was probably the end of it.

The following day, John stayed at home working in his study, windows open to catch any breeze that might waft through and relieve the oppressive heat. In early afternoon, he leaned back in his chair and closed his eyes. A completed editorial lay on the desk before him. Images and scattered thoughts floated through his mind as he drifted into the edges of sleep, but the sound of rapid footsteps outside yanked him awake. He glanced out the window in time to see a figure racing away from the house. John sprang up from his chair, stumbled on the rug in his groggy state, and headed for the foyer. By the time he opened the front door, no one was in sight. At his feet lay another envelope. He scooped it up and returned to the study where he compared its contents to the one received the day before. The penmanship matched, and the message, again in red ink, read: *Have you not read that Paul said women were to be discreet, chaste, keepers at home, good, and obedient to their own husbands? Rev. Stevenson, you are preaching the wrong message. Shame on you!*

John let the note fall to the table and sighed. How he would like to sit down with this misguided person and discuss the rights of women with him.

The second message did not sit well with Ella. "This

is harassment," she fumed, her jaw set after reading the note. "I think you should lay a trap. Stay by the door all afternoon, grab him when he appears, then shake a confession out of him. Torture him a little if you have to — maybe twist his arm or stomp on his toes."

"That would not be very becoming of a man of the cloth, even a retired one," John said, amused at her suggestions.

"Then I'll stay home and grab him and shake some sense into him myself." Ella snapped the dish towel in her hand for emphasis. "I am not a man of the cloth, and thus not restricted by those unspoken rules."

"Of course, my dear." He knew she was simply letting off steam, but understood the motivation behind his wife's anger.

However, her thoughts on being alert should the culprit reappear, and confronting him, appealed to John. Perhaps if he did so, he would get some answers. The following day in lieu of a nap, which was becoming more and more a habit in the warm afternoon, he plied himself with coffee, put a chair outside under a tree at the side of the house, and sat. Though partially hidden by leafy branches, he had a good view of the walkway to the front door. Two hours passed. He observed an occasional carriage, clipping along Washington Street and the humming of the bees visiting a nearby bush. John began to feel this was a terrible waste of time. Stretching, he decided to return to his study and put down on paper the thoughts he'd been gathering while sitting in wait.

He picked up the chair, then set it down again when

he spied a young man sauntering along the road. Dressed in knickers held up by suspenders over a striped shirt, his face hidden under the rim of a cap, he could have been a newsboy delivering the afternoon paper. Yet, something about his manner drew John's attention. The figure slowed, looked around, then promptly marched up the walkway, pulled back his arm and flung a brick at the house. A sudden earsplitting crash shattered the silent afternoon as the parlor window splintered into a thousand pieces.

John's astonishment immediately turned to anger. He rushed forward, grabbing the perpetrator by the arm. "Just a minute, young man. Damaging private property is going too far. If you have something to say to me, say it now in a civil manner, or I'm calling the authorities."

A wide-eyed look of terror swept across the face of the courier who screamed, then jerked free with such momentum that his cap fell to the ground. John stood speechless as a cascade of blonde curls tumbled loose. The person behind the mysterious afternoon deliveries—a woman—raced up the street away from the house. John made no attempt to follow. When she was out of sight, he leaned down and scooped up the cap which, along with clothing typical of a young man, had concealed her identity and gender.

Chapter Forty

FLAPDOODLE

John entered the house and picked up the brick which lay among shards of glass on the parlor floor, the now familiar white envelope tied neatly to one side. Pulling it from the twine, he opened the seal and read. The message was a repeat of the others. John shook his head, sighed, and retrieved a broom from the kitchen.

He was outside applying a make-shift repair to the damaged window when Ella returned home at the end of her work day. She walked across the lawn and stood there, a puzzled look on her face. "What are you up to, now, Reverend Husband?" Coming closer, her expression changed to one of surprise as the damage became apparent. She put her hands on her hips. "Oh, my. Have you been throwing rocks at the house?"

John pounded the last nail in and stood back to view the results. He had found a stray shingle from the barn roof to cover the jagged gap resulting from the shattered pane. "Guess that will do temporarily," he said, wiping his brow before responding to his wife. "No. Not me. Not rocks. A political brick did the job."

"What?"

He could feel Ella's anger rise to the surface like

steam from a shrieking teapot as she followed him into the house. He motioned toward the parlor where she sat, not even bothering to remove her hat. Pointing to the white envelope resting on the tea table, he told her the latest saga of the baffling messages and the surprising courier. "She had a hefty arm for a woman, that's for certain."

"Well!" Ella huffed and stood, her face turning scarlet. "Well! This has gone too far." She marched toward the front door, flinging it open. "I am going to put a stop to this."

"Wait a minute," John stomped after her. "Where do you think you're going?"

"I am heading right over to Violet's house to give her a piece of my mind. Surely, she is somehow responsible. This ridiculous harassment has gone too far."

John grabbed her arm. "Ella, take hold of yourself. You have no proof Violet had anything to do with this. The antisuffrage movement has been building lately, and it's not Violet's style. This could be anyone. Don't go off half-cocked and cause more trouble."

Ella stared at him a moment. He never spoke to her in such a stern manner, and it obviously got her attention. He felt her arm go limp. He loosened his grip, and she leaned into him. "Oh, John. It is just so frustrating. You work painstakingly at something meant for the good and then get punished for it. It's not fair."

They agreed it was time to report the incidents to the authorities. An hour later, when the marshal surveyed the damage, he scowled, pulled a notebook and pencil from his pocket, and wrote some hasty comments. "I'll make a report, but can't really do anything unless we know who's behind it." He scratched his head and thought a moment. "You say the messages have been delivered about the same time every day?"

"As far as we know. No one was home the first time the envelope was left."

"Tell you what," the officer said. "Tomorrow I'll come around about then. Maybe we can catch whoever it is."

After he had gone, and the door shut behind him, Ella remarked, "Well, that will keep the culprit away for sure, with the law standing right there. Now we'll never know who's doing this."

John shook his head. "It doesn't matter, Ella. I suspect she wouldn't have come back anyway. And we do know who it is in general— some misguided person who doesn't yet understand what is best for her and our country. We deal with this all the time, just in a less violent manner."

True to Ella's prediction, with the marshal's presence there for a few days, the incidents were not repeated. Somewhere in the city of Waterloo, a young woman felt she had been recognized and therefore would not risk arrest. Besides, in her mind, she must feel she had gotten her message across, so what was the point?

~ ~ ~

FRUSTRATION OVER THE STAGNATION OF WOMAN'S RIGHTS simply spurred John forward to continue fighting for the cause with his pen. For Ella, however, her anger flared—especially over the brick incident. The thought that there were women who were blind to the advantages voting would open to them seemed incomprehensible to her. She sometimes took out her wrath in the garden, tugging weeds as though they were the enemy. John worked alongside her, digging up root vegetables and pulling tomato worms off the plants—something Ella refused to do.

"Why don't these women understand?" she sputtered.

"Many of those who oppose suffrage have husbands with political power they can influence," John said. "Those women don't feel the need. They already have what they want—at least they seem to think so."

Ella sat back, a weed clump in one hand, wiping her brow with the other. "Maybe those high and mighty society ladies should visit the women who spend hours in the factories that have sprung up in Waterloo during the past few years. A conversation with women who have no voice in their work hours or wages, or have no control over their money, might change some minds. John raised his eyebrows at this. "What do you know of those women? Have you been to the factories?"

"Well, no, but I've met a few. The missionary society helps sponsor some of those families, you know." She sat there in the sun for a few minutes, a contemplative look spreading across her face. Suddenly she stood, handed John the weed she held, and marched toward the house.

He glanced at the straggly dandelion, tossed it aside,

picked up a basket of carrots and beets, and followed Ella. "Where are you going?"

"I have an idea."

An idea, John muttered to himself. *This may not be good.* He followed her into the house.

Twenty minutes later, Ella appeared from upstairs wearing a clean dress, her hair tidied, and her newest hat in hand. She stopped by a vase of flowers, freshly picked that morning, and extracted a red rose to tuck in her hat band. "I'm going visiting," she said. Without further comment, she swept out the front door.

She was gone longer than he expected, but John refused to worry. Two hours passed before he heard Ella's footsteps on the front walk. He greeted her at the door. She entered with a smug look on her face, removed her gloves and hat, the rose now slightly wilted. She continued into the kitchen where she poured herself a large glass of water, then sat at the table.

John pulled out a chair and sat opposite her, waiting for whatever she had to say. Ella's eyes held a mischievous twinkle.

"Well, you were right," she said after consuming the entire glass of water.

"Thank the Lord for that. It doesn't happen too often around here. Right about what?"

"Violet Cunningham."

John groaned. *What had his wife done!* "You didn't."

"I did." Ella beamed. "I visited Violet, and you were right. She had nothing to do with those horrible messages. In fact, she was downright decent to me—

invited me in for tea. We actually had a pleasant chat."

"Did you accuse her of brick throwing?" John tried to control his dismay. "And what about her husband, was he there?"

"Of course not—to the brick. But I had to determine if she at least knew who was involved. You've always said we need to talk these things out to make progress. As to her husband, I doubt she would have asked me in had he been there. He is the thorn in her paw, as you well know. And though she is of the class that you say does not feel the need for a woman's right to vote, I think she is tired of not having the right to decide for herself. What do you think of that!" Ella grinned so broadly, John doubted anything could wipe it from her face at the moment.

He shook his head and smiled back at her. "And what do you think changed her mind? What about all her ranting over the years about me misquoting the Bible?"

"Well, we know she has been reading *The Woman's Standard*. You and others keep putting some mighty convincing words in that publication. I'll give you some credit for her conversion." She hesitated a moment. "And then there is her niece Polly who lives with her. She must certainly be an influence."

"So, Violet is on our side now?" John felt a glow of triumph at the possible persuasion of such a stubborn woman.

"Almost. During our conversation, I reminded her that this was an election year, and only men can decide who will be president of the United States. I asked her, wouldn't she like to have a say in that important decision? The outcome certainly affects women as well as men." Ella paused, and her mood seemed to change. She clutched the empty glass in both hands and shook her head.

"A government of the people, for the people, and by the people? Hah! That's hogwash. Aren't we women people?" She abruptly stood, carried the glass to the sink, plopped it on the counter and left the room.

The wheels in John's head began to turn. He slipped into his study and began to write.

The presidential campaign is now on. That ancient spavined steed, "a government of the people, for the people, and by the people," has already been trotted out. This is no such government. In the so-called "North," with the exception of four states, we have a government of the people by the men and not necessarily the best men at that. In the so-called "South," the government is not even by men. It is a government for the people by the white men…

So long as more than one half of the people are systematically excluded from the ballot box; so long as the moral, educational, and religious half is not at all, or at the best, poorly represented at the polls; all talk in a republic of a government of the people, for the people, and by the people is simply flapdoodle or food for fools.

~ ~ ~

In the meantime, family joys and concerns continued. Letters from Ada told of Josephine's development. One included a photo of a bright baby draped in Ella's hand-knitted shawl.

"I think she looks like you, John. Don't you agree?" Ella said. She had framed the picture and placed it prominently on the piano where the baby's perpetual smile brightened the room. She looked like a regular baby to him, although definitely alert and intelligent, as any grandchild should be. John was simply happy for Abram and his lovely wife.

Constant thoughts about his other son were a different matter. Now that John Jr. was institutionalized, they never heard from him. Occasionally, Gaston sent a brief note that seldom included encouraging news. The most contact they had regarding Johnny came from friends living in Washington State who now and then made an effort to visit him. Their letters always tried to sound upbeat and pleasant and at least gave John some idea of the situation.

The national election came and went without votes from women. Theodore Roosevelt won with an overwhelming majority, the antisuffragists' assessment being that a woman's vote wouldn't have mattered one way or the other.

"That's a ridiculous assumption." Ella remarked. "How does anyone know what the outcome would have been when half the population can't speak for themselves?"

Chapter Forty-One

POLITICAL STUPIDITY

1906

An early winter wind howled outside as the year 1905 wound down. Ella sat in a chair opposite John's desk. She sometimes joined him in his study while he wrote, as he seemed to be there more than anywhere else in the house. As long as she promised to be quiet and not disturb his thought process, at least they were together. She often read, but tonight she knitted another baby shawl—this one blue. In October, Abram and Ada had blessed them with another grandchild, Gordon Keen Stevenson.

"I wish they were closer so we could enjoy those babies," Ella said. "Abram's job keeps them moving around so much. I scarcely know where to send this when I've finished." She stopped knitting a moment and sighed. "That must be hard on Ada—never knowing exactly where they will be living next." She shook her head, returned to her project, and began another row.

John flipped his pencil back and forth between his fingers as he watched the blue yarn gradually unroll from the ball in Ella's lap into a lacy pattern. His thoughts shifted to long ago when he and Anna's family grew each year—seven precious babies, one after another. He pictured the three little graves in

Shenandoah. *Dear Lord, may Abram and Ada's children all be healthy, happy, and live long lives.* Clearing his mind of the past, he refocused on the words he had written.

It is well known that the worshiping audiences of all our churches are composed of women by an overwhelming majority. It is well known that church membership also consists of women in a ratio of three or four women to each man. It is well known that women have no vote except in four western states. It ought to be well known that because of this condition of affairs, Christianity is practically disenfranchised. Nevertheless, somebody gets up every now and then and declares that if Christians would vote as they aught, our political corruption would immediately be reformed. All of which is pure political stupidity.

John reread what he had written and nodded to himself. This was a good opening paragraph. He continued:

The latest ignoramus along these lines is an anonymous writer in Collier's Weekly who says: "If Christians should vote their duty to God at the polls, they would carry every election and do it with ease. They would elect every clean candidate in the United States and defeat every soiled one. Their prodigious power would be quickly realized and recognized, and afterward there would be no unclean candidates upon any ticket, and graft would cease."

John chewed on the end of his pencil a moment as he perused what he had written, then with an "ah ha," and a smile, he added: *To make good sense out of this nonsense change the word should for could. Then it would read "If Christians could vote..."*

He continued writing what became an entire

column, pointing out the absurdity of yet another man's thoughts that blindly eliminated the Christian majority who could make his comments a reality—the women.

Though retired, John still attended meetings of the ministerial association to keep abreast of the Christian community. He mostly listened, but his peers were accustomed to his croaking voice and seemed undisturbed when he did speak. In one of his monthly letters to Sarah Whitney, now living in California, he expressed his frustration that even the pastors in the Waterloo churches often seemed not to get the message.

It amuses me much to sit in our ministerial association and hear the brothers discuss "cleaning up the town," apparently unconscious of any relation between their work and "votes for women." I pinch them once-in-a-while, but it seems to do very little good.

~ ~ ~

THE YEAR 1906 BLEW IN WITH BLUSTER. WIND WHIPPED snow flurries in circles, coating everything in white. When the sky cleared, the air was painful to breathe, and those folks who ventured out wrapped their faces in woolen scarves, coats buttoned tightly and collars raised high. However, with the river frozen solid, the youth braved the cold to don their skates and slide along the glassy surface. Bonfires along the banks warmed their frozen hands. When John bundled up to go out, he often stood on the bridge watching the gaiety, remembering when his own children were among the skaters. His offspring were now scattered beyond

Waterloo living their own lives: Abram and Ada always moving around, Maggie graduated from Nebraska University and a principal at a high school in Ohiowa, Irene now teaching kindergarten in New Orleans, and Johnny—lost in a world of his own in an institution on the west coast.

In the warmth of his study, John continued penning his editorials, now appearing more and more often in the *Waterloo Courier* as well as *The Woman's Standard*. In the April edition, he had the sad task of including tributes to Susan B. Anthony who, at eighty-six years of age, died on March 13th. *A great soul has passed from earth,* John wrote, concluding her biographical sketch with: *Speak of the American revolution and we think of George Washington; speak of the emancipation of the slave and we think of Abraham Lincoln; speak of woman's emancipation and we think of Susan B. Anthony.*

Ella read the remarks with a shake of the head. "She worked so hard and never saw her fight won. The best we can do is carry on and not give up."

"And right now, that is encouraging for Iowa," John said as they enjoyed an evening by the wood stove in the parlor. "The legislature is about to decide once again whether to allow the public to vote on an amendment to the state constitution allowing women to vote. Maybe the thirty-first time will be the charm. The petitions are filled with more signatures than ever before—especially those of men."

"And the one I passed around even had Violet Cunningham's bold scrawl. Don't forget that!" Ella boasted for the hundredth time.

John had to give his wife credit for her perseverance in garnering this new recruit. Violet had even convinced some of her followers to sign. These small battles won made the fight feel victorious, even though the war against suffragists still raged.

But once again, even with the many petitions, the measure lost.

~ ~ ~

ON SUNDAY, MAY 3RD, JOHN AND ELLA DRESSED FOR church, pulling out warm weather clothing for the first time in what seemed like ages. Ella sported a new hat, a luxury she afforded herself once a year as the chief bread-earner—this one, a smart beige felt with a silk rose in a soft yellow affixed to the band. They looked forward to the service with eager anticipation and curiosity. A Reverend Walter H. Rollins was to fill the pulpit with hopes from the congregation that he would become the next pastor, the Reverend Tanner having gone as well as his successor, Reverend Seecombe.

As John and Ella walked arm in arm the few blocks to Jefferson Street, a voice from behind called out to them. "Good morning, Dr. and Mrs. Stevenson."

They turned to see Mr. and Mrs. Alan hurrying to catch up. John doffed his hat and smiled. "Good morning to you this lovely day. Please join us."

The two men strode side by side with the women leading the way. "Any more bricks through your window?" Mr. Alan asked.

John shook his head. "Nothing that violent, just the usual rebuttals in the paper. Of course, worse than even a ton of bricks is yet another rejection by the legislature refusing to put the question of a woman suffrage to a public vote."

Clyde Alan shook his head. "A lot of pig-headed men running our state, Stevenson. Maybe they simply don't have wives as smart as ours, so they think it's a bad idea."

"On the contrary," John harumphed. "They probably do have smart wives, and that scares them."

Clyde laughed, and as they approached the church, he changed the subject. "Well, let's see how smart Reverend Rollins is. That's our immediate concern for the moment."

They entered the narthex, and John took Ella's hand, leading her to their pew. Sunbeams angled through the stained glass windows casting rainbow colors across the sanctuary. "It's like stepping into a magical kingdom," Irene had once whispered in awe.

"It is," John had responded squeezing her small hand. "The kingdom of God."

On this particular Sunday, a sense of nostalgia seized him. He had been instrumental in the construction of this beautiful place of worship, and now with Waterloo growing leaps and bounds, there was talk of selling it and building yet another larger church. Growth, of course, was good, but this was his church in more ways than one. Tearing it down would leave a painful wound. His melancholy was interrupted by loud and vigorous applause from the congregants as the Reverend Rollins stepped up to the pulpit. At the end of the service, John shook hands heartily with this new recruit. The man would be a good addition to Waterloo.

While the obviously capable Reverend Rollins took hold of the reins at the Congregational Church, John continued to tackle the ongoing issue of the close-minded members of the Iowa government. The May edition of *The Woman's Standard* was about ready to go to press. Only the important first page needed completing. John's mind and pencil flew.

The thirty-first general assembly of Iowa has come to an end. The general consensus of the Iowa opinion is that it was a good deal of a failure. Its vote on the question of submitting equal suffrage to the people was 42 ayes and 45 noes, 13 absent or not voting.

John again named names, noting that two men in particular who voted against the measure were Republicans... *however the majority of Republicans voted for suffrage, whereas the Democratic members voted almost unanimously against us... this is the season of Jeffersonian banquets when the Democratic orator loves to quote Jefferson's saying, "equal rights to all, special privileges to none."... from all such Democrats, good Lord, deliver us, because in this context, "all" of course does not include women.*

After putting down these remarks, John stood abruptly and strode outside, marching back and forth on the walkway along the street, gesturing and talking to himself, letting off steam.

Twenty minutes later, he re-entered the house, his anger subsided, his thoughts realigned. He would focus on Oregon which once again was putting the idea of women's suffrage to a vote. He searched through a stack of papers. Picking up a letter from an Emma Smith DeVoe of Oregon, he scanned her words: *I am working night and day in the Oregon campaign,* she wrote. *We had a splendid meeting in Jefferson. Mark my word, Oregon will carry for woman suffrage in June. When Oregonians hear the gospel of equality preached, they respond promptly. The men say, "I am with you. I'll vote for woman's suffrage." What more could we ask?* Mrs. DeVoe's positive remarks were to go on the front page of *The Standard* to counter the disappointment of the loss in Iowa.

John felt, as did many others, that the Oregon campaign would finally be successful. "Oregon has actually managed to get the question of a woman's right to vote on the ballot twice before," he told Ella. "Each time it failed, but the second time, forty-eight percent of the voters supported it. This year it's a referendum put there by the people themselves. That's a huge leap."

The possibility of one more state reaching its goal excited Ella. John could see it in her eyes. The National American Woman Suffrage Association had held its annual conference in Portland the year before, and Ella so wanted to be among the delegates from Iowa who attended. John had just smiled and shook his head, knowing it was beyond their financial means. In spite of her age, Susan B. Anthony had been among those who gave speeches, as well as Anna Howard Shaw, president of the national organization. Iowa's own Mary Jane Coggeshall was also among the delegates. A huge campaign had ensued, and now that the election was imminent, suffragists across the nation held their collective breath, anticipating another victory for their cause.

After the date for the vote in Oregon, John looked for news of the outcome. *We scanned the columns of the great political dailies in vain for information on this point. It may not have been worthy of their notice,* he wrote as he put together the July issue of *The Woman's Standard.* When news of defeat did begin to trickle out to the rest of the nation, commentaries often stated the results against the referendum were "large and decisive."

"That is not necessarily true," John pointed out to Ella. She had come into his study that sweltering summer afternoon with a cold drink for him, reading over his shoulder as he relayed to the readership the unhappy news. John took the glass from her and drew a long swallow. "The measure actually received forty-four percent of the vote. It was the liquor and other business interests who spent large sums in advertising that defeated it," he said.

Ella leaned against the desk, dabbing at her face with a handkerchief, the perspiration sticky and wet at her hairline. "Well, of course, isn't that always the problem?" She sighed. "The very issue that would make a difference if we women could vote is the same nemesis that won't allow it."

~ ~ ~

THE THIRTY-FIFTH ANNUAL STATE CONVENTION FOR THE Iowa Woman Suffrage Association was to be held in Ida Grove that September. John usually attended and always looked forward to these occasions. It was tremendously stimulating to be with a large group of folks together in support of the same cause. As he prepared for bed one night in late August, he was suddenly struck with an idea. He sat on the wicker chair in the corner, pulling off one shoe then the other. Holding a sock in his hand he thought for a moment, then blurted. "Come with me, Ella. You haven't taken time off from work in a long while. You need a break."

She lay on top of the coverlet in her summer nightgown, the still evening air too oppressive to crawl between sheets, and looked up from the book she was reading. "Come with you where?"

"To Ida Grove. You can be an unofficial delegate. You'll find it a splendid experience to mingle with all those like-minded people—men and women. It's very uplifting, and I know how discouraged you have been over the setbacks lately."

"Hmm," she murmured. "Let me think about it."

It didn't take much thinking on her part, and so three weeks later, they boarded the train for Ida Grove. John could feel Ella's excitement as they traveled west across the state. He squeezed her hand. "You'll be glad you came. You'll see."

They stayed in the home of a gracious couple— staunch suffragists—and the town was small enough they could walk to any destination. The three days were a whirlwind of speeches, reports, meeting old friends, and making new acquaintances. On their return, John got right to finishing up the October *Standard,* having saved the first page, as always, for the most current news and happenings in the push for woman's rights.

Ida Grove is a city set upon a hill. The equal suffrage convention raised that hill a foot higher. The weatherman must be an equal suffragist, for he gave the convention model autumn weather. The spirit of the meeting was joyous and sunny. The Hon J. L Bleakly in his address of welcome, said he was in hearty sympathy with the cause of woman's suffrage, had always voted for it and hoped to see the day when it would be granted. Rev. W. E. Kunz of the Presbyterian church, said that it was in sight, and that it was the greatest bloodless revolution in history.

Though John and Ella had returned with a glow for their cause, upon returning they were greeted with the news that the Congregational Church had entered into a contract with a syndicate to sell its property at the corner of Fifth and Jefferson Street. A new, larger building would be constructed on West Fourth and South Streets.

Ella understood John's mixed feeling regarding this "progress." She patted his arm and said. "It will still be a short walk, John, when the weather is good."

Chapter Forty-Two

ALL SWEPT AWAY

1907

As the beginning of another year unfolded, more pressing matters than the letting go of an old church building occupied John's mind. Lately, letters from Gaston and others regarding John Jr. brought a different concern. During his confinement, the young man had developed pulmonary tuberculosis, and the prognosis wasn't good. A longtime friend, Mrs. Uhl of Shenandoah, had recently visited the northwest institution and written John that his son's death by summer seemed inevitable. With this news hanging heavy on his heart, he responded to her note:

The sorrow is very hard to bear as I had built upon John a reliance in my declining years and a dependence for the rest of the family when I shall have gone. This is all swept away. Then it is hard because John was our first child and I had curted and carried him in those days long gone on the far away hills of Connecticut, and it was hard because he would not come East, would not write, such was the nature of his disease which gave his mind the twist to go away off somewhere and hide himself; to cut off the past completely. And so I could not be with him in his trouble. Your account of your visit is the only comforting word I have received. According to you, he seems to have been off his guard and more natural and thus your account more satisfactory.

Though John tried to concentrate on his editorials and other daily responsibilities, he couldn't get Mrs. Uhl's letter out of his mind. If he made the long trip to Washington State, would his son be lucid and know him? From other letters he had received, he wasn't too sure. He took long walks, even when winter winds snapped at his coattails and bit at his ears and fingers. He often was not home when Ella returned from work.

One such evening when they sat down for a late supper and he scarcely mumbled two words, Ella rested her elbows on the table and looked him in the eyes. "John, what is it? You are not yourself. This is more than thinking through an article for the newspaper. Something else is going on, and I have a right to know."

He could hear curiosity in her voice, but also concern, and perhaps a little bit of anger. He did not respond immediately.

"John!" This time the irritation in Ella's voice seemed to tear at the wallpaper in the small kitchen.

"I've been thinking," he said.

At that she huffed and folded her arms against her chest waiting for more than the obvious.

"I need to go to see Johnny." There, he had said it. "It means leaving you for a month or so, and an expense, but don't you see, Ella? I must see him before it's too late."

Tears sprang to Ella's eyes. "Of course you should go. Of course. And did you think I wouldn't understand? Oh, John, this has been eating away at you too long. Go!"

He boarded the train for points west a few days later, arriving at the terminus for the Northern Pacific Railroad in Tacoma, Washington, late on a March afternoon.

Exhaustion from a long journey and the churning anxiety at seeing his eldest son under difficult circumstances, made him decide a night's rest first would be wise. A friend had recommended the Tacoma Hotel. He hoped it was not far from the train station. To get there, he could have selected one of those new-fangled sputtering automobiles, but instead, he hailed a horse and carriage, and directed the driver to the hotel.

"The Tacoma? Good choice," the man said. "Best hotel north of San Francisco. You'll be treated like royalty. Famous people stay there, yes sir!"

Shortly thereafter, he pulled up in front of an elegant five-story building, complete with turrets, covering an entire city block. John feared the cost might be a bit much for his pocketbook, but he was here now, and a bath and bed sounded too good to go in search of other accommodations. A stiff breeze carried with it the unmistakable scent of bay water mixed with pungent evergreens, though dark clouds directly overhead threatened rain. A clear horizon show-cased a magnificent snow-capped peak. John had not been to this part of the country before, and he immediately understood the lure of the place. But weariness sent him to find his room.

He awoke early, and after a filling breakfast in the hotel lobby, engaged a carriage to take him to the State Hospital. John choked a little on the words when he gave his destination, though the driver seemed not to notice his discomfort. The carriage drifted in and out of a low fog as they traveled, and the cabby, a little too friendly, chatted continually. "Ah, the hospital. I had you pegged for a doctor right away."

John didn't correct him. It saved him the embarrassment of admitting his son was a patient there. After all, he was a doctor, wasn't he? Just not the kind that attended to medical needs. The man with the reins talked away. "Interesting history, that place. Suppose you know it was the old Fort Steilacoom military post for years. Then the state turned it into a hospital for crazy folks. Insane Asylum of Washington Territory, they called it."

John winced. He hadn't heard such a blunt name for the hospital. If he recalled correctly, Gaston had kindly referred to is as a sanitarium. The driver rambled on. "Guess some people got offended at that and more recently the name was changed to Western State Hospital. All the same, though, if you ask me."

By the time they turned into the drive, John's stomach felt clutched by a giant claw, and he thought he might lose his breakfast. However, even with all the talk, he wasn't prepared for the enormity of the place. The cluster of three-story brick buildings seemed to go on forever, covering acres of land and framed by the ever-present, towering evergreens. For a full moment John simply gaped.

"Here you are, Doc. It's all yours." The driver's flippancy brought John back to reality. He handed the man money and eased himself out of the carriage. He gripped the handle of his valise—full of gifts and letters from family and friends for Johnny—and forced himself forward.

A pleasant woman in a full-sleeved blue uniform covered by a long white apron, a crisp cap on her graying hair, led John up a flight of stairs and down an endless hallway, keys jingling in her pocket. Floor wax, rubbing alcohol, and a mix of more unpleasant odors dominated the long walk. Finally, the nurse stopped in front of a door, inserted a key into a lock and motioned John into a large room. There must have been twenty beds crowded into the space—all occupied.

The woman nodded to the second bed over. John approached, his heart in his throat. There against the sheets lay an emaciated version of his eldest son—his eyes closed. John whispered a deep prayer and laid a hand on the young man's arm. "Johnny?"

The lad's eyes opened, focused, and then a broad smile stretched across his wan face. "Papa?"

John felt he would burst with joy. This was not at all what he had expected. He pulled up a chair, and they talked. Johnny's mind seemed clear, and he spoke about the old times. It was as if the hallucinations and all the issues that had brought him to this place never existed. "I got a letter from Abram," he said, "though I must confess I haven't answered. Guess I haven't been too good about that lately. How are the girls and mother? I haven't heard much from them."

"They let me do the writing," John said. "I think they are not sure what to say, but they love you and you are always in their thoughts. Here, I brought letters from each." He opened his valise and pulled out several envelopes setting them on a small table beside the bed.

"And I brought this—just in case yours didn't get here with you." He added a copy of the New Testament to the pile of letters. A vase of flowers and a few magazines also lay on the table. "Pretty bouquet," John commented.

"From Miss Laing," Johnny volunteered. "She is good to me."

"Miss Laing?" John queried at the mention of the unfamiliar name.

A smile brightened Johnny's pale face. "Yes, a special friend. She is often here and keeps me company—sees to my needs."

This news warmed John's heart. *A woman to look after my son and care for him. Thank you, Lord.* Gaston had not mentioned this.

John stayed for over an hour until, in his weakened state, the lad drifted off. "I'll come back tomorrow," John whispered, and quietly left the room.

He found the nurse in charge and asked for a prognosis. She was frank, but kind. "If he should have one more severe hemorrhage, his recovery from that would be doubtful. The tuberculosis is in the final stages." Nothing was mentioned about Johnny's mental state, for which John was very grateful. Death was always hard to bear, but a disease of the body was somehow more acceptable than a disease of the mind.

John stayed a few more days, spending as much time with his son as possible. When it appeared the boy would linger for weeks, perhaps longer, John left for home, grateful that he had come and more at peace with what he had found than he had expected to be.

"You were sorely missed at the farewell service in the old church building," Ella remarked upon his return, "though your absence was understood. You might even have been embarrassed at all the tributes you received regarding the construction of that church. Now, until the new building is ready, services are being held in the West Waterloo Library. A very different experience, I might add."

John was sorry to have missed the last service in the Jefferson Street church—not really such an old building, just too small. But perhaps it was best he hadn't been there.

~ ~ ~

THE TELEGRAM ARRIVED MAY 15TH: JOHN OGILVIE Stevenson Jr. had passed the evening before.

Working through his grief, John immediately wrote quick notes to his other children and labored over an obituary in time for it to appear in the afternoon *Courier*. "I've instructed for the remains to be sent to Shenandoah," he told Ella. "I want him to be buried with the others. If we leave here on Friday, we can have a service on Sunday, May 19th." He'd had weeks to work through these details, knowing the end was coming, and was grateful now that plans were all in place.

Maggie joined them in Shenandoah, having the least distance to travel of the siblings. She kept saying, "I can't believe he's gone. It's not right. People are supposed to be old when they die." Then she would tell of a fond memory of her big brother, between sobs.

Amongst all the tears, the few days at Shenandoah also had happy moments. Old friends embraced John, and they talked of the years when he served as pastor of the church there. God blessed the day of the funeral with warm sunshine, and following the service, a group of faithful friends walked the half-mile to the large, park-like Rose Hill cemetery on the east end of town. Both John and the current pastor, W. A. Schwimley, prayed for Johnny's soul before the casket was lowered into the ground. They laid flowers on the grave, and the crowd gradually disbursed, murmuring parting condolences to John, Ella, and Maggie until the three of them stood alone on the hill.

John felt the presence of the Lord in the comforting breeze as he knelt before the grave markers of those who had gone before him, offering a prayer for his lost children. Tiny Donald and Louis, each on earth for such a short while—hardly long enough to get to know them—and Ruth, darling bubbly Ruth who lived a year and a half and whose death broke Anna's heart. The marker he had chosen for his adult son stood tall and proud in contrast to the others. John had chosen the inscription with great purpose. It read:

JOHN O. STEVENSON JR
A.B. TABOR: L.L.B. IA. UNIVERSITY
DIED TACOMA WASH 1907
IN THE PHILIPPINES WITH
CO. L, 51 IA. VOL. 1888-1889
GLORY GUARDS WITH SOLEMN ROUND
THE BIVOUAC OF THE DEAD

John and Ella arrived home two days later after a tearful goodbye to Margaret who returned to Nebraska. With great difficulty, John tried to close that chapter of his life. Though he knew, somewhere inside him, the pain would never completely go away. This special lad had held such promise. John realized his own salvation would be in continuing with his day to day obligations. As soon as he was home in Waterloo, he plunged into his responsibilities, forging forward with his writing.

Good things were happening, too. During services in the library basement, members talked excitedly of the new church on West Fourth and South Streets, gradually growing into a magnificent building. Though still not ready for occupancy, on July third, a happy throng gathered to witness the laying of the cornerstone. "It will be wonderful, John. Don't you think?" Ella squeezed his arm and smiled. She had been extra cheerful lately, and he suspected it was her way of lifting both of them from the inevitable doldrums following Johnny's passing. He appreciated the effort, and admitted it helped to have something as grand as the new church to look forward to. They often took an afternoon walk to the site to observe the progress.

More joy arrived with a telegram from Abram and Ada, now living in New York. Another baby girl had been added to the family: Dorothy Romaine Stevenson, born August 21st. *Everyone doing fine,* the message said. The very next afternoon Ella stopped by Black's department store on the way home from work to get more yarn. Her enthusiasm transferred to John, and his bogged-down world seemed to slowly upright itself.

On September 2nd, on completing that month's edition of *The Woman's Standard*, John stood and stretched. Afternoon sunshine brightened the study and he felt good, though his hay fever, not a big problem yet this season, was beginning to give him some restless nights. Leaning over the desk, he made one last change to a personal commentary for the issue. He was surprised to hear a knock on the front door. Laying down his pencil, he strode to greet whoever might be calling.

"Telegram, sir," the young man held out the familiar yellow envelope. John's high mood spiraled down like a kite without wind. His first thought was that of the new baby—such fragile little creatures—how well he knew. *Dear Lord. Please don't let it be that.* His hands shook as he signed for the document and handed the messenger a few coins. Closing the door, his asthmatic breaths suddenly came in short gasps. He took the few steps to the parlor to confront what he held in his hand, and sat stunned as he read the unexpected message. Cora, Ella's beloved sister, had died from complications during surgery. John covered his eyes with his hands and shook his head. How could he ever tell Ella?

After the initial shock and her tears of disbelief, Ella pulled herself together. The telegram had been from her sister Nellie who was on her way to Denver, Cora's home for the past few years. "I'll leave tomorrow," Ella said—her typical strength edging out a sob. "I'll stop by the law firm and let them know what has happened. I'm sure they will understand." With that, she flew upstairs and began packing a bag. John followed, thinking he might offer assistance, but he could only sit on the bed and watch while his wife sped around the room plopping things in an open satchel as she wiped away tears and blew her nose. "Besides a funeral, there will be so much to do—all her personal things, and books, and papers."

Once packed, she collapsed onto the bed beside him, kneading the wet handkerchief in her fingers, releasing a huge, sob-ridden sigh. "Professor Cora McDonald. She's irreplaceable, John. One of a kind."

He knew exactly her feelings—the same he'd experienced upon losing a bright, promising son. He reached for Ella's hand. "One of life's great mysteries, my dear, is not only death, but why such people are taken before their time. Yet, we can take comfort in knowing they won't be forgotten. Death immortalizes the influence of all good men and women. We know death does not end self or personality; Jesus Christ's resurrection proved this. Nothing essential ever perishes; nothing spiritual ever dies."

Ella squeezed his hand. "Thank you, John." They prayed together for two precious lives lost.

~ ~ ~

NINETEEN HUNDRED AND SEVEN DREW TO A CLOSE, leaving concerns about keeping *The Woman's Standard* afloat. Only six to seven hundred of the 1000 subscribers paid the monthly fee of twenty-five cents. With the cost of paper, mailing, postage, and the small amount John charged for his services, it was difficult to make ends meet. There was talk of abandoning it or perhaps combining it with another paper. Neither idea set well with John.

Mary Jane Coggeshall sent him a long list of questions regarding the situation, and he responded post haste, fearful of the publication's future. It had been his salvation and, he strongly believed, its contents were greatly responsible for any progress made toward Woman's suffrage in Iowa. This was one death he could not allow and felt he might be able to influence.

Chapter Forty-Three

MARCHING FORWARD

1908

Determined that *The Woman's Standard* would continue, John put together a plan at the beginning of the new year to keep it afloat. This included a suggestion that groups throughout the state affiliated with the Iowa Equal Suffrage Association be asked to contribute a share of the cost. *If we get this financial support and eliminate complimentary issues, I will be willing to continue as editor,* he wrote to the committee in charge.

When John received a reply from Vivian Robinson Webb, corresponding secretary for the I.E.S.A., he could hardly wait to share the news with Ella. "Listen to this," he said when she entered the house at the end of the day. He grabbed the one-page letter from his desk and followed her around as she removed her hat and coat and plopped with fatigue onto a chair in the parlor.

John cleared his raspy throat and commenced to read:
"Dear Sir,

Upon receiving your letter this morning, I immediately telephoned the members of the committee, and all are greatly delighted that you will undertake to carry on the Standard. The Des Moines club, I am sure, will make an effort to lift its share of the load.

You, with your experience, will know what is the best way to write up an appeal to the other clubs to come to our aid. Shall I correspond with some of them and tell them just the situation? Will be glad of any suggestions, and will do all I can to help."

Ella smiled, removed her shoes, and settled back in the chair. "Did you really doubt them, John? Where would they ever find someone to take your place and keep the paper going? They know there is no such person. Now, did you put those potatoes on to boil?"

Hopeful that the Suffrage Association would accept his offer, John had already completed most of the articles for the February *Standard* by the time he received Mrs. Webb's letter. As usual, when it was ready to send out, he took a copy to the *Waterloo Courier* on West Park Avenue. He always walked the short distance regardless of the weather, and enjoyed entering the newspaper building. Immediately upon stepping through the door he was assailed with the scent of ink and the echoing, rhythmic clank of printing presses. Men busy working to get the day's news out hollered to each other to be heard over the din of the machinery. It was a world all its own.

John approached the receptionist, a plump, pleasant middle-aged woman who greeted him with a warm smile. "Dr. Stevenson, I was hoping you would be by soon. Please wait here a moment." She disappeared through a door and reappeared shortly. "Mr. Hartman would like to speak with you."

This surprised John. His relationship with the editor was most often through printed responses appearing in the paper to some of John's comments, not personal contact. He followed the woman into a small, stuffy room dominated by a desk cluttered with notes, books, and newspapers. She closed the door behind her, muffling the clamor. Hartman, a slender, middle-aged gentleman in spectacles, stood and greeted John with a handshake, not bothering to don the coat hanging close by on a rack. The sleeves of his starched white shirt bore smudges of newsprint at the elbows. "Stevenson. Good to see you. Please take a seat."

When John left a half hour later, his step felt light—as though a few inches of air cushioned the soles of his shoes. He found himself whistling, something he realized he had not done during the past troubling year. Hartman had offered him a job. Would he be interested in writing a regular column for the paper? It seemed the man found John's editorials for *The Woman's Standard* enlightening, intelligent, and thought-provoking, and felt more of the same would be a good addition to *The Courier*.

Of course John heartily agreed, and he holed up in his study with renewed energy, spending more hours on his written thoughts now for *The Courier* in addition to the suffrage paper. An abrupt change in weather brought heavy frost and snow flurries, sometimes a problem for Ella getting to work, but was hardly noticeable to John while he sat at his desk, pen in hand.

~ ~ ~

ON APRIL 5TH, AS THOUGH ORDERED BY GOD, ANY lingering winter clouds parted, and more than 750 parishioners assembled at the dedication service for Waterloo's new First Congregational Church building on West Fourth and South Streets. The large, beautifully appointed sanctuary inspired awe and reverence. Of great satisfaction to John, the pipe organ from the former church had been included, a special piece of the history of Congregationalism in Waterloo… saved. On this auspicious occasion, its melodic notes accompanied a choir of over forty voices.

Guest preachers filled the pulpit and offered words from the scriptures befitting such an event. John, too, had been asked to speak at the dedication. He spent the early morning beforehand gargling with all the remedies for his throat, and felt his comments had been successful and understandable. For a brief moment he wished he were delivering a complete sermon, then overcame that notion and was satisfied to simply enjoy the beauty of the new building. What a glorious day!

"Have you ever seen so many people in church before?" Ella whispered to him. "I wonder if most will continue to come."

John nodded his agreement. He recognized many long-standing members, though suspected a number of the new faces had come out of curiosity. Which was okay, he figured, if the mood instilled a yearning to belong to such a splendid place of worship.

After the last words of the benediction were spoken, the respectful hush present during the service grew to a hum of voices as folks filed out of the large sanctuary to the adjoining hall for refreshments. During the reception, the Alans approached. "It was good to see you in that pulpit, Reverend. It seemed like old times to hear your golden preaching again," Clyde said.

Other friends joined in with like expressions. John smiled and thanked them, a little embarrassed at the attention he felt should be directed to Pastor Rollins and the two guest preachers. Caught up in the bustle of the crowd, he almost spilled the throat-soothing punch he sipped when he felt a light touch on his arm and found himself looking directly into the eyes of Violet Cunningham. She had gained a few pounds since he last saw her, and in place of the signature purple, she wore a simple, tailored dress and short cape in a soft gray. However, an ostentatious ostrich feather fluttering from the brim of her hat lent a typical defiance to the understatement of the rest of her attire.

"Reverend Stevenson, may I introduce my niece, Miss Polly Chase." John had been so surprised to see Violet, he had not noticed the smiling, red-headed woman standing by her side.

Before John could acknowledge her, she said, "Doctor Stevenson, it is a great pleasure to meet you. I read each of your articles in *The Woman's Standard* and see that you are now writing for *The Courier*. I do hope you will continue your crusade for woman's suffrage through that outlet. If you ever need any assistance in the cause, please let me know."

For a moment, John found himself at a loss for words, but quickly gathered his wits, in spite of the unexpected turn of events. He responded in as clear a voice as he could muster. "Thank you for your welcome comments. I will certainly keep your offer in mind." He turned to Violet with astonishment and amusement.

His former antagonist shrugged her shoulder, but John noted a mischievous gleam in her eye. "Beautiful sanctuary, Reverend," she said. "Too bad you won't be in the pulpit spreading your thoughts and biblical interpretations with that unique wit of yours."

"Spreading my thoughts by writing is equally satisfying, ma'am."

"Oh, yes," Miss Chase added. "You do such a grand job of it, and you must admit, Aunt Violet, you have even said so yourself."

With that, the two women headed for the refreshment table, leaving John chuckling in disbelief at the encounter. He liked to think his persuasive words had finally convinced the perplexing lady to soften her objection to suffrage for women, but he sensed the real influence had come from the experiences of a certain young lady who now resided with her.

It simply proves we must never give up, he thought. Just keep marching forward and our goal will be achieved, one antisuffragist at a time.

Chapter Forty-Four

CELEBRATIONS

Along with his editorials and articles, John continued to correspond with his children. In a letter dated June 27, 1908, to Abram and Ada, now living in San Diego, California, he told of the many changes going on in Waterloo.

We have more amusements than usual which comes I suppose with growing towns. The trolley cars now run up Jefferson Street along Washburn Pond, the Red Cedar Park, across the Black Hawk where the woods used to be, alongside of long rows of factories called Westfield across the river to Chautauqua Park and back to town via East Waterloo… A new concrete bridge is going in at 5th Street; and another down at 11th Street. New houses of all kinds are going up. New streets are being laid out and paved.

He also added exciting news related to both of Abram's sisters. One note recently from Irene had radiated with excitement:

Dear Papa, I have become acquainted with the most remarkable man. We met by chance on a train trip, and would you believe? He refused to get off at his stop so he could stay on and get to know me. We have remained in touch and are becoming good friends.

So John was not surprised when in May he had

received a letter from a Mr. Ray Bassett.

Dear Sir, I take the liberty of writing to you because I know you have heard of me. I want to ask of you one of the greatest favors one man can confer on another — that of asking for the hand of your daughter Irene in marriage. I love her with all my heart and believe she loves me, and shall always do all in my power to make her happy…

No date was set, but it seemed inevitable. John could only pray this man was worthy of his precious Irene.

In addition to that news, Maggie and her Mr. Wood finally decided to tie the knot. The wedding, a simple ceremony, would take place in the parsonage on July 16th. The big event set Ella in a whirl. Maggie arrived home the first of the month. John stood aside while the two women discussed wedding arrangements with animated excitement. The bride-to-be insisted that John officiate — a commitment he agreed to with only a slight hesitation. Surely, his voice would allow the few words necessary to solemnize the occasion. The arrival of Irene and Nellie added a special sparkle. During the busy preparations, Irene often talked of Mr. Basset, her own intended. John noticed how she posted a letter to Paris, Missouri, almost daily. He had to finally admit, even though his daughters had not lived at home for a number of years, they were no longer little girls, but grownup women with futures that didn't particularly involve their papa.

By the time Mr. Wood appeared, the day before the wedding, it seemed the walls of the old parsonage might come apart. Somehow, everyone fit in and voices and laughter filled the rooms just like the old days. John tried not to think about the missing family members. Abram, Ada, and their children could not come, of course—and Johnny? His presence, and Anna's, drifted through the air like nostalgic cologne.

Maggie, as beautiful as any bride, stood beside her groom, a wreath of flowers in her hair, wearing a simple pale blue outfit with a row of lace at the cuffs and neck. She told the other ladies she had fashioned the ensemble herself. "Something I can continue to use for church and special occasions," she said. Always the practical one, John noted.

Ella prepared an assortment of sandwiches for a special buffet for the guests, and Mrs. Alan created a lovely two-tiered wedding cake, complete with frosting roses. John thought the very reserved groom, dressed in a store-bought gray suit a little short for his height, was perhaps slightly old for Maggie. But it was evident he adored her, and that was most important. He had waited for her all these years while she finished college and found a teaching job—reminiscent of John and Anna's romance, but flip-flopped. The new Mr. and Mrs. Wood left for a honeymoon in Colorado, after which they would make a home on his farm in Ohiowa, Nebraska, where she would continue teaching.

Rather than an abrupt ending to the jubilation, two guests stayed on. Irene planned to remain until the end of August before she returned to her teaching position in New Orleans, and Nellie promised to be there until October. Though John was back in his study a great deal of time, writing, the other two women in the house kept a smile on Ella's face and a buoyancy in her demeanor...a good thing, he thought.

~ ~ ~

NOTABLE EVENTS REGARDING WOMEN'S RIGHTS HAD ALSO taken place that July. A State Supreme court decision brought good news for the suffrage movement, and John could hardly wait to spread the word through his writing. The year before, on June 20, the city of Des Moines had held a special election for approval to build a city hall. The 1894 proposition granting women permission to decide on matters involving the levy of a special tax or the issuance of bonds did not require women to register. They were to be provided with separate ballots and a separate ballot box for deposit of their ballots. However, for the June 20, 1907, election in Des Moines, none of the requirements were provided, and those women who attempted to vote were turned away.

Mary Jane Coggeshall and three other women, as representatives of the Political Equality Club of Des Moines, sued the city of Des Moines, contending that the election was invalid because the women had not been allowed to vote. Their suit was dismissed, but the plaintiffs appealed, and Justice C. J. Ladd of the State Supreme Court concluded that "the plaintiffs were entitled to vote on the question submitted... and were illegally deprived of that privilege." The election in question was voided.

John thought surely the roar of victory among the Iowa suffragists could be heard throughout the state.

He marveled at the continued determination of Mrs. Coggeshall at the age of seventy-two, and her never-wavering fight for women's rights. He wrote her a congratulatory letter commending her dedication. His contribution seemed so little in comparison. Yet, he knew many voices joined together kept the spark of progress alive.

But by August, the joyous time of visiting family and the wedding, along with the gradual advancement in the fight for women's rights, tumbled into the background. John awoke one morning wheezing and gasping for breath.

"Too much excitement," Ella said as she insisted he inhale steam from a pot of boiling water laced with herbs. "We'll just take care of it right now so you won't have to leave while the girls are still here."

The herbs helped a little, though temporarily, and the next night John made his way down to the parlor where he could sit upright in the overstuffed chair. He must have dozed, because in the early morning, Ella, dressed for work, touched him lightly on the shoulder. "John, Irene is not well. Nellie and I are taking her to the hospital. I'll go to work from there."

The fog of sleep evaporated from John's head as he observed the other two women behind Ella, Irene holding her head with both hands as though it might break apart at any moment, her eyes dark circles in her pale face.

Alarm struck John like a swift kick. He stood abruptly. "I'll go with you. Let me get dressed."

"No," Ella said. "Nellie is perfectly capable of

handling this. You stay here and take care of yourself."

They left him there, and after a self-treatment of steaming herbs, he paced, wheezing with each step. Just before noon, the door opened and Nellie appeared—alone. She dropped into a chair with a huge sigh. "It's typhoid. Probably contracted on a camping trip in Missouri on her way to Iowa from New Orleans. She was admitted to the hospital."

"Typhoid?" John sat stunned. His thoughts spun back to the terrible memory of the typhoid epidemic that had swept through Waterloo a few years before leaving a trail of death. He spent his waking hours in constant prayer for Irene's recovery and was thankful Nellie stayed on to help. Tension and anxiety gripped the household. His own health issues didn't help matters.

"John," Ella pleaded, after he sat up all one night again, wheezing and chuffing like an overworked locomotive. "You must get out of here for your own sake. Go to Wisconsin."

He shook his head. "Not yet. I'll tough it out here until I know Irene is okay. Then I'll go."

Nellie visited Irene in the afternoon, Ella at night, and John as often as he could, thankful Waterloo now had a real hospital only a few blocks away. Irene kept in contact with Mr. Bassett during this unexpected turn of events, and he anxiously made a trip to Waterloo to visit the patient. Thus, John and Ella met him sooner than intended.

"He's a fine young man," Ella remarked. "I'm so happy for both of them." She dabbed at tears with a handkerchief.

John whole-heartedly agreed with Ella's assessment of Mr. Bassett and felt the man truly loved their youngest daughter. He tried not to imagine anything other than a future together for the couple, the outcome of Irene's illness still an unknown.

The prayers and good care did their work, and by mid-August Irene had improved enough to sit up and eat. She came home at the end of the month, well on her way to recovery. Only then did John leave for Bayfield for his own relief.

~ ~ ~

BY THE TIME HE RETURNED TO WATERLOO IN LATE September, Irene was gone—well enough to go back to New Orleans to teach—and whatever affected John's lungs in Waterloo had blown away for another season. He could breathe more easily and would often break from his writing to spend time outside. The fresh air and stimulation of an Indian summer provided a welcome emotional tonic.

One Saturday morning in early October, he set about working in the front yard, cleaning out dormant flower beds and heaping leaves in a musty, fragrant pile. Leaning against his rake to rest, he chuckled as a light breeze tugged yet another leaf free from an overhead branch.

Neighbors out enjoying the weather brightened the day even more. A couple with a baby carriage strolled by and stopped to chat a moment before continuing on at a leisurely pace. Several houses up, a young woman in a bright green coat walked with a brisk, determined step in their direction. She greeted the couple and cooed at the baby. John smiled and resumed his raking, whistling a favorite hymn as he did so. It felt so good to be alive.

A pleasant voice interrupted his labor. "Hello, Dr. Stevenson. I expected to find you in your study working on one of your editorials."

Startled, John looked up from the growing pile of debris to see the lady in the green coat. At first, he didn't recognize her, then the smile stirred his memory—Violet Cunningham's niece.

"Miss Chase. What a pleasant surprise. Out enjoying the sunshine?"

"Yes, and I also have something on my mind. Do you have a minute?"

This was not an accidental meeting, he realized. The woman had come with a purpose. John's interest sprang into place. "Of course, please come in. I'll get Mrs. Stevenson." He leaned the rake against the house and motioned the young woman to follow as he entered the front door. Leading the visitor into the parlor, he offered her a seat, and went in search of his wife. He found her in the kitchen, shelling peas. "Ella, we have a guest."

Ella immediately donned her best hospitality mode. John could tell her curiosity possibly even outweighed his own. "Can I offer you a cup of tea, Miss Chase?"

"Oh, no thank you. Not on this warm day." The young woman looked around the room, and her gaze rested on the one piece of furniture that stood out. "My, what a lovely piano. I heard that you played, Mrs.

Stevenson. My aunt says you are very talented."

The Cunninghams lived in a large mansion across town. John figured it was filled with the most up-to-date, expensive furniture available, and suspected the compliment was to make them feel at ease in their modest home. After a few more moments of innocuous chatting, his inquisitiveness got the better of him. "You said you had something on your mind?"

"Yes. I do." And then she got right to the point. "I hope you will forgive the intrusion, but I understand the annual Iowa Equal Suffrage convention is to be held in Boone later this month. I would very much like to attend and wonder if you know of any others in Waterloo who might want to go. I would even be willing to help organize a group from here, if that would help." Then she added with a sly smile, "I think with a little push we can even get Aunt Violet to come."

John exchanged a knowing look with Ella. Here was another giant step forward in their own personal crusade—one he had thought at times might never happen. "That would be grand, Miss Chase. We only have a few weeks. Let's get to work."

During the last few days of October, Ella, John, Polly Chase, Violet Cunningham herself, and others from Waterloo, with communities across Iowa, gathered in Boone for the convention. And on the twenty-ninth, the crusade hit an all-time high when one hundred fifty women marched through the business district waving banners exclaiming: WE DEMAND A VOICE and FULL SUFFRAGE FOR WOMEN.

Among the protestors was Mary Jane Coggeshall,

John's friend and mentor. The shout for their rights echoed through the town and sparked an enthusiasm like an uncontrollable wildfire. John didn't know of any parades anywhere such as this. Certainly, there had been suffragists who had been part of traditional parades at various places across the nation, but none consisted entirely of women marching for their individual rights.

Following the event, a breathless Polly approached him, her face flushed with excitement. "Oh, Dr. Stevenson, this is so wonderful! I can feel victory in the air."

John had to admit, of all the events he had attended on behalf of the I.E.S.A., this had been the most stimulating. He hoped, as always after a rally with the Iowa suffragists, that victory was indeed around the corner.

Chapter Forty-Five

LETTING GO

1909-1910

John marveled at how life could change in such a short period of time. After the dark despair during Irene's illness, things up-righted themselves. Iowa still hummed from the uplifting rally in Boone, and then Irene sent a letter, adding yet another surprise to the mix of things.

Dear Papa,

The terrible scare I had while in Waterloo has got me thinking about life and what is truly important. If you and Mama think you are up to another wedding in the old parsonage so soon, Mr. Bassett and I would like to be married there in January. Please let me know ASAP if this is acceptable.

"Well, what shall we tell her?" John asked Ella the evening after the letter had arrived. They sat at the supper table during a November wind storm, the electric lights flickering on and off as Ella reread the letter for the umpteenth time.

He could almost see the wheels of thought churning in her head as she unconsciously drummed her fingers on the tabletop. "What kind of question is that?" she spouted. "You know what we'll tell her, John. The only doubt in your mind is you don't want your little girl to be all grownup and married."

"I didn't say that. I just needed to be certain you were up to another wedding here so soon. That was the question."

"Well, of course!"

He knew from the onset that this wedding would be quite different from the small, unpretentious ceremony the previous July. Both Irene and Ella had grand ideas. The date was set for January 13th. Irene came for Christmas and stayed on so plans could be made. The minute holiday festivities were aside, the place stirred with such fuss and commotion you'd think the circus had come to town. John had only one comment in regard to the ceremony itself, and early on motioned Irene into his study for a brief talk. He took her hands in his. "My darling daughter, as much as I would like to officiate at your wedding, I would prefer that Reverend Rollins do the honors. I hope you understand."

She kissed him lightly on the cheek. "If that is what you think best, Papa." And she let it go at that. He knew she shared his memory of his raspy attempt to speak coherently during the vows for Maggie and Mr. Wood. This was the only right decision, as disappointing as it was for both of them.

Irene and Ella spent hours shopping for dresses and accessories, the bride choosing a hand-embroidered silk, and Ella a lovely gown for herself. John tried not to think of the money. Thank goodness the groom was covering some of the cost. He was a junior partner in the successful Bassett Brothers store in Paris, Missouri, a family business that had been handed down through several generations. Most of the Bassett family planned to come to Waterloo for the event. Maggie would not be able to attend, so Mr. Bassett's sister Marie would serve as maid of honor. Out-of-town visitors were to be housed in a hotel. There was no other way.

The guest list kept growing, too many in John's mind, but the women insisted it would all work. When the big day arrived, somehow everyone squeezed together while Reverend Rollins did the honors of uniting the couple. Several church ladies had helped decorate the rooms and, after the ceremony, tables were brought out for an elaborate wedding supper. John later wrote to Sarah Whitney that he figured it *was the last grand function in the old parsonage we'll ever see.* And through it all, the weather was unusually mild, an added blessing.

After the tumult of the occasion, even the house seemed to breathe a sigh of relief, as though it had been lifted from its foundation and finally settled back down where it belonged. Through much of the wedding preparation, John had stayed in his study with the door closed—shutting out the chaos and buzz of excitement. He tended to his editorials and writing obligations. Underlying the frivolity in the other rooms, serious concerns simmered. The financial stability of *The Woman's Standard* continued to be an issue. One of the reasons publication continued was through the generosity of the Callanan Trust—a fund for which Sarah Ware Whitney served as trustee.

Those monies were dwindling and wouldn't last

much longer. John had written to Mrs. Whitney in December stating:

I do not know what will be the ultimate decision of the I.E.S.A. about continuance. They do not want it to stop, but they do not want to do much for it, at least a part of them do not. A final decision will be necessary inside of two more issues.

In January he wrote again:

Dear Friend,

I have heard nothing further from headquarters, but suppose I will hear sometime during the month.

Things continued to stagnate, and finally, on March 10, 1909, Sarah Whitney bowed out of the responsibility. She sent him the following letter to be passed on to the Iowa Equal Suffrage Association through its executive committee:

I would hereby make a formal transfer of The Woman's Standard, our official paper, to the Iowa Equal Suffrage Association hereby relinquishing all ownership and rights to said paper, also freeing myself from any debts or bills or other matters concerning said paper. The legal price of one dollar for the same may be placed to my credit on my subscription ... I wish for the paper's unlimited success in your management, and I also wish to thank you each and all for what you have done for the Woman's Standard the past ten years that it has been in my care.

Most sincerely,
Sarah Ware Whitney

Mrs. Whitney's resignation was not a surprise, just a

disappointment for John. He had enjoyed the personal relationship with Sarah over the years. The Association resolved to assume the support of the paper, and in the March edition, John announced the change to the membership, writing: *The larger the number of subscribers, and the more promptly paid the subscriptions due, the less will be the cost of the paper to the organization and the greater will be its value to the cause of equal suffrage.*

So, he continued on, writing his thoughts, pushing equality, encouraging the Violet Cunninghams and the male legislators to realign their thinking—challenges John enjoyed, even though progress was slow and frustrating. And during it all, his own health issues were beginning to sap his energy.

On April 21, 1909, a letter from Abram announced the birth of another daughter, Elizabeth Lee Stevenson, born in San Francisco, California. The evening of the day they learned the news, John donned his now well-stained apron and stood cutting up chicken at the kitchen counter for the soup Ella was making. As they worked, she spouted off about issues in the office and the automobile garage being built just off their alley. "And now Abram's new baby is born in San Francisco? Every time you hear from him they're living somewhere else. He drags his wife and those little children all over the nation!"

"Now, Ella, it's his job. Everyone wants a telephone."

"And speaking of telephones, I think it is high time we get one," she fumed. "We've had one at the office for several years. Wouldn't it be handy to call the children sometime?" She chopped celery and onions with such force John was afraid a finger or two would also end up in the soup.

He plopped the last bit of chicken into the pot and sighed. Ella had obviously had a bad day, and what was there to say? He could never repay her willingness to spend day after day at the law firm to earn a paycheck.

"Yes, Mother, you are right. We have electricity. Let's get a telephone, but I am not ready to get one of those noisy automobiles."

John responded post haste to Abram's announcement. *I am glad that mother and child are doing well, and hope that this may find both in the same continued condition.* He alluded to the possibility of a phone at the old parsonage—wishing Abram were there to install it. His letter also hinted at his growing health issues, figuring the lad should be aware that at sixty-nine years of age, his papa was not quite as spry as before. *I have not commenced gardening. The weather has been cold, and I have not as yet been able to get a man to spade it. I do not feel equal to spading now for myself as I used to. The fences too are falling to pieces and I will need to get them repaired.... .*

By midyear 1910, it seemed to take longer each time he put together *The Standard.* The letters often blurred as he wrote, and he had to stop and rest his eyes. He worried about his accuracy—concerned the Iowa Equal Suffrage Association would suggest he hadn't proof-read his work beforehand.

So, after working on the July edition, he carried several sheets of paper into the parlor. "Ella, could I impose upon you to read this to me?" He handed her his latest editorial and other comments scrawled across the page in large letters.

Ella put down her knitting with a little laugh. "Of course. Don't tell me you're asking for my opinion after all these years?"

He chuckled. "Hardly. Seems to me I've been getting that whether I asked for it or not. No, I want you to make certain the words are legible." He hesitated a moment and cleared his froggy throat. "Sometimes when I've been working too long, the page gets a little fuzzy."

Ella frowned, took the pages from him and began to read: "We speak of our nation as enjoying a government of the people, by the people, and for the people, but we are very far from..." Rather than continuing, she hesitated. "John, I can't make out this next word. What has happened to your beautiful penmanship?"

He looked over her shoulder at where her finger pointed on the page and read the word for her. "Realizing. It's realizing," he said, a little piqued that she couldn't make it out even though he had asked for her help. "The sentence finishes with 'we are very far from realizing any such a government.'"

Ella put down the paper and looked up at him, worry etched across her face. He sat beside her and massaged his forehead, suddenly feeling weary and not quite up to a task so important to him. "It's my eyes. The words blur and sometimes appear double. As much as I would hate to, I think I may have to give up doing *The Standard.*"

Ella reached for his hand. "Oh, John. It means so much to you. Are you sure? And what about the editorials for *The Courier?*"

He shook his head. "I can't give everything up. If you help with the proofreading, I can continue with that. It's only once a month or so, and the booklet for the church. I've been working on that for so long, I will finish it. *The Woman's Standard* is a bigger task. I'll keep it up for a while, with your help — maybe get a medical opinion about my vision."

In late August and most of September, he took his annual hiatus to Wisconsin to help his breathing. For the first time, Ella accompanied him, giving her a break from the office. She continued to help with the proofreading, and the next two editions of *The Standard* went out in a timely manner. His eyes felt better after the rest, and as always, his lungs cleared. A visit to a doctor regarding his eyesight resulted in spectacles that frustrated him no end. They kept slipping off his nose, but they did help. However, the more he thought about it, the more he decided it was time to give up the suffrage paper. He could still work for the cause in his other writing. In October, he mailed a personal letter to the Iowa Equal Suffrage Association in care of Mary Jane Coggeshall, telling her, as painful as it was, it was time for him to let go of his responsibility.

Once he had posted his resignation, John felt both relief and disappointment. Working with the I.E.S.A. had meant a great deal to him.

~ ~ ~

As November dawned, there was cause to celebrate across the nation. Washington State's male electorate ratified an amendment to the state constitution granting women the right to vote. "That makes five out of forty-six," Ella said, "and how many years have we been working on this? I guess that's progress."

"Yes, dear wife," John said. "It is indeed. Each one is a triumph. More will soon follow."

The next day, when a gilded envelope arrived in the mail, Ella's tone shifted first from astonishment to delight. "Will you look at this!" She jerked John awake from an afternoon snooze. He yawned and took the elaborate card from her hand. The sentiment written in an elegant scroll didn't quite register at first, then on a second read he laughed until tears spilled down his cheeks. Violet Cunningham had invited them to a gala affair at her home to celebrate the Washington State victory for women.

Ella had to have a new dress for the occasion, but John figured his church suit would be just fine. He wasn't about to put on airs. Still, he would go. He and Violet had been on a long road together. Why Mr. Cunningham, who made his money in the liquor business, would be willing to allow such a celebration in his home stirred John's curiosity. The man belonged to a group of businessmen who had fought a woman's right to vote from the beginning. Would he even be at the event?

Yet he was, and as John mingled with the crowd at the unexpected occasion, Mr. Cunningham, a heavy-set, bearded gentleman wearing a red velvet waistcoat under his expensive black suit, approached him.

"Reverend Stevenson, it's a pleasure to meet you. My wife has told me what a determined man you are. You must be very persuasive to make her change her mind. I know that's not an easy task."

John studied his host for a moment not quite certain how to respond. Then simply spoke his mind. "I'm surprised you are taking it so well. Congratulations on your open-mindedness."

Mr. Cunningham contemplated the drink in his hand, swirled the amber liquid and smiled at John. "Personally, I consider the entire idea folly and doubt it will come to pass in Iowa, or the nation, for that matter. We all know those western states who have permitted it are full of ignorant backwoodsman. Even so, the way I look at it is, just because women are given the vote doesn't mean they are going to vote away the saloons. Violet likes a little drink now and then herself. And of course, most women will undoubtedly vote on any issue the way their husbands suggest. You may find this whole endeavor is a snake that will strike and bite you, Reverend."

John wondered who was being naïve, himself or the Joe Cunninghams of the nation. He thought about Beatrice Cooper, Polly Chase, Mrs. Jenkins, and other victims of too much drink, and all the intelligent Christian women he knew and how he suspected they would vote on moral issues once they were granted that right. A warm feeling flowed through him. He returned Cunningham's smile and said, "We shall see."

~ ~ ~

THE LETTER HE HAD WAITED FOR FROM MARY JANE Coggeshall came the following week. John took it into his study and sat, eyeing the envelope for a while. After a time, he got up and walked to the window looking to Washington Street and beyond. The sky glowed a striking pink with the sunset, casting iridescent shades of the same in puddles from an afternoon rain. God's palette never ceased to amaze him. It always seemed to put things in perspective. He watched as the colors faded, then turned his attention back to the envelope on his desk. Sitting again, he removed the seal.

Dear Dr. Stevenson,

This "letting go" that you have written about is a serious business to us and the occasion of it must be a serious business to you. You have my sincere sympathy. It seems to me there has been a rather heavy hand laid upon you. May it grow lighter as the months go by.

What will become of our dear little "Standard," when its intellectual — capable — valiant and sweet-spirited father has laid it down?

I hope you will be at the Convention. We have always felt honored by your presence. Iowa suffragists owe a large debt of gratitude to you for your painstaking work for the Standard.

Yours hopefully,
Mary J. Coggeshall

John sighed, and with a tear in his eye, he bowed his head in prayer. In spite of the letter's hope that he would change his mind, he was resigned. He had been faithful to the call with the time he had been given. Although progress for women's rights in Iowa, and across the nation, were moving along slowly, and the goal not yet reached, he knew it would come to pass. It was time for others to take up the good work.

Epilogue

MARY JANE WHITELY COGGESHALL BRIEFLY TOOK OVER the editorship of *The Woman's Standard* beginning with the January 1911 edition, publishing it from Des Moines. The last issue appeared in November 1911 followed shortly thereafter with her death from pneumonia on December 22, 1911.

John Ogilvie Stevenson died December 19, 1912, of heart disease and complications from asthma. His completed history booklet for the First Congregational Church of Waterloo was published in 1913 as a memorial and prefaced with many tributes to him. A plaque in his memory was placed in the narthex of the church that is still in use today.

His last column for *the Waterloo Courier* had been written and was published the Saturday following his death. *The Courier* included a long obituary honoring him stating "Waterloo has lost a personality that cannot be replaced. Humanity has lost a friend."

Dr. Stevenson was first buried in the family plot in Shenandoah. Later his remains were relocated to the Elmwood cemetery in Waterloo, it is assumed at the request of Ella.

Ella Stevenson died in February 1920 and was interred next to her husband. Irene died of pulmonary tuberculosis on June 8, 1921, at the age of thirty-six leaving three young children. Abram and Ada had two more children, a daughter who died in infancy, and a son, John Ogilvie Stevenson III. Margaret and Frank Wood had one adopted daughter.

Like so many suffragists, neither Ms. Coggeshall nor Dr. Stevenson lived to see the fruits of their labors. While other states were successful, Iowa still struggled with the cause. Finally, on June 5, 1916, a referendum appeared on an Iowa State ballot which would allow men to vote to strike the word "male" from Article II, Section 1 of Iowa's constitution. It was defeated by 10,341 votes. After an investigation by the WCTU, fraud was suspected.

On July 2, 1919, the Iowa General Assembly ratified the 19th Amendment to the U.S. Constitution. By August 26, 1920, thirty-six states had ratified the amendment—making it a federal guarantee. With Tennessee being the last state, that amendment became law stating:

The right of citizens of the United States to vote shall not be denied or abridged by the United States or by any State on account of sex.

Congress shall have power to enforce this article by appropriate legislation.

Author's Notes

THE MAIN CHARACTERS IN THIS BOOK WERE REAL PERSONS, including John and Ella Stevenson and John's children, as were Ella's sisters, Cora and Nellie McDonald. Moses Cross, the Leavitts, and Sarah Whitney, were actual members of the Waterloo Congregational Church.

Violet Cunningham, Leroy and Beatrice Cooper and her sister Belva were created by me as vehicles to move the story along and emphasize the inequality of the laws at the time, plus the strong antisuffrage sentiment. All incidents involving them throughout the story, and those of the Alan family, are fiction. Any semblance of these characters to actual people is purely coincidental

Italicized segments throughout the book are taken directly from sermons and editorials written by John O. Stevenson, and letters written by and to him. His thoughts on divorce (Chapter Three) came from an article he wrote for *The Waterloo Courier* entitled *Divorce*.

Oberlin College, Oberlin, Ohio, was founded in 1833 by a pair of Presbyterian ministers and is committed to values of freedom, social justice, and service. It was the first college in the United States to admit black students and women and, as stated in Chapter Thirteen, the school after which Tabor College (no longer in operation) was formulated.

In regard to the legal rights of women in Iowa during the period of time this story takes place, the book *Legal and Political Status of Women In Iowa* published in 1918 by Ruth A. Gallaher was a great help.

However, sorting through the various improvements in Iowa law demonstrated even when a ruling was a step forward, the old English common law still dominated, not only in society, but often in the minds of the judges.

The commentary regarding the reception for John and Ella after their marriage mentioned in Chapter Four was an actual event written up in *The Waterloo Courier*. The Logan family of Waterloo was often mentioned in John's letters.

The parable of the horse and the umbrella is from one of John's newspaper articles in *The Waterloo Courier*.

Comments made by Cora McDonald in her speech in Chapter Ten were taken from a newspaper article she had written on the subject of woman's suffrage in Wyoming.

Chapter Ten. The incident regarding the cancellation of John's talk on Temperance at the Northern Iowa Union camp meeting is well documented in a number of newspapers.

John Jr. kept a diary the entire year of 1891. Some of his expressions and thoughts expressed in this book were gleaned from his written account, as was the incident of his leg injury.

It is not known if the Rev. Stevenson traveled to Tabor to receive his doctorate, but it gave me an opportunity to acquaint readers with that community plus the town of Shenandoah. I visited Rose Hill Cemetery while researching for this book and placed flowers on the graves of his infant children and that of John Jr. The inscriptions for each child are quoted directly from the markers.

Chapter Sixteen. Many of the reverend's observations regarding the Chicago World's Fair came from a sermon he preached following his visit to the fair. I don't know if the entire family accompanied him, but in the sermon he says "when we attended the fair." Cora McDonald was represented in the Woman's Building among notable women of the time. Whether she read her paper in person or it was simply posted is not known. Susan B. Anthony gave several speeches at the fair. John makes no reference to attending her talks, but they certainly would have been a draw for him. The quotes from Miss Anthony's talk on *The Moral Leadership of the Religious Press* were taken from her actual speech.

The Benedict Home in Des Moines introduced in Chapter Twenty-one, was a real institution supported by the Woman's Christian Temperance Union.

The revival in March and April of 1896 actually occurred and caused a huge stir in the community. John kept a notebook of the proceedings including his unhappiness with the evangelist. The incident is well documented in *the Waterloo Courier* and *Waterloo Daily Courier,* especially issues for April 20, 21, & 22, 1896. Quotes regarding the incident from letters written by Sarah Ware Whitney are true as are comments by John for *the Waterloo Courier.* He later wrote an editorial for *The Courier* on the subject titled *Revival Philosophy.*

Sarah Ware Whitney was an important presence in John's life. All quotes from her letters are real. The two corresponded often when she served as proprietor of *The Woman's Standard.* During much of that time, she lived in Southern California. I spent a day at the University of

Southern California archives photocopying the letters written by John to Sarah which are stored at that facility in the Amy C. Ransome Collection on Women's Suffrage.

John's health: Though many letters referred to his allergies as "hay fever" printed references, plus his death certificate, indicate the affliction causing his breathing problems was probably asthma. References to issues with his throat appeared as early as April 1878 in a letter from Anna to her parents. His use of cocaine, prescribed by a doctor for his throat, was mentioned in a letter dated Dec. 9, 1897, from E. Fletcher Ingals M.D. to Dr. Case in Waterloo. Dr. Ingals stated that some of John's problems were related to the use of the cocaine and he was appalled that any doctor would order it.

In Chapter Thirty-One, the letters dated June 7 and 12, 1899, to John from Elizabeth Cady Stanton regarding her book, *The Woman's Bible,* are authentic. The letters have been donated to the Grout Museum in Waterloo, Iowa, especially for their exhibit in 2020 commemorating the 100th anniversary of a woman's right to vote.

Mrs. Stanton's comments regarding Mrs. Martha Place, the first woman convicted of murder and sentenced to the electric chair, are true, as are John O. Stevenson's comments and rebuttals on the subject published in *The Waterloo Courier.*

Some of the letters received from John Jr. while in the Philippines, are written from my imagination with help from letters written by Henry Hackthorn of his same unit (Letters from the Philppines: The 51st Iowa Volunteers at War, 1898-1899 edited by H. Roger Grant

Palimpset) though not quoted directly. However, the description of the campaign in the "deep mud of the great Candaba swamp" are John Jr's own words.

All references to conventions are of actual events as are descriptions of the venues.

Chapter Thirty-nine. No record exists of there being threatening notes left at the parsonage; However, during this time the antisuffrage movement had accelerated, and many women, as well as men, were still very much opposed to the idea of their needing the right to vote. There is no doubt that the Rev. Stevenson, unafraid to speak his mind on the subject, received negative responses.

John's visit to his dying son in March 1907, is well chronicled in letters from a Mrs. J. Uhl of Shenandoah, and those he wrote to Abram—one written from the Tacoma Hotel during his time there. John Jr.'s subsequent death in May of that year is also noted in messages to Abram and lengthy articles in both the *Shenandoah World* and the *Waterloo Courier*. The death certificate reads death from Pulmonary Tuberculosis. It is evident from all letters regarding the tragedy that he suffered from Post-traumatic Stress Disorder related to his war experiences.

The weddings of Maggie to Mr. Wood and Irene to Ray Bassett were elaborated in the *Waterloo Courier*, as well as in letters from John to Sarah Whitney.

Ella's job is documented in the booklet *The History of the First Congregational Church*, written by J. O. Stevenson and published after his death. It includes pages of tributes to him, including one from *The*

Waterloo Courier that states: *It is worthy of note…to recall the sacrifice and desire of Mrs. Stevenson to help her husband. She stepped into the breach and became in large measure the bread winner. She mastered the art of stenography and became the office assistant of Gates & Liffring, serving in that capacity with a rare efficiency for the past twelve years or more.*

The last letter to John from Mary Jane Coggeshall was among his papers, and represents a very poignant goodbye and sincere appreciation for the many years of work he did on behalf of the Iowa Equal Suffrage Association.

Acknowledgements

A BOOK BASED ON HISTORY DOES NOT SIMPLY FLOW FROM the mind through computer keys; first one must find authorities on the subject, then spend hours of research before the writing can proceed.

Through telephone calls and countless emails, I learned early on that Iowans are friendly folk eager to help. A bouquet of thanks to the many who oversee the fascinating history of that state including: **Shari Stelling**, The State Historical Society of Iowa; **Becki Plunkett**, Special Collections Archivist, Iowa Department of Cultural Affairs; **Jerilyn Marshall**, Head, Liaison and Research Services Rod Library, University of Northern Iowa, Cedar Falls, Iowa; **Yvonne Keller** from the *Waterloo Courier* who took time to locate dates for some of the editorials written by John Stevenson during the early 1900s; **Joy Stortvedt** of the Shenandoah Public Library who located articles from *The Shenandoah World* regarding the illness and death of John O. Stevenson, Jr.

Mike Wendel of the Iowa Railroad Historical Society willingly advised me of train routes during the period of time the Rev. John O. Stevenson lived and traveled in Iowa. Also, my brother **Ken Beach** conjured up a fabulous book of railroad maps of the United States printed in the late 1800s.

I'm indebted to the **archivists at USC** who allowed me to access and photograph the Amy C. Ransome collection on women's suffrage containing many letters from John. O. Stevenson to Sarah Ware Whitney during the time she was proprietor of *The Woman's Standard*.

Genealogist extraordinaire, **Sharon Hoyt**, diligently dug into the past of Ella McDonald about whom I had only sketchy information. I would recommend Ms. Hoyt to anyone researching family roots. She is awesome!

Additionally, my son **Glen** and I traveled to Iowa where I got a "feel" for the area about which I was writing. During that trip I met with Iowans with knowledge of the Rev. Stevenson and/or the communities in which he lived during the late 1800s and early twentieth century. I am deeply grateful for assistance from the following: **Cindy Baker**, Historian, Congregational Church, Shenandoah, Iowa, who greeted us with enthusiasm and took time before our arrival to go through the church archives and lay everything out on tables in the basement for my perusal. She also located the Stevenson graves at the Rose Hills Cemetery. Thank you, Cindy. You are a gem! **Roger Lane**, Historian, Congregational Church, Waterloo, Iowa, provided additional information on the Rev. Stevenson's pastorate there, walked me through the beautiful sanctuary, and pointed out the plaque mounted in the foyer in the Reverend's honor; **Bob Neymeyer,** Historian, Grout Museum, Waterloo, Iowa, researched and answered many of my questions via email then spent time talking to me during my visit and directing me to archives and other museum staff helpful to my project; **Sue Pearson** of the Waterloo Library found information on Waterloo jails and hospitals during the Rev. Stevenson's life in the area, and showed me how to access newspaper archives once I returned home. She pointed out photos on the library wall pertinent to that era, including a huge bird's eye map of Waterloo circa 1906.

My special appreciation to **Leslie Payne** who edited the first half of the book before the process became stalled due to my husband's health issues and subsequent death; and to **Jan Holmes Frost** who picked up and continued the editing after I had taken a two-year hiatus from writing. Another edit done by **Molly Lewis,** whose expertise and knowledge of history during the time the book takes place proved invaluable. And special hugs to my beta readers: **Fran Wozencraft, Karen Atwater,** and **Carol Beach.**

A lucky find was **Barry McWilliams** of Everett, Washington, whose wife is a descendent of the Gaston family. He provided additional information regarding Ozro Gaston, law partner of John Jr., and clarified Ozro's connection to George Gaston, founder of Tabor College.

As always, a huge thanks for the ongoing support of my Fresno, California, critique group—the **Book Buddies**—who will forever be my guiding light.

Loads of thanks to **Jessica Therrien** and **Holly Krammier** of Acorn Publishing for their enthusiastic agreement to take me on as one of their authors.

And, of course, the book would not have happened without the encouragement of my family. Son **Glen** and his wife **Lisa** were always there to provide technical assistance when the computer failed to cooperate, and my daughters **Karen** and **Donna,** along with their husbands, **John** and **Ken,** continued to cheer me along the way.

Further Reading

- Not For Ourselves Alone, The Story of Elizabeth Cady Stanton and Susan B. Anthony, Geoffrey C. Ward and Ken Burns, Alfred A. Knopf, 1999

- Strong-minded Women — the Emergence of the Woman-Suffrage Movement in Iowa, by Louise R. Noun, Iowa State University Press, 1969.

- Legal and Political Status of Women in Iowa, An Historical Account of the Rights of Women in Iowa From 1838 to 1918, b Ruth A. Gallaher, Published at Iowa City Iowa in 1918 by The State Historical Society of Iowa

- A Modern Madonna, by Caroline Abbot Stanley Published 1906 by Grosset & Dunlap

- Founding Sisters and the Nineteenth Amendment by Eleanor Clift, John Wiley & Sons Inc. 2003

- Carrie Chapman Catt A Public Life by Jacqueline Van Voris, The Feminist Press 1987

- Carrie Chapman Catt, A Life of Leadership, Nate Levin, New Dialogue Press 1999

- The Woman's Bible A Classic Feminist Perspective by Elizabeth Cady Stanton, Dover Publications 2002 (Originally published in 1895)

- Woman, Church and State by Matilda Joslyn Gage, Forgotten Books 2012 (Originally published in 1893)

- A Century of Struggle, The Woman's Rights

Movement in the United States by Eleanor Flexner and Ellen Fitzpatrick 1996 The Belknap Press of Harvard University Press

- Splintered Sisterhood, Gender and Class in the Campaign against Woman Suffrage, by Susan E. Marshall 1997 University of Wisconsin Press

- The Emancipation of the American Woman by Andrew Sinclair 1965, Harper & Row, Publishers

- *Letters from the Philippines: The 51ˢᵗ Iowa Volunteers at War, 1898-1899* by H. Roger Grant, Palimpsest, Volume 55, Number 6, November/December 1974, State Historical Society of Iowa 1974

- The grassroots diffusion of the woman suffrage movement in Iowa: the IESA, rural women, and the right to vote, Graduate Theses by Sara Egge, Iowa State University, 2009

- *The liquor Merry-Go-Round* by Ruth A. Gallaher, *The Palimpsest* edited by John Ely Briggs, Vol XIV, No 6, issued in June 1933, State Historical Society of Iowa

- Suffrage in Iowa, an online exhibit. Created by the Iowa Women's Archives with funding from the State Historical Society, Inc.